Praise for

The Thirteenth Skull

by
Bonnie Ramthun

*"**The Thirteenth Skull** is one heck of a ride! From the first paragraph to the last this story is non-stop excitement where the hunters become the hunted. Loaded with thrills and perfect for those who enjoy walking just a bit on the dangerous side of life!"*
Detra Fitch—Huntress Reviews gives **The Thirteenth Skull** ★ ★ ★ ★ ★

*"A touch of intrigue, a tad of romance, a cupful of murder, a pinch of the paranormal and a whole lot of danger add up for great reading in **The Thirteenth Skull**, author Bonnie Ramthun's third novel."*
Julie Failla Earhart—Book Reviewer

*"Bonnie Ramthun scores again, assuring her reputation as a premier thriller writer. **The Thirteenth Skull** is her best yet, original, riveting, powerful. Readers will race to the heart wrenching—and unexpected—finale."*
Carolyn Hart—Agatha Award winning author of 34 mystery novels.

*"Bonnie Ramthun has created a marvelous page-turner set in the great West. **The Thirteenth Skull** is jammed with suspense, history, romance, and even some supernatural shenanigans— but what I enjoyed the most was the sense of place that permeates the story. The wind-swept eastern Wyoming Black Hills come alive with details that only a careful, and nature-loving, writer can provide. At the end, the diverse threads of the tricky plot come together, the ironic mix of characters saves the day, the white-knuckle tension is resolved, and the world is a better place. What more could anyone ask for from a book?"*
Manuel Ramos—author of the Luis Montez series including *Brown-on-Brown.*

More Praise for
The Thirteenth Skull

*"**The Thirteenth Skull** is another hair-raising tale of murder and suspense that will keep you on the edge of your seat all the way from the mysterious beauty of the Wyoming prairies into the deepest secrets of the ancient Aztecs. Bonnie Ramthun's sense of the American West is flawless and I wish I had her characters energy!"*
Marne Davis Kellogg—author of *Brilliant.*

*"Don't miss **The Thirteenth Skull**! An engrossing mystery with a breathtaking setting in the Wyoming wilderness, a smart, determined sleuth, and a plot with enough twists and surprises that you'll want to keep reading late into the night."*
Margaret Coel—author of *Killing Raven.*

*"This fast-paced suspense novel is believable enough to make your hair stand on end. Not only is this novel action packed but Bonnie Ramthun also expertly connects you to her characters and researches her subject to detail; the end result is high-tech and credible. **The Thirteenth Skull** will keep you hanging on the edge of your seat!"*
Susan Prieto—Teacher

"Bonnie Ramthun is like Sherlock Holmes meets the X-Files."
Robert New—Entertainment Attorney

Bonnie Ramthun

the THIRTEENTH SKULL

Loveland Press, LLC
Book Publishers
Loveland, Colorado

The Thirteenth Skull is published by:

Loveland Press, LLC
P.O. Box 7001
Loveland, CO 80537-0001
970-593-9557
www.LovelandPress.com

Production Credits:

Edited by: Barbara Teel
Cover Design, Layout and Production by: Sandi Nelsen

the
THIRTEENTH
SKULL

Signature
2005

DEDICATION

This one is for my husband, Bill.

ACKNOWLEDGMENTS

Grateful thanks to my group of friends who edit my work before a publisher gets a chance to look it over. My dad, Lee John Droege, my father-in-law Gary Ramthun, my English professor friend Jack Reardon, and my brother Nick Droege all provided insight and correction. My mom, Judith Butler, my sisters Roxanne Tomich and Allison Butler, my friends Lisa Shattuck and Suzanne Katchmar all pored over the pages and told me what went right and what went wrong.

Dr. Megan Silva provided me with answers about gunshot wounds, concussions, and brain injuries. She is desperately busy but takes time from her schedule to answer my questions to the smallest detail.

My publishers, Craig and Sandi Nelsen, allowed me to talk Loveland Press into becoming my new home. I wanted no one else for a publisher after seeing their spectacular work. They are everything an author hopes for and I appreciate their support.

Murray Rubin, my publicist, has worked tirelessly in my radio show publicity work. His efforts brought me into every market in the United States and overseas, and my fan mail reflects his efforts. He is more than a publicist, he is a true friend.

Finally, here's a story. Long ago I was heartbroken over a breakup with a boyfriend, right after my freshman year of college. My Mom and her friend, Ila Miller, got together in a gentle conspiracy. They sent me to northeastern Wyoming with Brit, Ila's daughter. Brit and I helped herd cattle and check on fences on the Miller's ranch near Devils Tower, Wyoming. At the end of this time I was sunburned and happy and confident in who and what I was. The boyfriend? I can't recall his name.... God Bless the moms, for knowing what I needed so badly. Thank you for your friendship, your love, and your sweet wisdom, and for giving me the summer that serves as an inspiration for this novel.

CHAPTER ONE

The Reed Ranch, Wyoming

"**O**h, no," Eileen Reed said. "We've got trouble. The archaeologist is here."

"The one who thinks her partner was murdered?" Lucy Giometti asked. She rose on her tiptoes to see out the kitchen window. They were both standing at the Reed Ranch's enormous kitchen sink, up to their thick yellow glove-tops in soapy water. Eileen was washing dishes and Lucy was rinsing. Lucy had pitched in to help Eileen with her mother's cook pans. Big cook pans, too, for a crew of hunters who were scouting the Reed Ranch and an additional crew of archaeologists who were excavating a buffalo jump.

"I think so," Eileen said, peering through the kitchen window at the dusty brown truck in the yard. The shadowy figure behind the wheel was looking down, rummaging for gum or cigarettes or perhaps some paperwork. Eileen kept scrubbing the pot that had held gravy. "Which is why Mom wanted me up here, me being a cop and all."

"A homicide detective," Lucy said with a little grin. She took the pot from Eileen's hands and rinsed it. "And me a little nobody friend of yours from back East, and let's keep it that way."

"Of course, Secret Agent Man," Eileen said from the corner of her mouth, trying to do a Bogart imitation. Lucy

Giometti worked for the Central Intelligence Agency and couldn't tell anyone that she did. Eileen knew, but only because of her own homicide work within the Defense Department. They'd met on a difficult case two years ago and hit it off immediately, two women who hunted bad guys for a living and liked it. Though they couldn't be more different in temperament and looks, Eileen had found herself with an unexpected best friend.

When Eileen became engaged she hesitated before asking Lucy Giometti to be her matron of honor. Would Lucy think she was pathetic, asking a friend a continent away to stand up for her, a friend that she saw maybe once a year? Lucy, at her call, had broken into whoops of joy. She'd never been a matron of honor, she confided to Eileen. Always a bridesmaid, and once a bride, but never the one to hold the bouquet while the bride accepted the ring. She was honored. She was thrilled, and she made Eileen laugh with relieved joy.

The wedding was now four months away and Lucy had come out to help Eileen with finalizing the thousand small details. Lucy had been enchanted with the idea of traveling to the Reed Ranch. She had done the fittings for her matron of honor dress, but she admitted the endless wedding details were wearing her out. Eileen, too, was relieved to be doing something, anything, else. They'd gleefully thrown the color swatches and bouquet pictures back on Eileen's desk, packed up Hank, Lucy's little boy, and headed for Wyoming.

The archaeologists were the main headache to Eileen's parents, and the reason Eileen and Lucy were in Wyoming. Paul and Tracy Reed had recently turned their cattle ranch into a guided hunting business. Elk, deer, mountain lion, wild turkey and bear were plentiful in the eastern Wyoming Black Hills. The Black Hills National Forest joined their property on the south. Six miles away the enormous stone trunk of Devils Tower created an additional attraction, although both Paul and Tracy had rejected the idea of renaming their ranch something trendy like "Devils Tower Ranch and Hunt Service." The Reed Ranch it remained, and even with the plain name the Reeds were doing very well.

In late May Paul started working on the new bunkhouse, a lavish log cabin that would hold rich hunters in near-hotel accommodations. He'd started the first clearing work with his backhoe and braked to a stop within minutes, confused and a little frightened. The dirt under the green grass was packed with bones, so thick and white they looked like outcroppings of chalk. After sitting still for a minute or two, looking at the bones, Paul got off his backhoe and took a look.

To his relief, he found they were buffalo bones. The bones were packed to a depth of six feet and it was then that Paul realized the bluff above the bones had been the site of a Native American buffalo jump. Six weeks later the Reeds were picking out a new site for their bunkhouse and a crew of archaeologists from the University of Wyoming were practically wetting themselves at the foot of the bluff. Now one of the archaeologists was missing, some extremely rich hunters were scouting at the ranch, and Tracy Reed had called her daughter for help.

"So do you think the missing archaeologist is dead?" Lucy asked. They'd been roped into cleaning dirty dishes the morning after they arrived, which didn't bother Eileen. On a ranch, work was whatever needed to be done, right now. Lucy, easygoing and cheerful, pulled on cleaning gloves and set to work.

"I don't know. He's missing, but that doesn't mean anything. He could be tossing the dice in Las Vegas with a downy thing he picked up at a bar. You know? Missing doesn't always equal dead."

Hank Giometti trotted into the kitchen with a black and white Border collie at his side. He was wearing a bright red T-shirt and shorts. His curly black hair was dusty and his cheeks were flushed. He was grinning. The collie, named Zilla, was panting. They had the same grin.

Zilla sat down and wagged her tail. She was a champion cattle dog, now a housedog after an accident with a bull. With three legs she was as quick as most other dogs were with four and her passion for herding things never left her. Tracy Reed, Eileen's mother, had named Zilla after a Hebrew word that meant "protective shade." Eileen thought Zilla's name fit her perfectly.

Lucy, Hank, and Eileen had arrived at the ranch late at night. Hank, when he awoke, fell in love with Zilla at first sight.

Hank went right to Lucy and threw his chubby arms around

her legs. She bent over and planted a kiss on his dusty curls, keeping her wet gloves in the sink.

"How are you, baby? Need a diaper change?"

"No, no, no," Hank announced. "Blocks!"

"I had many a wonderful hour with those blocks," Eileen said with a smile, turning her gaze away from Hank and looking back out the window at the figure who was still sitting in the truck. "My dad made about a million of them for me. I'm glad he kept them around."

Hank had spent much of the morning building towers in the living room with Zilla's attentive help. When they got tall enough, he would knock them over and squeal with delight. Zilla would yip encouragingly. Eileen and Lucy had been listening to the silence, crash, squeal and yipping while they washed dishes.

"Mommy," he giggled, clutching Lucy. Zilla wagged her tail.

"Oh, hey, she's getting out of the truck," Eileen said. Lucy stood up on her toes, looking out the window. Hank, apparently satisfied with his mommy visit, left the room with Zilla at his heels. There were more blocks to stack, squeal and yip over.

"Mom doesn't like these University ladies. She hasn't said, but I can tell," Eileen said. "Not that we've had much time to talk, you know." She scrubbed hard on the next pot.

Outside, the door to the dust-spattered truck finally opened. Out stepped a woman in jeans and a blue work shirt, a woman with a shoulder-length spill of honey blonde hair so thick and shiny it glittered like gold in the sun. She had a face to match the hair, fine-boned and full-lipped. Her eyes were sky blue and she had thick, naturally arched brows that were drawn down in dislike or temper. As she shut the door the rest of her body came into view. She had full, boys-fantasy size breasts, a hand span waist, and lush hips. She was, in short, spectacularly beautiful.

Eileen looked at Lucy. Lucy looked back at Eileen. Lucy's gloves were dripping with soapy water and her hair was uncombed. She had a smudge on her little nose and her eyes were still tired from the long drive the day before. Eileen knew she didn't look any better than Lucy.

"Let's kill her," Lucy suggested solemnly.

Eileen started snickering. She leaned over the soapsuds and tried to stop, knew that she couldn't, and leaned back. She roared with laughter, and Lucy laughed, too.

Suddenly the door to the kitchen burst open and Tracy Reed shot inside, her tall lanky body telegraphing distress.

"Jorie's here," she cried. "She's back and she's going to ruin *everything.*"

"We know," Lucy said.

Eileen snorted and Lucy sniffed hard.

"What is wrong with you two?" Tracy asked. She looked at them and her face relaxed. "Got the giggles, I see."

"I guess so, mom," Eileen said. She thought about explaining and then didn't. She'd just start laughing again.

"Well, get it together," Tracy said. "If Jorie starts harassing my hunters again I'm going to lose them, I know I am."

"Harassing?" Lucy asked. "How's that?"

"She's an anti-hunter, anti-beef, anti-everything type," Tracy said with an exasperated flapping of her hands. "You know the type. Militant feminist. Human hater. Thinks we should all live in tepees or better yet just die off. Plus she hates Howard Magnus. *Hates* him."

"That's not good," Eileen said, stripping off her gloves. She regarded her pruney fingers. "You never got to that part."

"You've only been here since last night," Tracy said. "I just got to the point where we have a famous rock musician scouting our business and the three of you were already asleep on the couch."

"It was a long drive," Eileen said meekly.

"I'm glad you're here, honey," Tracy said with one of her lightning changes of expression, smiling at Eileen with a look that lit her face. Eileen grinned. She loved her mom. She reached out and Tracy hugged her.

"Blocks!" Hank announced again from the doorway, Zilla at his heels.

"Knock 'em down!" Tracy said without missing a beat, grinning at Hank. She and Hank hit it off within seconds of his arrival. Tracy liked kids.

"Hello? Hellooo?"

"That would be Jorie," Tracy said with a grimace. She let go of Eileen and ran her hands through her flyaway gray hair. "In the kitchen, Jorie," she called.

Jorie Rothman walked through the door and Eileen sobered instantly. Perhaps the head archaeologist, Dr. McBride, was getting sloppo in some bar in Gillette or whooping it up with whores in Las Vegas, or maybe he really was dead. If he was dead, Eileen was going to have to be very careful not to mess this one up. She didn't want to let her folks down.

"Hello," Jorie said, in a chilly, surprised little voice, looking back and forth between Eileen and Lucy. Jorie was even more stunning close up. She had white, even teeth and flawless skin. She wore no makeup and her long, capable-looking hands were bare, though seamed with dirt. Her nails were chipped and dirty. Her shirt and jeans were reasonably clean but not new.

"This is my daughter, Eileen," Tracy said with a satisfied look. "She's a homicide detective from Colorado Springs. Do you remember, I told you about her? And this is her friend, Lucy Giometti. Lucy is visiting from Virginia."

"Hello," Jorie said. Her full lips tightened just a bit when she looked at Lucy. Eileen smiled inside. Eileen thought of herself as not particularly attractive, but she knew Lucy Giometti was. Lucy was short and perfectly shaped and had masses of curly black hair surrounding a lovely heart-shaped face. She had a triangular little smile that reminded Eileen of a very young Elizabeth Taylor. Lucy was more than a match for the glittery charms of this Jorie woman, even though Lucy had red eyes and a smudge on her nose.

"This is my son, Hank," Lucy said. Jorie gave Hank the kind of flickering glance that dismissed him as a human being.

"Nice to meet you. Are you going to work on this murder case?" Jorie asked, directing her question to Eileen.

"I'll go check Hank's diaper," Lucy said smoothly, picking him up. He laid his head against her shoulder and smiled at Jorie as Lucy left the room. Zilla ghosted along behind with her quick three-legged gait, wagging her tail.

"I'm here to help my mom and dad," Eileen said. "I'm sure you're very concerned about your friend and I'll do what I can."

"That sounds like bullshit," Jorie said waspishly. "Same kind of bullshit your dipshit county sheriff tells me every time I talk to him."

"Well," Tracy said with satisfaction, dusting her hands together. "I'll get back to my work, then. Paul and the hunters will be coming in from the South Ridge this evening and they're sure to be tired and hungry. Why don't you two sit in the family room so I can get supper started?"

"Sure thing, mom," Eileen said, suppressing a sigh. "This way, Miss Rothman."

Eileen glanced at her mother as they left the kitchen. Tracy grinned widely and gave Eileen a little wave that meant *she's all yours now*.

Tracy had decorated the family room in a western style, with leather couches and an enormous elk head over the mantle, softened with shelves of bright books and lamps and a thick wool rug. Tracy had pulled the blinds and curtains open earlier and the room was drenched with light. A few dust motes danced in the air. Outside the window there was a lovely view of her parents' land as it fell away towards the distant Belle Fourche River. Trees shaded the house and made the grass outside the window look cool and green. Eileen took a calming breath, enjoying the soothing smell of sun warmed leather and old books.

"Have a seat," Eileen suggested. "Tell me everything. I'm the good guy, remember."

"Whatever," Jorie said, looking at the leather couches with disgust.

"Jorie," Eileen said, as she took a seat on the leather armchair and deliberately relaxed into it. "Two months ago I testified at the trial of a man who raped and killed a young environmental engineer. The man had been polluting a creek and she found out and he killed her." There was a lot more to the story than that, of course, but Eileen was telling what she thought Jorie should hear. Eileen knew that she didn't look much like a cop. She was never going to scare people with her imposing authority, or cow them into confessing. Jorie's face reflected what Eileen had seen ever since she became a cop: A look of suppressed or even open contempt. This look was often replaced by one of surprise when the handcuffs went on or when the verdict came back guilty.

"I caught him, and he's going to prison. If something happened to your friend, then I'm going to find that out, too."

Jorie looked at her for the first time, her eyes so blue Eileen had trouble looking at them. Her thick brows raised a little and for a moment Eileen thought she had her, thought that whatever person lived behind the perfect features would come out and they could connect. Then the brows drew down and Jorie shrugged elaborately.

"I'll tell you what I know," she said.

Lucy came in from the living room and sat down in the other big armchair.

"Hank's back at his blocks," she said. "Can I listen?"

"Do you mind?" Eileen asked. Jorie gave Lucy that glare – which looked like jealousy, Eileen secretly chortled – and then shrugged again. Jorie liked to shrug, Eileen was finding out. It seemed to be her predominant gesture.

"My boss is Dr. Jonathan McBride. Was, I think. He's a professor of Archeology at the University of Wyoming. His specialty is Plains tribal hunting techniques before the Spanish brought the horse to America."

"Which means buffalo jumps," Eileen said, tucking her feet up in her armchair. Jorie remained at the edge of the leather couch, her rounded haunches barely touching the edge. She laced her fingers and settled them on one knee. Lucy crossed her legs and put her elbows on her knees, making herself a collected little package. Sitting that way she didn't look much bigger than her son.

"What's a buffalo jump?" Lucy asked. "We've been so busy I haven't asked yet."

"A buffalo jump is the primary way the Lakota and other Plains tribes hunted buffalo," Jorie said. Her face became more animated as she spoke; evidently she shared her professor's passion on the topic. "Before the fifteen hundreds, when the Spanish brought the horse, the Native Americans had no way to reliably kill a single buffalo. So they would slowly drive a buffalo herd towards the edge of a bluff or cliff. Then they would stampede the animals off the cliff and the fall would kill or cripple enough buffalo so the people would have what they needed."

"How would they stampede the buffalo?" Lucy asked.

"Here's the good part," Eileen said. She, too, knew about buffalo jumps. She grew up in Wyoming and schooled in South Dakota. Every schoolchild learned about the Plains tribes and how they survived. "Or not, depending on your point of view."

"Yes," Jorie said impatiently. "But it was a tremendous honor to be chosen."

"Chosen for what?" Lucy asked.

"To lead the buffalo herd over the cliff," Eileen said. She nodded at Lucy's stunned expression. "No, not suicide. The Lakota would dig a hollow right underneath the lip of the cliff. Then the young boy—"

"Boy?" Lucy breathed, eyes wide.

"Boy," Jorie said. "Between ten and fourteen, when boys are strongest and most agile. And aren't yet warriors."

Lucy looked around automatically, with the expression that Eileen was beginning to think of as the Mother-Radar look, even though Lucy knew Hank was happy with his blocks in the living room.

"The boy would cover himself up in a buffalo head and cape, and slowly lead the herd towards the cliff," Eileen continued.

"That doesn't make sense," Lucy said. "How does a ten-year-old in a buffalo skin look like a buffalo?"

"Buffalo aren't that bright," Eileen laughed. She stretched her arms behind her head. It felt good to sit down after all those pots and pans. "They look at silhouette, not size. Outline and smell is what counts. Plus, the tribe would sometimes light a grass fire to spook the buffalo even more. They wouldn't do that in a year like this one, because it's been so dry. But in wet years, they'd spook 'em with fire."

"Then the boy would start running towards the cliff edge. The buffalo would follow, believing that they were running to safety, then stampede, and the boy would flip off the edge of the cliff and into the hollow beneath," Jorie continued.

"And tons of buffalo steaks and chops would fall past him. It was a very risky and very honorable challenge for a warrior-to-be," Eileen said.

"And if he missed?" Lucy asked.

"Then they honored his memory," Eileen said.

"Actually we're hoping he missed," Jorie said. "The herd that fell off this cliff was absolutely huge. There are so many bones at the bottom of the cliff we think perhaps this was a bigger stampede than the tribes people intended. If the boy missed his perch, we'll find him underneath all the buffalo. With luck, he'll have everything with him. A complete skeleton, maybe even tools and artifacts. Talismans. A treasure."

"Have you gotten to the bottom yet?" Lucy asked, and then shivered elaborately. "Sorry. I just keep thinking of Hank."

"We're almost there," Jorie said. "Then Beryl and I had to return for a funding meeting at the University. Jon was gone when we got back. Just gone! He wouldn't have left. He sent us to the damned *funding* meeting, he was so excited about the excavation. I've never known him to miss a funding meeting. If the dig looks like a good one, we'll want to bring a whole crew of graduate students up here."

"That was when?" Eileen asked, though she already knew.

"Three days ago," Jorie said. "And your sheriff, that King idiot, he wouldn't—"

"King?" Eileen asked, sitting forward abruptly. "Not *Richard* King?"

"Rick, not Richard," Jorie said. "Anyway, he's a complete creep. He said we couldn't even file a missing persons report for at least a week, not without some suspicion of foul play—"

"Eileen," Lucy suddenly asked. "What's the matter?"

"I know him," Eileen said, swallowing past an acid lump of dismay in her throat. "I know Richard. Jorie, I hope your boss shows up with a hundred hickeys and a hangover, because I don't know if I can work with Richard King. Or, rather, if he wants to work with me."

"Hey, guys, here's some soda pop," Tracy said, bursting through the door with her customary speed. She cradled three glasses in her hand, glasses clinking with ice. "You hungry yet? Lunch in fifteen minutes, sandwiches. Gotta go." She set down all three glasses on a table next to Eileen and shot back out the doorway. Eileen very carefully avoided looking at Lucy, knowing if she did she'd start laughing. Tracy obviously did not want to be captured by the tenacious and unpleasant Jorie Rothman.

"Thank goodness," Lucy said, capturing a glass with a sigh. "It's been so hot these past few days." She took a deep swallow of her soda pop and stopped in mid-swallow. Eileen, handing a glass to Jorie, saw the stillness and turned to Lucy.

Lucy set her glass down.

"I don't hear Hank," she said, and leaped out of her chair.

"I'll be right back," Eileen said, bolting after Lucy.

In the living room there were blocks scattered across the floor, but no Hank and no Zilla. The door to the front porch was open, as it had been all morning, and the screen door showed an inviting slice of blue sky and green grass.

"Hank!" Eileen and Lucy shouted together.

"Who's Hank?" Jorie asked from behind Eileen. "What?"

"You better stay here," Eileen said. She left for the kitchen with Lucy at her heels and in the short shadowed hallway between the sunny family room and the sunny kitchen Eileen felt her arms brush up with sudden goose bumps.

The kitchen was full of a mixture of delicious smells. An enormous pot with a boiling chicken was on the stove for Tracy's chicken noodle soup. Tracy, hands lathered with flour, was rolling out dough for apple pie. The apples, peeled and sliced and covered with cinnamon and sugar, lay in a ceramic bowl. Tracy looked up and saw Eileen's face and dropped the rolling pin.

"What?" she asked, eyes widening.

"Hank," Lucy said in a little voice.

"He's okay," Tracy said. "He just wandered off. Zilla is with him, Lucy. We'll find him."

She stepped to a rack by the door, which held a leash, an old raincoat, and a dog whistle on a chain. Despite her calm words her hands were shaking. She stepped to the open kitchen door and blew the whistle. Eileen winced and covered her ears – though she couldn't actually hear the tones, she could sense a kind of high pressure on her eardrums.

There was silence, and then impossibly far away, like a dog in a dream, they heard Zilla barking.

CHAPTER TWO

The Reed Ranch, Wyoming

Lucy could hardly breathe as she followed Tracy and Eileen towards Zilla's barking. She couldn't understand how Hank could have gotten so far, so *fast*. She'd only left him for a few minutes.

The Reed Ranch sat in a fold of land in wooded hills with a gorgeous view down into a river bottom and across a valley to the slopes of mountains. Devils Tower lay six miles south but Lucy couldn't see it. She was glad. When they'd driven up she'd seen the Tower at a distance and it made her feel distinctly odd. The Tower was the remnant of an ancient lava eruption, fluted like the trunk of gigantic tree stump. It didn't look natural looming against the horizon. Lucy's eyes hurt just looking at it, it was so gigantic and still and black. She almost felt as though it were looking back at her, and didn't like her very much.

The main building of the Reed Ranch, a frame house painted a cheerful yellow and white, was set apart from the other outbuildings. It sat within a small forest of tall pine and aspen trees. A green and shady lawn stretched south and west of the house. To the north, where the road came into the ranch, there was a straggly flower garden. Lucy found out why the garden was so ragged her first morning at the ranch; she'd woken to see four deer munching happily at the flowers, enormous ears flicking back and forth ceaselessly, tails flipping happily. Tracy came out with her apron and shooed them away and the deer bounded off like mischievous children.

Tracy was heading towards the farthest set of outbuildings, a small yellow-painted barn and a chicken coop next to a tiny log cabin. The cabin was neat and tidy, but the roof of the small barn had a pronounced sag, and the chicken coop had a raspberry bush growing through the screening of the sides. Behind the outbuildings was the start of the forest, deep and green.

In the other direction, where the level land started to slope down towards the Belle Fourche River, there was a modern looking structure. It was large and metal and had a huge door. This building held a bewildering array of trucks and tractors and even a snowmobile. Beyond this building there was another barn, a big one, with a corral. There were some other buildings next to the barn that looked like horses might live there. Lucy, who knew next to nothing about rural life, wasn't sure.

As they came closer to the log cabin Lucy could see movement, and nearly fell over her feet as Hank and Zilla came into view. Hank was unharmed, dusty from head to toe, jumping up and down and laughing.

"Oh thank God," Lucy gasped.

"He's okay, he just wandered off," Eileen said. "I was never worried, were you?"

"Not for a second," Lucy said, and laughed shakily.

The day was hot and breathless and smelled like dust and pines and horses. Now that they could see Hank and Zilla more clearly, Lucy realized that the little cow dog was acting strangely. Hank was trying to jump past Zilla towards the cabin, but every time he did Zilla would block him. He tried to push by her and she wagged her tail harder, but she didn't move. He tried to dodge left but Zilla anticipated him and placed her blocky little body in front of him. Hank giggled and tried to dodge right. Zilla wagged her tail and blocked him again. Hank looked back and saw his mother.

"Mommy!" he crowed. "Look! Zilla!"

"That's the old homestead, Lucy," Eileen explained. "The log cabin is where my great-grandparents first lived when they came here. Now we just store stuff there. We don't even use the old chicken coop any more."

"That's where they lived?" Lucy said, looking at the sagging old log structure. "It looks like a dog kennel."

"They raised three out of their seven children there, as a matter of fact," Tracy said absently. She was looking at Zilla and frowning.

"What is going on?" Jorie said. Lucy glanced behind her. Tracy still had on her flour smeared apron and Jorie followed behind, looking impatient. "Can we get back to the ranch now? This is a waste of—"

"Something here is dangerous," Tracy said, her eyes on Zilla.

"Pick up Hank, Lucy," Eileen said abruptly. Lucy picked up her little boy, who settled into the crook of her arm. His body was warm and sweaty and dirty and smelled rather strongly of collie. And wasn't there something else in the air? Something thick and bland? She thought there was, and she looked at Eileen. Eileen nodded back, a brief movement of her chin. She smelled it too.

Tracy stood looking up and down the homestead. Lucy looked too. There were no cars coming up or down the ranch road that led to the highway. There was nothing moving in the hot, still day but four women, a small boy, and a collie dog. A few chickens scratched in the yard down by the big barn. High in the air down by the river bottom a hawk floated in big, lazy circles. There wasn't a cloud in the sky.

"Stand down, Zilla," Eileen said. She suddenly held a very businesslike SIG-Sauer in her hand, gleaming like a black jewel in the sun.

"What's that?" Jorie said in a high voice. "A gun? What do you need a gun for?"

"Something is dead behind my old chicken coop," Tracy said. "Can't you smell it? The death?"

"I smell it," Lucy said. Jorie nodded, her face suddenly confused.

"Something might be back there that's not dead," Tracy continued calmly.

"Something back there?" Lucy asked sharply.

"Cougar, bear, wolf, they all defend their kill, Lucy," Eileen said. "With me, Zilla." Zilla fell into place with Eileen, tail no longer wagging, her head and ears up and alert.

"Wish our dog Fancy was trained that well," Lucy muttered into Hank's ear, and shifted him so she was more comfortable. She half expected Eileen to come running back around the corner of the chicken coop with an enormous bear at her heels, a vision at once so horrifying and funny she felt a rise of nervous laughter in her throat.

"Not a wolf," Tracy said to Lucy, as though they were holding drinks at a cocktail party instead of guns in the midst of what Lucy felt was a completely deserted state. Wyoming was empty, empty. There was simply nothing. As far as Lucy could tell there were hills, trees, streams, bluffs and hollows and herds of antelope and deer and jackrabbits, but no people, all the way from the Colorado border to the Reed Ranch. To a girl raised in Baltimore, Maryland, the state of Wyoming was terrifyingly empty.

"Why not a wolf?" she asked, swallowing past a dry patch in her throat. Hank twisted in her arms to look at her face, his little mouth suddenly pursed in concern. "Everything's fine, Hank."

"Wolves are noisy. We'd have heard them howling over a big kill. And they don't dine this close to us, anyway. They're very polite, wolves."

Eileen walked back around the coop with no fanfare. Her gun had disappeared but her face was pale and thoughtful.

"I think we've found the missing archaeologist," she said to Jorie. "I'm sorry."

Jorie gasped and started forward. Tracy put a hand on her arm.

"No, dear," she said.

"You can't go back there," Eileen said.

"I have to," Jorie screamed. "It's Jon? He's dead? You don't know it's Jon!" She started forward again and Lucy joined Tracy, stepping in front of Jorie. Tracy put her arms around the younger woman.

"I don't know if it's Jon," Eileen said. "But there's a dead man back there, and I don't know if it's murder or not. It doesn't look like an animal attack."

"I need to see him," Jorie sobbed, trying again to move forward. Her face was shiny pale except for two bright red patches on her cheeks. Her mouth was drawn down and distorted. Lucy saw this with sympathy and a dawning interest. Jorie looked like a lover, or a wife. She wasn't acting like a colleague.

"No you don't," Lucy said at the same time as Eileen and Tracy.

"He might be alive," Jorie shouted through her sobs.

"He's extremely dead," Eileen assured her. "Let's get back to the house and call the police right away, and Dad too."

"Right, then," Tracy said briskly. "Lucy, you give Hank a bath right away. Lots of soap and scrub him good. Eileen, you get the tub out and scrub Zilla down. I'll take Jorie inside and we'll make the calls."

"Hank?" Lucy whispered to Tracy. "Did he – see? Did he touch him?" Tracy gave her a big smile, as reassuring as a hug.

"No, Lucy. I think Zilla caught the scent and followed it over here, and Hank followed her. But Zilla wouldn't let him get near the cabin or go behind it. You saw that, remember. And there aren't any tracks in the dirt but Eileen's. Look."

Lucy did, and tried to nod as calmly as she could when what she wanted to do most was burst into relieved tears.

"But just in case, we're going to scrub the two of them very well and have Dr. Peterson check Hank over when he gets here. Just in case. Let's move, girls."

Jorie resisted, her blue eyes clouded and red, her mouth trembling.

"Can you get hold of Dad?" Eileen asked. She was grave and unsmiling but Lucy could tell she was excited. But of course that was her job. Finding dead people was all in a day's work to Eileen Reed. Lucy, on the other hand, was an analyst. She only dealt with dead people on paper. A dead person right in front of her wasn't in her job description. She swallowed hard, trying not to think about what was behind the cabin.

"You're sure? He's back there? Jon is back there?" Jorie said again.

"I'm not sure of anything yet," Eileen said. "Come on, Jorie, let's get you inside and get you some water. You need to sit down for a few minutes."

Lucy followed Eileen as she led Jorie back to the main

house, her head buzzing with the July heat and her heart hammering with fear for Hank. By the time they got back to the main house Hank himself had calmed her. He was his usual cheerful self, sitting happily on her hip and watching Zilla trot along behind them. As they walked through the kitchen door his head started to droop on her shoulder.

"Upstairs for a bath, Hankster," she said. She walked to the stairs and looked back. "I'll be right back down, okay, Eileen?"

Eileen looked over at her, glanced at Jorie to make sure she wasn't looking, then dropped her an enormous wink and grinned at her. Eileen couldn't wink. She had a lovely oval face with high angular cheekbones that gave her an ice-queen look that Lucy envied, but when she winked she screwed up one side of her face and squinted both eyes into slits and turned her face from ice-queen to clown. Lucy smothered a giggle.

"No problem," Eileen said. Truly, she thought, with the two of them together, what *could* be a problem?

Eileen stood quietly over the body. Lucy was bathing Hank and Jorie had gone to the jump site to tell her colleague. She'd be back far too soon, but at least that gave Eileen some time.

She stood in the hot sun, feeling a lot less assured than the image she projected to her mother. Eileen was never sure how she solved cases. Her personal theory was that she just kicked at rocks until something came crawling out. So far, something had always crawled out.

Doctor Jon McBride, Professor of Archeology at the University of Wyoming, lay sprawled and three days dead in front of her. His face was in the dirt and weeds that grew against the neglected back of the chicken coop. The khaki of his shirt and the denim of his jeans were swollen tight. His corpse was starting to rot and the gases were bloating him. Eileen looked closely, beyond the bloating and the smell, and saw that he was originally a powerfully built, athletic man. His hair was gray and wiry, long and tied in a ponytail, and the skin at the back of his neck was seamed with a thousand fine wrinkles. The soles of his boots lay up, well worn. They were less elderly than the leather below; he was a man who had his boots resoled rather than buy a new pair. Eileen could see one hand. It was outstretched and the nails were dark at the edges. Blood? Paint?

She could see no gunshot wound, no knife wounds. Of course there was the front of his body, but she wouldn't touch the scene. She'd leave that to Richard King, her old high school classmate. She grimaced and raised the digital camera she'd borrowed from her mother. Richard had to have changed enormously since high school. Richard had been such a loser back then. How had he become a sheriff?

She took dozens of shots, carefully walking around the body and shooting from all angles. Perhaps because she was being careful to leave no tracks, she saw the ant trail. It was tiny and she might have missed it, but she was being meticulously careful. She didn't want Richard to have any excuse to get upset with her. Could he still be pissed off about prom night at the park?

The ant trail. What about the ant trail? There were several trails leading to the body, and the flies were already making good inroads into the exposed skin of Dr. McBride's ankles, hands and head. In a few days the body was going to be boiling with maggots. But this ant trail led away from the body, not to it.

She followed the trail, placing her feet carefully and silently. She'd long ago blocked out the smell from the body but it was still a relief to take a few steps away. The trail led to a small dried pool of blood covered in a carpet of dead ants. The ants had stuck and died in the blood. Flies buzzed past her head on their way to the body. Their sleepy buzzing sounded in Eileen's ears and thrummed in her head.

The second dried splatters of blood, a few steps beyond the first, gave her what she needed. Dr. McBride hadn't been at the ranch at all. He'd been heading *for* the ranch. Eileen stood up from the third dried splash of blood and looked down McBride's back trail. She hadn't been to the buffalo jump yet, but she knew where it was. She had a favorite tree down at the bottom of the bluff, a cottonwood so tall and thick it was a Tolkien forest all by itself. When she was eleven she spent hours in the tree with her collection of Barbie dolls and her *Lord of the Rings* books. By her seventeenth birthday it was gone, blown down in a fall thunderstorm.

The cottonwood tree was the site of the buffalo jump.

McBride was heading for the ranch from the buffalo jump when he died. Eileen looked at the blood and back at the body, almost entirely hidden in the summer grass. She wanted to turn the body over. She wanted to so badly she could taste it, like a bitten lemon in her mouth. What had killed him?

CHAPTER THREE

Highway 94, Colorado Springs, Colorado

"**A**m I dead?" Joe Tanner asked Sully.

Sully laughed and sprawled back in the whiteness that surrounded them.

"Naw, you're not dead, Joe. You've been in a car wreck. Just like mine, remember? And if you don't get the hell out of the car, they're going to come back and finish you off. Just like they did to me."

"Wait a minute," Joe said. "What is this place? Is this heaven?" He looked around, seeing more clearly. The clouds were white and pristine but there was sky of sorts above them, a clear pale sky with lines of clouds touched with every hue of the rainbow. Joe used to look at thunderclouds as a child and imagine flying up into heaven on their very tops. This was like that, only better. More beautiful. He felt absolutely wonderful. Every inch of his body tingled with energy. Sully, in front of him, floated in the clouds.

"Are those wings?" he asked in dumb wonder. Sully laughed again and stretched one wing out to her side. It was enormous, covered with feathers deep and strong, and colored a delicate and perfect pink.

"Cool, huh?" she said. "I'll tell you, being dead is pretty

great. Dying wasn't so hot, but heaven is fantastic."

"This is heaven?" Joe asked. Sully was dead, he knew that. Harriet Sullivan had died in a car crash over five years ago. He'd been engaged to marry her when she died. Three years later, when he'd met Eileen Reed, he was still grieving at Sully's sudden and senseless death. Only when he fell in love with Eileen was he able to finally accept Sully's death and move on.

"Not heaven, Joe," Sully said. "You're not dead. And I'm just an image, like these nifty clouds. This is just a – a communication place, a way for people near death to see and talk to creatures like me."

Sully had never been a very attractive woman, really, but he'd loved her for her spirit and her mind and her smile. Now she looked the same but not the same. Every inch of her was perfected somehow, beautiful beyond description. She wasn't the Sully he'd known, the Sully who had faded in his mind like an old color photograph. Suddenly he realized what she'd just said.

"I'm near *death*?"

"Damn near," Sully said grimly. "But we have some time to talk. Just a little. Usually we don't do this sort of thing, you know."

"We?" Joe asked in a weak voice. He looked down at himself. Yes, he was still dressed in his jeans and T-shirt, the same ones he'd worn to work that morning. He checked his right finger, where he wore a silver band that Eileen had given him. A promise ring, she called it.

"The ring's still there," Sully said. She was dressed in something light and fluttery, white and rose-colored like her wings. "Eileen is your life now, Joe, and you're going to need her help to get yourself out of this one. They've targeted you just like they targeted me. Even if you get out of the wreck tonight you're going to have to figure out a way to stop them."

"Who are *they*?"

"Remember the unsolved murders at Schriever Air Force Base?"

"Yes," Joe said, then felt a rush of fear and anger through his body. "Your car wreck wasn't an accident? You were *killed*?"

"I was killed," Sully said, and shrugged. Her wings rose, a poem of light and structure, and Joe was caught in their beauty.

They were so perfect. Joe was taken by a desire to touch those wings, to feel them alive and warm and beating like a heartbeat.

"Pay attention," Sully said. "You're not going to die like me. Not if I can help it."

"Yes," Joe said. "Could you – fold those away?"

"Oh, of course," Sully said, and folded her wings behind her. "Better?"

"Yes."

"Okay, then, listen up. They came back to the wreck and I was still alive. I wanted to live, Joe, then, as badly as you do. As badly as Eileen does. I was struggling to get out and they came up and when I asked for help the fat one took my chin and the back of my head and snapped my spine." Sully pursed her lips and shook her head. "It took me ten more minutes to die, and the worst part was that I couldn't say goodbye to you. It's long over now, Joe, don't cry."

"I'm not crying," Joe said, and wiped his face with the bottom edge of his T-shirt.

"Anyway, here I am, and I've got lots of work to do so I'm going to have to be quick."

"Work?"

"What, you think heaven is just sitting on clouds playing harps?" Sully grinned. "In medieval times people worked themselves to exhaustion every day without a rest. So their vision of heaven was a place of eternal rest. Harps and so forth. We modern types, that would be hell to us, a place without anything to do. Heaven is perfect, absolute perfection, you see? So I have the perfect work for me."

"What do you mean?" Joe asked. He wanted to stay with her. He wanted to stay and listen to her talk, forever. She looked at him, squinted at him, and shook her head. "Joe, you're smarter than you look, I forgot that. You can't stay here much longer or you won't want to leave. Listen. You're less than twenty yards from the auto junkyard at the bottom of the hill. Remember?"

"I remember," Joe said. "But—"

"Shut up," Sully said. Her head rose and she looked around her for the first time. Her smile disappeared and she looked wary. "You have to get out of the wreck. Get to the junkyard and you'll find the owner's house about a half mile down the road. You can call the police from there. They'll be back to look for you and if they find you they'll snap your neck just like mine. Understand?"

"I understand," Joe said. Sully's unease had transmitted itself to him. The hair on the back of his neck was standing in stiff bristles. His arms brushed up in gooseflesh. But wasn't this a dream? How could he have goose bumps in a dream?

"Then you have to get to Eileen. Get to her. That man, the fat man, he'll come after you. He won't stop until you're dead, or he is. He kills people like you, Joe. You've been targeted and I don't want to see you die like me."

"I hear you, Sully, but—"

"No more, Joe," Sully said. She unfolded her wings. Her beauty was blinding and heartbreaking. "I have to go, and so do you."

"Why do you have to go?" Joe cried. "Stay, let me stay."

"You'd need a bit of training to stay with me," Sully said. She rose up in the clouds and there was something in her hand, something ancient and sleek and long, like a spear married to a laser gun. Her wings beat and Joe's eyes were dazzled by rainbow. "Go, Joe. Live. We'll meet again. I have work to do."

"What work?" Joe called, but she was above him, wings beating. He saw what she was looking at and his heart staggered inside him. There was something coming towards them through the clouds, something loathsome and black and covered with spines and teeth. It was swimming in the clouds, eyes and head above them like an ancient crocodile. It looked something like a dragon but it was something more, something so evil his eyes couldn't find a way to see it. It reared up and a rotted, slavering mouth opened. Eyes opened, eyes like visions of hell, and it looked at him. It *saw him.*

"I fight these, now," Sully said serenely. Her wings beat sharply in his direction and Joe sank abruptly into the clouds and all breath and light left him then.

Joe hurt all over. He was cold but he was covered with sweat. And his glove compartment was open. How irritating. His insurance papers had spilled out along with ancient gum sticks, crumpled Taco Bell napkins and half a dozen straws still in their paper sleeves. He tried to reach out and snap it closed but his arm wouldn't work properly. He kept hitting the steering wheel instead, his fingers scrabbling uselessly at the warm plastic.

There was something he had to remember. Some dream he was having, about Sully. The wings....

There was no transition of consciousness. One moment he was trying to snap his glove compartment closed, muzzy-headed and confused, and the next he was all there, cold and aware and remembering everything. Sully. The dragon. He was in his car, and he had been forced off the road, and if he didn't get out and follow her instructions he was going to end up murdered just like her.

Something in him cried to stay, let go, so he could go back to the clouds. But stronger was his memory of how Sully had described her own death. His hands fumbled with his seatbelt latch. The man, the fat man, snapped her neck and left her to die, paralyzed, alone. Joe wiped his forehead and his hand came away bloody. The seatbelt latch let go and he fell against the driver's side door. The car was at an angle in the ditch. The window was black with mud and weeds. He stood up in the car and pushed open the passenger side door. It was heavy, and wanted to fall back on his head as he lurched out. His right arm was coming back to life, sending shooting pains from his fingers all the way to his shoulder.

The night came alive around him as he crouched beside his crumpled Honda Civic. He could hear thousands of crickets reeping in the grasses and further away the deep sound of frogs. The stars were thick above his head in the summer darkness. The smell of fuel and burnt rubber and oil and a sharp stink of blood filled his nose. His nose was bleeding too, he noticed.

Don't leave a blood trail, Sully whispered in his head. Joe nodded and wiped at his nose a few times until he could see he wasn't bleeding too badly. The forehead gash was right above his hairline. His hair was matted and sticky with blood but it, too, seemed to be clotting up pretty good. So then, no blood trail.

Joe took a deep breath and stood up, remembering with razor clarity the look of Sully's lance. He wished he had it now.

With that thing, whatever it was, he had the feeling he could hold off an entire army.

The road stretched on the other side of the ditch, clear and empty and blameless. Joe drove this highway every day, and had for years. He was near the bottom of Junkyard Hill, and although he still had no memory of his accident, he could see the tire tracks and the gouges in the grasses that led to his Honda. The gouges were as good as a trail of smoking flares. They would find him immediately when they came back. He had to get out of there.

He turned around, knowing what he would see. Behind him stretched the fence that surrounded an enormous auto junkyard. Joe had been there once last summer with his friend 'Berto, scouting for side mirrors for 'Berto's '67 Mustang. The junkyard owner was an enormous tattooed man who looked like a Hell's Angel except when he donned his Santa Claus outfit each Christmas and made hundreds of children happy at the mall. Joe couldn't remember his name. Tom? Todd? T-something. Joe stepped carefully through the grass and climbed the fence, a chain-link affair with slats of green plastic woven through the links. T-guy didn't bother with razor wire or barbed wire on top. He built the fence so people wouldn't have to look at the junkyard as they drove by; he was required to have the fence as a zoning requirement of the county.

As Joe dropped to the ground in the junkyard his eye was caught by a twinkle down the dark highway. Suddenly he had no breath. They were coming back to make sure he was dead. He checked the ground beneath him. Dry. He would leave no tracks. Silently he ran down an alley where the buildings were stacks of wrecked cars. He knew where the T-guy's trailer was but he had to see these men. He *had* to. His head throbbed and the pain in his right arm stabbed at him. *They* had done this to him.

The car lights swept quickly down the highway. The lights went out as the car purred quietly to a stop next to the tire tracks. Joe peered through the slats of the fence well down the road from his car, but close enough to see.

A man got out of the car. He was huge, tall and fat enough to make the car rock back up on its springs when he stood up. His face was moon-like, unreadable in the darkness.

"The fat man," Joe breathed silently. He never wanted to kill anyone before this. His bloody fingers clenched into fists. This man had killed Sully.

Fat man looked around, hitching at his pants. Another man got out and ran lightly around the car. He was smaller than Fat man but still substantial, a plank next to a pallet of lumber. Fat man nodded at Plank man and he leaped into the ditch. Joe heard a faint plonk as Plank landed on his Honda.

Plank said something to Fat man. Joe couldn't understand the words. The language wasn't German or Spanish, but it certainly wasn't English. Fat man said something back, incredulous. The smaller man said something back.

Fat man stood and looked at the junkyard with narrowed eyes. Joe took a deep breath and stayed absolutely still. Behind him was a maze of uncrushed cars, a buffet of car parts that he and 'Berto had wandered through the summer before. There was a rattling sound from the highway and Joe's mouth filled with a taste like old pennies as he realized Plank was *in the junkyard*. He'd climbed the fence, swarmed over it, and he was looking for Joe.

Joe had taken two steps towards Plank before Eileen's voice spoke in his head. *Pick your battles*, she said. Sully spoke up, then, too. *Stay alive*, she said. Joe wondered irritably if they'd taken up residence permanently inside his skull. Hopefully they wouldn't start talking to each other about his performance in bed. He crouched low and scuttled into the maze of junkers, keeping his body low and making no noise.

It was amazingly difficult to keep down and keep going. He wanted to stand up and find out where Plank was, or Fat man. He didn't think Fat man was capable of climbing the fence but maybe he'd found a way in. Picked the lock of the gate, perhaps, or cut the chain that closed the gate. For the first time Joe wondered who the fat man was and who had sent him. He remembered Sully telling him that the fat man was after him. He knew why, but how had the fat man known about what he'd done?

Six months ago Joe had come up with a unique computer solution to a very sticky problem in his field. He programmed computers for war games in Colorado Springs, Colorado. These war games were fought by the highest levels of military soldiers and defense analysts. He'd loved his job since he landed it seven years ago. War gaming was like the best of Dungeons and Dragons crossed with video games, and Joe had been a gaming fanatic since before he'd reached his teens. He watched Star Trek reruns; he lived in his parents' basement in high school and filled it with computer equipment, and in just about every way fulfilled the computer geek profile. Becoming a war gamer was the ultimate job to him and he loved it.

When another programmer was murdered during a war game Joe was too upset to register the impact of Eileen Reed, the homicide detective who'd interviewed him. His girlfriend Sully's accidental death – a murder, he amended now – was still so fixed in his mind he couldn't focus on the grave, quiet woman who asked him about the murdered gamer. Later he saw Detective Eileen Reed, fell in love with her as hard as a man could fall, and still couldn't understand what this beautiful strong creature saw that attracted her to him. He was just Joe Tanner, a man with a Star Trek uniform in his parents' basement closet, and he played video games for a living with such passion that he sometimes forgot to eat.

But fall in love with him she did, and now they were four months away from their wedding day. And in the past six months Joe had developed a new method for fighting terrorist attacks in gaming, a new way of organizing what was essentially a game board. He was inspired by Eileen Reed, he knew, fed by her intelligence and her own passion for solving problems. They were two sides of a coin, one who liked to solve massive battles and another who solved individual ones.

The reaction to his new programming was gratifying, he thought glumly as he crouched against the side of a crushed minivan and started to shiver in the cold night air. They'd played six war games in the past three months with his new concept and more and more high-level officers showed up. The Gamers counted the importance of the game on the number of stars on the shoulders of the men and women who played. At Joe's game last week there were twenty-six stars, a record. Someone among all those stars wasn't playing for the home team. Joe wiped at his forehead and winced. Someone now wanted him dead.

Three cars from the minivan he spotted the T-man's house. It was a doublewide trailer with a white picket fence and a lawn and a flower garden. Joe could smell roses in the darkness. Beyond the trailer he could see a vegetable garden with a patch of corn that looked tall and glossy. T-man liked to garden.

Outdoor lights suddenly clicked on, bathing the front of the trailer in a brilliant white light. Joe saw a flicker by the dark back door, where the corn grew. He took a shivery breath, wondering what to do.

The choice was taken out of his hands. There was a meaty hand placed on his shoulder and a cold, thin blade touched his throat. Joe stopped breathing, his belly freezing into ice. He thought of Sully and wondered if she was finished fighting the dragon thing yet. Maybe she could come meet him when the killers finished the job.

"What's going on, kid?" The voice, even at a whisper, was familiar, warm and deep. A Santa Claus voice. It was the T-man.

"Somebody's trying to kill me," Joe whispered, trying not to pass out. There were black blots falling in front of his vision, like giant snowflakes. "Accident. They came back to finish me off."

"You're friends with 'Berto Espinoza, right?" The whisper came again. The knife blade disappeared from Joe's throat without fanfare. The huge hand stayed on his shoulder.

"Yeah," Joe whispered. He swallowed past an incredibly large ball of dry in his throat. "Help me. They're in your junkyard."

"Back in the salvage area," the T-man said calmly. Joe creakily turned his head. The T-man crouched against the same minivan Joe was leaning against, less than a foot away. He was wearing black baggy pants and a soft black jacket. A watch cap covered his head. He wore a black piece of cloth over his mouth and nose, like a cowboy bandana. Under the jacket Joe could see the edge of a striped pajama jacket. The T-man's feet were bare. His feet were enormous, with long toes that gripped the ground like a monkey. He smelled like old beer and old pot and interrupted sleep. He carried a wireless computer screen in one hand and he positioned it so Joe could see.

The screen was split into six views, all of the junkyard, all crisp black-and-white. In the salvage area where Joe and 'Berto liked to rummage for parts there were two men, one gigantic and the other plank-like, walking silently in the rows with small black guns held at the ready. The Fat man must have cut the gate chain to get in, and that had alerted the T-man.

"Why do they want you dead?" the T-man asked. Joe couldn't see the top part of his face in the darkness. Had he blacked it out, somehow? And what was he, to be woken in the middle of the night and look like that?

"Sully told me they kill people like me," Joe said. He felt confused. Had he told the T-man about Sully yet? "I figured out something useful and now they want to kill me. I work out at Schriever—"

"Say no more," the T-man said with a brisk nod of his not-there face. "I know about Schriever Air Force Base. Don't really want to know what goes on out there." He produced a small object from his pocket and pressed a button. It was a cell phone, Joe realized with relief. The T-man must have modified his phone; it showed no light and made no sound.

"Hi, Marie, it's Todd Whitemore. I've got some intruders here at the salvage yard and they look armed to me. Can't tell. Send some of your big boys, right. Send an ambulance, too, we've got a vehicular out here."

Todd Whitemore powered off the phone and turned to Joe with a flash of teeth.

"The posse will be here in ten, maybe eleven minutes. Let's see if your boys are equipped."

"Equipped with what?" Joe asked.

"Police band radio," Todd said briefly. He looked at the computer screen and nodded. "There they go."

On the screen Joe could see Fat man and the Plank man conferring urgently. They made their guns disappear and headed rapidly for the now open gates of the junkyard. They were gone before Joe heard sirens.

"Damn," Joe said.

"You need to get to a hospital," Todd said. Joe watched as the big man took off his watch cap and bandana and pulled his black jacket over his head. He rubbed his face against the soft black material of his jacket. His hair and beard were snow white and tousled and his face, free of the blacking, looked round in the dim light. His pajama jacket was wildly striped. Todd stood up and stripped off his black pants, revealing pajama bottoms as loudly striped as his top. He balled up his black clothing and cap and grinned at Joe.

"You look completely different," Joe said stupidly. Todd had gone from dangerous commando to rumpled homeowner in pajamas in about five seconds.

"That's the idea," Todd said. "Come on inside, when the cops get here they're going to want a statement. Is your friend Sully somewhere around?"

"She's dead," Joe said.

"In the car? Are you sure?" Todd said sharply.

"She's dead a long time ago," Joe said, and rubbed at his forehead.

Todd regarded Joe for a moment.

"Let's get you inside," he said finally. "You've got a hell of a bump on the head. Looks like a cut on your arm too."

"I better not tell them about Sully," Joe said as Todd helped him to his feet. The ground seemed too far away, as though he was wearing stilts.

"This way. What's your name?"

"Joe Tanner," Joe said. Todd nodded as though he knew the name.

"Best to keep her to yourself," Todd said. "The police don't take kindly to apparitions."

The brightness of the man's porch light was overwhelming. Joe realized he'd forgotten the T-man's name again. There were bright flickering lights, silent now, approaching the junkyard entrance. The T-man opened his front door and hauled Joe into a warm dark kitchen. Tiny blue gas jets lit a stove and the air smelled pleasantly of sweet baking; apple pie, maybe, or cobbler.

"Hang on, I'll be right back," the T-man said, settling Joe into a kitchen chair. He disappeared down the hall with his commando outfit and his computer in hand. He returned a few seconds later, striped pajamas glimmering in the dark, and flicked on the kitchen lights. Joe hissed and covered his eyes. The light felt like knives.

"Concussion, man," the T-man said. "You're going to have to spend the night at the hospital."

"They'll kill me there," Joe said into his cupped hands. "I have to get to Eileen. That's what Sully said. I have to get to Eileen."

"You'll die if you have a bleed in your skull and you're not at the hospital," the T-man said. Joe lowered his hands and squinted at the man. In the warm glow of the kitchen lights and with his tattoos covered by his pajamas he looked astonishingly like Santa Claus. Santa in his summer striped p.j.s. "On the other hand, once they give you a scan and you're clear you can get out. I've left AMA a few times in my checkered career. That would be Against Medical Advice, and docs don't take kindly to it."

"Who are you?" Joe asked in bewilderment.

"Just a junk man," the T-man said, and winked. Bright revolving lights lit his face and he turned to the door. "But I think those men meant business. They looked like professionals to me. Is your Eileen out of town?"

"Yeah," Joe said, "she's in—"

"Stop," the T-man said, holding up his hand. "I don't want to know where she is. Just in case someone comes around asking questions."

There was a brief double-knock at the door and the T-man turned.

"Come on in, Shelly," he said with a grin. "Nice to see you again."

Shelly Hetrick stepped into the kitchen. She was tall and dark and almost as enormous as the T-man. Her hair was in a complex series of braids and her eyes widened as her eyes met Joe's.

"Joe Tanner," she said. "Are you all right?"

Joe gave her a weak grin. He knew Shelly. He was beginning to know all the cops in town. One of the advantages to marrying a cop was finding out the people behind all the uniforms and badges. One of the disadvantages was getting a speeding ticket from someone who worked with your future wife.

"I'm doing okay," he said. "I was run off the road. And

then they tried to come after me."

"He's concussed, but he's right," the T-man said calmly. "Someone cut my front gate chain and two men were looking in the yard for him. They had guns. They took off right after I called you."

Shelly Hetrick stepped aside to allow the ambulance crew in, two competent looking young paramedics. She frowned and hooked her thumbs in her leather belt.

"You look like hell, Joe," she said finally. "Let's get you to the hospital. I'll get a statement from Todd and then I'll come right over to the ER."

Joe looked at Todd who nodded slightly, his face showing nothing. Joe had no intention of being there when Shelly Hetrick came by. He had a strong feeling if he stayed at the hospital more than a few hours no one would be taking a statement from him, ever.

CHAPTER FOUR

The Reed Ranch, Wyoming

Tracy Reed was long gone to bed, after getting a warm kiss and hug from Eileen and warm hug and kiss from her husband. She would be up before dawn baking biscuits and bread and then feeding chickens and horses. By the time Eileen and Lucy would arrive in the kitchen she would have a mountain of dirty dishes for them. Lucy had gone to bed when Tracy did, Hank's small head soundly asleep on her shoulder.

Then it was just Eileen and the guys. Her mother had filled her in on the stories of these men, and although none of them looked like a murderer, any one of them could be. Eileen passed on the cigars but she accepted a small glass of whiskey. She made the drink last all evening, taking small sips now and again. She smiled. She observed.

Howard Magnus didn't look much like a rock star. He was small, for one, and his graying curly hair was neatly clipped in a ponytail at the back of his head instead of forming a wild mane around his face as it did in the pictures Eileen had seen of him. There were wrinkles around his eyes and mouth and his hands looked weathered and knobby. Howie had more money than Eileen could really comprehend, but he didn't look like a multi-millionaire, a killer guitar player and a successful music producer. He looked like somebody's nice grandfather. Except for the eyes.

His eyes were blazing sapphire blue, a perennial wild eighteen. Eileen liked him.

Howard Magnus didn't pack his bags and leave when Tracy Reed told him about Dr. McBride's death. He didn't much care for the archaeologists but he did care, very much, about hunting. He'd seen dead bodies before, he assured Tracy and Paul. Rock music was a fatality-inducing industry and he wasn't the running-away type, never had been. Howie drank and smoked until his wild blue eyes were bloodshot. His hair started to escape his ponytail and formed a fuzzy mane around his head looking more like his rock star pictures.

Jimmy Arnold smoked a cigar and made his whiskey last as long as Eileen did. He seemed to enjoy himself but there was a reserve about him that caught her interest. He never really joined in. Jimmy, part of Howie's entourage, was his brother-in-law. He was tall and dark-skinned, bald, and had muscles that bunched visibly underneath his white shirt whenever he moved.

Mark Plutt, another Howie friend, seemed to be an uncomplicated, happy computer businessman. Eileen's mother told her that Mark owned a software company that sold millions of games every year. He looked like a computer geek, from his skinny body to his black-framed glasses. He had a sweet, youthful smile and a shock of light brown hair. Howie had searched him out when Mark's company developed and sold a tremendously successful video game in which deer hunted down the hunters. Howie, a world-renowned hunter, was both offended and tickled by the game where beer-guzzling deer in Day-Glo orange vests tracked down hapless fat hunters. Mark and Howie had hit it off and Mark had been convinced to come along on Howie's scouting expedition to the Reed Ranch. This was their first trip together. He wasn't a hunter but he liked to hike, he'd said, and scouting for elk and deer sounded like fun. Since it wasn't hunting season there would be only picture-taking.

He drank wine, not whiskey, and knocked off most of a bottle by himself. He shared stories and he, like Jimmy and Howie, told them well.

Nolan Simmons, the last member of Howie's group, was a comedian. He was in his twenties, pudgy, with rosy red cheeks, brown eyes and hair, and an infectious, lopsided smile. Nolan was the son of some famous producer or another, Tracy told Eileen, born into so much money he never had to do a day's work in his life. He spent most of the year touring on second-rate comedy circuits, trying to break into the Big Time with his stand-up routine. Every once in a while he would tire of whacking cockroaches and eating diner food and he'd take a vacation with his father's money. One of his father's oldest friends was Howie.

Eileen would have expected him to dominate the conversation with his funny anecdotes and stories, but he only interjected an occasional joke. Howie chose his companions well, Eileen thought, not a jerk in the whole bunch.

One of them might be a murderer.

"Time for me to walk down to check on the women at the jump camp," Paul said. He looked tired, and Eileen remembered he'd spent the day on horseback scaring up deer and elk to show off to his clients. Spending the day on a horse in the back country was heaven, but tiring heaven.

"I'll go with you, Dad," Eileen offered. Jorie and the other woman, anthropologist Dr. Beryl Penrose, had refused to stay at the ranch house and had returned to the buffalo jump site. Eileen, who hadn't shared her discovery that Dr. McBride was probably attacked at the jump site, had tried hard to get Jorie and Beryl to stay at the house. They were immovable.

"I'll get your jacket," Paul said to her. The family room smelled of cigar smoke and whiskey and horse-sweaty men. Before she'd gone to bed Tracy had turned on the ceiling fan and opened the French doors to the night, which removed the worst of the cigar smoke. Howie and his friends had the vacation attitude; they were ready to drink and smoke and talk all night long.

"After riding a horse today you'll feel tomorrow like you've been dipped in cement, Mark," Howie said, drinking down the last of his whiskey. "Good thing Mr. Reed has a nice spa out on the back deck."

"The new bunkhouse will have three hot tubs," Paul said, holding Eileen's jacket for her. The night was beautiful and clear but cool. Paul shrugged into his own jacket. "Don't stay up too late, gentlemen, I'd like to show you around Devils Tower tomorrow. By truck, don't worry, Mark. We'll give you a day to get your hind end working again."

"Good night," Eileen called, and a half-drunken chorus followed her out the door. Paul closed the French door and whistled softly for Zilla. Zilla appeared instantly, tail wagging. Eileen looked up in the sky and was dizzied by the number of stars. Down in Colorado Springs, where she lived, the night-lights of the city cut out most of the stars. Here at the ranch there was nothing in the way and the stars packed the sky.

"Beautiful night," her father said.

"Yeah."

They started down the path to the buffalo jump, shoulders bumping and Zilla trotting silently at their heels.

"Do you think one of the hunters killed him?" Paul asked.

"I'd hate to think it was," Eileen said. "In order to know who, I need to know why. And I need to know how. The entry wound looked strange to me, not like a typical knife wound. The sheriff took the body, and I don't know if he'll share autopsy information with me."

"He will, Eileen, give him a little bit of time," Paul said with a smile in his voice. "He's never really gotten over you, you know. He's a good man. He's just got to come to terms with you. He tried so hard to date you after you broke up with Owen, and you never looked twice at him. It was hard on him, but it was a long time ago. He'll come around."

"I wish I had your confidence," Eileen said. She'd never told her father about what Richard had tried to do the night of her high school senior prom. There were rumors that came back to her parents, eventually, about Richard trying to kiss her at the park and then falling into the pond when she shoved him back.

There was more than that to the story, though, which she hadn't shared with her dad. Richard had been terribly drunk, more than most of the mildly tipsy crowd that was partying at the lake. He'd come up to her that night and talked to her as she stood with her friends. Most of the prom goers were at the lake, leaning against the rows of parked cars and drinking or smoking or talking. She hadn't encouraged him, in fact she was as distant as she could be, but somehow the dark and the late hour and the lines of her pretty prom dress made his drunken mind think she wanted him as badly as he wanted her.

He hadn't just kissed her, he'd *lunged* at her, pawed her, grabbed her breast in a clumsy grip that left her with a bruise the shape of his thumb across the top swelling of her breast. He'd forced her against the car and had his tongue in her mouth before she could do more than wheeze in surprise. What astonished her most, as she struggled, was the laughter and whoops from prom goers who thought she had asked to be kissed, or liked being kissed, while her backbone ground against the door handle and his fingers bruised her skin. Didn't they know? Couldn't they see?

She'd done more than shove him into the lake that night. She'd kneed him solidly in the crotch, pushed him away, and gave him a solid punch like her father had taught her, an upper cut that crossed his eyes and sent him stumbling backwards into the shallow water of the lake.

There were more catcalls, this time of derision, aimed at a soaking wet Richard who stumbled out of the lake, fell to his knees, and vomited on the shore. Eileen had left the lake immediately, graduated the following month and was gone into the Air Force before summer, but she'd never forgotten the awful feel of his hands bruising her. She'd never spoken to him again. She was sure he'd never forgotten his public humiliation at her hands, either.

The night grew colder as they walked the short distance to the jump camp. She smelled the tang of bug spray as they walked over the last mild rise. Below them lay the camp. A jumble of tents and tables glimmered white in the darkness. There were no lights.

"They must be asleep," Paul whispered. "I hope."

"Look at Zilla, Dad," Eileen whispered. Zilla stood, tail wagging slowly, unconcerned.

"Let's not bother them," Paul whispered. "Looks like everything is okay. I'll leave Zilla on guard."

Paul whispered to Zilla and she sat, wagging her tail. They turned and started the short walk back to the main house. Eileen linked her arm through her dad's and snuggled her hand into his pocket. His warm hand, roughened from years of work, closed around hers.

"We're glad you're here, punkin," Paul said.

"Don't call me punkin," Eileen giggled. "I'll lose all my authority as a detective."

"Okay, punkin," Paul said, and kissed her cheek. "I like your friend, too. She does a good 'I'm-just-a-mom routine,' doesn't she?"

"A very good routine," Eileen said. "I think we might just be good enough to catch us a murderer."

"That's my girl," Paul said. They walked in comfortable silence the last twenty yards to the main house. The house was dark and silent. Everyone was in bed, exhausted from the busy day. Eileen, energized, felt like she could go all night. When she had been trying on wedding dresses with Lucy just three days before she could barely keep her eyes open she was so tired and bored, and now a murdered man had her all charged and ready to go. She was weird, but Joe knew that about her. He loved her anyway. Thank God.

Eileen kissed her father goodnight and walked to her room, missing Joe suddenly and ferociously. She needed him desperately right now, not to help her but just because he was good and clean and...Joe. She unstrapped her guns and took off her clothes. She put on pajamas and brushed her teeth and then, instead of going to bed, sat in her old rocker by the window. Her room had been turned into a guest room for hunters long ago but her old rocker remained. She liked it better now than when she had cluttered it up as a teenager. Her mother had furnished it with clean, spare furniture and simple lamps.

Eileen turned off the light. She looked out the window into the night sky. She could see her favorite constellation, Orion, the hunter with his sword and belt of stars. If Joe were awake and looking up, he would see the same stars. She got into bed and lay still, composed for sleep, looking at the ceiling, thinking that she would not sleep tonight. Then she closed her eyes and she was gone.

Colorado Springs, Colorado

"I guess this takes our friendship to a new level," 'Berto

Espinoza said.

"I'm sorry about this, man," Joe Tanner said. The shot the nurse had given him was beginning to wear off and his head was starting to hurt.

"Let me get us some coffee, okay? Then you can start over again. I'm half asleep and I'm thinking you told me you saw Sully tonight."

"I did," Joe said, touching his head. "Hey, you wouldn't have any painkillers, would you? Good stuff, like when you had that knee surgery last year?"

"Didn't they give you a prescription at the hospital?" 'Berto asked. He got up and walked to the kitchen. 'Berto's apartment was pin-neat, which meant the hired maid had done his place that week. Roberto Espinoza was the worst computer-geek slob Joe had ever met. Chairs were for hanging boxer shorts and sweaty socks over, beds were never made, and trade magazines and paperback books piled up everywhere. If he didn't hire a maid 'Berto's apartment would be uninhabitable.

"What?" Joe asked, blinking. The two 'Berto's in the kitchen merged into one, a disapproving look on his face.

"Didn't they give you a prescription?"

"I left AMA," Joe said. "Against Medical Advice. I'd be dead right now if I'd stayed."

"Sully told you that," 'Berto said. "Our friend Sully. The dead one."

"Sully told me. Now *believe* me, or kick me the hell out of here," Joe said angrily. What did that doctor do, put staples into his brain? His forehead wound was burning. The doctor had stitched him up while they were waiting for the CAT scan machine. Joe had sleepily let the strange bell shape of the CAT surround him and measure him. The strange printout that the doctor showed him was incomprehensible, a bizarre swirl of colors and blots that didn't look anything like a brain. The picture was his brain, however, and it showed that there was no internal bleeding inside his skull. He was going to be okay.

Ten minutes after the nurse settled him in his hospital bed, Joe was sliding quietly out the basement service door, dressed again in his muddy, bloody clothes. Two harrowing hours later, ghosts of the fat man and his plank-like friend haunting every shadow, Joe had finally knocked on 'Berto's door.

Now 'Berto, in sweatpants and a ripped and ancient T-shirt, raised his eyebrows and shrugged elaborately. Then he walked out of the kitchen and down the hall to the bathroom. He emerged with a bottle of pills in his hand.

"Here you go, hermano," he said. "Take one, not two. I weigh more than you do. And better not go to work until they're out of your system. You don't want to get caught in a random drug test."

"Don't worry, I won't be going to work for a while," Joe said. "And thanks." He swallowed the pill and lay back against the couch as 'Berto made busy sounds in the kitchen. Beans were ground, water was poured, the heavenly smell of coffee floated to his nose. The pill made the biting snarl of the stitches go away. Finally the ache in his head subsided to a low, faraway drumbeat. He opened his eyes. Steaming in front of him was a cup of coffee, hot and black. 'Berto sat on the other couch, sipping from his mug.

"I hope I don't get you killed," Joe said muzzily.

"You won't," 'Berto said, with a matter-of-factness that in anyone but 'Berto would be arrogance. He'd been raised in the worst part of East Los Angeles and had avoided bullets, drugs and gangs to graduate at the top of his class at UCLA. To 'Berto, guns and drive-by shootings were part of the landscape, nothing more. "Want to tell me the whole story?"

"I do, and I will," Joe said. "And after I get done I hope you're going to let me borrow your car and some money."

'Berto's eyebrows climbed and he took a sip of coffee. "Okay," he said, as casually as though Joe asked to borrow a piece of gum and a glass of water. "Some clothes, too. Whatever you need."

Joe leaned over his coffee cup, trying to control his face. The drug was making him loopy. He felt absurdly like weeping, because for the first time since he'd woken on a pink-edged cloud with his dead girlfriend hovering in front of him, he felt like he just might be able to stay alive.

Memorial Hospital, Colorado Springs

"He didn't say why he was leaving?" Officer Shelly Hetrick was astonished. And concerned.

"He didn't just walk out. He disappeared out of here, Officer," the doctor said, rubbing his forehead. He was a tall, fat man, taller than Shelly Hetrick, and he looked tired. "The nurse didn't see him go. I didn't seem him go. Nobody did."

They were standing in front of Memorial Hospital. The doctor had been standing outside the entrance smoking a cigarette when Hetrick arrived. He said he was the attending doctor and he told her that Joe had left AMA, against medical advice. The night was deepening towards morning and the July air felt cold. The doctor hunched over his cigarette, looking as worried as Hetrick felt.

"But that's crazy," Hetrick said. "He had a concussion. A bad one, by the look of him. Didn't he?"

"A concussion, but no fracture or internal bleeding. I'd say he wouldn't be able to drive a car or walk more than a few blocks without falling down. Maybe you can check the area. We've called his house but there's no answer. Perhaps you could check? Does he have a girlfriend or family in town?"

"Sure, Eileen," Hetrick said absently. "He said someone was after him. Maybe he thought they'd come after him in the hospital. That could be why he left against medical advice."

"He's a sick man, Officer," the doctor said, stubbing out his cigarette. He then did an odd and, to Hetrick, touching thing. He leaned over and picked up his flattened stub of a cigarette and put it in his jacket pocket. He was a smoker, but he was no litterer, this doctor. "His girlfriend is Eileen, is that right? Can I call over there? Eileen – what?"

"Eileen Reed," Hetrick said. "Don't worry, I'll check over there. If he comes back in, could you call the police department? He paid his bill, right? He's not in trouble here?"

"He's not in trouble, he had his insurance card and he made his co-payment. I'm just worried about him."

"Me, too, Doctor," Hetrick said. "What was your name, again?"

"Dubois," the doctor said, shaking her hand with a friendly smile on his big face. "Doctor Dubois."

Westside Colorado Springs, Colorado

"That's the answer," Rene Dubois said in satisfaction. The stethoscope and the white medical coat were stored in the trunk, just in case he needed to be a doctor again. "That's why he lived."

"Why?" Ken said. He opened the wrapping of his fourth taco, neatly positioned it on his lap, and took a swig of pop. Rene looked at him and shook his head. Ken was a good man, but he didn't make connections.

They were sitting in Rene's Lexus, parked on the street in front of Eileen Reed's apartment building. The Lexus was shiny clean and unmarked. The car in which they'd run Joe Tanner off the road was back in the driveway where they'd originally stolen it. The headlights were broken and the passenger side was crushed along the entire length of the car, marked with blue paint from Joe's Honda. The owner was going to be one surprised commuter when he got up tomorrow.

Detective Eileen Reed, Rene thought. *Detective* Reed. Her face, oval and intelligent and lovely, looked directly at him from his laptop screen.

"Joe Tanner is going to marry Eileen Reed," Rene said. "Eileen Reed, who killed a child killer named Teddy Shaw. Eileen Reed, who caught the so-called 'UFO murderer' down in the Great Sand Dunes. Homicide detectives don't get big press, but that one was a huge case. What else? Oh, look at this. Eileen Reed, who caught the killer at that interesting weather station, Schriever Air Force Base. The weather station that really isn't a weather station at all, but a missile defense development facility."

"Oh, yeah, I remember that guy. The Schriever killer took out Art Bailey, too. We had Bailey targeted, remember?" Ken said, wiping taco sauce off his lower lip with a paper napkin. "You were happy as a clam that guy got took out."

"Taken out," Rene corrected. "Yes, I was. This article doesn't mention Joe Tanner. He was working out there during the murders, and that's how he met Eileen Reed. There's no other way they could have met. Tanner isn't the kind of guy who picks up girls in bars, and Detective Reed doesn't look like the kind of woman who hangs out in them."

"I'll say," Ken said, leaning over to look at the woman's picture. "So what does she have to do with Tanner getting away tonight?"

Rene sighed and leaned back in the leather seat. It creaked luxuriously beneath him. He relished the touch and feel of the leather. He enjoyed the silky smooth power of the laptop that hummed under his fingers. Power and luxury, these were things he appreciated.

"Simple," he said. "Tanner fought back. He smashed his car into ours, remember?"

"I remember," Ken said. He folded up the empty taco papers, tucked them neatly back into the fast food bag, belched, and took a long sip of his soda. "That was strange. He didn't act like the others did. He smashed into us like he knew we were coming. Like he knew what we were going to do."

"He didn't know we were coming," Rene said. "He acted like a cop. Like a soldier. Full reaction, without hesitation. The reason our jobs are so easy is that most people haven't gone through the moral argument of kill-or-be-killed. They try to comprehend that we're going to kill them, and that it's okay to fight back, and by the time they figure out they should fight back they're already dead."

"Tanner's figured that out."

"Exactly. He's already there. That's why we didn't force him off the road into the ravine, but just into that shallow ditch. That's why he was gone by the time we turned around and checked the area. His girlfriend is a cop. He's probably got a concealed-carry permit that she makes him carry. I imagine they practice on the range once a month or more. He's not going to be easy."

"Sounds like fun," Ken said with a smile.

"We don't get paid to have fun," Rene said. "We get paid to do a job. I'd rather break his neck like a chicken, like that girl we did a couple years ago. The easier the better."

"Oh, yeah," Ken said. He took a long swig of his pop and

the straw made a gurgling sound as he drained the cup. "Hmm. Why was she targeted, anyway?"

"She was the best programmer in missile defense, at the time," Rene said. "Now Joe Tanner is." He typed on the laptop, searching for any other information about Eileen Reed.

"So why are we waiting? Can't we just go in and pop them and go home?" Ken said. He was tired, Rene knew. Rene was tired, too. Setting up the trap for Joe Tanner had taken several days. Forcing Tanner's car into the ditch had taken harrowing minutes and the search of the auto junkyard and their escape before the police arrived had been nerve wracking. Now it was coming up on four in the morning and Joe Tanner was still alive. They weren't used to failure, either of them.

"They aren't there," Rene said shortly. "And we don't want to make our hits obvious, remember?"

"Oh," Ken said. "How do you know they aren't there?"

"No lights. They'd be up, if he were there. She's a cop and a good one, by the look of it. She wouldn't sleep until she'd seen the accident scene. She's not up, ergo she isn't there."

"So we have to find them."

"Yes. I hesitate to ask around the police department. That's more risk than I'm willing to take. Impersonating a doctor was close enough for me. And I don't want to enter her apartment before I find out more about her."

"So we'll go in tomorrow?" Ken asked.

"Tomorrow night, perhaps," Rene said. "We're going to have to kill her to get to Tanner, I believe. Taking her is going to be a trophy hunt, like hunting lions in Africa. Dangerous, but very satisfying. We'll have to be well prepared."

"Okay, boss," Ken sighed. "I could use some sleep first."

"We'll both get some sleep. Then we'll start, my friend. We've a lot of work to do."

Rene folded away the laptop. He put the Lexus in drive and pulled out of his parking place.

CHAPTER FIVE

Buffalo Jump, The Reed Ranch, Wyoming

"That's a long way to fall," Lucy said, looking up at the top of the bluff. Eileen stood next to her, imagining tons of buffalo falling helplessly over the cliff, coming down at them like a brown and black avalanche. The image was so real it made her stomach contract and her hands go cold. The morning sun was behind them, lighting up the bluff in gold and green. The grassy meadow where they stood was once a flood plain from the Belle Fourche River, a flood that cut away at the plains until it made a series of bluffs like crumbling steps down to the river. The Reed Ranch stood another quarter-mile east, in the last and oldest of the gigantic sheltering steps.

Eileen looked for the stump of the cottonwood tree that once stood in the meadow where the archaeologist's camp was erected. The stump was still there, an enormous circle of crumbling old wood. Some pieces had been hacked out of the stump for firewood and Eileen felt an unexpected and unjustified anger. What, the University archaeologists were supposed to leave the stump alone because little Eileen Reed once played with her Barbie dolls there? The rest of the camp was neat and tidy, with a main work tent whose open sides revealed a series of tables. The tables were loaded with trays and boxes and tools.

"There they are," Lucy murmured. Hank was on her hip

and Zilla trotted behind them. Hank had gotten tired after a few minutes of walking but Lucy wasn't going to let him play by himself anymore. From now on, Hank and Zilla were part of the team.

Beryl Penrose and Jorie Rothman rose out of the earth beyond the worktable, each in sturdy stained coveralls, with cameras around their necks and small wicker baskets under their arms. They appeared to be arguing. Beryl was a round woman with a round face and round hands, like a person made up of circles. Her eyes were bright and dark and her short black hair had an almost purple cast under the light. She was in her forties, perhaps even her early fifties, but she had several gold earrings in each ear and one small ring in her eyebrow. She was an expert anthropologist, Tracy had told Eileen and Lucy, the part of Dr. McBride's team that would examine any cultural artifacts that the team found at the buffalo jump.

"Good morning," Eileen said cheerfully. Jorie looked away from Beryl and saw them. She looked surprised and annoyed. Her pretty blonde hair was braided down her back and secured with a rubber band. Her face was covered with fine brown dirt and her hands were filthy. She clutched her wicker basket to her side and glared at them.

"We're fine, go away," she said. "We don't need you here."

"I just wanted to see how you're doing and to see the dig," Eileen said mildly.

"Why do you want to see the dig?" Jorie said. "You don't need to see it."

"Jorie—" Beryl said with a smile. "Don't be so rude. Good morning, Eileen. Lucy. Hank."

"Good morning," Lucy said with a smile. Hank hid his face in Lucy's neck. After a moment or two his little hand came from around Lucy's neck and he waved.

"Is this the main dig?" Eileen said. She moved towards the cut in the ground where Beryl and Jorie had just emerged. Jorie moved to stand in front of Eileen.

"You don't need to see it," she repeated, her chin thrust forward.

"What are you hiding?" Lucy asked. Hank wiggled to get

off her hip and she let him down into the dirt. He wandered towards the tables under the tent and Beryl's eyes shifted to Hank. She held out a hand as though she wanted to stop him, her face dismayed.

"Zilla, guard," Eileen said, and Zilla whisked in front of Hank before he reached the tables or the cut in the earth behind the tents. Hank was delighted; this had become his favorite game. He tried to dodge left, then right, giggling. Zilla intercepted him every time, panting and smiling her doggy smile.

"We're going to have to show them, Jorie," Beryl said gently. She moved forward and stood close to Jorie, her hands making soothing gestures.

"Show us what?" Eileen asked.

"The skeleton," Beryl said.

There was a small, loaded silence. The morning breeze stirred Eileen's hair and she smelled flowers and pine and freshly dug earth. Eileen looked from Beryl to Jorie and then back again.

"Well, now," Eileen said.

"But he's at least five hundred years old, we think," Jorie said. "He's not – uh, *fresh*."

"This skeleton is a significant find," Beryl said. "I don't mind that you see this, but please, please don't touch anything. You might ruin a priceless clue to this person's origins."

"Did you find it?" Eileen asked. Beryl shook her head, her bright black eyes looking puzzled and frightened.

"I think Jon found it first," Jorie said. "We only discovered it this morning when we took his tarp off his dig site. We hadn't touched it before because we thought he might come back and—" She trailed off, her face drooping in lines of loss and pain.

"I'd like to take a look," Eileen said.

"All right," Beryl said. She blinked and rubbed a hand across her forehead, leaving a dim clean streak amid the brown dirt. "I'm not thinking very well since I learned about Jon. Please don't disturb the site."

"We won't," Eileen said.

"I don't want to bring Hank down there," Lucy said nervously.

"He'll be fine," Beryl said. "Just put him on your hip and

don't let him touch anything. There's nothing there that will bother him, unless he doesn't like dirt."

"Ha, ha," Lucy said darkly. Hank was two hours out of a clean bed and he was already covered with dirt and grass. Eileen remembered her own childhood and grinned at Lucy. She, too, was always filthy when she was little. Some kids just had a liking for dirt.

"Zilla, guard," Eileen said, waving her hand in a half-circle around the camp. Lucy picked up Hank. Zilla, after a reproachful look at Eileen, set off on a quick tour of the camp. Eileen knew Zilla wanted to stick close to her new little master.

"The cut isn't that deep," Jorie said. "We put a ladder in to help us up and out so we won't break down the edges."

Eileen took a deep breath and walked to the cut in the earth that her father had originally made, then widened, with his backhoe. Paul had turned up bones with the dirt and now a murderer had come. Sometime many years ago a thousand buffalo, maybe more, had died in confusion and pain here. And a human, too, if Beryl and Jorie were correct. The ground should be red instead of brown with all the blood spilled here.

Eileen hadn't told anyone but Lucy and Sheriff Richard King about the back trail of blood. The trail that the dying Jon McBride had left led from the direction of the buffalo jump camp. Whatever happened to Jon McBride had perhaps started at the excavation.

"Follow me," Jorie said, her blonde hair shining in the sun as she backed down the ladder. She hopped down and turned her face up towards Eileen. The cut was about six feet deep, deep enough to swallow Jorie, and about four feet wide. Eileen turned around and followed Jorie. She looked at Lucy as she started to step downward and saw her friend with a worried, scared look on her face, Hank resting on her hip and clutching a handful of her hair like a little monkey.

Eileen was about to drop Lucy a wink to reassure her when Beryl Penrose turned away to set down her wicker basket and pick up another tool. For the second that Beryl was turned away and Jorie was blocked from Lucy's view, Lucy changed. She grinned at Eileen and winked, then switched instantly back to a worried looking mom. Eileen almost fell down the rest of the ladder. Damn, Lucy was good. She'd fooled Eileen, who should certainly know better. Lucy was all there, Hank on her hip or no.

"Down this way," Jorie said, as Eileen stepped to the rough dirt floor. "Watch the bones."

"What bones – oh," Eileen said. The bones were dark brown, dirt-colored, except where the backhoe had snapped them in two. The broken bones poked out, jagged white, like reaching teeth. Eileen immediately suppressed an image of the cut in the earth snapping closed on them and then chewing.

"Whoa," Lucy said behind her. "Hank, don't touch, honey."

"Down here," Jorie said, gesturing. Twenty feet along the cut, Jorie crouched on the dirt floor. Eileen joined her, Lucy and Hank and Beryl following. The cut had been widened there and there was a tarpaulin and some tools propped against one side.

"We reached the bottom of the jump just this past week," Beryl said quietly.

"The bottom of the jump?" Lucy asked.

"The place where the first of the buffalo hit. That's where we were hoping to find the Sioux boy, if he missed his perch," Jorie explained.

"You found him," Eileen said. "He *did* miss."

"That's the strange part," Jorie said. Her cheeks were stained bright red with excitement, even in the shadows of the cut. "I don't think this is our young Lakota warrior at all."

Beryl reached out and pulled the tarp away from the wall of the cut, moving slowly and taking care not to disturb the earth beneath.

"Would you look at this," she said in a low voice. Eileen stood speechless. She heard Lucy's little gasp at her elbow but she couldn't take her eyes off what she was seeing.

Huddled in the dirt wall was the skeleton of a man. He was curled up, knees and head facing out and slightly down. Buffalo bones were packed on top of him. The remains of some sort of head covering were still apparent, though the skin and cloth had long since rotted away. There was a glint of beadwork and some dim yellowish metal along the top of the skull.

Whatever he'd been curled around was gone. The dirt where his midsection had been was freshly gouged out and some tattered remnants of something that looked like skin or paper dangled in the new hole.

"Something's been taken from here," Eileen murmured.

"We've looked in Jon's tent," Beryl said. "There's nothing there. Whatever he took is gone. Did you see the top of the skull?"

"That's gold, isn't it?"

"I believe so," Beryl said. Her breath was faint and light, as though she were having trouble breathing. Jorie was red-cheeked with excitement. She took a paintbrush from her bag and started brushing a round stone that rested close to the crushed remnants of the man's hand.

"Did the Sioux have gold?" Lucy asked.

"Some, that they mined from the Black Hills," Beryl said. Hank kicked his legs against Lucy's sides but showed no desire to get down. He didn't look scared, Eileen thought, just happy to be with his mom in this strange dirt place. "But this gold, this doesn't look like Black Hills gold."

"I've seen that color," Lucy said slowly. "In the Smithsonian. But – that couldn't be possible."

"That's what we're arguing about," Jorie said, her hands working busily with the brush. "Oh, jeez, Beryl look at this."

They all leaned forward as one as Jorie moved her hands aside. There, exposed by her paintbrush, was a circular stone medallion. It was carved strongly and deeply with a fierce looking animal that looked directly out of the medallion. The animal's tongue hung down to its paws and around the edge of the circle was carved what could only be human skulls, rough-hewn and ugly.

"What is that?" Eileen asked.

"A jaguar," Beryl whispered.

"A jaguar surrounded by human skulls," Jorie said.

"Okay," Lucy said shakily. "What's the joke?"

"Fill me in, someone," Eileen said angrily. Her arms were packed with gooseflesh and her scalp was prickling. The eyes of the stone jaguar seemed to glare directly at her. The pupils of the jaguar were a cloudy green color. Jorie brushed gently at the eyes and the green came alive with depth and fire. The fire that only an emerald could bring. The jaguar's eyes were emeralds.

"The joke is, what is an Aztec warrior doing at the bottom of a buffalo jump in Wyoming?" Jorie asked.

"An Aztec warrior?" Eileen repeated. "Aztec? As in, South America?"

"Central Mexico," Lucy said. "The Aztec empire was in central Mexico. Why was he here?"

"It's possible he walked here," Beryl said. "There's no reason he couldn't. The question is, why?"

"He was walking along the bottom of the bluff, maybe," Lucy said. "And then – pow! – he's buried under a ton of buffalo."

"Like being caught in a prehistoric car crash," Eileen said.

"Maybe whatever is missing will tell us more," Jorie said. She was clearing the dirt out of the carved skulls of the medallion. Her paintbrush moved with feathery light strokes, coaxing dirt out of the stone.

"Whatever it was, Dr. McBride took it," Eileen said. "And now Dr. McBride is dead."

"There are a lot of questions to be answered," Beryl said. "All I know is that this could be the find of the century. We have to protect this site. We have to make sure we find out all the answers. This jaguar medallion itself is priceless."

"Yes," Eileen said. "I think we'd better make sure word of this doesn't get out quite yet."

She suddenly longed to be at the surface, away from the empty hands of the skeleton. The eyeholes, packed with dirt, seemed to look at her mournfully. *All these centuries protecting my treasure*, the eyeholes said. *And now my treasure is gone, my arms are empty.*

"I'll stay down here," Jorie said. She rummaged through her wicker basket and came up with a sturdy looking digital camera and a metal ruler. She positioned the ruler and started taking pictures of the stone jaguar. Eileen felt another chill pass over her skin as she followed Beryl back to the ladder that led out of the cut. Jorie was oblivious to her surroundings, focused so intently on her find that anyone could sneak up behind her and –no, wait. The entry wound in Dr. McBride was in the chest, not the back. Who-ever had killed him had been facing him.

The sun felt good after the cool earth. Hank wiggled to be down as soon as they were a few steps away from the dig. Beryl, who had accompanied them, sat down in a folding camp chair under the main tent.

"I can't squat for hours like I used to," she said, massaging her thigh muscles and grimacing. Hank and Zilla, reunited, were acting as though they hadn't seen each other in days. Zilla jumped high in the air and did acrobatic spins, landing within inches of Hank but never touching him. Hank giggled and finally managed to throw his chubby arms around the dog's neck. Zilla stood still, panting, while the little boy hugged her.

"This is so exciting," Lucy said to Beryl. "Is there a way to prove the man came from the Aztec Empire?"

"Carbon dating his bones will give us his age, and DNA testing could give us his race," Beryl said. "Best of all are the artifacts he's carrying, the medallion and the gold work, and anything else that might be in the vicinity of the body."

"And whatever artifact he was holding in his arms," Eileen put in.

"That, too," Beryl said, her eyes darkening.

"So why didn't the Sioux find him? Why was he left there?" Lucy asked.

"They never saw him," Beryl said. "When the natives drove a herd over the cliff the most they could skin and butcher before the animals rotted was maybe a dozen."

"Yeah, once they got as much as they could they'd leave," Eileen added. "The smell must have been horrific. So much for the old myth about natives never wasting resources."

"They wouldn't dig their boy out, if he'd missed the perch?" Lucy asked, looking up at the cliff edge. If there'd been a hole dug in the bluff edge it was long eroded away.

"They'd sing songs about him, Lucy," Eileen said. "But they wouldn't waste time actually trying to *find* him. Sorry."

"I see," Lucy said, and brought her attention to the present with an obvious effort. "So what about the object the Aztec was carrying? Was it worth killing someone over?"

"If it was anything like that medallion, I can see why someone would decide to murder Dr. McBride. That medallion alone could get you knifed in any back alley," Eileen said. "That's a motive, right there. Treasure. Money." Far overhead there was a plaintive screech as a hawk circled the bluff. A faint scraping noise came out of the pit where Jorie worked, and Hank and Zilla became fascinated with Eileen's cottonwood stump that stood in the center of camp.

"I wish Jon were here," Beryl said dully. "I wish none of this had happened."

"We all do," Eileen said gently.

"Hank and I need to get back," Lucy said. "Eileen can we walk back along the bottom of the bluff? I'd like to see the river bottom today, since the weather is so nice. I've never been to Wyoming, before," she said with a friendly smile to Beryl.

"Sure," Eileen said. "We might have to switch off carrying Hank, though."

"No problem, if you don't mind."

"Not at all," Eileen said. She turned to Beryl, who sat in her camp chair as though she'd be there all day. "When the sheriff gets here I'm sure he'll want to see you, so could you and Jorie come up for lunch? We'll try to keep this as discreet as possible."

"Thank you," Beryl said. She looked distracted and exhausted, even though it was still morning.

Lucy picked up Hank and settled him on her hip. Eileen gave a wave and they started south. Zilla trotted with her lopsided gait behind them. As soon as they were beyond the first curve of the river bottom Lucy stopped abruptly.

"You know why the Aztec civilization was so thoroughly destroyed?"

"Why?" Eileen asked. She knew nothing about the Aztecs, but that was going to change as soon as she could get to her parents' computer and the Web.

"Because they had lots of gold," Lucy said. "Lots of gold and lots of jewels. I bet you a fin that when we find our missing stuff it's going to be treasure, and lots of it."

"What's a fin?" Eileen asked, and Lucy looked aghast.

"A fiver. A five-dollar bill, you Western geek. Jeez, you'd think you never watched gangster movies."

"Never had the taste for them," Eileen said. "I always liked

John Wayne and Clint Eastwood, myself."

"Oh, *that's* original," Lucy said, rolling her eyes. Hank wiggled to get down. "Not yet, sweetheart." She looked at Eileen. "I got what you wanted."

"You did?" Eileen asked, startled. "When Beryl came up with us I thought we'd lost our chance to get a sock from Dr. McBride's tent."

"Not a sock, but something almost as good," Lucy said. "I picked it up when Beryl was looking at Hank and Zilla." She produced it from her pocket. It was a worn chisel with a wooden handle, an archaeologist's tool. The handle was stained golden brown by the sweat of a hundred digs and printed along the side were the words that made Eileen crow in delight: Jon McBride.

"Excellent!"

"Thank you, thank you very much," Lucy said modestly. "Shall we?"

"Zilla, here!" Eileen said. The dog whisked up to Eileen and sat down, an expectant look on her intelligent face.

"Get a good smell, Zilla baby," Eileen said. "Thank goodness Dad taught you how to track." The dog sniffed the wooden handle intently, and then sat back down in front of Eileen, panting.

"Wow," Lucy said. "She'll really track by scent?"

"That's how it's done," Eileen said. She took a deep breath. "Zilla, track. Zilla, track!"

Zilla took off at a run, back along the bluff towards the camp. Eileen and Lucy exchanged nervous glances and followed. Zilla took them back to the camp and Eileen spent the minutes trying to come up with a story that Beryl Penrose or Jorie would buy. Luckily when they reached the camp Beryl was back in the cut. The sound of Jorie and Beryl's voices was low but perfectly audible in the still air. Zilla sniffed around the cottonwood stump and then took off in a direct line, straight into the woods, following the curve of the bluff and heading towards the main ranch house.

"The game is afoot!" Lucy whispered to Eileen. They plunged into the trees behind the dog.

Chugwater, Southeastern Wyoming

Joe looked longingly at the bottle of pills 'Berto had given him. Then he put them in his backpack and shoved the pack to the floor of the Mustang. His head ached so badly he thought it might actually explode, like something out of a bad horror movie. But the pills made him sleepy and tired. Sleepy and tired was not the prescription for the long, straight stretches of Wyoming that lay ahead of him.

Sleepy and tired was certainly not what he should be while driving around in 'Berto's car. 'Berto's darling, a lovingly restored powder blue '67 Ford Mustang convertible, had an engine that kicked like a rocket jet at the slightest pressure on the accelerator pedal. Joe had never driven 'Berto's car before today, though he'd driven around with 'Berto many times. He still couldn't believe 'Berto was lending him the most precious thing he owned.

"Might save your life, Joe," 'Berto said, waving off Joe's offer to return the keys. "This car can outrun the wind. Don't have too much fun."

Now Joe was sitting in a Chugwater, Wyoming gas station and there was no way the fat man and his friend could have followed him. Joe was wearing 'Berto's clothes, driving 'Berto's car, and was wearing 'Berto's Ray Ban sunglasses and a soft baseball cap that covered the bandage on his head. Even so, he was paranoid all the way north from Colorado Springs until the traffic started to fade away close to the Wyoming border.

Joe opened a can of soda pop and swallowed some ordinary aspirin. He rested the cold soda can against his cheekbone. The impact that had split a twenty-stitch gash in his head had given him a hell of a shiner below his right eye. At least he'd had a good shower and a shave before he left 'Berto's place. 'Berto had designer taste in clothes, too. Joe was wearing some sort of soft, loose cotton trousers and a button-up shirt. Joe never wore clothes like that. Another reason why the fat man and his friend were certainly left in the dust.

Eventually, of course, Joe was going to have to go back to Colorado Springs and his job. When he did, he had every intention of going in as the hunter, not the hunted. Joe took a long swallow from the can of soda and started the Mustang's engine. The July sun flooded the Wyoming prairie with light and made the highway shimmer in front of him. The Mustang roared happily as he muscled it back onto the highway and headed north towards Eileen.

CHAPTER SIX

The Reed Ranch, Wyoming

The morning was warm and sunny. The woods were green and gold and magical. A unicorn would not seem out of place in those woods. Lucy dodged around a branch and wanted to swing right into the tree like Tarzan, swing into the tree and follow Zilla by leaping from one to another. Hank seemed weightless on her hip. He had a good hold on her. His legs were wrapped around her hips and his little hands were entwined in her hair. He was grinning madly.

Zilla was in the lead, followed by Eileen. She chased Zilla through the trunks and the crunchy green plants that she'd told Lucy were called kinnikinnick. Kinnikinnick, what a hilarious name. Lucy was caught by laughter again, caught but good, and she couldn't let go or Beryl and Jorie might hear her. Sound carried incredibly far in the enormous empty stretches of Wyoming. There was no traffic, no people talking, no lawn mowers or building air conditioners or construction machines. There was nothing but the wind in the pines and the thin cry of a hawk, and Eileen's running footsteps three trees ahead of Lucy.

"Wait, Zilla, slow down," Eileen said urgently.

Ahead of Eileen, Lucy could see Zilla's feathery tail wagging. She'd stopped immediately when Eileen called her. Her little body shivered with the effort of holding still. Lucy caught up to

Eileen and Zilla and she put a hand on Eileen's shoulder, struggling to catch her breath.

"Let me take Hank, if he'll have me," Eileen said. She was grinning, hair tangled. She was enjoying this as much as Lucy. She reached for Hank and to Lucy's surprise her little boy held out his arms to Eileen. He settled in on her hip and looked intently at her face. He didn't smile and Lucy prepared herself for an outthrust lip and a wail of anguish. Instead Hank turned his attention to Zilla. He pointed at her and kicked at Eileen's hips like a rider trying to get a horse to trot.

"You okay?" Eileen asked Lucy. Lucy raised her arms above her head, free of Hank's weight, and took a deep breath. She felt like she could outrun Zilla now. She nodded. "Zilla, track!"

Zilla bolted, her paws digging up trenches in the pine needles that covered the ground. Eileen and Lucy followed. Hank made little crows of excitement as he watched Zilla's wagging tail.

The trail that had begun as a straight line now began to waver. Zilla slowed down, too, her sensitive nose buried in the fragrant pine needles of the forest floor. She sniffed and snuffled, then raised her nose and sniffed the air. Eileen came to a stop well back, letting Zilla have space. Lucy stopped at Eileen's shoulder. Eileen pointed at her feet. Lucy looked down and saw a rust-red splotch on the kinnikinnick leaves at Eileen's feet. The splotch was dried blood and Lucy felt a surprising rush of satisfaction. They really were tracing Dr. McBride's steps.

"Keep your eyes open," Eileen murmured to Lucy. "Look for anything he might have dropped."

But it was Zilla who found what Dr. McBride had hidden. Her tail suddenly started wagging so fast it was a white blur. She barked sharply, then stopped and took a strange stance. She stood on her three feet and leaned forward, almost toppling over her one front leg. She quivered, but she didn't move, and her nose stayed absolutely still.

"What is she doing?" Lucy said. She gathered Hank from Eileen's hip without taking her eyes from Zilla. Hank put his arms around her neck and she kissed his cheek. He was watching Zilla, his eyes round and fascinated.

"She's pointing," Eileen said. She put her hands at the

small of her back and stretched, absently massaging the muscles, relieved to be free of Hank's weight. "Look where her nose and her eyes are aiming and you'll see what she's pointing at. I didn't know she knew how to point. Maybe Dad's training her to be a bird dog."

"Can we get her to track again?" Lucy said. She couldn't take her eyes away from Zilla. The little dog was absolutely still, except for the faint trembling of her body. Even her tail was stiff, thrust straight behind her as though she were trying to turn her entire body into an arrow.

"I think she still *is* tracking," Eileen said in a low voice. She produced her gun with the effortless ease that Lucy found amazing. Lucy felt like one of the Three Stooges when she drew her gun. Eileen held her gun as though it were a part of her. "Let's see what she's looking at. Stay here, okay?"

"Okay," Lucy said. She shifted Hank on her hip and saw another splotch of blood in front of her. This one was big, far too big for a cut or a scrape. This was a lot of blood, blood that came from a human who was dying as he stumbled through these woods. Lucy felt ashamed suddenly of her delight in the beautiful day and the company of her friend and her little boy. Dr. McBride didn't deserve to be dead, with no way of ever enjoying again the beauty of the blue Wyoming sky.

"Lucy," Eileen called. "Zilla, come." Zilla broke her stance and leaped forward to join Eileen. Eileen was standing in front of a lightning blasted tree, Lucy saw as she joined her friend. The giant old tree had broken in half and taken a whole section of woods with it when it crashed to the forest floor. The pile of dead and rotting trees were covered with kinnikinnick and small shrubs. A row of shelf mushrooms grew along the trunk of the largest tree. A squirrel chattered madly at them.

Behind the splintered trunk of the old tree there was a hollow made of broken trees and shrubs. A nest of red mushrooms spotted with white grew at the foot of the old tree trunk.

"Don't touch those," Eileen said as Lucy and Hank joined her. "They're poisonous."

"Okay," Lucy said. She looked at the splash of dried blood that spread across some pine needles at the front of the natural cave. How could anyone lose that much blood and live? Oh, that's right, he hadn't. Flies buzzed in the quiet air.

"You okay?" Eileen said.

"I'm fine."

"Good. I'm going to crawl in there. Hang on."

Eileen stepped over the blood patch and crouched down. She edged into the cave, a space barely large enough to contain her, and stopped.

"Do you have anything made of cloth that I can use?" Her voice was muffled and strained. Lucy unzipped her small fanny pack and dug out a disposable diaper. She always carried a few diapers and wipes. If she didn't, she needed them, without fail. She leaned forward and placed the diaper into Eileen's outstretched hand, the only part of her that was visible from the tiny cave.

A moment later Eileen was backing out of the cave, holding an object wrapped in the diaper. In her other hand she held a bundle wrapped in a scrap of tarp. Lucy had seen those tarps at the archeological dig. Eileen stood up and shook her head rapidly back and forth, making her dark red hair fly madly about her head.

"Don't tease me, just check me for spiders," she said nervously.

"Eileen Reed is afraid of spiders," Lucy said, brushing at her friend's shoulders and hair with her free arm and laughing. Hank patted at Eileen's shoulder, giggling. "No spiders, you wimp."

"I'm not afraid of spiders, I'm terrified of them," Eileen said. She was grinning, her eyes blazing with excitement. "Guess what I have in this here diaper?"

"Show me," Lucy commanded.

"No," Eileen said. "Not where Hank can see. It's the murder weapon."

"Oh," Lucy said. Hank, who was ignoring the adult talk, reached for Zilla.

"Let's walk away from this area very carefully," Eileen said. "I think the sheriff will rope this place off too. Then I can show you the thing in the diaper. And we can both look at whatever is in this tarp."

"Okay," Lucy said. "Lead the way."

Eileen walked ahead and Lucy very carefully followed in her footsteps. Once they were over a gentle hill from the downed trees Eileen stopped in a small clearing. The late morning sun was bright and warm. Indian paintbrush flowers nodded their bright red heads above the grasses of the meadow. Lucy could hear the low buzzing of bees. Hank wiggled to get down and after a careful look around, Lucy let him.

"Zilla, good girl!" Eileen said. "Go play." Zilla immediately began her ecstatic reunion dance with Hank. She jumped and twisted and Hank giggled and ran in circles, chasing her. "We're really close to the ranch house," Eileen said in a low voice. "It's just over that rise at the end of the meadow, there."

"Let me see," Lucy said. Eileen opened the diaper. Lucy stood with her head close to Eileen's and they peered within, as though they were checking an extraordinary poop from her little boy, one so spectacular that it simply had to be seen. There within the diaper was the most horrible looking stone knife Lucy had ever seen. It was a length of shiny dark obsidian that had been chipped until it was double-edged and sharp. The rock was streaked with thick, chunky red stuff at the point. Lucy swallowed hard. This wasn't a bloodstain, this was gore. There were pieces of Jon McBride on that knife, along with his blood. Lucy looked away.

"The fatal wound was made with this knife, I think," Eileen said.

"Looks Aztec," Lucy said faintly, looking at her son and the little three-legged Border collie and trying hard not to pass out. They were trying to catch two white butterflies that were doing a complicated sort of dance above the meadow flowers. "So McBride carried it off with him. Why? And what's in the tarp?"

Eileen carefully rewrapped the stone knife and laid it at her feet. Then she cradled the bundle in her arm and unwrapped the tarp. They both gasped. The object within the tarp, revealed to the sun, caught the light and flared like a torch with every color of the rainbow. Lucy squeezed her eyes to slits against the reflected light.

"Is that a *diamond*?" Lucy asked.

"I don't think so," Eileen said. She sounded like she'd been kicked in the stomach. "It couldn't be, could it? It's as big as my head."

The thing in the tarp was made out of some perfectly clear substance, life-sized, and carved into the shape of a human skull. The eye sockets looked up at them mockingly, the teeth bared in a death grin. It was the most beautiful thing Lucy had ever seen, and the most terrible. Draped around the top of the skull, like a crown, was an oval of gold set with dully flashing gems. The largest one looked like an emerald as big as Lucy's thumb. The tight-fitting crown was grimed with dirt but the skull itself was as clean as though it had been polished minutes ago.

"Treasure," Lucy whispered. "We've got ourselves a problem, girlfriend."

"We sure do," Eileen said. She wrapped the tarp around the skull and looked at Lucy. "Whoever stabbed Dr. McBride wanted this stuff badly enough to kill for it. Now we have it."

There was silence between them. In the meadow, Hank panted and giggled and chased Zilla and the butterflies. The sun felt hot on Lucy's dark head. She felt her heart pick up speed, but in a good way. Eileen couldn't keep her solemn expression any longer, and she grinned at Lucy. Lucy smiled back.

"We're going to be harder to kill," Lucy said.

The Reed Ranch, Wyoming

"You moved evidence," Sheriff Richard King said furiously. Eileen kept her relaxed pose against the family room fireplace mantle. This took so much effort that a line of sweat ran down the small of her back. The day had only gotten hotter, the way mid-July days can get, and the family room was packed. Tracy, who was sitting with Paul on the piano bench, had opened the French doors and turned on the fans but the room was still warm.

The crystal skull sat on the mantle, crowned with the dirty circlet of gold and gems. Jorie Rothman and Beryl Penrose sat side by side on the leather couch. They were still grimy from the buffalo jump dig although they'd washed their faces and hands. They couldn't keep their eyes off the skull. Beryl, in particular, seemed to have disconnected entirely from the crowded room. Her round face was distant, her eyes focused on the glimmering skull.

Howie Magnus and his friends crowded together on the

other couch and the two armchairs. Howie was clearly enjoying the whole scene, his strong musician's hands laced over his knees and his eyes bright with interest. His brother-in-law, Jimmy, sat composed and mute as a statue to his left. Nolan Simmons, the comedian, and the software tycoon, Mark Plutt, slouched in the armchairs like little boys called in from their summertime play. Lucy stood next to Tracy and Paul. She'd put Hank down for a much-needed nap and had just entered the room. She folded her arms and glowered at Sheriff King.

Sheriff Richard King didn't notice her attention, though Eileen thought that he would be a smarter man if he would. She wouldn't want to be on the receiving end of Lucy's smoldering glare. King was angry, but he would have been angry if he'd walked through the door and Eileen and Lucy had been sitting in white dresses, drinking iced tea and leafing through Vogue magazines. He had it in for Eileen, and her discovery of the crystal skull and the murder weapon only added fuel to the fire. He had grown taller and had filled out since high school. His dark blond hair was receding but it looked good on him. His skin had cleared up and if not for his expression of bitter anger, he would have been quite a nice looking man. Eileen sighed to herself.

"I had no choice," Eileen said calmly. "We had no idea if we were being watched or followed. Once we found the knife and the skull—"

"How did you do that, anyway?" Mark Plutt asked. Sheriff King turned his narrow, furious face to Mark. Mark Plutt, software tycoon, didn't blink at the sheriff's angry gaze.

"Just an accident," Eileen said blandly. "We were taking a walk through the woods back to the ranch house and Zilla got all excited."

"I see," Mark murmured, with a blandness that mocked Eileen.

"That's moving evidence," Sheriff King said.

"Certainly, and under the circumstances we were justified," Eileen shrugged. "We were under conditions of imminent threat. If we left without the objects who knows if they would have been there when we returned? I didn't want to stay there alone, or leave Lucy and Hank there, either. We needed to stay together."

Tracy stirred on the piano bench and Eileen saw Lucy put a gentle hand on her shoulder. There was a sudden, sharp tang of fear in the air. Unless the murderer was a drifter with intimate knowledge of the Reed Ranch, the murderer was in the room at that very moment. No one else could have killed Dr. McBride. Eileen saw glances, lowered eyes, and a slight drawing away, one from another.

"I'll have to see where the objects were left," King said. "And I'll have to secure the items as evidence—"

"In my safe, Sheriff," Paul Reed said, right on cue. Eileen breathed a mental sigh of relief that her father had come home early enough for her to prep him. Sheriff King didn't hate her dad. Paul would succeed where she would certainly fail.

"What? Mr. Reed, you know I have to—"

"I've seen the evidence room at the station, Sheriff," Paul said calmly. "A ten-year-old with a good crowbar could break in there. This object is priceless."

"I could get oh, five or six million or so on eBay, no questions asked," Nolan Simmons commented. Howie's comedian friend nodded appreciatively at the treasure. "That's just for the crown. I don't know what the skull would fetch."

"It belongs in a museum!" Jorie said hotly, unconsciously aping the movies, a line said many times by fictional archaeologist Indiana Jones. A wave of smiles enveloped the room and Jorie looked around, confused, and then realized what she'd said. Her face flushed scarlet all the way to the roots of her hair. This made her look even more fetching, Eileen thought sourly. She caught Lucy's eye and quickly looked away from Lucy's bright, cynical smile. She didn't want to start laughing.

"I don't mean that I want to sell it," Nolan said patiently. "Just that if somebody stole it *they* could sell it. Jeez."

"I have a safe here, Sheriff, you've seen it," Paul said. His face, lined with age and reddened from the morning's scouting session, was as solid as bedrock. Eileen carefully looked at the floor, trying to see in her peripheral vision if anyone in the room was fidgeting, twitching, sweating, pale and shiny with guilt. No one seemed guilty, though everyone was sweating.

"I'll photograph the skull and the er – jewel thing, and we'll store it here," the sheriff said, grudgingly. "But I'll need to ship the stone knife to Rapid City for fingerprint and DNA analysis."

"All right," Paul said.

"Tell them to be careful," Beryl said suddenly, rousing out of her trance. "That thing looks like it might be Aztec as well. Tell them it's a priceless artifact and they have to treat it that way."

"Of course, ma'am," Sheriff King said.

"Well," Tracy said briskly, standing up from the piano bench. "That's settled, then. Paul, you were going to take Mr. Magnus and his friends north this afternoon? There are some excellent meadows that the deer and elk just love. Paul will drive there, Mr. Simmons, no horses," she added with a smile. "We'll give you a rest from horseback riding."

"We'll get back to the dig, of course," Jorie said. Beryl nodded and visibly collected herself. She was fascinated with the skull. Here was the first mystery – what had been taken from the Aztec skeleton – already solved. Eileen hoped the second mystery would fall apart as quickly, and they would be able to jail a murderer.

"I need to see where you found these things," Sheriff King said to Eileen.

"Of course," Eileen said levelly.

"I'll go, too," Lucy said. "Hank should sleep for two hours or more, he's very tired. As long as you can listen for him?" she asked Tracy. Tracy, already on her feet and retying her apron, nodded.

"Of course. If he wakes early he'll just have to help me make cookies. I don't think he'll mind. We'll be fine, you go on. Take Zilla with you."

Sheriff King glowered at the carpet and Eileen realized he didn't want Lucy along. He wanted her alone. Eileen cast a timeless female glance at Lucy, the glance that meant *don't-leave-me-alone-with-this-creep*, and Lucy answered with a tiny squint of her eyes, a double almost-wink. *Of-course-not-girlfriend.*

"Let's saddle up, boys," Howie said with relish. "Didn't you say something about black bear, Paul?"

"There's some good blackberry bushes just coming into fruit," Paul said calmly. "No guarantees, but we could get lucky.

That's why we're in the truck this afternoon, too."

"So the bears won't get us?" Nolan Simmons asked curiously.

"So the horses don't throw you on your head and run all the way back to their stable," Paul said. "Horses do *not* like bears. Nervous horses mean bear, or lion. Remember that, this fall, if you're hunting here."

"I will," Nolan said, visibly impressed.

"Bye, honey," Paul said to his wife, and kissed her cheek. A moment or so later Paul and the hunters were gone. Jorie and Beryl slipped out after them, two women in stained khakis with dirt in their hair and under their nails, obviously anxious to get back to their Aztec skeleton. If not for Jon McBride's death, Eileen thought, they would be the two happiest women on the planet right now.

"Go take your photographs, Richard," Tracy said. "I have shortcake to make for dessert tonight, and I need my girls back so they can help me out in the kitchen."

"Yes, ma'am," Sheriff King said. "The camera is in my car. I'll be right back."

As soon as he left the room Eileen drew a deep breath and let it out in a huge sigh, as though she'd been holding her breath forever. It felt as if she had.

"Good girl!" Lucy said admiringly. "You kept your mouth shut the whole time, practically. I wish I could do that."

"Nice work, punkin," Tracy agreed. "Get back as soon as you can, hear? I have strawberries to cut up for the shortcake."

"Oh, Mom, you and your elaborate cooking," Eileen groaned. "Couldn't we just have leftover apple pie?"

"Somebody polished it off in the middle of the night," Tracy said. "Not a smidgeon left this morning. Those boys are using up a lot of calories chasing around after the wildlife. They eat a lot, and we plan to keep them happy. Howie is paying a lot just for this scouting trip. The guide service next fall is going to make us a bundle, if he chooses our service."

"He will, Mrs. Reed," Lucy said. "Even without the excitement of a murder, he'll be back. He loves it here. Can't you tell?"

Tracy grinned and nodded. "I know," she said happily.

"Now catch us that murderer, girls. And don't let it be Howie."

"We'll do our best," Eileen said dryly.

"Ahh, Richard," Tracy said, looking through the doorway. "I need to get to the kitchen. Why don't you take the pictures you need. Eileen, and Lucy, why don't you freshen up and drink some water before you go back out? You don't want to become dehydrated; it's such a hot day."

Zilla heard the car first, with her phenomenal collie ears. Eileen and Lucy were in the front hall, ready to retrace their steps with the sheriff, when Zilla came racing down the front stairs. She skidded to a stop at the front door and stood, ears raised, tail down.

"Car?" Eileen said.

"Nobody she knows," Lucy said. "Look at her tail. It's not wagging."

Eileen opened the door and Zilla bounded out. The highway was over half a mile away, and a simple gate marked the road that led to the Reed Ranch. There was no elaborate sign, though Tracy and Paul had discussed an entrance sign at some point in the future. The Reed Ranch sat in a fold of hills and wasn't visible from the highway. The only cars that came down the ranch road were locals, paying hunters, and the Schwan's truck. Schwan's delivered frozen food and ice cream and Zilla knew the deliveryman, Doug, as well as she knew Paul and Tracy. Tracy told Eileen she suspected Doug was the only human who could possibly tempt Zilla away from her owners. Doug had been slipping Zilla ice cream sandwiches since she was a puppy.

Eileen rolled her shoulders, suddenly feeling tense. She couldn't hear the car but she knew there was one coming. Zilla stood alertly at the end of the lawn, where the road turned into the ranch yard. The trees were in full July leaf and the shade at the front of the house was soothing and green. There was the sound of bees humming and the smell of grass and horses. The bees got louder and then they weren't bees at all, but the sound of a car engine.

The car came over the final rise and it was a light blue Mustang convertible. The Mustang was trundling along slowly, almost at idle. The car wavered to one side of the road, hesitated, and then straightened. The person behind the wheel wore a dark baseball cap and glasses. His hands were close together on the wheel and his head was hunched close to his hands, as though he were almost blind. Eileen knew the car. It was Roberto Espinoza's car, his cherished Mustang.

"I think that's Joe," Eileen said, in a voice so soft it felt as though she spoke no louder than the sound of the wind in the trees.

The car slowed to a stop in the ranch yard, blocking the sheriff's car. Eileen flew down the steps and across the lawn. The Mustang was hot from the sun and the man sat behind the wheel, eyes closed, and he was Joe. Joe, with an enormous bruise that covered half his forehead, Joe with two days of beard growth and black sunglasses and a hat that didn't conceal the white bandage underneath. He sat with his head back against the headrest, unmoving, hands still poised on the steering wheel as though he were driving.

"Joe," Eileen said in a hoarse little voice. Joe rolled his head towards Eileen and took his hands off the wheel. He fumbled the sunglasses off his face and Eileen bit back a strangled sound as she saw the shiny bruised eye socket, the bloodshot eyes.

"Hey, Eileen," Joe said, and gave her his sweet smile, the one she loved so much. "Give me just a minute to collect myself, damned Wyoming highway. Just about kills me to drive across all that emptiness."

"Amen," Lucy said from Eileen's elbow.

"What happened?" Eileen said in voice that felt strength less. "What happened?"

"A lot," Joe said. "First, since I'm here, I'm going to take a couple of 'Berto's pain pills. Then before I pass out in your bed—" He leered at her for a second and Eileen grinned, feeling immensely better. If Joe could give her that look, he was going to be just fine. "—I'm going to explain. But first—"

"Who is this?"

Joe winced. Sheriff King's voice was loud and sharp, and so close that Lucy and Eileen both flinched.

"This is Joe Tanner," Eileen said. "My – my—" she floundered, so concerned about Joe that she forgot the word that meant two people were going to be married. For a second her brain seemed to thrash like a fish caught on a hook. "My – my beloved."

"Your *what?*" King said.

Lucy snickered, and put a hand to her mouth. Joe blinked through his tiredness and grinned at Eileen.

"Fiancé, I mean," Eileen said, feeling a wave of heat in her face and remembering the word at last.

"I prefer beloved," Joe whispered, closing his eyes and leaning his head back against the seat. He reached out blindly with his hand and she caught it in her own, feeling tears rise and forcing them ruthlessly back down. She was *not* going to cry.

"What's going on here?" King said flatly.

Eileen didn't have to look at Lucy. Lucy knew Eileen needed her help.

"Looks like Joe was in an accident, and he's come up to see Eileen," Lucy said briskly. "He needs to get inside, and get some sleep. I'll take you to the place where we found the – er, the objects, Sheriff. Eileen needs to stay with Joe right now."

"Come on, Joe," Eileen said gently, opening the door to the Mustang. Joe was wearing some sort of soft cotton trousers and what had to be a silk shirt. It felt warm and soft to her touch and molded itself to his chest as she helped him out of the car. The shirt, the pants, the baseball cap, they frightened her, even more than 'Berto's car. The car might be borrowed but the clothes added up to a man on the run.

"Backpack in the back," Joe said. Eileen hooked the pack with one arm and put her shoulder under his arm. He leaned into her heavily and sighed as they walked into the shade of the trees on the front lawn.

"Bed upstairs, babe," Eileen said. She spared one glance at Lucy, who waved her on. Sheriff King stood scowling at her side, a tall pole of a man next to the compact curves of her friend. Eileen reminded herself that Lucy could more than handle herself. She had Zilla, too, to help them find their way through the woods. Joe was important right now, not Lucy or Richard King or anybody else. Joe was hurting, he was in trouble, and she had to help him.

CHAPTER SEVEN

West of the Reed Ranch, Wyoming

"**S**o what's your story, anyway?" Lucy asked abruptly.

"Excuse me?" the sheriff said, his dark look momentarily replaced by surprise.

Lucy was pleased. She meant to be surprising. They were walking briskly west, Zilla trotting ahead of them. The mixture of pine and cottonwood trees that covered the steps of the ancient riverbed was fast approaching and Lucy hadn't the faintest idea how to find the deadfall where they'd found the skull and the murder weapon.

She was from Baltimore, a very old city, and she prided herself on being able to find her way around in any metropolitan area. But these were woods, Wyoming woods, and the only structure in sight was the ancient homestead cabin and chicken coop where Dr. McBride had been found. Sheriff King walked quickly, his camera swinging in one hand.

"I was wondering what your story was. I know about you and Eileen," Lucy said.

"You do?"

"We're women, if you've noticed," Lucy said with exaggerated sarcasm. "Girlfriends. We've told each other things you'd never tell another soul. We compare tampon types, for God's sake. I know about you."

Sheriff King flushed and looked away. Lucy grinned to herself. Tampon talk always disconcerted and embarrassed men. It was a cheap shot, but she was willing to use it.

"So what do you know?"

"Eileen went to prom with Owen Sutter and his new girlfriend Molly, because they were all friends. The three had been friends since they were kids, right? So Eileen was already on her way to college and flight school in the Air Force, which you know all about. She left after a few years and went into police work, but she was on fire to get out of Wyoming and Owen wasn't, so they had broken up months before the prom. She told me it was better when Owen was with Molly, because that's the way it should have been in the first place. Things just felt right. Eileen didn't have a boyfriend and didn't want one, so she went solo but traveled to the prom with Owen and Molly, and you thought you had a chance with her and you tried to make out with her."

Lucy stopped and drew breath. Damn Wyoming, anyway. The air was too thin out here, five thousand feet above sea level and a thousand miles inland. The air was thin and dry, too. She wasn't feeling tired, just out of breath, but it didn't suit her to let King know that. She wanted to connect with this man and she needed an excuse to make conversation. So she stopped and gasped and gestured for a little time to recover her breath.

"That's her story?" King asked, stopping. "That's what she told you?"

"Well, I would go on but I seem to be running out of breath out here," Lucy said finally, with a smile she considered her very best. The sheriff wasn't immune. His expression lightened and he fumbled at his side for his water bottle. Lucy took it gratefully, ignoring her own water bottle. The sheriff might not know how powerful a symbol sharing water represented, but Lucy did. She handed it back with a grateful sigh and a shrug.

"She hit me," King said after taking a drink from his bottle. He didn't look at her when he said it.

"I imagine she would hit pretty hard," Lucy said, trying to keep her expression mild and friendly. She was now determined to make this man a friend, or at least to make him friendly. She thought the whole case might revolve on whether they could get this man, the local sheriff, to cooperate. "Worst would be the rejection, I suppose."

"Yeah," the sheriff said, his face darkening into his usual glower. "I fell into the lake. In my tuxedo. In front of *everybody*."

"Not in front of me," Lucy said. When he looked at her, she pointed her finger at him. "Listen to me, Sheriff. Do you know why this state scares the crap out of me? There's nobody here, for miles and miles. Things seem incredibly large out here, and incredibly important. Maybe something that happened a long time ago still seems important because everyone knows the same stories. Maybe things aren't that important. Come on, I'm not that much of a wimp."

She started walking and Zilla wagged her tail and gave a happy little rowf. She'd been lying in the shade of a leafy tree, her nose settled on her one foot. Lucy suddenly had an idea. Perhaps she could find her way to the deadfall after all, without having to admit to the sheriff that she didn't know where the hell she was going.

"Zilla, find, find," she said, waving her hand the same way Eileen had done down on the river. Lucy's heart thudded hard as Zilla scrambled to her feet and started nosing back and forth. Would she find Dr. McBride's trail again, or was she simply sniffing for rabbit?

Zilla wagged her tail briskly and gave a sharp bark. She headed up the grassy slope and into the trees, then turned and looked at the sheriff and Lucy with an inquiring expression.

"Good girl, Lassie," Lucy said under her breath. "I mean, Zilla."

"So what do you mean, things aren't so important?" Sheriff King asked after a minute of silent hiking. Lucy didn't smile, although she wanted to.

"Just that. Things aren't so important. Back in Baltimore, where I grew up, you could move twenty miles away and nobody would know you from Adam. There are lots of people back East, have you ever been?"

"I went to California once," the sheriff said in a low voice. "Never east. Always wanted to go to the Capitol, see the Declaration of Independence."

"You should go," Lucy said. "It's great. There's a guard there all the time, did you know that? So nobody can take pictures. The room is dark and quiet and there isn't a lot of light, and the Declaration is under about a foot of bulletproof glass. Gives me the shivers just to look at it and see the signatures. Damn, I have to stop again."

"You do go on," King said, but he said it kindly. Lucy stopped for breath and looked down the slope where Zilla waited impatiently. She recognized the meadow with all the tiny flowers, wasn't that where they'd looked in the diaper and saw the knife? Only a few minutes to the deadfall, then. She couldn't fake another oxygen stop.

"Well, yeah, I do. But you should go. But watch out. Go into a bar in Georgetown and you'd never make it out alive, Sheriff."

"Why's that?" King said, his face darkening again. Lucy laughed internally. It was all too easy.

"Because the women there would fight over you like a bride's bouquet in one of those funny home videos. They'd probably carry you off on their shoulders like a trophy. You're a fine looking man, don't you know that? Or aren't there any women in Wyoming other than Eileen Reed and her friend Molly what's-her-name?"

The sheriff looked as though he'd been struck. His face reddened again and then paled. Lucy wondered if he'd ever been complimented before. Didn't women flirt out here? *Were* there any women out here?

"Molly O'Neil," he said in a low voice. "Molly Sutter, now."

"And Eileen Reed. She's a great woman and she's about my best friend in all the world, Sheriff, but she isn't the only woman in the whole world. She's a Wyoming ten, but she's a Washington seven."

There was a small silence and Zilla gave an impatient woof at the bottom of the small hillock. Lucy put a hand on her hip and glared at Sheriff King.

"Ok," she said, with an exaggerated sigh. "She's a ten in Washington, too. *Damn* it."

Richard King threw his head back and laughed, his hands on his belt and his eyes closed. Lucy laughed with him, her voice a silvery tinkle through his lower range, and she wasn't faking her laughter. She could almost see the tension draining out of him.

"Who *are* you?" he asked, when their laughter finally tapered off and ended.

"Just a friend from back East, Sheriff," Lucy said with a shrug and a smile. "Just Eileen's friend. Maybe yours too, if you'll have me."

She held out her hand, little and strong, and he shook it with a crooked little smile that looked almost shy.

"Let's go find that deadfall, Lucy," King said.

The Reed Ranch, Wyoming

"I was thinking my brain was actually going to explode," Joe said dreamily. He was on Eileen's bed, wrapped in a comforter even though the day was warm. Eileen didn't try to get him through a shower before she put him to bed. She made a mental note to change the sheets before she went to bed that night. Joe was filthy. His hair, unwashed, was matted with blood and sweat and dirt. Dirt was grimed into his knuckles and creased his neck. The bandage was still white but was starting to fray at the edges. Joe had swallowed two of Roberto Espinoza's pills and collapsed on the bed, obediently drinking a full glass of water.

"Drink some more water, Joe. You don't want to get dehydrated," Eileen murmured, echoing her mother.

"Sure," he said, raising his head with an effort and drinking another half glass of water. Letting his head fall back onto the pillows, he sighed. "Damn highway was going to kill me. I couldn't take anything more than aspirin or I'd fall asleep. Haven't slept in – what, two days?"

"What happened, Joe?" Eileen said. She smoothed his dirty hair back from his brow, feeling a fierce protective love and a consuming fear. Had he hurt someone, even by accident? Had he done something wrong?

"Got run off the road," Joe said. His eyes started to lose

focus and grow blurred and soft. "They killed Sully, remember? She talked to me, told me to get out of the wreck and hide. I saw them – they killed her, they want to kill me."

Eileen abruptly reached to the bedside table and picked up Joe's water glass. She drank the rest of Joe's water. She shoved her worries about Lucy and Sheriff King, her thoughts about Dr. Jon McBride and his potential murderer out of her mind. They were gone. She brushed her mental table clean and focused.

"Professionals," she said. "Contract killers."

"Yes," Joe gasped, and his hand nearly crushed hers. "You believe me."

"Of course I do," Eileen said calmly. "Get some sleep, love. I won't do anything until you wake. I'll keep you safe. We'll take care of this. Go to sleep."

Joe's hand relaxed in hers and his eyes closed as though he were waiting her permission to let go, to finally sleep.

"I love you," he whispered. "Sully told me—"

"Sully told you what?" Eileen whispered, but he was gone. Eileen sat for a few minutes longer, feeling confused. Harriet Sullivan was his old girlfriend, his fiancée, killed in a car wreck over five years ago. Wasn't she?

Joe snored and rolled on his side. He pulled the comforter up to his chin and drew his legs up like a little boy, like Hank sleeping his happy toddler sleep in the bedroom down the hall.

Eileen held Joe's hand, leaned over it, and rested her cheek against his grubby skin. His skin was warm and she could feel the slow steady pulse of his heartbeat underneath. She breathed through her confusion, her fear, until the tears that threatened her moved back inside her and were gone.

Eileen finally kissed his shoulder gently, then got to her feet and headed for the door. There would be time, later, to figure all this out. Right now she had to rescue Lucy from the clutches of the sheriff.

Colorado Springs, Colorado

"Two more minutes and we're out of here," Ken said. Rene

didn't answer. He was sorting through Eileen's filing cabinet and was elbow deep in *Bride's* and *Modern Bride* magazines. He stifled the urge to throw the things down to the floor and stomp on them. The magazines were the most offensive, heavy and scented so thickly they made him feel like sneezing. The girl, the detective, Eileen, had more than magazines to confound him. She had filing folders full of invitation samples, other ones for catering companies. Then there were dozens of brochures for reception halls, from the Stanley Hotel in Estes Park to the Broadmoor Hotel in Colorado Springs. She had folders for disc jockeys, florists, bridesmaid's outfits and tuxedos for the groomsmen. She had catalogs that listed bridesmaid's gifts and other catalogs that offered centerpieces for tables at the receptions. The amount of information was staggering.

Rene continued to sort through the satin and silks of a bride's planning, his head pounding fiercely. In all this, there was no indication of a second home like a mountain cabin or a favorite place to stay. He shuddered at the thought of checking on all the hotels Eileen was looking into for a wedding reception. Eileen had pictures of her mother and father and pictures of Joe Tanner. She had pictures of a black-haired girl who was holding a little baby boy. She had pictures of a handsome older man who looked eerily like her, perhaps an uncle or a cousin. She had addresses in her address book but her only address for her parents' house was a post office box in Hulett, Wyoming.

"Less than a minute to go before we have to leave. I think she went to Hulett, Wyoming." Ken said. He was gloved and masked just like Rene, and the shower cap they both wore looked ridiculous on his wiry brown hair. It made him look like a cross between a circus clown and a psycho. Rene didn't want to know what he looked like. His head pounded.

He sneezed into his handkerchief for the twentieth time. The detective bitch had a cat, to top things off. The cat was nowhere to be seen, evidently shipped off to friends. This was another sign that Eileen Reed was out of town for more than a day or so. The cat hair and dander remained. With the heavily scented bridal magazines the smell was enough to drive Rene out of his skull.

"I think so, too," Rene said. "Time to clear out." He stripped his gloves and shower cap off before they left the apartment. He took a last look around and the apartment, a simple three-room affair with big windows that faced south, was pristine. Unless she was looking for intruders, she would see nothing wrong. Rene had no intention of giving this young lioness his scent. Leave her surprise for when he killed her.

He saw a final scrap of paper on the kitchen counter and put his gloves back on with a sigh. The receipt for a matron-of-honor dress was the jackpot. Lucy Giometti was the black-haired girl with the baby, if the measurements on the receipt looked correct. Best of all the dress was to be delivered for final alterations directly to Lucy's home address.

The address was listed. Great Falls, Virginia. But at least it was a start.

"So where is Hulett, Wyoming?" Ken asked, as they drove away from Eileen's apartment. Rene's head was already starting to clear and he sighed heavily in the Lexus's air-conditioned breeze. The hour was almost noon, and he was hungry. Being discovered in Eileen's apartment was least likely at eleven o'clock, when most people were at work. They had their false badges at the ready, but didn't have to use them.

"False badges aren't going to work in Wyoming, Ken," Rene said heavily. "Do you know how many people live there?"

"Not many?"

"Less than the population of Denver, in a state as big as Colorado. I've driven through there. We'd stick out for miles, you and I. Maybe we can find out more about this Lucy Giometti. She might be the answer. Her and her adorable little brat."

Ken nodded, leaning back in his seat and closing his eyes. Rene knew that Ken hated to burgle. Ken loved to kill, that was what satisfied his soul. He loved to kill and he loved listening to music. Rene thought that Ken might have a chance to listen to a lot of music while they drove through the empty spaces of Wyoming. Though Ken didn't know it, Joe Tanner was a priority higher than they'd ever had. This one was going to be the last hit, the one that broke the camel's back. After Joe Tanner, there was no one else who was ready to step up and play a thermonuclear attack and win. They were going to have to go into Wyoming and kill him there, like it or not.

Now all they had to do was find out where Eileen's mother and father lived. That should be possible. It might be best to kill everyone at the Reed household. Set it up as a transient serial killer, the kind that Eileen Reed was so good at catching and putting behind bars.

Humming softly to himself, Rene steered the car towards home and a good meal. There were many plans to make.

CHAPTER EIGHT

The Reed Ranch, Wyoming

"**Y**ou couldn't do better than this?" Howie asked Eileen, gesturing at Joe.

"He cleans up real nice," Eileen drawled. Joe, still muzzy-headed from his nap and the pills, was trying to get through his head that Howie Magnus was in front of him. He'd had Howie's poster on his wall when he was just hitting his teens, and knew every song on Howie's *Black Magic* collection by heart. He bet he could still sing every verse.

"Nice to meet you," he said. Howie grinned at him, re-markable blue eyes sparkling in his weathered face. He looked smaller and older than his posters and his albums, all but the eyes. The eyes were exactly Howie.

"You just drove into a prize shitstorm, fella," he said. "You show him the skull yet, Eileen?"

"Not yet," Eileen said. "I thought I'd let him get settled in before we started all of that."

"Is this about the missing guy?" Joe asked. Getting his bruised head around the sight of Howie Magnus was like swallow-ing one of 'Berto's horse pills. 'Berto's horse pills weren't helping his brainpower, for that matter. Still, there was enough wattage for him to realize there was a lot going on, none of it good.

"Yes," Eileen said crisply. She was dressed in light khaki

pants and a white cotton T-shirt. She wore a light blue button-up shirt, open, over her T-shirt, which Joe appreciated. She looked delicious. If he saw her nipples through the thinness of that old T-shirt he'd go absolutely crazy. He hadn't seen her for nearly a week, after all, and there was nothing bruised below his waist.

Then again, he knew why she was wearing two shirts on such a hot day. The second shirt hid her holster at her waist. Joe was confident she had her other friend, her revolver, fastened to her ankle. Eileen was carrying her weapons at her own parents' home. This had to mean trouble.

"Where's Lucy?" he asked.

"Getting Hank dressed after his nap," Eileen said. "Dinner in about fifteen minutes, and you're going to meet more people. Everyone you meet was here when Dr. McBride was killed, except for Lucy and Hank and me."

"Hank, right," Joe said. The little baby, the boy who'd been inside Lucy when she and Joe and Eileen had saved the world from nuclear war. He surely wasn't tracking that well, because it suddenly occurred to him that Eileen had just told him that the missing archaeologist was now the dead archaeologist.

"I think I'll get this fella a cup of joe," Howie said, rising to his feet with compact grace. "He looks a bit stoned from his meds. I'm going to get a cup for me, too, even if it is before dinner. I think I'll be drinking coffee tonight instead of whiskey with my cigars. Story time should be interesting. Tonight looks like your night to tell all, Mr. Tanner."

"You won't be disappointed," Joe said.

"Thanks, Howie," Eileen said. "Joe takes cream only, just like me. Bring a cup for me, would you?"

"Of course," Howie said, disappearing through the doorway to the kitchen. Joe sat looking at the empty doorway. Howie Magnus was getting him a cup of coffee. Amazing. His mind wandered to Sully doing lazy flips and turns, wings outstretched, her laser lance in one relaxed hand, watching him and laughing, and he felt so dizzy for a moment he had to shut his eyes.

"Joe, you need to rest," Eileen said anxiously. She touched his hand and he took it, holding the warm length of it in his own.

"I'm all right," he said. "No more pain pills, after this one.

It's aspirin or nothing, from now on. I hate the way they make me feel."

"No fractures, no bleeding?"

"Nothing but a concussion, and that's going away," Joe said. "Now tell me, what happened? The guy that's dead, he was murdered?"

"He was murdered," Eileen said, still holding his hand. "We found him by the old chicken coop. He was attacked near the archaeological dig, and whoever did it left him for dead. He wasn't. He got up and made it almost the whole way here before he collapsed and died. Before he died he hid a few things, which Lucy and Hank and I found."

"What things?"

"Here's coffee," Howie said, coming through the doorway with a wooden tray. "I added a cup for Lucy, she's in the kitchen with Hank. She'll be along in a minute."

"What about Mark and Nolan?" Eileen asked.

"They're setting up some targets for shooting practice tomorrow," Howie said, setting the tray down on the coffee table and taking his own black coffee from the tray. He sat down and sipped, eyebrows raised over the rim of the cup. "Your dad is directing, they're setting up. Jimmy is taking a shower. I excused myself because I'm old and tired."

Eileen laughed and Joe surprised himself by laughing with her.

"Okay, I wanted to meet Eileen's boyfriend. I took a quick shower and hustled down here. I was thinking she'd called up her muscle-bound buddy to help her out when she wrestles the bad guy into handcuffs, but you don't look like a cop."

"I'm not," Joe said.

"Hey, Joe," Lucy said, coming through the door with a small boy on her hip. Joe hadn't seen Lucy face-to-face since she was pregnant, over two years ago now. He hadn't really seen her that afternoon when he'd driven in; he was too busy trying to keep his brains from leaking out of his ears.

Lucy was just beautiful, he thought, and he'd thought that when she was bulging with pregnancy. She had a glorious mane of dark hair and a lovely face and eyes. Best of all, she was Lucy, personality blazing like a bonfire. She was thinner now but still rounded in a way the fashion magazines frowned upon but Joe did not. He found himself grinning like a happy pup.

The little boy in her arms, with curly dark hair and dark eyes, must be her son Hank. He looked unsmiling at Joe and Joe smiled at him. Hank hid his face in Lucy's neck as she leaned over and gave Joe a big kiss. Joe was probably a nightmare to a small boy; bruised, one eye bloodshot, white bandage covering his stitches. At least he'd showered and shaved, so he looked a tiny bit more presentable.

"Hi, Lucy," Joe said. "Hello, Hank. I'm sorry I look so awful. I'll be all better soon."

Hank kept his head in Lucy's neck and she shrugged. She walked around the couch and took a seat on the other side of Joe with Hank clinging to her like a little barnacle. She took the coffee Howie had brought in and sipped it, then relaxed into the couch.

"He'll get over it," she said. "How far did Eileen get? Did she get to the skull?"

"What skull?"

"I'll have Dad get it out tonight," Eileen said. She handed a cup of coffee to Joe and he took a hot mouthful that cannoned down his throat and lit him up like a light bulb. The mere smell was enough to revive him, earthy and sweet and bitter at the same time. "It's a crystal skull, Joe, along with a crown of rubies and emeralds in about two pounds of gold. That's not all."

"Oh," Joe said. There didn't seem to be anything else to say. He drank more coffee.

"It's Aztec, or so the archaeologists think," Lucy continued, her barnacle son now peeking with one bright eye from her chest. He saw Joe's glance and hid his face again, but Joe could see him smiling. "They have the skeleton that wore it down at the buffalo jump, along with a few more artifacts. A jaguar medallion that's surrounded by skulls, worked in turquoise and maybe emeralds."

"Emerald eyes," Howie said, his own glittering like jewels.

"I didn't know you'd been down there," Eileen said smoothly.

"I haven't," Howie said. "I'm a shameless snoop. I heard you and your mom talking about it in the kitchen."

"Howie wouldn't be welcome at the dig," Lucy said. "There's the anthropologist, Beryl Penrose, and the other archaeologist, Jorie Rothman. They don't like the hunters and the hunters don't like them—"

"On the contrary," Howie protested. "I think Mark and Nolan would both like to become extremely friendly with Jorie."

"So friendly she'd walk funny for days," Lucy said dryly.

"Jorie is pretty?" Joe guessed.

"You have no idea," Lucy looked past Joe at Eileen and they both smothered smiles in their coffee cups.

"So that's the situation. Howie is the head of a group of hunters who are scouting out my parents' ranch. Beryl and Jorie worked with Dr. McBride. Anyone could have killed him, and as Nolan puts it so well, anyone in a dark alley would be happy to kill Dr. McBride for what he was carrying."

"Which you now have," Joe said. Howie looked at Joe over the top of his coffee mug, his eyes suddenly interested. He looked at Eileen and nodded.

"It looks like you picked a smart one," he said. "I'll have to check back later on the looks when he's healed up."

There was a bobbing motion at the door. Zilla came through the door and around the couch. Hank released his mother and squealed with joy. Zilla bounced ecstatically up and down on her one front leg and Hank slid to the floor so he could throw his chubby arms around the little dog.

"Zilla's amazing, even by cattle dog standards. She's fetching us for supper, that's why my mom sent her in," Eileen explained to Joe.

Joe had no desire for food, but he knew he had to eat. He stood carefully and slowly, like an old man. Eileen took his arm and made it appear as though he were escorting her, not taking half his weight as he negotiated his way carefully from the room. Howie and Lucy, along with Zilla and a joyful Hank, went ahead. This gave Joe enough of a chance to steal a kiss, his first one, from his future wife.

The kiss was long and deep and wet enough to make him want to forgo supper and head directly upstairs. Eileen grinned at him.

"Down, boy," she said. "Separate bedrooms in this house, you know. We're not married yet."

"Oh, that's right," he groaned.

"Old-fashioned they are, but there are lots of woods around here," Eileen teased. Then her smile fell away from her face and Joe knew what she was thinking. He was thinking the same thing. There would be no romantic trysts in the woods with a blanket and a picnic basket. There were monsters out there. Murderers.

"I'm sorry—" he started, and she put a finger to his lips.

"Kiss me again," she said. "Forget everything, for right now. Kiss me again."

Colorado Springs, Colorado

"Los Angeles," Ken said. "Why do you want me to stay here while you're there?"

"Research," Rene said tersely, folding shirts carefully and packing them into his suitcase. "Wyoming. Find out everything about it. Tell me when Hulett was founded and who founded it. Find out why they named it such a ridiculous name. How many people live there, how long it's going to take to get there from here, where are the gas stations and the police stations and the speed limits. I need to know everything. Find out about Lucy Giometti. What her neighborhood is like, where she works, everything."

"I can do better work at my home in Newark," Ken began, but Rene was already shaking his head.

"I also need to know about Detective Eileen Reed, and that means you stay here. I need to know about the Colorado Springs police. Who is her partner, what does she do, every bit of publicity on her cases. When I get back we'll need to leave so make sure the Lexus has an oil change and is clean. Go buy some new music and enjoy yourself. Eat that damned fast food I refuse to look upon."

Ken laughed. He was a good man, Ken, solid and smart and dependable, despite a regrettable taste for fast food. Rene was going to need him badly in the days to come, when he'd gotten through with his business in Los Angeles.

"Is there going to be a problem, not killing Joe Tanner on the first try?" Ken asked. He was sprawled on a comfortable couch in the living room. They were in a Residence Inn close to the Colorado Springs airport, a place where business types spent days or weeks or months. Their long stay would draw no interest from the innkeepers, unlike a more transitory place. Best of all, Ken was free to fill the living room with his elaborate music sound system and his computers. Rene would return in a few days. Another day to recuperate and then it would be off to Wyoming and a nice little murder spree.

"No. If we fail again, then perhaps. But we won't fail again." Rene folded a tie in precise thirds and laid it gently in his suitcase. He didn't tell Ken that the contractor, in this case, was actually Rene himself. Some things Ken didn't need to know. Rene's laptop was packed. After his plane took off he would play dozens of games of Free Cell, the computer solitaire game. Free Cell was his way of meditating, of solving problems in the back of his brain while the front of his brain was involved with queens and jacks and red eights.

"Not a chance," Ken said. He put his hands behind his neck and stretched out on the couch. He was probably already dreaming of the enormous greasy bucket of fried chicken and some low sort of beer to go with it that he would buy after Rene left. Rene could hardly keep himself from shuddering. "I'll have a Ph.D. in Wyoming trivia by the time you get back, boss," Ken said confidently. "And I'll know everything about our little pussycat Eileen and her matron-of-honor girlfriend Lucy."

"Eileen will be a pussycat when she's dead," Rene said. "Until she is, she's dangerous. Don't forget that."

"Okay," Ken said, unfazed at the rebuke. "I won't. I'll drive you to the airport."

Rene took his briefcase and his bag and left the suite, Ken following behind. The sun was heading towards the range of mountains that lay to the west of Colorado Springs. The day was hot and still. Puffy white clouds floated across the sky. Rene set his bag in the back of the Lexus. Good weather lay ahead. Rene took it as the best kind of omen.

CHAPTER NINE

The Reed Ranch, Wyoming

"**I** don't want to leave," Howie said calmly, stretching an arm to the cigar humidor.

"You're a suspect," Eileen said, not unkindly. She thought Howie was a wonderful man and he could single-handedly launch her parents' new business into orbit, but he could still be the murderer.

"I know," he said, removing a cigar and admiring it. "So if I'm the murderer and I'm staying here to fool you, I'll trip myself up and you can arrest me. If I'm not, which I'm not, maybe I can help."

"I vote for Howie," Joe said. His pain pills had worn off during dinner and his eyes were sharp again. The plain aspirin he'd swallowed was working fine, he'd assured Eileen. She knew that was a lie but she let it stand.

Lucy was curled up on one of the big armchairs. Zilla had somehow wormed her way into Lucy's lap and was watching the proceedings alertly, her head stretched out on Lucy's knee.

"Zilla says stay, and so do I," Lucy said. She looked fresh and radiant, her eyes as alert as the little collie dog in her lap. Her hair was still wet from an evening bath she'd taken with Hank, who was sound asleep in the little bedroom they shared. Eileen was grateful Lucy had enough energy to stay up and powwow. She needed her.

"I'm biased, I'm hoping to get his business this coming year," Paul Reed said quietly. "I'll leave the decision to you, Eileen."

"All right then, Howie, you're in," Eileen said. "Light up that horrible thing and let's get on with it."

Nolan Simmons, the comedian, had left for bed the same time as Hank. He was visibly thinner than when he'd arrived, despite Tracy's plentiful cooking. Horseback riding and walking at a high altitude were whipping him into shape faster than any fat farm. He was exhausted, and so was Mark Plutt, the software tycoon. Plutt had the opposite problem; he was thin and slight, without any reserves. He, too, was eating huge meals. Despite the murder, or maybe even because of it, they were both having the time of their lives.

Jimmy Arnold, Howie's brother-in-law, had deftly removed himself after dinner without a single visible signal from Howie. Eileen was sure there had to be one. Jimmy was a mystery. He was general manager of Howie's extremely successful catalog empire and was therefore a millionaire in his own right. There was a flavor of equals about the two men. In any case, they were friends of such time and depth that they communicated without words. If Jimmy were the murderer, Eileen was convinced Howie would risk his life to help him.

Tracy had gone to bed as soon as Lucy returned from her bath. Tracy carried a paperback book and a glass of cold water. She'd be up at five a.m. again; cooking huge meals that would be devoured to the last scrap.

The two University women, Jorie and Beryl, hadn't joined them for dinner. Paul and Eileen had walked down to the jump site and made sure they were settled for the evening, which infuriated Jorie, of course. Everything seemed to provoke anger from Jorie. Eileen was tired of it.

There had been, before supper, an interesting conversation in the kitchen of the ranch.

"I won't eat with those men," Jorie said. "They're hunters. They love to see dead things. Men love to *eat* dead things. They're hunters."

Tracy sighed audibly and did not say anything, but continued her supper preparations.

"You could eat just the potatoes and the corn," Eileen said. "Why don't you stay? We don't have a problem with your being a vegan. You can stay." She really wanted to keep Jorie and Beryl at the ranch. She wasn't sure the jump camp was safe. "Besides, I'm a hunter too, and I'm not a man."

"Then what do we need men for?" Jorie said, in the same bitter needling tone. She was beginning to give Eileen a headache. "What does anyone need with men? What are they even for?"

"You don't know, Jorie," Tracy said in a gentle voice. "I hope none of you girls ever have to find out."

"I know," Lucy said, surprised. She was cutting carrots for the evening salad. Hank sat at her feet, chewing messily on a cracker. "Of course. Just look at Hank. *He's* why."

"Men aren't just sperm producers, Lucy," Tracy said. "Just as we aren't baby incubators."

"Oh, well, I know, but…" Lucy trailed off, chastened.

"I guess making lots of love wouldn't be the reason, either," Eileen said with a grin. Lucy felt better. Jorie grimaced. Tracy smiled and shook her head.

"No. Let's not talk about this now."

"Ever," Jorie said in an undertone that reached everyone. Her lovely face was flushed and angry, and she turned and left the kitchen before Eileen could say anything more.

Eileen looked over at Lucy with raised eyebrows, and Lucy nodded in understanding.

"Poor Jorie," Tracy said, and went to wash her hands in the sink.

"Yeah, poor Jorie," Lucy said. "She's going to miss out on barbequed chicken."

Now with supper consumed and the evening drawn down into night, Eileen sat in her parents' family room and prepared to think her way to a killer.

"So here's the murder hunters," Howie said, lighting his cigar and puffing out a cloud of blue smoke. Lucy rolled her eyes and Eileen smiled. Paul opened a window and turned on the fan. Eileen looked at her companions, missing Dave Rosen, her homicide detective partner, more than she thought she would. He was brilliant but he was in Colorado, more than eight hours away. Joe Tanner sat with her on the couch, his long body draped in unfamiliar clothes. Lucy sat on the chair, Paul returned to his seat on the other armchair and Howie reigned on the other couch. The hot July night outside the screened French doors was black and still. A few moths beat against the screen.

On the mantle, joining their group, the crystal skull grinned at them all. Oddly enough, Eileen was undisturbed by the skull. It was a perfect representation of a human skull, as clear as rock candy. The eye sockets were carved deep and the teeth were perfectly formed in bas-relief in the stone. The overall effect was cheerful, somehow, as though the skull were smiling.

Joe loved the skull. He'd run his hands over it again and again, handling the artifact more than any of them had. The dirty golden circlet with the inset jewels didn't interest him. He'd removed it and set it on the mantle. When he'd put the skull back on the mantle he'd left the crown off.

"Here we are," Eileen said. "We explained to Joe what was going on before dinner, Dad. So here's my first question of the evening. Why did the murderer kill Dr. McBride?"

"For the skull and the crown," Howie said immediately, pointing at the skull with his cigar. Paul nodded. The skull grinned.

"So why didn't the killer take it?" Lucy asked. "After he stabbed him with that stone thing, why didn't he take the stuff?"

"They fought," Paul said. "And the murderer ran away, not knowing he'd killed McBride."

"No signs of struggle," Lucy said, "at the camp. No tables overturned no collapsed tents or scattered tools."

"Maybe they fought in the ditch where the skeleton was found," Eileen said.

"We should look for dirt and marks on Dr. McBride," Joe said. "Evidence he'd fought someone. Skin under his fingernails, maybe?"

"There were no defensive cuts," Eileen said, remembering the body when it had been turned over. "Just the one stab wound. If there was a fight, the killer was too quick for Dr. McBride to defend himself."

"So if the killer was that quick, why didn't he take the loot?" Joe asked.

"There has to be something else," Eileen said. "Something we're not seeing."

Lucy stroked Zilla's head and blinked slowly, her eyes unfocused. "Maybe this murder doesn't have anything to do with the skull and the crown after all," she said. "The murderer didn't care about the jewels. They hated Dr. McBride and wanted to kill him."

"Okay," Eileen said. "Why would anyone hate Dr. McBride? Could someone have come up here and killed him for some other reason? Someone that traveled here, killed him, and left?"

Paul frowned, then shrugged. "Sure," he said. "Someone could come through the woods, sneak past Zilla. But they'd have to be a helluva woodsman to get in and out."

"A Lakota Sioux could," Eileen murmured. "One of the warrior types."

"What do you mean warrior types?" Lucy asked.

"There have been several lost generations of Lakota," Eileen said. She shrugged, feeling uncomfortable with the topic. "Almost all of them seemed to turn to drink or abuse drugs. Lately, though, there seems to be a renewal among the tribes. They're turning away from booze and apathy, as though they're finally finding a way. I don't know how else to describe it, and I haven't been living up here so I'm not sure if that's my opinion or—"

"No, you're right," Paul said. "Some say it all started after the birth of the white buffalo. If you believe that sort of thing. I don't, but if the symbol of the white buffalo helped the tribes, I'm all for it."

"White buffalo?" Lucy asked.

"A real albino buffalo," Eileen explained. "I've seen pictures, he's a beauty. The prophecy of the Lakota — and other Plains tribes, if you really want to get into legend — is that the birth of a white buffalo calf means the return of the great buffalo herds and the return of the American tribes."

"So maybe one of the new generation of White Buffalo Lakota knew Dr. McBride? And disliked him enough to murder him?" Lucy asked.

"Sure, but why would one of the Lakota hate Dr. McBride?" Paul asked.

"We could ask around the reservation," Eileen said. "Carefully."

"Maybe one of them heard about the jump and thought his ancestors were being desecrated," Joe said.

"Nobody knows about the skeleton but us. Dr. McBride found it the day he died. It would be impossible for a Lakota to find out about the skeleton, get here, and kill him."

"And he'd take the loot, for sure," Joe said. "It belongs to his ancestors, anyway."

"Not really," Lucy said. "It belonged to an Aztec warrior, so technically it belongs to Mexico."

"Maybe the Aztec was bringing it to the Lakota," Howie said, and stopped everyone's breath in an instant. Eileen felt an almost audible click in her brain as her jaw dropped open. Lucy looked like she felt; eyes wide, mouth open. Joe grinned.

"Of course!" he said. "That's what he was doing way the hell up here. He was an envoy, maybe, or a priest or shaman or something."

"No wonder Beryl is so thrilled," Eileen said. She felt a growing excitement. "Whoa, to establish that the Aztec nation and the Lakota nation were in contact more than five hundred years ago. What an incredible link."

"How do we know this skeleton is really five hundred years old?" Lucy asked. "They don't have portable carbon-dating kits now, do they?"

"No," Paul said. "As soon as the Spanish arrived and left horses here, the Plains tribes stopped running buffalo off cliffs. They started hunting them on horseback."

"Oh, of course," Lucy said. "And the Aztec didn't survive the Spanish invasion, because they had gold and the Spanish had the smallpox virus. So it had to be five hundred years ago."

"Exactly," Eileen said. "Too bad we can't put the murder together that cleanly."

"So maybe Dr. McBride was killed by a rival archaeologist. You know, like that little dude in the Indiana Jones movies that always tried to steal Indy's stuff," Joe said.

"Sure, *there is nothing you can possess which I cannot take from you*," Lucy said, with a passable French accent.

"That doesn't work," Paul said, as everyone nodded in agreement. He continued anyway, voicing what they all knew. "The skeleton was found the same day he was murdered, or Jorie and Beryl would have known about it. No rival archaeologist, just like no vengeful Lakota warrior, could have known about the skull and made his way here in time to kill Dr. McBride."

"Okay, then, let's look at the people who were here," Eileen said. "You and your hunters, Howie. Jorie Rothman, Beryl Penrose, and my parents."

"And mystery killer X," Joe said, his face suddenly grave. "Someone who comes out of nowhere and tries to kill you."

Interest sharpened towards Joe. Eileen opened her mouth but Joe held up a hand, stopping her.

"When we're finished with Dr. McBride," he said, "I'll tell my tale. But one thing at a time."

"Thanks," Eileen said. She was a person who liked to focus on one task at a time. She liked to line up problems one by one and knock them down. She even washed dishes that way. "First things first. Dr. McBride. Did you meet him, Howie?"

"Sure," Howie said, puffing on his cigar. He gazed through the smoke at the ceiling, his blue eyes narrowed in thought. If he was the murderer, he was concealing it incredibly well. "I met him the second day we were here, less than a week ago. He was excited about the buffalo jump. He knew who I was and blinked at me a couple of times while we shook hands. But he was much more interested in his dig. He wanted to talk to Paul about borrowing something."

"A tarp. He thought it was going to rain and they were short a tarp," Paul said.

"Did it rain that day?" Eileen said.

"No," Paul said.

"That must have been the day he found it," Lucy said. Zilla had dozed off. Lucy smoothed Zilla's soft head, her face in frowning thought. "Where was Jorie Rothman? And Beryl Penrose?"

"They were already on their way to the funding meeting in Laramie," Paul said.

"Separately or together?" Eileen asked. She had a little notepad and she flipped it open to make some notes. Joe swung his legs onto her lap so she rested the notepad against his shins. It was a very unprofessional position, but she didn't care. She loved the sensation of his legs resting against her lap. It was frustrating to think about spending the night apart when they hadn't seen each other in so long. But her parents' rules were unbending and she had no intention of breaking them. After all, tomorrow there was the potential for a walk in the woods with a picnic lunch and a big blanket, murderer or no murderer.

"Separately, I think. They each brought their own cars up here, unlike Howie and his crew. But they aren't on vacation. They knew they'd have to travel back and forth from the University of Wyoming in Laramie," Paul said.

"Okay, then, what about your boys, Howie? Nolan and Mark and Jimmy?"

"No alibis, any of them," Howie said. "None for me, either, I'm afraid. This was our second day here so Paul was letting us get our feet under us. I think Nolan spent some time in the stable, checking out the horses. Mark was in his room on his computer all day trying to straighten out some mess at his company. Jimmy took a hike along the bluff. He took Zilla with him so he wouldn't get lost but he was gone most of the day."

"And you?" Eileen asked.

"I was with Paul most of the day, but I took an afternoon nap. I know that sounds pitiful, but I've been working on some new material and I wanted to catch up on some sleep. I'm not eighteen any more." Howie shrugged and grinned at them with his eighteen-year-old eyes. "So I could have done it too, you see."

"How about jealousy?" Lucy suggested. "Jorie and Beryl both love Dr. McBride. He decides he loves Jorie more than Beryl and she kills him out of jealousy."

"Why not Beryl more than Jorie?" Joe asked, and then frowned at the grins. "Oh, that's right, Jorie is a hottie. I haven't met them yet, you know."

"We know," Eileen said and patted Joe's shins.

"I don't think the jealousy thing will pan out," Howie said.
"How come?"

"Because Nolan Simmons gave it his best shot the other day and Jorie turned him down cold. He's a good-looking kid and he's been brought up right. His dad and I are good friends, go way back, and he never spoiled Nolan. Nolan doesn't miss with the ladies, not usually. Anyway, Jorie told him she didn't swing that way."

"Swing?" Paul said blankly.

"She's lesbian?" Joe said. "Damn, all the pretty ones. Except for you, of course, sweetie."

"Don't call me sweetie," Eileen said absently. "Really, she told him that?" She looked at Lucy who was frowning and shaking her head slowly.

"I didn't think so, either," she said.

"What?" Howie asked.

"She acted like Jon McBride was her lover, not her colleague. I'd swear she was in love with him, which is where I got my theory. Which is now shot to hell, if she's a lesbian."

"She was just very upset, perhaps," Paul said. "A friend's death can do that to you." His face, lined and weathered, was sagging with weariness. He had an enormous burden on his shoulders right now, Eileen realized, and she was keeping him from his rest. He wasn't a young man anymore, no matter how much he could still do.

"Let's stop beating this dead horse," Eileen said, closing her notebook with a snap. "We need to get to bed. There's someone I want to call tomorrow."

"Who's that?" Howie asked.

"Alan Baxter," Eileen said, looking at her dad. He frowned a little and that pierced to the core of her. Then he met her eyes and nodded gravely.

"Of course," he said. "Don't worry about me, punkin. We've had that talk already."

"Thanks, Dad," Eileen said.

"Why Alan?" Joe said.

"Who is Alan?" Howie asked.

"My birth father," Eileen said levelly. "I was adopted at four, and I found my birth father last year. His name is Alan Baxter and he lives in the San Luis Valley, in Colorado."

"Does he live with Marcia?" Paul asked. "Is that why you're going to call him?"

"Don't ask," Joe said to Howie, smiling at his confused expression. "I'll fill you in on all the details. Marcia Fowler is Alan Baxter's friend. She's a sweetie. Plus, she's an expert in every strange legend and off-the-wall theory you've ever heard of. She's a former schoolteacher and she's spent her whole life investigating paranormal activity."

"Paranormal activity," Howie said with a grin, puffing on his evil cigar. "This just gets better and better. What, you think the *skull* killed Dr. McBride?"

"Just a hunch," Eileen admitted, tapping her pencil on her notebook. "Crystal is a new-agey kind of thing. Marcia wears a crystal around her neck all the time. So perhaps the crystal skull has some sort of paranormal meaning."

"That's right, you found that so-called UFO murderer," Howie said. "Big press. You even had a little glossy article in *People*, didn't you? Hero detective and all that."

"Yes," Eileen said.

"Camera hog," Lucy teased. Eileen flashed a quick, grateful smile at her. Lucy had helped in that case; her research at the Pentagon had helped Eileen solve the crime. Lucy didn't get any publicity since no one in the media had discovered that someone from the CIA had been involved. If *that* tidbit had gotten out the publicity might have been bigger and more uncomfortable than a tiny snip of an article in *People* magazine.

"Alan and Marcia don't live together, they're working their way around to getting together in a grumpy, old-folks kind of way," Joe said. "That's my take on it, anyway. The whole little community of Crestone is full of spiritual people. There's more Navajo influence than Lakota down that way, but I wouldn't be surprised if someone knew everything about the Aztecs. Marcia, probably. She knows everything."

"Just as long as these two don't spill the beans to the press," Howie said. "We don't want that. I don't want that. No *People* articles for me."

"None of us want press," Lucy said. "Including Jorie and Beryl. Their careers are at stake."

"Alan and Marcia wouldn't give a journalist the time of day," Eileen said. "So let's get to bed. We'll talk to Alan and Marcia tomorrow, and find out all about crystal skulls and Aztec priests."

"What about Joe?" Howie said. "Don't we get to hear about his adventure?"

"I think," Eileen said slowly, "that I had better listen to Joe's story alone. He works at a high security Air Force base. It might have something to do with his work, and if it does, it's classified. Not even you can listen, Dad," she said. "I'm sorry."

"I'm not," Paul said without regret. "I'm tired. Let me know whatever you can, and try not to stay up too late."

Howie stubbed out his cigar and rose to his feet. "That's my cue too. I don't want to hear any government secrets. I have enough trouble with the IRS. Miss Lucy, you going up with me?"

"I'll put Zilla out first," Lucy said smoothly. "Then I'll be right along."

Los Angeles International Airport, Los Angeles, California

Rene sat in first class waiting for the plane to dock. Out the window the airport screamed with light and color. Planes stacked up on each runway, lights flashing. Baggage carriers trundled like slow beetles under and around the docked planes. He tried not to look, not to remember. He couldn't stop his memories. Los Angeles International Airport was the departure point of his delightful, happy childhood. LAX was the end of the dream.

He and his father had flown to Paris from Los Angeles International Airport. They had flown back to France in disgrace, in bewildered and bitter anger, and there six-year-old Rene had found that although he was a citizen of France, he had been raised as an American child and he didn't fit in at school at all. America was denied to him, and France turned its back on him, the thin French boys with their skinny strong arms and the rocks they threw at him. He survived. He loved Paris now, he loved France. He despised America with all his heart, every crass piece of her. He reserved his deepest hatred for this city, Los Angeles.

Los Angeles took his father, Jacque Dubois, and made him a minor celebrity. Dubois was a cinematographer in the days when cinematographers were just another member of the film crew. Dubois was one of the first to elevate the craft into an art form. The way he arranged light and form, when he was allowed to, was just short of miraculous. He had a way of arranging women in light so that they looked spectacular, moody and mysterious and inexpressibly lovely. Actresses started requesting him by name. He was beginning to realize wealth and work when the last remnants of the McCarthy era, already over, struck him down.

Rene turned in his chair, looking away from the window. He thought of his father, the way he'd been when Rene was a young boy. His father was tall and handsome, lean and brown-haired, with eyes like dark flashing jewels. He held a cigarette as though he were ready to flick it aside and fight a duel at any moment. His laugh was a cascade of sound, infectious and joyous. He was everything a little boy would want in a father.

Then someone in Hollywood, even though the House Un-American Activities Committee was disbanded, decided that Jacque Dubois' membership in the French Communist Party was enough to cause him to be blackballed. Senator Joe McCarthy had been in his grave a year, dead of drink, when Jacque Dubois was brought down.

McCarthy was the junior Senator from Wisconsin in 1950 when he began a meteoric, spectacular political career by claiming he knew of Communists working in the United States State Department. His claims of Soviet-controlled Communists actually turned out to be correct, years later when the Soviet Union fell and journalists began to ferret out Communist documents of the era. But it was McCarthy's lists of American communists, and the Hollywood film people that were on the list, that terrified the film industry.

Blackballing, where companies refused to hire anyone on a special blacklist, was elevated to a high art in Hollywood in the fifties and early sixties. It carried on past McCarthy's quick disgrace at the hands of other, outraged senators, who passed a censure of the man that ended his career. Joe McCarthy died less than three years after the HUAC committee was disbanded, died in Bethesda Naval Medical Center of what was kindly called peripheral neuritis but which was really high-octane whiskey and lots of it. But in Hollywood, where backstabbing was a way of life, blackballing continued like a virus gotten loose and still raging.

Without a single morsel of proof or a trial, Jacque Dubois had been convicted and sentenced to the death of his career by whispering innuendo, by the blackball, by the fear of another Joe McCarthy and a new HUAC committee. Or perhaps by other jealous cinematographers, who resented Dubois' brilliance, or even by directors jealous to share the limelight with a mere camera boy who refused to stay in his place. Rene never found out. Without work or the possibility of work, Jacque Dubois was forced to return to France.

Worst of all, he hadn't really been a Communist at all. He joined the party years ago, in France, in order to date a girl that wasn't even Rene's mother. A lark, as he would have called it. Just for fun. Nothing he did could clear his name. No appeal would give him a job that he loved more than his life itself.

Rene avoided Los Angeles International Airport whenever he could, just to keep the worst memories of his life safely locked away.

Yet they clamored at him now, as rudely as the boys in his new school where he started in a thick and unfamiliar uniform, a small boy trying to speak French that he barely understood. He went home every day to a father grown more depressed and despondent by the day, a lamp whose wick had blown out. When Jacque Dubois died, when Rene was eighteen, only his body stopped working. His mind had long since gone.

The plane rolled forward, and Rene tried to relax the bunched muscles of his jaw. He had business to attend to. Since murder was his business, he had murder to do. Doing it in the hated city of Los Angeles would only make the finish sweeter.

CHAPTER TEN

The Reed Ranch, Wyoming

"**I** don't feel guilty at all," Lucy said. "Where are the paper napkins?"

"Under that cabinet to your left," Eileen replied, sliding a second frozen pizza onto a baking sheet. "Joe, I know there's beer in the fridge."

"I'll get some for you and Lucy," Joe said, "but I better not, not with the pain pills and all. They might not be all the way out of my system yet."

"Then we'll all have milk," Lucy said, smiling at Joe. He looked worlds better than he had that afternoon, but he was still bruised and shaky. A pizza would do him good, pizza and a glass of milk and maybe some cookies to finish it off. No cookies for her, though. She wasn't built to burn calories like Joe and Eileen were. She slapped the napkins on the table and went back for plates. Zilla hopped nimbly out of her way. Joe sat at the kitchen table with a jug of milk and three glasses. Zilla curled up at his feet as he carefully poured the tumblers full of milk.

"I feel great," he said. "You know?"

"We know," Lucy and Eileen said together, and smiled at each other. Lucy did feel great. With the others safely off to bed they were free to talk at last.

"And it's not just the pizza," Eileen said. "Here's the first batch, let me cut it up and we'll eat."

"You eat, I'll talk," Joe said. He reached down and started patting Zilla's head. "I hope you believe me. Okay, here goes. I must have been driving home from a war game. I don't really remember. The first thing I remember was waking up on the clouds...."

"Oh, my God," Lucy said in her squeakiest, tiniest voice, when Joe had finished. It was the best she could manage. She felt like the time when she was six and she'd fallen off the back yard swing set and landed flat on her back.

Her pizza lay, untouched, on her plate. Eileen hadn't touched hers, either. Her face was pale and distressed. Zilla, undisturbed, snoozed with her head on Lucy's foot.

"I guess that means you believe me," Joe said. His hand was pressed to his forehead, right below the stitches.

"Eat some pizza, Joe," Eileen said. "You need some food."

"Okay," Joe said. His face brightened as he picked up his pizza. "I feel better, actually."

"Of course we believe you," Lucy said, still feeling dazed. She took a bite of pizza, cooled to perfect munching temperature. Her security clearance was higher than Joe or Eileen's. The reason she'd met Detective Eileen Reed and computer programmer Joe Tanner was because of her analyst job with the CIA. She'd been given an old file several years ago, a file that contained a series of murders of missile defense scientists. She had a copy, in the CIA computer database, of Harriet Sullivan's autopsy results and the police report of her accident.

She'd never solved the murders. She and Eileen, together, had caught a serial killer at Schriever Air Force Base, where Joe worked now. But the earlier murderers and accidents like Sully's were never solved. Many believed them to be a series of coincidences, which was why Lucy's file was on inactive status.

"I dreamed that Sully described her murderer," Joe said, "and then they came for me, too. Do you think Sully was just a dream?"

"It doesn't matter. Dream or not, it got you out of that car before they came back," Eileen said.

"We have to find out who they are," Lucy said. Her pizza was gone to the last scrap and she tried to suppress a longing for Tracy's chocolate chip cookies. "I never thought the trail would pick up again. There hasn't been a murder added to my file since we met out at Schriever."

"I would have been a new one," Joe said. "And I still will be, if we can't figure out who they are. We have to go back sometime, you know."

"Unless they decide to come up here," Eileen said coolly. Joe flinched visibly, startled. Lucy turned to Eileen. Eileen shrugged, eyebrows raised. "Why not?"

"They don't know about you," Joe said. "Nobody knows about you and me."

"Joe," Eileen said with a funny, rueful sort of smile. "I've been planning our wedding for months. We bought my engagement ring. I've been talking to caterers, florists, music services, and places for the reception. We told my pastor, remember? Everybody in the police department knows about you now."

"Oh, shit," Joe said, his hands to his face. "I forgot."

"Don't worry," Eileen said.

"Why?" Lucy said. She looked out the kitchen windows as though Joe's murderers would drive over the hill from the highway at any second. How far behind Joe could they be?

"Because my parents don't have an address," Eileen said. "They only have a post office box. How are Joe's bad guys going to find this place?"

"Ask at Hulett," Lucy said. "How's that for starters?"

"Butch knows everyone in town," Eileen said. "He runs the Conoco station, and that's the only gas station. If strangers start asking about the Reed place, they're going to call the sheriff. I'll call the post office tomorrow, and talk to Sylvia, and we'll have Dad talk to Butch and to the sheriff. But they won't risk coming up to Wyoming." Eileen stared at her plate and stirred the crusts of her pizza with a finger. "I bet they'll set a trap in Colorado Springs," she continued. "Which means we'll just have to set a bigger one."

"Thank goodness," Lucy said, her thoughts going to Hank, so sweetly asleep. She couldn't risk endangering him. Not for anything, anybody.

"Don't worry about Hank," Eileen said, voicing Lucy's thoughts. "We won't let anything happen to him."

"I know," Lucy said. But she didn't know. As they finished stacking the dishes and turning off lights, Lucy realized she was very worried, indeed.

"So sneak down the hall," Lucy said sensibly, looking in Eileen's doorway. Lucy was washed and brushed and in her cotton pajamas. She closed the door and came to sit down on Eileen's bed. Eileen wore a satiny peach-colored shirt that came down to mid-thigh.

"I like your pajamas," Eileen said, her face scrubbed pink and her hair held back by a flowered band. She looked no more than sixteen.

"I like yours," Lucy said. "Kind of sexy."

"Joe likes satin," Eileen said. "So I've changed my sleeping clothes. I used to wear big T-shirts to bed. This was my compromise, a satiny shirt thing."

"It's great," Lucy said. "So why won't you sneak down the hall? You're going to be married, you know."

"I know," Eileen said. She shrugged, and smiled ruefully at Lucy. "It would be cheating. I can't cheat on my mom and dad. Dad, mostly. My mom certainly knows that I'm having sex with Joe. She asked me, when we first got engaged."

"She did?" Lucy asked, fascinated. "What did she say?"

"Just that I should make sure we were compatible in bed, if we hadn't already figured it out. She told me this hilarious story about a virgin bride who married the son of the richest man in town. And the richest man was—"

"A doctor. A lawyer. The veterinarian? The mayor?"

"The undertaker," Eileen said, poker-faced. Lucy started to laugh and put both her hands to her mouth. "So there they are on their wedding night and her groom asks her to sit in a bath full of ice for fifteen minutes, then lie real still on the bed."

Lucy grabbed one of Eileen's pillows and pressed it over her face. She leaned into the quilt and howled.

"Okay," she said finally, brushing tears of laughter from her eyes.

"So I confessed to Mom that yes, we were excellently compatible in bed, and she was very happy but she told me to make sure I never told my dad. So I just can't, no matter how much I need to hold Joe right now."

"I understand," Lucy said. "And I'm glad. I don't know if I could resist my bad side."

"There's always a blanket and a picnic lunch, tomorrow," Eileen said with a wicked little grin. "That doesn't count, does it?"

"No, indeed," Lucy said. "I have to confess I've never actually done it outdoors. I've always wanted to, like in the romance novels, but I just never had the opportunity and space."

"Wyoming has lots of space," Eileen said. "I didn't do it indoors until I was halfway through college. It just seemed more private to be all by ourselves."

Lucy blinked at Eileen. "If I wasn't in Wyoming right now I'd think you had a screw loose," she said. "But now I know exactly what you mean."

"Hey," Eileen said, her face suddenly thoughtful. "I just had an idea. How about you bring Ted out here? This is getting messy, you have to admit. If Ted's here you can split the time with Hank, there'll be two people to look after him. Plus, you can take a blanket and a lunch one day and I'll look after Hank. Fulfill a fantasy, what do you think?"

"I can't," Lucy said slowly, and shrugged her shoulders at Eileen's crestfallen expression.

"Why not?"

"I can't tell you. It's too embarrassing," Lucy said. Eileen reached across the little bed and took Lucy's shoulders in her hands.

"You can tell me anything," she said. "We're friends, right?"

"Okay," Lucy said, but she didn't look at Eileen. She looked at her cotton pajamas and the little winged pigs that floated among puffy white clouds. "It's money. We can't afford a round-trip ticket for Ted. I'm on part-time status at the Agency and Ted, he's a teacher you know. Not exactly big bucks."

"Oh," Eileen said.

"We could afford my trip out here, and we can afford to come out in September for your wedding, but that's it. I don't want to go into credit card debt, I hate credit cards."

"I let you pay for gasoline, and you paid for lunch in Wheatland," Eileen said. She looked angry. "I let you pay. You let me let you."

"What?" Lucy said, smiling.

"You know what I mean," Eileen said. "Lucy. Your trip this fall is paid for, no questions asked. And you know I'm not going to make you pay for the hideous bridesmaid's dress we picked out."

"It's a beautiful dress," Lucy protested. "And I'm not going to let you—"

"Shut up," Eileen said. "You saved my life. Twice."

"So far," Lucy said, and she did start to cry, she couldn't help it. She reached out for Eileen and they hugged. First they were laughing and now they were crying together. Ridiculous. Eileen reached out and got them tissues from the bedside table. The pretty rocker that sat by the bed was festooned with Eileen's collection of holsters and guns and ammunition. Lucy felt better, looking at them. They were anything but girly.

"Time to get to our lonely beds," Eileen said, blowing her nose with an enormous honk.

"But not for long," Lucy said. "I can't wait to call Ted. I'll call him as soon as we're up."

The Reed Ranch, Wyoming

"Okay, Eileen, we're both here now." Alan Baxter's voice rose tinnily from the speakerphone in Paul Reed's tiny office. "Sorry it took so long."

"No problem," Eileen said. It was afternoon, and she'd been waiting for his return call since nine in the morning. The longest day on record, and catching Joe alone in the kitchen and kissing him until they were both panting didn't improve her temper. With no way of knowing when Alan would call back, they couldn't slip out into the woods. The day was again cloudless and hot, a heat wave that felt as endless as the blue sky overhead.

Lucy sat on the floor in the hallway, playing with Hank and listening in. Tracy Reed had kept Eileen's childhood collection of toy cars and dug them out that morning for Hank. Hank was in heaven, rolling the little cars up and down the hallway with Zilla as a fascinated audience.

Joe came in and sat on the edge of Paul's desk. Tracy followed, wiping her hands on her apron and then wiping a lock of gray hair off her forehead. She already looked tired. Paul and the hunters had long gone, off to another promising ridge that might hold elk and deer. They were on horseback, despite Nolan's half-hearted protest, and wouldn't be back before dark.

"Do you have the camera set up?"

"We've got it, and we have the skull, too," Eileen said. Joe positioned the digital camera on top of Paul's computer. "Ready?"

"We're ready," Marcia Fowler's voice came out of the speakerphone. "We've got a camera here too, so we'll aim it us."

"We'll aim it at us, too, before we introduce you to our new friend," Joe said. He aimed the camera behind Paul's seat and gestured for Lucy and Tracy to move into the picture. Lucy picked up Hank and they crowded behind the desk. Joe pressed a few keys on the computer and two sharp pictures sprang up on the screen.

In one were Eileen, Joe, Lucy, Hank and Tracy, crowded together. Hank waved at his picture on the screen and then smiled as his image waved back at him.

In the other, Eileen could see her birth father, Alan Baxter. For a moment she could look at no one else. He looked so much like her. Or actually, she looked so much like him. They were still finding out about each other. Her mother had kidnapped her as a baby and tried to kill herself and her baby daughter on a highway outside Rapid City, South Dakota. She'd only succeeded in killing herself. Paul and Tracy Reed, who later adopted Eileen, had rescued the little girl from the car wreck. Eileen, who never knew her last name, had found her father only a year ago, and she still felt a surprising jolt every time she saw him. *My father.*

"Hi, Eileen," Alan said, with his beautiful slow smile.

"Hi, Dad," Eileen said.

"Hello, Mrs. Reed. Joe, and is that Lucy?"

"This is Lucy," Lucy said, and waved. Hank waved with her. "I'll be listening in but I have to go play some Matchbox cars with Hank."

"Hi, Lucy," Marcia Fowler said. She was sitting with Alan Baxter and looked radiant. Eileen thought suspiciously that she looked like a woman who'd just done what she wanted to drag Joe out to the woods and do.

"Hi, Miss Fowler," Lucy said. Hank wiggled impatiently and she waved again. "Gotta go."

"You've told her the story?" Eileen asked Alan.

"Everything you told me," Alan said.

"Let's see it," Marcia said impatiently. She was a small woman in her sixties, with gray hair and large, dark eyes.

"Here we go," Joe said. He walked behind the desk and tilted the little ball of the camera eye down. Sitting on a dark blue towel and grinning his cheerful grin, the skull appeared on the computer screen. He was wearing the crown of dirty gems and dull gold, exactly as Eileen had found him in the scrap of tarp.

The reaction couldn't have been more satisfying. Alan opened his mouth in astonishment. Marcia nodded peacefully, as though greeting an old friend.

"That crown isn't a crown," she said.

"It isn't?" Eileen asked.

"No, it's a necklace."

"What is it made of?" Alan asked. "The skull. It's rock crystal, isn't it?"

"We think so," Eileen said. "We don't know for sure. So what do you think about this thing?"

"I have a question, first," Marcia said firmly. "I want to know how you feel around it. Just tell me how you feel."

Eileen looked at Joe, who shrugged, and Tracy, who tugged at her ear and shrugged her shoulders as well. Lucy poked her head in from the hallway.

"I feel goofy," she said loudly at the phone. "Goofy in a good way. Cheerful. Like he's smiling at me."

Eileen laughed. Lucy was so unabashed. And so perfectly right.

"She's right," Tracy said. "I feel kind of happy."

"Me, too," Joe said.

"Yeah, I have to agree," Eileen said. "Weird."

"What does that mean?" Joe asked. "The feeling goofy part. And how did you know we'd all feel good around it?"

Joe turned the camera so Eileen and Joe came back into camera range. Marcia nodded and smiled at him.

"Thanks, Joe," she said. "I'll tell you what I know. This is really out there sort of stuff, though."

"We're comfortable with that," Joe said impatiently. "Marcia. This is *us*."

"Okay, then," Marcia said. "This has to do with the Aztec civilization, and before that, the Mayans. I'll be as brief as I can. You know the Aztecs existed in Central Mexico for thousands of years. Their major city, Tenochtitlan, is now Mexico City. They had advanced knowledge of the solar system, of medicine including brain surgery, and some say of computers and space travel."

"Space travel," Tracy said flatly.

"Computers?" Joe asked.

"There was a capstone to a tomb, found in the lost Mayan city of Palenque in southern Mexico, in 1949. On it was a carving that clearly showed a man in a spacecraft pod. He has oxygen tanks and a helmet and the pod shows flames out the bottom."

"Skulls, dear," Alan Baxter said easily. "Aztecs, not Mayans." Marcia blinked and nodded her head.

"Oops, don't mean to get off track, there. You know the direction my brain always heads off into." Eileen smiled and shook her head as Joe rolled his eyes. Marcia was a UFO believer, a member of the Mutual UFO Organization. She was also one of the most knowledgeable people Eileen had ever met. Marcia seemed to know something about *everything*, and when it came to odd knowledge she was astonishing.

"Okay, no more Mayan. They were gone before the rise of the Aztecs. The Aztecs also made lots of human sacrifices, as you've probably heard," Marcia said, obviously trying to get back on track.

"The whole rip-the-heart-from-the-chest thing," Eileen said, thinking uneasily of the wound in the center of Dr. McBride's chest. Would the coroner find that McBride's heart was missing?

That would mean the killer had followed McBride all the way to the chicken coop at the ranch, perhaps followed his blood trail as they had done? Eileen saw an immediate image of a gasping, dying McBride with a shadowy Aztec priest standing over him, bloody heart in hand. She squeezed her eyes shut and opened them again, trying to erase the image.

"Exactly," Marcia said. "They saved skulls. Who knows why, nobody knows. But they revered them. They practiced human sacrifice on an unimaginable scale, but otherwise they had a lawful, peaceful, advanced culture before Cortez and his band of merry men showed up in 1519. This is all fact. Now I'm going to delve into theory."

"Ready," Joe said.

"There is some indication they had some sort of advanced data storage system, a sort of computer that held the accumulated wisdom of their civilization. And the form that this information was stored in was...."

"A human skull," Eileen breathed. "Of course!"

"Exactly," Marcia said. "The skull is where the brain resides, and the Aztecs worshipped the skull. These computers were used as oracles. I've never seen one until today, but I hear—"

"Until today," Tracy interrupted. "You mean you think this skull is one of them?"

"It certainly matches the description," Marcia said tartly.

"Go on," Joe said. He put his hand on Eileen's shoulder and the warmth of his hand felt very good. For some reason she was nearly shivering, even though the day was warm and her father's study was stuffy and hot.

"Okay, the legend of the skulls is that they're data storage devices, and that may or may not be true," Marcia said, settling down into her chair again.

"Every modern computer stores information on a magnetic medium," Joe said. "But I've read there are some experimental companies that are attempting storage in laboratory grown crystal. It's not so far-fetched."

"Whether or not they had advanced computer technology, they certainly used the skulls as oracles," Marcia said. "The legend goes that the priests who cared for the skulls received a prophecy about the invasion of Cortez, the Spanish Conquistador that crushed the Aztec civilization. So before he landed—"

"How many skulls were there?" Lucy interrupted, speaking at knee level from the hallway. Behind her Hank crawled down the hallway making a sports car sound.

"Thirteen," Marcia said. "Twelve in a circle and the thirteenth in the center. One of the skulls, called the Mitchell-Hedges skull, was the first to be found and I've seen pictures. It's glorious, and smaller than yours. Supposedly the twelve in the circle were female skulls and the thirteenth was a male."

As one, everyone in the room turned to look at the skull on the chair. He grinned up at them, unmistakably male. Eileen would have bet her pension on it. Their skull was a man's.

"The thirteenth skull," someone whispered. Eileen didn't know who spoke. Joe turned the camera eye back to the skull. Eileen saw Marcia and Alan staring at their computer screen. They, too, were looking at the skull.

"Go on," Eileen said. She had a feeling she knew what was coming, and from the look on Joe's face he knew as well.

"The priests seemed to know Cortez was coming and that he'd destroy their civilization. Montezuma, the leader at the time, was a weakling. The priests knew that. So their prophecy, or their visions, or whatever, told them to scatter the skulls to the different North American civilizations. Then someday they would be brought back together again."

"The Lakota Sioux," Eileen said, and blew a deep and trembling breath. "Incredible."

"That's the legend," Marcia said. "The ancient Mayan city of Luaantan in Belize had one, and that was the Mitchell-Hedges skull. It was found in a pyramid that some say is Mayan but others believe might be an extremely ancient Incan. The Navajos are supposed to have a crystal skull secretly hidden under a mountain on the reservation somewhere in New Mexico. There was supposedly one found along the banks of a river in Texas. Who knows where that was supposed to go?"

"Who knows what happened to the warrior who carried it?" Lucy said quietly from the hallway floor.

"And then there's ours," Joe said. "Our guy almost made it,

can you imagine? He'd found his way all the way to the Lakota Sioux."

"And then he's buried under about a million buffalo," Tracy said, shaking her head. "That's incredible."

"We have to tell Beryl and Jorie," Eileen said. "They have to know this."

On the computer screen, Marcia looked at Alan and shifted uneasily in her chair.

"Uh," she said, and then stopped. "Are those the archae-ologists? Or are they anthropologists?"

"There's one of each," Eileen said. "What's up?"

"Okay, well, there's something else I need to tell you."

Lucy stuck her head in the doorway and Eileen, Tracy and Joe all leaned closer to the screen. Joe turned the little ball of the camera again so that Marcia could see them.

"Ready," Joe said. "It can't get any wilder than this."

"Oh yes, it can," Marcia said uncomfortably. "Ahem. I edited the legend somewhat. The legend that talks about the crystal skull computers is from a whole series of legends about, well, hmmm."

"What is it, Marcia?" Eileen nearly shouted. Marcia believed in little gray aliens who abducted humans and shoved probes up their butts. She was convinced that the government was in cahoots with three-fingered gray guys and she was hesitating? Eileen wanted to reach through the computer screen and shake the little schoolteacher.

"Atlantis," Marcia said and shrugged her shoulders. "The legends say the crystal skulls came from Atlantis."

There was a profound silence in the room. Suddenly there was a burst of laughter from behind them.

"I'm sorry," Lucy said, clutching the doorway. "I can't help it."

Then they were all laughing helplessly. Marcia smiled at them sadly, raising her hands in the air in a *see-I-told-you-so* gesture.

"So be careful what you tell your University friends," she said. "Archaeologists and anthropologists tend to get pretty feisty about Atlantis legends. If you know what I mean."

"I'm sorry, Marcia," Eileen said, wiping at her eyes. "It's

Lucy's fault."

"Is not!" came Lucy's voice indignantly from the doorway.

"It's always Lucy's fault," Joe said. "I swear."

"No, really, thanks for the warning," Eileen said. "This is fascinating and I'm glad we know about the skulls. I don't know how this helps find our murderer."

"I have an idea," Marcia said.

"What?" Eileen asked.

"Ask the skull," she said, and pointed at the screen. "Figure out how it works, and *ask it.*"

CHAPTER ELEVEN

Marriott Hotel Conference Center, Room 1420, Los Angeles

"**S**uch a beautiful view," Chin Leh said, looking out the window.

"Lovelier every year," Rene said in liquid Chinese. He had a flair for languages. Though he couldn't read or write Chinese, he could speak it quite well. Chin Leh was a representative of the Chinese government, an Undersecretary for Hong Kong, and was delighted to run into a fluent Chinese speaker at the taxi stand at the airport.

They discussed the pleasures of Hong Kong, the jewel added so quietly to the crown of China, over a lovely dinner of Thai food. They discussed the latest Merlot from France and the grape crop from the Napa valley. Finally they retired to Chin Leh's room, where the Chinese bureaucrat ordered a bottle of brandy. He had received all the signals from Rene, all the proper small glances and looks, and was undoubtedly looking forward to an evening of sexual adventure with the enormous Frenchman.

What he received was death, and quickly. Rene was in no mood for games. He had business in Wyoming to attend to. Rene broke the smaller man's neck with his garrote, careful not to snap through the skin. Chin Leh died with only the smallest expression of surprise on his face. Rene wiped his prints, poured out the bottle of brandy, and left the room within thirty seconds of Leh's death. He would receive a fat check for this, the other half of a payment made by a Hong Kong rival of Chin Leh's.

As the door closed behind him Rene walked quickly to the stairway. His heart was beating far too fast for a man his size. He couldn't help it. He didn't crave power, or wealth, or women who were required to submit to him. The death behind him meant less than nothing to him. It was the death yet to come he craved. He craved revenge, a lifetime worth of it, and he was determined to get his full measure. He was going to drink it like fine wine, and it was going to be delicious.

He walked down three flights, then left the stairwell and hastened to the elevators. He had to get to the airport and back to Colorado. He couldn't wait to kill Joe Tanner.

The Reed Ranch, Wyoming

"What *is* this?" a woman asked in a loud voice.

Joe felt like the time when he was ten and he'd been caught going through the hall closet looking for his birthday presents. He jumped.

Eileen and Lucy were no better. Lucy dropped the screwdriver she'd been holding and uttered a little shriek. Eileen started violently and Joe saw her draw her gun. It was the first time he'd ever seen her do that. She was incredibly fast. It was like a magician's trick.

Then the gun disappeared, as quickly as it had come. Joe wasn't sure the girl had even seen Eileen's gun. She was looking at the dressmaker's dummy they'd hauled down from Tracy's attic sewing room. The dummy was draped in an old black tablecloth Tracy had rummaged up for them. Lucy had been attaching a dowel to the neck of the dummy when the woman entered.

The woman had to be Jorie Rothman. Her face was beautiful, with high cheekbones and full lips. Her hair was thick and blonde and her body was as promising as her face. She was gorgeous, but there was nothing about her that interested Joe. Even in a single flashing glance he could see the seething anger and bitterness that dominated the girl. If she didn't get rid of that interior ugliness, the face she wore at fifty would be very different from the one she was blessed with now. She stood with her fists on her rounded hips, her brows drawn together and her face thunderous.

"We're checking out a theory," Eileen said coolly.

"Whose theory? Who gave you permission to get the skull out?"

"Joe Tanner, meet Jorie Rothman," Lucy said with a little grin. She picked up her screwdriver and continued the awkward business of setting the sharpened dowel into the neck of the dummy. "Jorie doesn't hold much with polite niceties."

"Nice to meet you, Jorie," Joe said. Jorie frowned at him, evidently noticing him for the first time.

"Who are you?"

"Joe Tanner," he said, and held out his hand. "I'm engaged to Eileen."

"What happened to your face?" she said, ignoring his hand.

"Car accident. I came up to recover," he said, and offered a smile. She pursed her lips and folded her arms and looked up through her lashes at him. She was angry, but she knew what she looked like to men. The stance pushed her lovely breasts up and swung a mass of glittering hair over one shoulder. She was a piece of work, this Jorie. Joe could see Lucy working the screwdriver, her black eyes narrowed dangerously.

"So what are you doing with the artifact?"

"We spoke to an expert on the Aztec civilization," Eileen said. "She said that the skull may be set up to move and, er…" she trailed off and Joe saw a stain of red climb her cheeks. Joe knew how she felt. It seemed ridiculous, all of a sudden, to expect a rock crystal artifact to come to life and tell them who killed Jon McBride.

"It might be a form of recorder," Lucy finished smoothly, driving the last screw home as Eileen held the dummy. "We're just checking it out, that's all, Jorie. Could you get the necklace from the towel over there?"

It worked. Jorie picked up the necklace, scowling, and was directed by Lucy to drape it over the shoulders of the dress dummy.

"Time for the skull," Eileen said nervously. Joe felt the same way. The family room, full of sunlight and ordinary things like couches and tables, seemed charged with a sort of bright light.

"What *are* you doing?" Jorie said again, but her eyes were on the skull. Joe picked up the skull. The jawbone dropped slightly; it was a separate piece of carved crystal, as beautifully detailed as the head, attached to each corner by a crystal pin.

"Is there a hole, like Marcia said?" Lucy asked.

"Yes," Joe said, and handed the skull to Eileen. She took it carefully and set it on the sharpened dowel. The skull wobbled for a second as she searched for the hole in the bottom of the skull.

It was positively eerie. The skull settled onto the dowel, turned lightly, and looked directly at Jorie. She made a tiny little squealing sound and then put a hand to her mouth as though disgusted at herself.

"It looks like those dog statues with the bobbly heads," Lucy said. She was grinning in delight. Then her mouth dropped open. As she spoke, the skull bobbed around and looked at her.

"Whoa," Eileen whispered, and the skull slowly spun to face her.

"Does it work for me, too?" Joe said softly. The skull bobbed in his direction, nodding gently as though agreeing.

"This is nothing more than a simple trick," Jorie said, folding her arms nervously. "This has nothing to do with a murder investigation. You're playing around with a priceless artifact and I don't—"

"Oh, Jorie," Lucy said. "We're just trying to figure out what we're dealing with here. The skull may contain information, and if it does we might be able to get the information out of it."

"Right, by asking it?" Jorie said scornfully. Joe was beginning to understand why Lucy and Eileen had that bitten-lemon look when speaking of Jorie. "You think you'll get the answer like you're consulting a magic eight ball?"

"We haven't tried that one, yet," Joe said cheerfully. The skull, as though relieved, bobbed in his direction. "Let's ask it a question and turn it over. What do you think, Bob?"

"*Bob?*"

"Sure, Jorie, we had to call him something," Eileen said casually. Lucy worked her lips, obviously trying to keep from bursting into laughter.

"Yeah, he seems like a Bob to us. Doesn't he look like a Bob to you?"

"He does not look like a *Bob*," Jorie spat.

"Well, he doesn't talk, anyway," Joe said. "We were just checking to see if he might."

"And who told you he might talk?" Jorie asked. She leaned a hip against the couch and shook her hair back over her shoulder, gestures graceful and naturally enticing and each one aimed at Joe. Joe would have thought a lesbian would have been flirting with lovely Eileen. Lucy, too, was a petite little beauty. Why was Jorie aiming her pointy big breasts at him?

"A friend of mine, a retired schoolteacher who specializes in odd knowledge," Eileen said calmly. She didn't appear to notice that Jorie was interested in Joe. Joe wasn't sure that *Jorie* knew. Lucy, however, threw a hot dark glance at Jorie and tapped the screwdriver she was still holding against her palm, as though contemplating how it would look bouncing off Jorie's golden head.

"Jorie?" A voice called from the hall. A woman who had to be the other University scholar entered the room and stopped dead, eyes round and mouth falling open in stunned surprise. She was older than Jorie and heavier, with bristly short dark hair and a round, cheerful face.

"Hi," Eileen said in resignation. "This is Joe Tanner, my fiancé. Beryl Penrose, Joe. She's an anthropologist."

"What are you doing?" Beryl whispered. She never took her eyes off the skull and her expression became even more stunned as the skull, barely moving now, shifted slowly in her direction. Joe thought he might be able to explain the skull's movement to the sound of a voice, watching it slowly turn to face Beryl. If the skull were still, it wouldn't shift to follow voices. It had to be moving to react to the vibrations of a voice the way a tuning fork could cause glasses to vibrate. Given time, he bet he could write a mathematical equation to describe the movement. Still, the trick was amazing and terrifically spooky.

"They're calling it *Bob*," Jorie said, sounding all of eight years old. "They were trying to make it *talk*."

"And boy don't we feel foolish now," Eileen said, with a sigh. "Let's put it away, guys, before Sheriff King comes along and figures out some way to arrest me. It's beautiful but it definitely isn't going to—"

"Wait," Beryl said. She walked past Jorie and approached the skull. Her face was rapt. Joe liked her much more than Jorie. She smelled strongly of bug spray, sunscreen lotion, and dirt. He noticed the three gold earrings in one ear and a small loop in her eyebrow. Her hand, grimed with dirt, touched the brow of the skull as gently as a moth. The skull bobbed happily at her, grinning his eternal fixed grin. Reflections from the light shining on the crystal made water-like reflections dance on the ceiling of the room.

"Such a beautiful artifact," she said finally, turning from the skull. She looked at Eileen and Lucy. "You've obviously discovered the Atlantis legend."

"*Atlantis?*" Jorie said in a high, breathless voice.

"Atlantis, dear," Beryl said absently. "Don't worry, I'm not upset that you got out the skull. But I'm not a believer in the Atlantis theory. I believe that the Aztecs were an incredibly advanced civilization all on their own. But I do know about the Atlantis legend."

"So you think this skull may be a data storage device?" Joe asked. Beryl turned her gaze to Joe. She had beautiful, intense hazel eyes and thick, expressive brows. She made Jorie look like a plastic doll in a discount store, and she must have seen Joe's obvious admiration. Her brows twitched slightly and her mouth curled in an amused smile.

"Yes, I think it may be. The Atlantis legend is the white man's way of explaining away the accomplishments of the Aztecs. Of course primitive brown men couldn't possibly have had an advanced culture, so white men from the destroyed island of Atlantis must have founded the Aztec civilization and given all their technology to the inferior natives. It's a racist concept, and I despise it."

"That's what our schoolteacher friend said," Eileen said, nodding.

"Well that's one point in your friend's favor," Beryl said. "I don't think we have the technology to pull data from this device. Or to put it another way, we don't have the magic to make the skull talk. I think we need to study this skull, and by we I mean scientists. Not detectives and their friends." She looked at Eileen, Joe and Lucy sternly. Joe felt like hanging his head like a child caught with a forbidden treat.

"We have no mojo," Lucy said mournfully, irrepressible as always. Beryl laughed.

"Exactly," she said. "I'd like you to put the skull back in the safe, please."

"Yes, ma'am. Back in the safe, Bob," Joe said to the skull, which bobbed around to look at him. Was it Joe's imagination, or did the skull look unhappy?

CHAPTER TWELVE

Los Angeles International Airport, Los Angeles, California

Rene gazed moodily at the Los Angeles air traffic control tower. It sat across the tarmac in the sparkling California sun, looking like a silly robot spider from a B-grade horror movie. He was stuck again, waiting for his flight to be called, and he was trapped again into thoughts about his father.

Jacques Dubois never hated the actor who became President, Ronald Reagan. Perhaps Rene, his son, fixated on Reagan because he was visible. It didn't matter, ultimately. McCarthy was long dead; most of the committee members were faceless. But Reagan testified before Joe McCarthy's House Un-American Activities Committee. He testified out of principle, Rene had read, not out of a desire to save his career. Reagan genuinely hated communism and the American Communists who were so obviously run by the Soviet Union. His principled actions, his all-American attitude, his good looks, gave gloss and meaning to McCarthy's witch hunt. And he was *visible.* Always on television or in the movies, always smiling, playing the hero.

Reagan was long gone into politics when Jacques Dubois was blackballed in Hollywood, but Rene became convinced the actor was ultimately responsible for the destruction of his beloved father. Six-year-old Rene *hated* Ronald Reagan. He hated him with a child's uncomplicated purity.

Rene at eighteen was working at a wine shop in Paris when he was recruited, abruptly, into a branch of the Russian Mafia. His father was near death with the lung cancer that was stealing his life away. Rene carried tons of boxes of liquor and wine and spent the money on heroin to help kill his father's pain. The Russians that were going to enforce protection money for the shop were in the midst of administering a beating to the shop owner when Rene came out of the stockroom.

Rene had very little memory of the fight. He remembered the taste of his own blood in his mouth, and the pain of a broken finger. But the rest was a blur of ecstasy. Every untutored blow was joy; the joy of released anger that had festered inside him for so long it was like a monster finally let free of its chains. One man later died of his injuries, and the other never walked again. Rene thought he would be targeted for assassination and was, instead, issued an invitation to join. His father died without ever knowing how Rene could suddenly afford the finest heroin and hashish. At that point, he didn't notice much. Rene cared, though, that his father was as comfortable as possible in his final miserable year of life.

When Ronald Reagan was elected President, Rene was incandescent with fury and rage. He was an assassin, although a novice one. He was beginning to plan his own attempt when John Hinckley, Junior, stepped out of a Washington crowd and shot the American President. Rene had a copy of the tape showing the shooting. He'd played it until it wore out, then he had it digitized so it would never wear out again.

He liked watching Reagan get shot, which was undeniable. But he also watched the fully automatic weapons appear magically, as though conjured, by Secret Service agents. He studied other attempts, successful and failed: Oswald's assassination of Kennedy, Squeaky Fromme's attempt on Ford, even the assassination of Abraham Lincoln.

Ultimately he decided he couldn't kill the President without being caught. He thought about other options. He'd recently finished a contract assassination. He kidnapped a Taiwanese diplomat's mistress, a young thing with a pout much like little Iris in *Taxi Driver*, John Hinckley's favorite movie. The diplomat, madly in love with the girl, had driven right into Rene's hands while trying to save her. He and the girl were together now, forever, at the bottom of an oil barrel filled with cement. Even at the end he was trying to protect her, trying to cover her body with his as Rene filled the barrel with liquid cement.

Rene thought about Reagan's children, his wife, his former wife. All of them had potential, but none called to him. Obsession, after all, was an arcane and elegant thing. It had to be satisfied in its own way.

Rene stirred in his lounge chair and blinked sleepily at the air traffic control tower. Why did Reagan's missile defense system call to him so powerfully? Why did it beg to be destroyed? He wasn't sure, and it didn't matter. Killing scientists, just because they worked in missile defense, turned out to be terrific fun. He was still a contract assassin but took time out at least once a year to indulge in his hobby. Quietly, always masked as a suicide or an accident, but always the most brilliant, the most far-reaching scientists and engineers. After a while it became a game he couldn't stop playing. Reagan was long gone now, Dubois was getting old, but he couldn't stop. Every death filled him with a joy that was curdled like old milk, sour and sweet at the same time....

"Sir?" The touch brought him upright with a jerk and he winced at the sharp, hot pain in his neck. He'd been sound asleep and his neck was stiff.

"Yes?"

"Your flight, sir, I noticed you were sleeping. Your flight is being called." The airline attendant was square and blocky, an unattractive woman, but attentive. The VIP lounge was always well staffed.

"Thank you," he said, searching for his case. He was fuzzy-headed with exhaustion. He needed a good night's sleep before they headed into Wyoming. Ken would be waiting, a mere three hours away, and he would have information, and there would be food, and finally, bed.

The flight was called again and Rene boarded the plane, feeling the anticipation tingle pleasantly in his belly. Time to kill.

The Reed Ranch

"I can see why you call him Bob," Howard Magnus said, cigar in hand. Jimmy Arnold sat in the leather armchair with a glass of soda pop in his hand, looking at the skull with the first expression Eileen had seen on his face. He looked interested.

The crystal skull sat back on the dressmaker's dummy, swiveling to follow the conversation, glowing like a lamp. Eileen had protested, but Joe and Lucy had pleaded. They knew Bob was lonely in the safe. Jorie and Beryl avoided the ranch when the boisterous hunters were there, so the chance of being discovered playing with Bob were slim.

"We'll keep him out for a little while," Paul said, with an affectionate look at Eileen. "Then we'll put him back." Hank was in bed, after racing around with Zilla for an afternoon where absolutely nothing happened. Lucy's husband Ted was coming into the Rapid City, South Dakota airport tomorrow morning and Lucy, at least, was humming with pleased anticipation.

Eileen rolled Joe's engagement ring slowly back and forth on her finger and wished desperately that she was married, too, and could take Joe to bed tonight. Particularly after the way that Jorie wench had flipped her hair and pouted after him. She wondered if Joe had seen her jealousy. She hoped not. It was embarrassing to be jealous, and it was the first time it had ever happened to her. The emotion was hateful and ugly, like feeling a spider crawl on her. Worst of all, there was nothing she could do to brush it away. She was jealous.

Joe sat right next to her, his thigh pressed to hers, warm and solid and reassuring, making her feel simultaneously ashamed of her jealousy and mad with desire for him.

"Well, I'm going to bed," Tracy said, standing up and stretching. "You hunting types would do well to hit the sack early, too. Paul has a big trip planned tomorrow and you'll need the rest."

"Yes, ma'am," Mark Plutt said, already glassy-eyed and yawning. "I've never been so tired. Or slept so well, actually. I have trouble sleeping back home. Running a big company, you know, there are always problems. So many worries and I can't get them out of my head. But not on this trip."

"That's what I told you," Howie said with a grin, savoring his cigar. "Wait until hunting season this fall. Every smell, every sight will be sharper and clearer than you've ever felt in your life. Then that trophy elk will step into the clearing and you'll feel like your heart is going to leap out of your chest."

"Howie?" Lucy asked, after taking a deep breath. Bob, who had been following Howie's words, moved gently around to face her. That afternoon Joe and Eileen had contacted Marcia Fowler again and discussed the skull's curious behavior. Marcia was thrilled. She told them she'd read of crystal gazing, or scrying. Evidently rock crystal had a particular vibration, and if the skull had been carved precisely it could vibrate to human voices and thus seem to follow them. This was comforting but nothing about Bob, so far, seemed frightening to Eileen. He was a happy skull. No one felt nervous under his rippling crystal gaze.

"You're going to ask me about hunting, aren't you?" Howie asked. Lucy jumped a little.

"Yes, I was," she said. "I don't understand hunting."

"Do you like to cook?" Howie asked.

"Well, yeah."

"When you cook a really fine meal, like a fancy dinner or a Thanksgiving feast, don't you just feel great? Tired, maybe, but fulfilled and happy and satisfied?"

"Yes, I do," Lucy said. "Is that what hunting makes you feel like?"

"It's a start, but there's more than that," Howie said thoughtfully. "If Mark decides to go hunting and shoots a trophy bull next year he'll be putting delicious meat on his family table, and that's very satisfying. And he'll get a beautiful antler rack to hang on his wall, if that's what he wants. But when you bring down a game animal there's a satisfaction that is almost impossible to describe. We've been hunters, providers, for a million years. That's what we're meant to do, we men."

Eileen looked at Tracy, who hadn't left for bed. She looked at them both, deliberately, and shook her head a tiny fraction. Not that, either, her shake said. Eileen was determined now to pin down her mother and find out what she thought men were for.

Howie was continuing, however, his cigar sending up an obnoxious ribbon of smoke, his beautiful voice like rough music. "Trophy elk, the big bulls, usually don't make it through their seventh winter. By the time our hunting season starts they've already fought and mated. Lots of the herd bulls have used their reserves to keep and impregnate a harem of elk cows. They don't have enough stamina to make it through the winter anyway."

"So you take them out before they starve?" Mark asked. He didn't sound convinced, and Lucy remembered that he wasn't a hunter.

"Or before the wolves get them," Howie said. He put the cigar in his teeth and grinned. "I consider death by Howie's arrows a bit better than being hamstrung and devoured by wolves."

Mark looked unconvinced, still, and Eileen thought about Mark Plutt driving a ceremonial Aztec knife into the chest of Dr. Jon McBride. Ridiculous. Mark was uneasy about shooting a game animal. Surely Mark couldn't be the killer.

"Howie's arrows?" Lucy said. "But I thought—"

"We're archers, Lucy," Eileen said, surprised. "Didn't I tell you? I'm sorry. It just slipped my mind, I guess."

"We always carry side arms, of course," Paul said. "But that's for protection, not to hunt. It's tough to hunt an animal with a rifle, but that's nothing compared to hunting it with a bow and arrow. Did you want something, dear?"

Tracy, who was sitting next to Paul, smiled and pressed her hand on his.

"Thanks. I was just going to ask Eileen if she would mind going into Hulett and getting a gallon of ice cream for us. We're getting low what with the midnight forays and all, and I could use a gallon before Doug comes with his truck."

"Doug?" Lucy asked.

"The Schwan's man," Eileen said. "Sure, Mom. Any special flavor?"

"Whatever looks good," Tracy said.

"I'll take you," Joe said. "I've got 'Berto's Mustang. We'll be back before we left."

"Don't go that fast," Lucy said with a smile. "You don't want to get a ticket from Sheriff King."

"Heavens, no," Joe said with a groan. "Come on, babe. Let's take a drive."

"Don't call me babe," Eileen said. She was suddenly thrilled. The day was as hot and breathless as every other day had been, but with the close of daylight the air was beginning to cool and freshen. Driving in 'Berto's mustang with the top down would be heaven.

"I'll put Bob away," Lucy offered. "You two kids go have fun."

"And we'll toddle off to bed," Howie said. "After we talk more boring hunting talk, while I finish this fine cigar."

Eileen didn't hear any more. She was flying up the stairs like a teenager, to grab her purse and comb her hair and change from her jeans into a light summer skirt and a fresh new tank top that clung to her breasts and showed off the soft skin of her shoulders. She couldn't wear her ankle holster with the skirt but her SIG-Sauer fit nicely in a clamshell holster at the small of her back. She tied a light cotton sweater around her waist to hide the bulge of the gun and grimaced at her reflection. What she wouldn't give for a glittery golden mop like Jorie's, right now, instead of her dark red.

"You look ravishing," Tracy said from the doorway. She was smiling. "Take your time, punkin. If you know what I mean."

"Oh, *Mom*," Eileen said, feeling her face grow red in an instant. "Am I that obvious?"

"Only to your mother, maybe," Tracy said. "I'm off to bed. We're going to start interviewing in August for a new family for the cooking and cleaning job. I'm probably going to hire the first ones who answer the ad, I'm so tired." She shrugged and held out her arms. "You and Lucy have been lifesavers, you know. Hug me, dear. Then run a comb through your hair and find your man."

CHAPTER THIRTEEN

Highway 24, North of Devils Tower, Wyoming

"**A**hhh," Joe said, "this is the life." His hair blew back in the evening wind. His black eye was beginning to lose its puffed appearance and was now starting a rainbow stage, patches of dark purple fading to orange and brown. There was even a greenish tinge where the brown faded out. Eileen didn't care. He was Joe, and his arm was around her, and they were finally alone.

The road was deserted in both directions, a ribbon of gray that ran through pine trees and into prairie. In the distance Eileen could see a herd of antelope, white hindquarters flashing in the evening light, as they bounded over a ridge. The air smelled of sage and pine and sun-heated grass. Eileen was glad she hadn't put on perfume. The air was perfume enough. Joe wasn't driving particularly fast but with the top down their speed seemed much higher. He had his arm across the seat and his fingers touched her bare shoulder.

Eileen felt a sensation like slow molasses running through her. Every breath seemed to be a little less than she needed, as though she couldn't get enough. She shifted in the seat and tried to get more of Joe's hand on her shoulder, like a cat trying to get a petting hand to a particular spot.

"Hey, Joe," she said. "There's a place I'd like to show you."

"Where?" Joe said. His fingers started rubbing her

shoulder lightly. She found it difficult to speak.

"Just two miles up. It's a scenic overlook of the Belle Fourche River. It's not marked; it's on Ivan Zehr's ranch. He lets locals use the road."

"Okay," Joe said. He seemed as taken with the silence as she was. The two miles sped by in a blur of trees and grasses and far bluffs rising in the distance.

"Here," Eileen said, finally, seeing the seldom used gateposts at the bottom of the small hill. And the boot was still there! Joe turned off the road and traveled slowly down a track to the gatepost. A cowboy boot sat on the left post, a cracked leather thing that curled like an ancient piece of dried fruit.

"What the hell is that?" Joe asked.

"A cowboy boot," Eileen said.

"Is the track much worse than this?" Joe asked. "I don't want to bang up 'Berto's car, he loves this car."

"It's easier past the posts, and I don't want to bang up 'Berto's car either," Eileen said, unbuckling. "Don't worry, love. I'll be right back."

She got out and flew down to the gate. Her sandaled feet didn't seem to touch the ground. She removed the boot and placed it on the middle spoke of the gate, then pulled the gate open so Joe could drive in. Once he'd passed her she closed the gate and ran back to the car, trying to control the hammering of her heart. So close, now.

"What's with the boot?" Joe said.

"So no one else will bother us," Eileen said. "I'm taking you to our own private make out spot. Been this way for a hundred years, I think. Someone replaces the boot when it gets too old."

Joe didn't put the car in gear. He turned to look at her, and until that afternoon Eileen wouldn't have recognized the expression on his face. After Jorie and her pouting lips, though, she knew. Joe was jealous.

"Did you park here with that Owen Sutter guy?" he asked.

"Oh, Joe, you know I did," Eileen said, instantly frustrated. They weren't going to have a fight now, were they? "But everybody parked here. Mom and Dad, they came here. And I never—" she stopped, embarrassed and flustered.

"You never what?" Joe asked.

"I've never been in love, until you," she said huskily.

Joe's expression lightened. He blew out a sigh and put out his hand. She took it and he squeezed her hand, hard.

"Look at me," he said. "I'm sorry. Show me this place. I want to see it. But you do understand we're parking in a deserted lover's lane, and there's been a murder in the county, and it's getting dark...."

"And I'm a cop," Eileen said.

"That helps," Joe admitted. "But if you're going to tell me about a legend of a guy with a hook who creeps up on people in this place, well—"

He put the car in gear and drove slowly down the over-grown grassy lane, smiling as Eileen laughed. The two ruts were still used, although not recently. They led over a small hill, hiding the highway behind them from their view, and then led up to the top of a small rise.

Joe drew a deep breath as they crested the top of the hill. Eileen grinned. It looked just the same, even after all the years between high school and now. Beyond them was a hundred miles of nothing but mountains and valleys, shrouded in the coming dusk. The Belle Fourche River wound slowly by at the bottom of the bluff, lit golden orange by the setting sun. It was wild and gorgeous and empty as far as the eye could see.

"How beautiful," Joe said.

"As gorgeous as you," Eileen said. "Unbuckle, damn it." She unbuckled her seat belt and as soon as he was unbuckled they were kissing, as frantic as teenagers, tongues together and teeth clicking off each other. She swung her leg over him and straddled his lap, her back against the steering wheel.

Joe reached into her hair with both hands and held her head, the same way he would sometimes hold her head when she was exploring him with her mouth.

She unbuttoned his soft 'Berto shirt as his hands left her head and traveled up her back to the hooks of her bra. She was caressing his chest, pinching his nipples with her fingers by the time he finally unhooked her bra with clumsy fingers and captured her freed breasts in his hands. He pinched, lightly, and she arched her back and threw her head back. Above her, the stars were already beginning to show in the indigo depth of the sky. She could hear the rustle of the river water at the bottom of the bluff, no noisier than Joe's panting breath.

"I am so excited," she said, stripping off her shirt and letting her bra fall from her arms. "I can't tell you."

"I think," Joe said, burying his face in her breasts, "I know."

His hands traveled up her thighs and to her hips. Eileen unsnapped her clamshell holster and put her SIG-Sauer on the dash. She unsnapped and unzipped her skirt and lifted it over her head. Joe left her breasts for a minute and looked at her hips.

"Is this a thong?" he asked. "This is a *thong*. You're wearing a *thong*."

"Just for you. It's actually sort of comfortable," Eileen said, snapping a strap that led over her hip. "Do you like the pattern? Big hearts and stuff?" Lucy, in fact, had insisted that Eileen buy the silly thing. They had been shopping for bridal lingerie and Lucy had informed Eileen that men loved thongs. That she had to buy this silly silky one with the red hearts on it. She was very glad, now, that she had.

"Oh, God, I'm going to come right now," Joe groaned, closing his eyes. His hands held her hips and rubbed her back and forth over his lap.

"Don't," Eileen laughed. "We still have to pick up ice cream, you know. Unless you brought a change of pants."

"Let's get them off, right now," Joe growled. Eileen eagerly unsnapped and unzipped. The steering wheel was in the way, so she shifted over and let him pull his pants off. The bucket seats of the Mustang were spacious, covered with old leather meticulously maintained.

"Back seat?" he asked hoarsely.

"Right here," Eileen said, patting the passenger seat. She spread her skirt on the seat and Joe shifted over. She knelt above him and let him strip the silly underwear from her, and when they were around one ankle she pushed his hands aside and settled on top of him, slowly as she could stand, feeling every warm inch as they came together.

He didn't take long. She used her thighs to move up and

down on him and as he took her hips in his hands he shuddered and groaned and buried his face in her breasts. She kissed the top of his head.

"I love you," she whispered.

"I love you, too," he panted. He leaned his head back so they could kiss. "Did you come?"

"Not the right position for me," Eileen said. "I think you did, though."

"Lean back against the dash," Joe said, his face still flushed and red and his breath fast. "Stay on me."

Eileen leaned backward, her thighs still folded on each side of Joe, their bodies still coupled. He touched her with gentle fingers and she closed her eyes and let the sensations build in her. The dashboard dug into her back but she didn't notice anymore. Eyes open, staring up where stars covered the sky; she opened her mouth and screamed his name.

As he pulled her trembling body close for a kiss, she heard a far-off yipping of coyotes in the darkness of the hills.

"They're wondering, what the hell kind of coyote was *that?*" Joe laughed, kissing her breasts.

"A loud one," Eileen panted, still shuddering. "I never actually screamed before."

"I shall make you scream every night," Joe said, his eyes half-closed in satisfaction, his arms caressing her bare back. "My wife."

"We should get dressed," she said sensibly, but she didn't move from him. "Mosquitoes won't stay away forever now that the wind has died down."

"I know," Joe said lazily. "But you are so beautiful naked. I'd like to—"

He broke off and they both turned their heads. There was a car engine sound coming from the track behind them.

"Someone's coming," Eileen hissed. "They shouldn't—"

Joe was already scrambling for his trousers and shirt. She grabbed her bra and tank top and spent frantic seconds getting the clasp of her bra closed. She whipped the tank top over her head and pulled her skirt over her hips, then snatched her holster and gun from the dash. She snapped the holster to her skirt band. Joe, his trousers on, was trying to button 'Berto's silky shirt. Car headlights swept over them as Eileen adjusted her skirt and Joe finished buttoning.

"My panties," Eileen hissed. Joe grabbed them from the seat and started to give them to her when bright revolving lights lit them both. Joe crushed the panties into a ball and closed his fist around them. Eileen turned and squinted at the revolving lights, feeling her fear and embarrassment give way to anger. The revolving lights meant police, and there was only one policeman in the county.

"Sheriff King," Joe said, as Richard King got out of his car and approached Joe's side of the car.

"Eileen," King said with loathsome satisfaction. "And John, right?"

"Joe," Joe said pleasantly. "What's up, officer?"

"Richard, what are you doing here?" Eileen said. "You know about —"

"It's Sheriff King, now, Eileen," King said. He stood outside Joe's door with his hand on his holster, the way all cops are trained when they approach a vehicle, but it still burned Eileen's blood. She was a fellow cop. Cops treat each other differently.

"Sheriff, then," she said. "Why did you come up here? I put the boot on the gate."

"We've had a murder in the county," King said with condescending patience. "Remember? We've got a curfew right now, and we don't need any couples parking in the woods. Is that what you were doing? Parking?"

"Just looking at the scenery, sir," Joe said. Eileen could see the line of Joe's shoulders and he was tense. King was like a man made of stiff wire.

"Anything else?" he asked.

"Richard – I mean, Sheriff," Eileen said. "We were doing a little sightseeing and making out. Give me a break."

"And doing what? Smoking dope? Doing cocaine? One of those big city things you picked up in all your travels?"

Eileen was getting more than angry now. She was getting nervous. King was not acting right.

"Of course not," she said. "What's going on?"

"What's in your hand, then?" King asked Joe. "You've got something in that hand, and I'd like to see it. Now."

"It's nothing, really, just some —" Joe started to say.

"Now, please," King said in a near whisper. He moved his hand on his holster and Joe slowly raised his hand. The panties tumbled out and dangled by one delicate strap from his finger. He grinned ruefully at King and shrugged.

"Couldn't get them back on in time," he said. "Sorry, dude."

For endless seconds King stared at Eileen's panties, his jaw clenched so tight Eileen thought his teeth would splinter. She had her hands ready to reach her own hidden gun and wondered if she could outdraw him. There was real murder in his eyes.

Then something died away in him. He shifted on his feet and looked away and the moment was gone. Eileen realized her spine was running with hot sweat.

"Get home," he said roughly. "I'm trying to keep this county safe. Just get on home."

He turned without another word and stumbled back to his car. A few moments later the revolving lights clicked off and the engine roared as he backed down the road. Eileen let her head fall against Joe's shoulder. He blew out a deep breath and put his arms around her.

"That was scary as hell," he said. "I thought for sure he was going to try and kill me."

"I haven't had a chance to explain about Richard," Eileen said quickly. "I never—"

"Oh, I already know. You never dated him, but he sure wanted to date you."

"How did you know? Did Lucy—"

"I'm a man, hon. Everything about that weird little exchange told me what King wanted to be to you. If you two had been together there would have been a whole different conversation. He would have said something nasty about the kind of underwear you wore in high school, or how he broke you in for me."

Eileen shuddered. "I didn't—"

"I know. Let's forget about him. We've got ice cream to

get, right? Don't let him spoil our date." He hugged her close, but Eileen could smell the strong odor of anxious sweat coming from him. She loved him, smelling that scent, loved him so fiercely she felt tears prickle to her eyes. He'd been afraid, but he was still trying to protect her. Her own damp back told her how afraid she had been. Richard King was a very dangerous man, and his anger was aimed directly at her.

La Creperie, Colorado Springs, Colorado

"Tell me something good," Rene said, after swallowing a delicious morsel of crepe. They were seated in a small restaurant in the center of downtown Colorado Springs, a French restaurant that was actually quite high-quality, even by Rene's standards. Ken ate his broccoli and chicken crepe without enthusiasm, but Rene relished every bite of his burgundy beef wrapped in layers of perfect, succulent crepe. A good wine sat in front of them, another difference between them. Ken preferred beer, the common rice-brewed beers like Busch or Miller Lite. His tastes were simply horrible, it couldn't be denied. Rene drew the glass to his lips and took a mouthful of rich, dark Merlot. The taste of the beef, the earthy tones of the Merlot, the delicious feeling of being well-rested, filled Rene's heart with contentment. Best of all, there was going to be killing done. Perhaps a lot of it.

"I've got something we might want to use," Ken said. "I swear I could drive around northeastern Wyoming with my eyes closed right now. I know all about Devils Tower, too. That's the big tourist draw up there, just in case we need to travel up there. It's July, so there's lots of tourists. We won't stand out. So I found —"

"I believe we do have to go up there," Rene said with a small shrug. "Time to take care of this business, and best to do it quickly."

Ken sat for a moment, thinking, and then nodded his head. He took a drink of wine and a bite of chicken crepe, undoubtedly longing for a big greasy burger and a fat glass of beer. "Okay, then, I might have something for us," he said. "Remember the matron-of-honor girl, Lucy? The one with the little boy?"

"Yes," Rene said, thinking of the girl's picture. She was very pretty, with a great head of curly black hair. Something about the small, secret smile she had was very alluring. He liked to kill beautiful women, he had realized long ago. The prettier, the better. It satisfied him. Killing children didn't bother him much, but he took no pleasure in it. Killing men gave him a different sort of satisfaction. A beautiful woman was like wine, a man like a hearty meal. To kill an entire houseful would be an interesting buffet. And the dessert, of course, would be the engaged couple. Joe Tanner and Eileen Reed. What a pleasure this would be.

"Okay, I called her home number and pretended that the dress shop had lost the measurements. I needed her phone number so I could call her and get new measurements taken for the alterations."

"Very nice," Rene said. He took a bite of food and waved Ken to go on.

"Her husband is named Ted and he was packing to go on a trip to meet her. I gave him the number here. So when he calls, we can get directions—"

Rene wiped at his mouth with the napkin. "Did he say the airport he was flying into?"

"I didn't ask," Ken said. "Why?"

"Let's go," Rene said. He frowned. There was a delicious dessert that he really didn't want to miss, a chocolate confection also wrapped in crepe. Ah, well, when he returned. He swallowed the last of his wine and stood up from the table. Ken waved the waiter over and paid quickly. Rene didn't say another word until they were in his Lexus and he'd pulled out his laptop. "He has to fly to a connecting place somewhere. Passenger planes don't fly to Devils Tower. That means someone has to pick him up and take him back to the – what did you call it? The Reed Ranch. And that means —"

"That means we can intercept them at the airport," Ken said, chagrined. "I didn't think of that."

"No, Ken," Rene said. "You were unaware how urgent the job had become. Your plan was brilliant. His name is Ted, Ted Giometti? Let's see what we can do."

Rene, among other identities, was a licensed travel agent

under the name Victor Blanch. As Blanch he had access to plane reservations information across the country. Just another tool in his assassin's box.

"There he is," Ken said, finding the name first in the flight list. "Rapid City, South Dakota. He's flying in tomorrow morning."

"There are seven empty seats on this plane," Rene said with satisfaction. "Looks like we've got a flight to catch tomorrow."

Highway 24, Devils Tower, Wyoming

"We should finish this before we get home, you know," Eileen said, taking another spoonful of chocolate chip ice cream and feeding it to Joe. "Everyone will be jealous we didn't bring home the gourmet stuff for them." He took the ice cream in his mouth, relishing the smoothness and sweetness on his tongue. The air blew through the car as he drove in the darkness. The headlights, giant old Detroit monsters, lit the road for miles ahead of them. Joe kept a close eye for deer. The small grocery was closed when they got to Hulett so they bought two quarts of ice cream at the Conoco gas station. Plus a pint of gourmet chocolate chip ice cream, Joe's favorite.

"I could eat the whole pint," Joe said. "Then I could eat you."

"Mmm, mmm," Eileen said, her mouth full of ice cream. He stole a quick glance and saw that lovely satisfied look on her face, the look that he gave her. He smiled and let the breeze blow through his hair. Life was good, in this moment and at this time. Whatever blood and pain and joy the future held, that was in the future. Now was what mattered.

"I was thinking that we could take Lucy and Hank to Rapid City tomorrow," Joe said. "I've never seen Mount Rushmore. It would be a fun road trip."

"Actually, I was going to ask you if you would take Lucy and Hank. I shouldn't leave the ranch. I'm supposed to be helping Mom and Dad catch the murderer, and I haven't got a clue yet."

"Yeah, but you found the skull and the crown – er, necklace

thing," Joe said. "You're making progress. Do you have anybody in mind?"

He saw Eileen wriggle her shoulders into 'Berto's comfortable seats. The spoon was in her mouth. She rested her other arm against the outside door of the Mustang. She looked at the road ahead of them and took the spoon from her mouth. She was ready to talk.

"Look at the list of suspects. First, my parents."

"You have to include them, I suppose," Joe said, accepting another bite of ice cream after she dug into the pint in her lap.

"Right, but they have no motive. If Dr. McBride was trying to rape my mom, maybe, but then Dad would have shot him and then called the police right away. He's not the sneaky type. And my mom? She has everything she wants."

"Except grandchildren," Joe said serenely.

"Yeah," Eileen said, and poked him in the ribs. "Stop teasing me. So then we have the hunting crew. Howie, Jimmy his brother-in-law, Nolan the comedian, and Mark the Texas software tycoon. All of them wealthy, happy, uninterested in Aztec priests and Atlantis legends."

"Then there's our two University types," Joe added, as Eileen took a bite of ice cream. "Jorie, the pretty and very mean little blonde piece, and Beryl the older and very sweet anthropologist."

"Jorie could have killed him; maybe he made a rape attempt. She doesn't like men. Remember she told Nolan she was a lesbian."

"She acts strange," Joe said. "I'd swear she was trying to flirt with me, even though her mouth was whining continuously. Creepy."

"Creepy," Eileen said with obvious satisfaction.

"Jealous," Joe said. "My girlfriend's jealous."

"Your fiancée is jealous. Keep away from my husband, says Eileen," Eileen said. "Last bite of ice cream." Joe took the last bite from her spoon and spoke through a mouthful.

"So maybe Dr. McBride was raping Jorie and Beryl comes along and pow, stabs him with the knife."

"Then they call the sheriff and get off the hook through

self-defense," Eileen said. "This seemed much more sneaky than that. More planned. More enraged."

"Somebody else, then, Mr. X. What about all those desserts that keep disappearing?" Joe asked.

Eileen stopped moving abruptly. Joe saw this from the corner of his eye. He watched the ribbon of road unspool in front of him. Fairly soon they'd reach the ranch boundaries. Eileen would have to direct him to the gate. It was far too easy to miss.

"I thought the hunters were eating the extra desserts," she said. "But maybe it's someone else."

"Whoever it is knows Zilla, though," Joe said. "Or she'd raise the roof. My vote is for Sheriff King. He seems angry enough to kill someone. Anyone."

"I guess I'd have to include him," Eileen said reluctantly. "Although then I'd have to include Butch at the Conoco station as well. Maybe I'll head into Hulett tomorrow and ask around. Someone local might have a story that could open this up."

"While I'm driving Lucy to the airport. You'll just have to promise me after this is all over to take me to Mount Rushmore."

"Sure," Eileen said absently. "The gate's coming up, about a mile now."

Joe stopped at the gate as she directed him. He let her unlatch the chain. He wondered where the trails were going to lead. He felt cold and unhappy suddenly, because he could not find in his heart the idea that he and Eileen would ever be a contented, carefree couple driving up to see Mount Rushmore. He felt something rushing upon them, and it was as bad as the crocodile thing he'd seen in his vision, or dream, or whatever it was. He would be ready, he promised himself, as Eileen got back in the car and they headed down the road to the ranch. He would be ready.

CHAPTER FOURTEEN

Spearfish, South Dakota

The early morning was already breathlessly hot. Joe pulled off Interstate 90 and stopped at a Texaco station. Hank, who had fallen asleep in the back, stirred and then settled back into his car seat again, his dark little head drooping forward. The top was up on the Mustang and the air conditioning kept the car nicely chilled for the little boy. Stepping out from the car felt like stepping into an oven, even at nine in the morning.

"Whoa, it's hot," Lucy said. "I'm going to visit the girl's room, then get myself something cold. You want anything?"

"Bottle of water. Distilled, not that spring stuff. God, I sound just like Detective Rosen, Eileen's partner. He's corrupted me with his pure water obsession."

"I'm getting a diet Coke," Lucy said. "Which means I'll have to pee again in an hour, but we should be there by then, right?"

"Yep," Joe said. "That's the plan. Let me fill this hog and we'll be on our way. We won't miss Ted's flight."

Lucy grinned and gave a little wave at him as she trotted off to the restroom. Eileen had given her an abbreviated, whispered report on the previous night's adventure before Lucy and Hank and Joe had left. By the time Eileen had finished with the part about the panties, Lucy had been heaving with laughter, hands plastered over her face. Eileen, who had looked pinched and concerned, was at first upset by Lucy's reaction. Then she grudgingly shrugged.

"Okay, it is kind of funny," she admitted.

"God, it's a riot," Lucy whispered. They were in the hallway between the kitchen and the family room, trying to swap information before Lucy had to leave. Eileen was planning on taking her Jeep into town and asking some of the locals about Dr. Jon McBride. She was also planning to do a bit of quiet investigation of Sheriff Richard King. "Eileen, I don't think Rick is a bad guy. He's just got an enormous chip on his shoulder about you. I think maybe seeing your panties in Joe's hands was enough to knock some sense into him. You're not eighteen anymore, and neither is he. People move on, you know."

"I hope so," Eileen said.

"And what panties, anyway, right?" Lucy giggled. "I mean, if you want anybody to see your panties those would have to be the ones, wouldn't they? The thong with the hearts and all?"

"And the gold trim," Eileen sighed and rolled her eyes. Then her solemn mouth twitched. She blinked, and then they were laughing, hands over their mouths, and that was where Eileen's mom caught them and shooed Lucy out the door where Hank and Joe were waiting.

Lucy found Joe's distilled water and got a soda for herself. She resisted the urge to buy a big package of nacho cheese Doritos. The last thing she needed was to kiss Ted with Doritos breath. Joe was at the counter when she got there, paying for gas with a wad of cash that Eileen had produced for him. Lucy nodded at the cash and paid for her own small purchases with cash as well. Best not to leave any sort of credit trail for the fat man and his friends to follow. She and Joe had spent much of the drive discussing the missile defense murders. Lucy ached to know the fat man's name, or where he was from. She thought that there was a possibility that he might be the author of the entire list of dead scientists that had plagued the program since its very beginning.

When she and Joe got back in the car and headed out, Joe was uncharacteristically silent and grim. Lucy drank her soda pop and enjoyed the lovely rolling hills, covered with thick forest, which surrounded them now. These were the South Dakota Black Hills, full of gold and silver, now the location of Mount Rushmore and countless vacationing families. They'd been passing motor homes and minivans since they'd crossed the border into South Dakota.

"Can we see Mount Rushmore from here?" she asked Joe.

"Afraid not, it's tucked back into the hills to the west," he said, a lighter expression coming across his face. "I looked up the location just in case. I just hope it's not – not disturbing, like Devils Tower."

"Exactly!" Lucy said. "That's the word I was trying to think of."

"That's what I feel, too. I don't like it."

"Like it's looking at you."

"Yeah," Joe said. "Exactly. Maybe if Ted's feeling up to it we can cruise on up and check Mount Rushmore out before we go back. See something friendly, for a change."

"I'd like that," Lucy said, grinning. Joe's face, however, fell back into a worried, gloomy look.

"I'm nervous about being here, I guess," he said. "Most of all I'm worried about changing Eileen's focus. She needs to find out what happened to Dr. McBride, and with me here I'm just distracting her."

"Oh, right, she'd be much happier here trying to find a killer while you're trying to avoid another one down in Colorado Springs," Lucy said. "Yeah, that would make her real happy. Don't be silly, Joe, she hasn't lost focus. We've all just been looking in the wrong places, I think. There's something here other than Bob the crystal skull and his jewels and the Atlantis legend. It's all fascinating stuff, but I don't think it has a thing to do with McBride's death."

"I don't think so either, really," Joe said. "Still, there's something there." He trailed off and for a few minutes there was silence. "You don't think I'm causing her to lose focus?"

"No, Joe," Lucy said. "Me, I've lost focus. I really don't give a rat's butt right now if Dr. McBride was killed by Aztec ghosts or Howie Magnus. I want to know who the fat man is. I want to set you up as bait and see if we can draw him out. I want to catch him and put him behind bars for the rest of his life."

"I want him dead," Joe said abruptly, "and I don't care if

you know it. I want him dead. He killed Sully. I don't know how many people he killed, but we'd be a damn sure further along in missile defense if our best people hadn't gotten killed."

"I know," Lucy said. "Believe me, I know. I've got the missile defense file. I know who's dead."

"But you don't know what he's done," Joe said, and clutched the wheel until his knuckles turned white. "Most of what we do in missile defense is secret. But the big tests are made public, and a lot of those have been failures. There aren't that many brains around, you know. Kill off five or six in an industry and you can wreck the whole industry."

"An anti-John Galt," Lucy murmured.

"Who?"

"John Galt. He was the hero of a book called *Atlas Shrugged*, by Ayn Rand. I read it in college and I thought it was really good. This guy named John Galt went around convincing the motors of the world to quit. You know, the real motors; the people who make things go. So he caused civilization to fall because he got the men and women with brains to quit."

"Hey," Joe said. "I should read that."

"I think you'd like it," Lucy said. "But Galt didn't kill people. He just wanted them to stop working for the government types, the looters. Your guy wants to kill people."

"He kills people," Joe said. "I don't know why he wants to kill people in missile defense. Back in the Cold War days I'd say he was a hired killer from the Soviet Union, but that doesn't make sense. China? They haven't been in the game that long. Japan? Who knows."

"We need to know his name. Could you remember his face?"

"Yes, I could. Absolutely."

"Okay, then," she said. "We'll start from there, after we wrap up McBride's killer."

"That easy, huh?" Joe gave her a sideways grin and she smiled back.

"Oh, sure. Eileen said she might have an idea who did it."

"Did she tell you who she thinks it is?"

"No, she didn't, the skinny wench. She said wait until we're back with Ted and she'll tell us if her suspicions are correct."

When they drove into Rapid City Lucy realized how accli-mated she'd become to the vast emptiness of Wyoming. The traffic seemed overwhelming, the number and color of buildings and businesses seemed too loud and jammed together. Joe rubbed his head briefly but shook his head when she asked him if he was hurting. They left the bulk of Rapid City behind and took the Radar Hill Road exit.

The Mustang purred up and around an enormous hill where there was, indeed, a large radar.

"I don't see the airport," Lucy said.

"The radar is for Ellsworth Air Force Base," Joe said. "If you look behind you you'll see the base."

Lucy twisted around and saw the familiar outlines of a military base, complete with runways and hangers and dull tan buildings.

"What does Ellsworth do?"

"They store nuclear weapons there," Joe said shortly. "See those bunkers in the distance? That's where the nukes are. The kind they load on planes and drop. I guess they're slowly getting rid of most of them. More power to *that*."

"Amen," Lucy said fervently. She turned back and saw a tiny cluster of buildings on top of a small plateau. "I guess that's the airport?"

"That's the airport," Joe said. "How could the fat man and his plank buddy know that I'm in Rapid City?"

"They can't," Lucy said, suddenly feeling uneasy.

"Exactly," Joe muttered. He hunched a little over 'Berto's steering wheel, looking left and right with palpable unease. "It's just being back in a city, that's what it is. Fat man can't find me in Wyoming because there aren't enough people there. I don't think that makes much sense, but...."

"Oh, it does," Lucy said. "Ever since cities began putting cameras on traffic lights I've become as paranoid as a conspiracy chat room. And I'm one of the people the conspiracy nuts talk about. You know, working for the Agency and all."

"Daddy," Hank said suddenly from the back seat. "Daddy here?"

"Soon, baby," Lucy said, turning around to see Hank blinking dazedly and looking out the windows.

"Not baby," he said firmly.

"Big boy, want some water?" Lucy asked.

"We're almost to the airport," Joe said.

"Do they have passenger pickup, or do we need to park and walk?" Lucy asked, consulting her watch as she handed back a covered cup of water to Hank. He took it and sipped from the plastic straw at the top with greedy little-boy pleasure. Joe laughed. It had a strained sound Lucy didn't like.

"What?"

"We're talking about the Rapid City Regional Airport," Joe said. "You blink, you miss it. We'll park in front and Ted will come walking right out to us from baggage claim, which is on the same level as parking, the one cafeteria, ticketing and check-in."

"That's useful," Lucy said.

"You should see Cheyenne, Wyoming's airport," Joe said. "The one time I flew through there the same woman who sold tickets to us went outside and put big ear muffs on and waved the plane in, then she put gloves on and loaded the bags on the airplane, then climbed right on board with us and served drinks. It was wild."

"So we don't have to get out of the car, you're saying," Lucy said. "I'll get out anyway, if you don't mind. I need a big Hollywood kiss from my guy."

"Oh, right," Joe said, embarrassed. "Sorry. I'm still thinking about the fat man."

"Don't worry," Lucy said. She found Hank's shoes and untied them, opening them up so Hank could fit his fat little feet inside.

"Here we are," Joe said, turning from the little two-lane highway onto the airport access road. The heat shimmered off the alfalfa fields and a small herd of cattle stood under a single tree, crowded together in the shade.

Lucy saw a tiny little airport building appear in front of them, a cheerful building that looked like a child's set of piled up blocks. There was a colorful double row of small airplanes sitting on a huge stretch of concrete and behind them a plane suddenly flashed down. Lucy jumped, thinking it was Ted's plane, but then realized the color was dark brown. A UPS package jet, then. At least the airport was big enough to handle jets. Joe took a hand off the wheel to point at a tail rising behind the small airport building. The tail was a passenger jet, and it was already on the ground. Lucy felt a great burst of happiness inside her. Ted was on the ground, and she was going to see him. Until this moment she hadn't let herself believe she was actually going to see him. She missed him terribly, even though they'd only been apart for a week.

"It's Daddy, Hank," she said in a high, breathless voice. "We're going to see him."

"Daddy, Daddy, Daddy," Hank sang, kicking his feet.

"I'll pull up in front," Joe said. "Tell me if you see him."

There was a small crowd of taxis and cars parked in the passenger pickup area. Joe pulled in an empty spot and kept the engine running. Lucy unbuckled and turned around to slip Hank's shoes on his feet.

Joe's mouth dropped open. Everything jammed up inside his brain as he saw Ted walking with the fat man and his plank-faced friend. Ted was talking with them politely, his face showing a mild puzzlement at their obvious friendliness. Ted was carrying a single bag. He also had a leather valise swung over his shoulder. Fat man was smiling at Ted, responding to something Ted had said. The fat man's enormous round face was as cheerful and as inhuman as a painted balloon. His eyes blinked like a doll's eyes, dark and blank and soulless, and Ted Giometti didn't know there was a killer behind the eyes.

Then with the instinct of humans who are being watched, all three men turned their gaze to Joe behind the wheel of 'Berto's Mustang. The plank man reacted instantly, eyes narrowing and his hand reaching for Ted's elbow, obviously meaning to grab and hold him. The fat man turned his balloon face to Joe and a small smile touched his plump little mouth. Their eyes met and they looked at each other for the first time. Joe felt a crusted hate boil out of him, a hatred so pure and naked he felt the stitches on his head immediately pound into furious, screaming pain.

"Ted!" Lucy suddenly screamed, directly into his ear. Joe

realized he was shouting wordlessly.

Ted's smile dropped from his face. For an eye blink his expression was stunned and confused. Then Ted Giometti's face flashed comprehension and he did an amazing thing, something Joe couldn't believe. He spun elegantly on his toes, his valise and his small bag spinning with him as he twirled. His arm ripped out of the plank-like killer's grip and his valise caught the other man in the gut. Ted finished his ballet-like twirl with a strange, odd dip of the shoulder that brought the fat man stumbling to his knees, clutching the center of his chest. Then he turned and ran like a greyhound towards the Mustang.

"Go, Joe, go goddamn it, go!" Lucy screamed. Joe put the Mustang in gear and there was an earsplitting roar as the engine cycled up. Ted dove neatly through the open window and landed on Lucy. He wasn't a small man and Lucy's screaming stopped abruptly. Joe squirted smoke out of the Mustang's tires and saw all activity at the little airport come to a total halt as he shot out of the parking space like a bullet from a gun. The rich choking smell of burning rubber filled the car. The Mustang flashed by the fat man, still trying to haul his enormous bulk to his feet, and the scrambling plank man, who was digging furiously in a bag at his feet.

"Hank, Hank," Lucy wheezed. Ted reached the back seat by flipping over the front seat as neatly as he'd dove in the window. He did something to Hank's car seat that Joe couldn't see, but suddenly Hank was lying flat on his side in the back with his father's body covering him.

"Shit!" Joe finally shouted. His voice was hoarse; he'd been screaming wordlessly, like an ape. That was the first word he'd gotten out. Lucy, who was breathing again, climbed over the seat as Joe shot out the exit to the airport. There was no tollbooth to negotiate since they hadn't parked. He would have blown through the tollbooth, if he had to, but he would have hated to bang up 'Berto's car.

"How long until they have a car? Seconds?" Lucy screamed over the roar of the Mustang.

"Seconds," Joe said. "Shit, Lucy, oh God. Did he get a shot off? Is Hank okay?"

"Hank's okay," Ted said in a remarkably calm voice. "Lucy,

come back here and cover him. Joe, I need to drive."

"Are you kidding me?" Joe snapped. He was frantically searching for a police car, but not to ask for help. A Rapid City cop would be dead before he drew his gun if he tried to take on the fat man and his friend. Joe didn't want to ask for help, he just didn't want to be stopped. He wove in and out of the sparse traffic, trying not to break the speed limit too extravagantly. Once they were on Interstate 90 he could make the 'Stang walk and talk.

"No," Lucy said. "Joe, Ted used to drive cars for a living. You need to switch."

"You're not making sense," Joe said.

"Honey," Ted said, scrambling into the front seat. "Not you Joe, I mean Lucy," he said, as Joe threw him a surprised glance. Ted Giometti looked like what he was, a mild English teacher. He was tall and thin with a slight rounded belly and with his black hair thinning out on top. He had pale skin and hair that grew along the backs of his hands and out the top of his sporty yellow polo shirt. His face looked shocked, but not because of the fat man. Ted was looking at Lucy. "I didn't know that you knew."

"He was a Mafia chauffeur," Lucy said tightly. "There, I said it. Pull over and let him drive, Joe. Honey, I think I'm going to throw up."

"Don't," Joe and Ted said in unison. Joe, in fact, felt a lot like throwing up himself. His head ached fiercely and his stitches throbbed. He shot through a yellow light that turned red before he was completely into the intersection, and he ignored a chorus of honks behind him. No cops, yet. He pulled over to the side of the two-lane highway and jammed on the brakes, making his decision. He unbuckled and shifted over as Ted scrambled over the top of him to get to the driver's seat. Ted took the Mustang up to speed on the shoulder, and then shifted onto the highway.

"Let's put our seatbelts on, shall we?" Ted said smoothly, as though he were giving a busload of tourists a scenic tour. "This is a very nice car, Joe," he added. "We can outrun anything back at the airport with this. Unfortunately it's a powder blue '67 Ford Mustang and everyone who sees it is going to remember it. And it's easy to spot if they have helicopter backup."

"I don't know about backup," Joe said, buckling his seat

belt and still fighting nausea. Hank, Lucy, Ted, they were all in danger. Because of him. "Take Radar Hill Road, there'll be a sign saying 'I-90.'"

"Helicopter?" Lucy said from the back, where she was still sheltering a bewildered Hank. He wasn't crying but wasn't happy with his current squashed circumstances, held prone on the back seat with his car seat still buckled around him and his mother crouched over him. Joe looked back and gave him a little wave. Hank looked unhappily back at him.

"Helicopter is a possibility, isn't it? I'm used to hits where they're backed with lots of money. Back in the bad old days, of course."

"They found out at the FBI academy," Lucy said softly. Joe looked back at her and she was near tears. Her hair was in wild disarray and a button had popped off her sleeveless summer shirt, leaving it hanging askew. A piece of flowery, lacy bra was revealed in the gap where the button had been, something Joe was sure she was wearing for the reunion with her husband. She was staring at the back of Ted's head. Joe, helpless to leave the conversation, glanced at Ted. His hands were resting lightly on the wheel and his eyes flicked professionally back and forth from the front of the road to his rearview mirrors. He was driving the car so smoothly Joe didn't realize until he saw the speedometer that they were going 90 miles per hour on a highway where the regular traffic was going only 65.

"So they broke open my juvenile files, the ones sealed by a court order, is that it? Then they came running to tell you what you'd married?"

"That's right," Lucy said from the back seat. "That your dad was a Mafia chauffeur and you were being brought up into the ranks. Your dad was clean as could be; he was a bodyguard. Then he got killed and you got sent to your aunt."

"He died protecting Mary Lisoletto and her unborn child," Ted said, his face as smooth and unconcerned as though he were discussing Chaucer at an English teacher's party. "That was his job, and it would have been mine. But I got sent to my Aunt Lisa and she got my juvy records sealed and that was that."

"And I don't care, Ted," Lucy said. "I've known and I don't

care. I didn't care then and I don't care now."

"Cop," Joe said tensely.

"Saw him," Ted said serenely. "Look at the speedometer."

Joe did. It showed a sedate sixty-five. He hadn't even noticed the car slowing down. Had Ted even hit the brakes?

"We'll be taking Highway 90 across to Spearfish," Lucy said. "But first we have to get through the traffic around Rapid City."

"We could lose them in Rapid City," Ted said calmly. "They're behind us."

Joe and Lucy swiveled around in their seats to look behind them. Joe could see nothing.

"I don't –" Lucy began.

"Look at the dust cloud, half a mile back," Ted said. "They ran a car off the road, either passing or cutting in too close."

There was a dust cloud, faint and far back. Joe would never have seen it if Ted hadn't pointed it out. Behind them was a string of cars, summer tourist sedans and recreational vehicles and an occasional truck. Ted passed a slow moving truck pulling a trailer and as he cut back onto the two lane highway Joe realized there wasn't more than a three second gap before the oncoming traffic swept by. The day, hot and clear and cloudless as all the previous ones, made the road waver like silver water in front of them. Joe realized he was running with sweat. Ted had turned off the air conditioning, to give maximum power to the engine. Joe remembered an episode of Star Trek where Captain Kirk had his crew cut all power except to the shields. The crew had waited, sweaty and frightened, until the Klingons had made the fatal mistake of —

"I told you Joe was run off the road," Lucy said crisply. "By a man and his companion. Evidently these two are responsible for the deaths in my missile defense file. Here's Radar Hill Road."

Ted made the turn and accelerated up the hill, passing a truck in a no-pass zone and sending Joe's heart into his mouth. He turned his mind with difficulty back to the conversation.

"I thought the missile defense file was classified," Joe said to Lucy.

"He's my husband, Joe," Lucy said with a shrug. Her face was still pale and strained but she no longer looked as though she was going to throw up. "And of course I'm not supposed to discuss anything with him. But still, there are some parts of my life he knows about."

"I guess I see the point," Joe said. "Eileen knows what I do, too."

"The fat man, getting back to business here, may be a very successful hired killer," Lucy said. "We need to lose him in Rapid City so he doesn't find his way to the ranch...."

"He won't," Joe said. "Eileen said her parents have a mailbox address in Hulett, remember? That's all they could find, even if they know about Eileen's folks."

There was a brief silence in the car as Ted negotiated another hair-raising passage, this time of an ancient camper. The last curves of Radar Hill Road were approaching quickly. Joe chewed unhappily on his lip. It was Lucy who finally voiced what they were all thinking.

"So how did the fat man know about you, Ted?"

"I was just thinking the same thing," Ted said. "I told Cindy and Bob that I was going, they're taking care of Fancy and watering the plants."

"Fancy!" Hank said suddenly. "Zilla!" Joe glanced around and saw Hank smiling. He'd obviously decided that traveling sideways didn't hurt, so he had adapted. Lucy had shifted over so that she was sitting next to him on the back seat. She'd put her seat belt on but she still had her body ready to shield her son's.

"That's right, Fancy the dog. Who else did you tell?"

"Nobody," Ted said, puzzled. Then he raised his eyebrows. "Oh, wait. The dress shop called from Colorado Springs. They said they needed to get your measurements again for your bridesmaid's dress, and I told them—"

"That you'd have me call them. That you were going to see me," Lucy said heavily.

"That must have been the fat man or his plank friend," Joe said. "They have some way of looking at airline reservations. This means they know that Lucy is Eileen's matron of honor. They have her name and address. And that means they know that Eileen is my fiancée, and that means—"

"They've been in Eileen's apartment," Ted said flatly. "We can't try to lose them in Rapid City. We've got to stay ahead of them."

"They'll just get ahead of us and wait on I-90, if we try to go into Rapid City," Lucy said. "Or get to Hulett ahead of us and wait for us there."

"Eileen said she was going to Hulett today, to talk to some of the locals," Joe said. His hands were clenched around the seatbelt that crossed his middle. He tried to sound as calm as Lucy and Ted.

"So it's a race," Ted said. "One that I think we can win. Once I open her up on the Interstate there's nothing that's going to catch us."

"Unless they have a helicopter back up," Lucy said.

"In which case, you dump me and run for it," Joe said.

"I don't *think* so," Lucy said hotly.

"I don't either," Ted said. "We dump Lucy and Hank, and you and I run for it."

Joe saw Lucy open her mouth, eyes flashing. Then she closed her mouth and bowed her head. She patted Hank gently on his tousled curls.

"Then they pick Hank and I up and all of a sudden your options are even worse," she said. "No, we're going to have to stick together on this one."

Joe leaned back in his seat and looked up at the canvas top of the Mustang. Here the car showed some age; the canvas was faded to a soft gray above him. He tried to think of a way out but he could not. He could think of a dozen ways to handle this in the movies; a look-alike Mustang, an empty truck with a ramp out the back, a fake storefront in Hulett with a hidden garage in the back... every idea would require as much preparation as a movie set. There was nothing they could do, the four of them, except run as fast as they could.

"We'll swing through Hulett and pick up Eileen," Joe said. "Then we'll get to the ranch. They won't be able to find it."

"They will, eventually, you know," Ted said gently.

"I know," Joe said grimly. "By that time, we'll have worked out a plan. We just need some time."

"Just a little time," Lucy said.

"Then let's rock and roll," Ted said. "Here's the Interstate."

CHAPTER FIFTEEN

Interstate 90, Rapid City, South Dakota

"**W**ell, this isn't going well," Rene said tightly. They'd switched cars in Rapid City and were now certainly well behind Joe Tanner and his friends. Ken, wisely, said nothing. Rene was in a towering rage. So close, and they'd missed Joe Tanner again. They hadn't had a chance to get to their weapons, checked nice and legal in their baggage. Guns are perfectly acceptable on airlines as long as they're declared, unloaded, and safely inside checked baggage. Their unloaded and therefore useless guns sat on the ground in their bags as Rene and Ken had struggled to get to their feet. The humiliation of being dumped off their feet by a paunchy English teacher was just about the worst insult of all. How had he reacted so quickly? He was even quicker than Joe Tanner, who'd fought desperately as they'd forced his car off the road. Ted hadn't known who they were until Tanner started shouting, and yet he slipped from their grasp with all the liquid grace of an eel.

"We'll get them," Ken said.

"Yes," Rene said. He concentrated on driving in the heavy mid-afternoon traffic.

At the airport they'd stolen an Oldsmobile with an elderly couple still in it, two people who'd just seen their grandchildren on the plane back to Dallas, Texas. The couple was still alive, against Rene's wishes. Ken had prevailed, arguing that a stolen car would provoke a cursory search but a murdered set of grandparents would set off a manhunt. Ken had been doing a lot of research into the Black Hills area. He recommended keeping a low profile.

With no chance of catching Joe Tanner and his companions, they abandoned a high-speed chase. Ken found a substantial sedan in a motel parking lot and with the help of a frightened desk clerk, got the keys to the motel room of the sedan's owner.

The sedan, a late model Chrysler, was luxurious enough for Rene's tastes. They left the grandparents, the Chrysler's owner, and the desk clerk in the hotel room, bound and gagged and terrified. But alive.

Rene still didn't think leaving the people alive was a good idea, but Ken was adamant. A stolen car wouldn't start a manhunt like a motel room full of dead people would, and they still had to find and kill Joe Tanner and his annoying girlfriend Eileen Reed.

With the Chrysler and a new, stolen set of plates at a gas station down the road, they made a stop at a supermarket for a portable cooler, food and drinks and ice. The chase was now a steady hunt. They were set for about twenty-four hours. By then the job would have to be done.

Interstate 90, Spearfish, South Dakota

"So how did you two meet, anyway?" Joe said. Lucy took a swig of water from Joe's distilled water bottle. Lucy didn't feel so much like throwing up, now. Still she couldn't stop thinking about what would have happened if she'd gotten out of the car. Her seat belt had been unbuckled at the airport. She was ready to get out when Joe started shouting. What if Joe hadn't seen the fat man, if he'd been rummaging in the glove compartment for some chewing gum, or if he'd been drinking water and hadn't seen the two killers? Would Hank be alive at this moment? Probably not, Lucy kept thinking sickly. Probably not.

The highway unreeled in front of them, almost impossibly fast. Ted had the speedometer at a trembling 94 mph, just shy of a very large ticket. On an Interstate where the top speed was supposed to be 75 this wasn't too extravagant. On the other hand, there were slow moving trailers and recreational vehicles dotting every mile. Ted wove through these like a slalom skier, passing so quickly and deftly that Joe was sprawled out in the front seat, as comfortable as if they were traveling to a picnic lunch.

"We met at a wedding," Ted said. He looked relaxed, but Lucy could see the bunched line of his shoulders. She could also see the lift of his eyebrows and the smile that curved his mouth ever so slightly. He was having a great time. Ted could have been a race car driver, she'd thought before, if he'd been born in to a racing family instead of a criminal one. She'd never shared this thought with him before because that had been a secret between them. Lucy patted Hank on the head and gave him another animal cracker. He was upright again. Once they'd gotten through Rapid City Ted had allowed her to raise his car seat and adjust him so that he was sitting. She knew how to tip his car seat over and protect him. At any second she was prepared to do that.

"My brother's wife, Carolyn, her sister was getting married. Larry's actually my cousin; he's my aunt's son. He always wanted a little brother and then I turned up. I taught him how to drive, and now you know how funny that is."

"I can stop pretending that I don't know why you're such a crazy driver," Lucy offered, catching a microsecond of Ted's glance in the rearview mirror. His eyes were crinkled and she felt a rush along her body as sweet as cool water. He wasn't angry with her. He was all right with her. *They* were all right. Everything was going to be all right.

"So Carolyn's sister is getting married and I got dragged along to the wedding. They knew I was single and Carolyn's sister had lots of girl friends. The old matchmaker story."

"One of the girlfriends was Lucy," Joe guessed.

"You got it," Lucy said. "I didn't catch the bouquet. I was already off in a corner with Ted, talking about Shakespeare."

"Not a word of which I remember," Ted said. "I was trying not to stumble around in circles and dribble spit down my chin. I was gone, babe, the moment I saw you."

"I'd kiss you right now, but I don't think it's the right time."

"Not at 94 miles per hour, no," Ted said. "But consider yourself kissed anyway."

"Ah, that's what bothers me," Joe said. "I always thought about you as being the regular guy, you know, Ted the English teacher. Nothing surprising about Ted. Among all these weird and brilliant people I know, you seemed the only normal one."

"Should I say thanks to that?" Ted asked dryly.

"Why would I marry a dull man, Joe?" Lucy asked in surprise. "I know it seems strange, a cop's daughter marrying a criminal's son, but—"

"Criminal's chauffeur, if you please," Ted interrupted. "Joe, everyone is weird and brilliant in his own way and his own time. I figured that one out long ago. Maybe it was my lifestyle when I was growing up. Every seemingly dull person you meet has some incredible moment in their lives; something that happened to them that would make your mouth fall open in astonishment if you knew about it. Everyone does. And if it hasn't happened to them yet, it will."

"Some have fewer dull moments than others," Joe said. "Still no sign of them?"

"No sign," Ted said. "We're going to come up on Highway 111 in about twenty minutes. If there's backup of some kind, that's where it'll be. Let's get ready."

Lucy was breathing quickly in fright and readiness when Ted took the Mustang off the highway in a long, tearing curve. The tires made a thin, high squealing sound and as he straightened out on the northward highway he shifted abruptly over to the right side of the road. They passed a slow-moving recreational vehicle in a single gulping roar, kicking up a cloud of dust that made Ted say something under his breath that Lucy hoped Hank couldn't hear. Then they were on the clear highway and away, already at sixty miles per hour and accelerating.

"Highway 24 in 9 miles," Ted said. "What's the road like up ahead?"

"Twisty," Lucy said.

"There are a lot of curves," Joe said at the same time.

"Is there an exit onto Highway 24, or a stop sign?"

"Stop sign," they both said again, and grinned at each other.

"Okay," Ted said. "What is that, off to the left?"

Lucy looked and saw a deer browsing in a hollow. Two

fawns cropped grass with her, fawns as delicate and lovely as a drawing. She caught a millisecond of a view before they were gone, lost in the back stream of the speeding car.

"Those are deer," Joe said. "I'm amazed you spotted them."

"I'm trained to spot things," Ted said, a delighted smile on his face. His eyes remained cool and watchful, flickering between the road and the mirrors. "Those were real deer, huh?"

"There's more where that came from," Lucy said, thinking of Tracy's flower garden. "Tomorrow morning I'll show you a whole bunch of them, right outside the window."

"Whoa," Ted said. "I'd like that." He looked left, then right, and took a hard left turn onto Highway 24, ignoring the stop sign that sat at the intersection of the two highways. For a few minutes there was silence as Ted drove at impossibly fast speeds on the twisting two-lane highway.

"Do you think I could ride a horse, too? I've always wanted to do that, never had a chance to, yet," Ted asked, as they came down a corkscrew section of road. He had both hands on the wheel but he looked utterly relaxed.

"Considering the circumstances, I'm not sure we'll get a horse ride this trip," Lucy said, smiling at the back of her husband's head. "But we'll come back for the wedding this September, and we'll come up here, I promise. We'll get a horse ride then, won't we Joe?"

"You bet," Joe said. Lucy could see the muscles in his jaw bunching as he set his teeth. "We'll party like—"

"What the hell is that?" Ted said, and Lucy could tell the measure of his speed by the way the Mustang skidded, back end loose and frighteningly out of control, at a single twitch from his hands on the wheel.

"Don't do that!" Joe cried, sitting straight up in his seat, face white.

"Sorry," Ted said. "But what the hell is *that?*"

"Devils Tower," Lucy said, looking on the horizon and seeing the humped, looming shape of the Tower. She looked away after a second, unable to keep her gaze on the thing.

"We can't see it from the ranch," Joe said. "Lucy and I

agreed that we liked it that way."

"That's Devils Tower," breathed Ted, taking tiny glances away from the road so he could look at the vision on the horizon. "I saw it in that old movie, you know —"

"*Close Encounters of the Third Kind,*" Joe said. "Yeah, I know."

"It's very big," Ted said. He took the Mustang down a corkscrew road and sighed when the horizon swallowed the view of the monolith. "I think I'm glad, too, Luce. That's one big piece of rock."

"We're coming into Hulett," Joe said, sitting forward in the Mustang. "Get ready to look for Eileen."

Hulett, Wyoming

Eileen was standing on the sidewalk of Hulett's one main street, talking to Sheriff Richard King, when the Mustang shot by them. They both stopped talking, mouths open, as the Mustang squealed like a pig. The tires left extravagant black skid marks on the highway and the Mustang rocked to a stop in a cloud of gray smoke.

"Holy shit," Eileen said. She had spent the day investigating her own personal murder theory, most of it in the one local bar but for the last two hours with Sheriff Richard King.

The bar was the easy part. The Fawcetts, the bar owners that she'd known as a girl, were long gone, but the new owners knew Paul and Tracy Reed well enough. They were a couple from Minnesota and they thought Wyoming was quite tropical. They spoke in the soft, singing accent of the Minnesotan, and they'd turned the smoky dim little Sportsman's Bar into a scrubbed clean tavern called the Tower Pub and Grill. Most of their business came with the summer tourist traffic but they kept up a good clientele of locals during the winter months.

The summer day was hot and cloudless and the Tower Pub's small grouping of tables was packed.

"I'd love to talk, but we're just swamped," Lisa Olsen told Eileen. She was short and plump, with blonde-gray hair braided in a crown on her head. Her face was pink with the heat and the exertion. Her eyes were china-blue and kind, but she was obviously strained. "We lost a short order cook yesterday so I'm trying to handle tables and the kitchen, too. Maybe later this afternoon?"

"I waited tables all through college," Eileen said, holding out her hands. "I've been scrubbing dishes at my mom and dad's business, so how 'bout I pitch in?"

Lisa Olsen blinked twice at Eileen, then grinned and shoved her waitress pad and a pen in Eileen's hands.

"Bless you, child," she said. "Give me an hour and when the lunch crew clears out I'll tell you whatever I can remember."

"It's a deal," Eileen said. "Menus?"

An hour later Eileen had only to figure out the tabs. She sat down briefly to finish up the last of the six tickets and when she stood from behind the register there was Richard King. He was sitting at the window looking moodily out into the street.

For a moment Eileen was suffused with anger and embarrassment. She'd never worn daring underwear before and the first time she did, Richard King had to be the one to see it. She shuffled the tickets in her hands, wondering what to do. King took off his hat and rubbed his hands across his forehead and through his thinning hair. His face was turned from her but she could see his shoulders and they drooped with tiredness.

She had Rosen, her partner. She had her captain, Harben, and an entire police department. King had nobody but his car and a huge territory and two Sundance cops who had too much to do already. He'd never reinvented himself, never left the area and tried to become something or someone else. He'd stayed, and endured. She had to respect that. Even if she didn't like him, she had to respect him.

She collected a glass of water, a coffee cup and a menu. She passed out tickets with a smile and a nod, not seeing any of her previous customers. She set the water glass and the cup in front of Richard King.

"Do you need a menu?" she asked, and when he turned his face to her she was smiling her very best lets-be-friends smile. His face, open and weary, snapped shut like a clam.

"What are you doing here?" he asked harshly.

"Just helping out Lisa and Karl," Eileen said. "I wanted to

talk to them, too, of course. Do you want some coffee?"

"I'm handling this investigation," he hissed. "You don't need to interfere."

"I'm trying not to," she said, keeping her expression steady and welcoming. "Do you take your coffee black?"

"Cream and sugar," he said. Eileen left the table instantly and got the coffee pot, the cream and a sugar container. She remembered Lucy's story of sharing water with Richard, how she'd gotten him to be friendly with her. Coffee had to help. Lisa made excellent coffee.

"Here you go," she said, pouring a cup expertly to an inch below the brim. "And here's a menu, just in case. Did you get the autopsy reports back yet?"

"Yes," he said. She watched as he took a sip of coffee. Nothing overtly magical happened. He didn't suddenly smile and break into a Broadway tune and dance around the room with her. But he did, very slightly, shift the tense line of his shoulders. It was a start.

"How about the meatloaf sandwich?" she asked. "I've seen everything here today and that's the best. Open face, maybe, with gravy? And fries?"

"All right," he said, eyes still narrowed. "I suppose you want me to share the autopsy reports with you."

"Not really," Eileen said, writing a ticket. "I want you to get some food in you, and some coffee, and then we can talk a bit if you want. I was just thinking that you don't have a partner."

"I don't need anyone to take care of me," King snapped. He took another sip of coffee. Still no Broadway tunes, but Eileen had hopes.

"City cops all have partners," Eileen said. "Mine is named Rosen. He's the best partner there ever was. Really. You'd like him, I bet."

"City cops," King said in a low voice. He hadn't looked at her after the first glance.

"That's me," Eileen said brightly. "I'll be right back." She snapped the ticket onto the short order cook's window and winked at Karl Olsen, a tall thin man who was cleaning the grill and watching her without watching her. She took a quick coffee turn around the restaurant and then put the pot back on the burner and sat down at the table with Richard. She sighed gustily and pushed her hair back from her forehead. "Hot," she said.

"Yes," he said.

"Look, I'm sorry about last night," Eileen said. "And I'm even more sorry about high school. That was a long time ago—"

"It was a long time ago," King said. "I've forgotten all about it. I'm worried about what's going on at your parents' ranch. I'm afraid whoever killed Dr. McBride is going to kill someone else."

"Me, too," Eileen said. "So tell me something. Was his heart still there?"

"What?" King asked.

"Was Dr. McBride's heart missing?" Eileen asked patiently.

King's expression was answer enough. "I'm not going to discuss it," he said. "You don't have a private investigator's license and you haven't been assigned to this case."

"So it wasn't missing," Eileen said, mostly to herself. She'd had about enough of Richard King, that was sure. Karl rang the bell and she fetched his meatloaf, and then refilled his water glass and his coffee cup.

"Thank you," he muttered.

"You're welcome," she said. "The cherry pie is to die for, if you want dessert later." She gave him what she hoped was a non-grumpy smile and headed over to the kitchen where Lisa Olsen was scrubbing the short order area.

"Thank you so much," she said as Eileen sat down in a handy kitchen chair. "You're an angel. You wouldn't be interested in a job, would you?" Her face dimpled into a smile.

"No thanks," Eileen laughed. "I like what I do just fine."

"Your mom and dad are sure proud of you," Lisa said. "What with catching that murderer who tried to make it look like UFOs did it. And that child killer, too. You were in *People maga-zine!*"

"I should have guessed you'd know about those," Eileen said, thinking of Richard King and trying not to wince.

"Sure, Tracy brings all the newspaper clippings to crafts night. We get together and make quilts for the nursing home in

Spearfish. We're all coming down to the Springs for the wedding this September, too. We wouldn't miss it, not after all this time Tracy's waited and all—" she stopped, eyeing Eileen. "I've said too much, haven't I?"

"No, I know all about the grandchildren thing," Eileen sighed. "I'm surprised they don't examine Joe's teeth like he was a good breeding stallion."

"Wait until the wedding," Lisa giggled. "I remember mine like yesterday. My great aunt—"

"So here's my question," Eileen interrupted. Lisa looked like she was going to settle right in for an afternoon of wedding reminiscences. "Did Dr. McBride ever come in here with anyone else?"

"Sure, he was in here the first trip up here. He had that silly intern, Rochelle something-or-other. They were canoodling like two kids, drunk as could be. Luckily your dad was letting them spend the night at his place. Karl called Paul and he came in and got them and drove them to his place. McBride apologized to us, later, said he was just amazed at the opportunity to excavate such a perfect archaeological site. Said he was overcome. I remember he was in here, too, with the crew he brought up. There was a nice roundish lady and another girl, um."

"Beryl Penrose and Jorie Rothman," Eileen said. "Forget about trying to be nice. Be gossipy and catty and insulting. I won't tell a soul."

"Well, okay," Lisa said doubtfully. She finished the short order table and took off her apron. She stepped into the other room where Karl was busy preparing food for the evening rush. She returned with two glasses of tall lemonade, fresh and pulpy and full of ice. "My reward to myself," she said, handing a glass to Eileen. "I don't know why we got into this restaurant-bar thing. But I do have fun, mostly."

"So McBride came in with two new girls," Eileen said, after taking a long drink of lemonade that chilled her to coolness in three delicious seconds. "What happened to the Rochelle girl, the one he was making out with?"

"She was just an intern," Lisa said. "And I heard from that Beryl Penrose person when she came in for lunch one day that she was dropped like a stone when Jorie Rothman joined up. Guess she was just heartbroken, but she wasn't the first one."

"McBride was a chaser, huh?" Eileen asked.

"I guess so, a ladies man, we'd call him in Minneapolis. I thought he had his sights set on Beryl, at first, though Jorie, um, well."

"You are remarkably nice," Eileen said flatly. Lisa looked taken aback, then laughed.

"Okay, that Jorie girl is just a complete b-i-t-c-h," she said, spelling the word out in a whisper and flushing an even brighter pink. "She wanted some kind of guarantee that we hadn't cut the meat and vegetables in the same area of the kitchen, can you imagine? Like vegetables should have their own shrine? And the way she talks, well, you know."

"I know," Eileen said. "Makes it worse that she's such a pretty thing, doesn't it?"

"I guess it does," Lisa said, surprised. "She's almost an offense against God. To be given such a gift of beauty and to – step on it, I guess. To be so ugly inside."

"Well if I were a chaser – er, ladies man, I'd go after Beryl," Eileen said. "She's a sweetie, don't you think?"

"Oh, I do," Lisa said, brightening immediately. "She's very nice. McBride mostly talked to her, the one night the three of them were in here. Ah, what a sad thing to happen, eh? He was such a nice looking man, full of fun. Maybe a little on the wild side, but he had such a nice laugh."

"That was the only time they were all in here?" Eileen asked. "What about the hunting crew, Howie and his friends?"

"Haven't been in here," Lisa said. "They're too busy scouting, I guess. And I'm not too proud to say that Tracy's cooking puts ours to shame. She's an artist, I'll tell you. She gave me the cherry pie recipe we use, the topping is so simple but it makes the tartness of the cherries—"

"I know," Eileen said. "I could tell it was Mom's recipe. Mom is a great cook, that's true. So no one has dropped by for a drink or a chat with the locals? No one —"

"I need my check, please," Richard King said from the short order cook opening. Lisa Olsen jumped like she'd been pinched but Eileen merely turned in her chair and observed him coldly. She'd been expecting him to interrupt as soon as he figured out she was in the kitchen pumping Lisa for information.

"Sure," she said. "I'll get it."

"I'll get it, Eileen," Lisa said. "You've helped so much. Can I pay you for your time? We—"

"Don't bother," Eileen laughed, and got to her feet. She smiled at Richard King with her teeth in her smile. "I'll just keep my tip money, is that okay?"

"Of course," Lisa said.

"I'll walk you out, Sheriff," Eileen said. "Thanks for speaking with me, Lisa. It was so nice to meet you."

"You too, Eileen dear," Lisa said. She opened her arms and Eileen stepped into her embrace without hesitation. They hugged and Lisa kissed Eileen on the cheek, her lips warm and kind. "See you at the wedding!"

"Of course," Eileen said.

"You don't need to walk me out," King said.

"Of course I do," Eileen said. "I want my tip. Plus, there's something I need to speak to you about, and it doesn't have anything to do with the McBride investigation."

"Oh," King said. "What is it?"

"Outside," Eileen said. "This is something between you and me." She waved at Lisa and Karl as they left the little tavern. The bell attached to the tavern door jingled behind them. The day was still and breathless, hot and bright. Eileen narrowed her eyes against the sizzling heat and took a deep breath of the dusty, sage smell of the air. Even in a town, Wyoming still smelled like sage and dust. She wished for a thunderstorm, for the wet smell of the earth and the look of the sky packed with gray thunderheads. She looked at the sky and saw nothing but hazy blue.

"It's hot, and I have work to do," King said. Eileen almost snapped, right then. He was so rude, even after she'd gotten him food and drink and spoken to him with kindness and respect. She swallowed hard, as though she were trying to get down a particularly large pill.

"Okay," she said finally. She looked up and down the main street, which was also Highway 24. There was a gas station and a small grocery and that was it. Two gigantic recreational vehicles were being pumped at the gas station. An elderly man was cleaning one of the vehicle's windshield with a bottle filled with blue liquid. She could smell the tartness of the cleaning solution all the way across the street. "Here I go. My fiancé, Joe Tanner, works for a defense contractor down in the Springs. The reason he's up here is that he has reason to believe someone tried to run him off the road."

"I'm listening," King said. He took a wrapped toothpick from his pocket and began to unwrap it leisurely.

"That someone, or someones, may be a group who have been killing people like Joe for quite a while. He's a scientist and he does some top-secret work with the defense department. So the reason I'm telling you this is—"

"Because they might follow Joe up here, is that it?" King said. He put the toothpick in his mouth and chewed it. "What a piece of work you are, Eileen Reed. You come in here and do your best to screw up my investigation, and then you're telling me your little boyfriend might have someone chasing his back trail?"

"Screw up your investigation?" Eileen said, at very near top volume. "Screw up *what*, Richard?"

"Rick King, not Richard," King said, eyes narrowed. "You've been poking around messing with my—"

Whatever his words were going to be were lost in the enormous roar of the Mustang. The toothpick fell from King's lip as the Mustang skidded to a stop on the highway, blowing an enormous cloud of stinking gray smoke into the air.

The car reversed and, tires howling, screamed backwards up the street. It spun to a stop directly in front of them. Eileen looked down and saw that the Mustang was parked neatly between the lines of the parking space. Ted Giometti stared out from behind the windshield at her.

"Holy shit," Eileen said.

"Eileen," Joe Tanner shouted, leaping from the Mustang. Behind Ted Eileen could see a pale, disheveled Lucy and a happy Hank. Hank had cracker smeared around his mouth and he was smiling, bouncing up and down in his seat and waving at her.

"Joe?"

"Gotta go, Eileen, we've got to go," Joe panted. "Get out of here, guys, go, we'll take Eileen's Jeep."

"Step on it, Joe," Ted said. "Don't explain here." The Mustang reversed out of the parking spot a second later, coming to a smoking stop on the highway like something out of a Hollywood movie. Then the Mustang was gone, accelerating down the highway with engine bellowing.

Eileen could see the elderly man with the windshield-cleaning bottle, standing stock still and staring down the highway at the disappearing Mustang. She was already fumbling for her keys, trapped down the deep pocket of her khaki pants.

"It's them, they somehow got Ted's airline reservation and they met him at the airport," Joe was saying. "We gotta go, honey, I don't know how far they are behind us."

"What's this all about?" King said.

"What I just told you," Eileen snapped. There, she had her keys. Her Jeep was parked four slots away. "Don't tell them where we live, Richard. Don't believe them if they tell you they're police, or FBI, or anything. What do they look like, Joe?"

"The leader is tall and fat, his friend is tall and built like a plank," Joe said hurriedly. "I don't know what else to tell you. They want to kill me and I don't think they'd mind killing anyone who got in their way."

"I'll call you later today," Eileen said. "Richar – I mean, Rick. Please. We've got to go." She already had her keys in her hand and Joe was tugging at her arm, not gently.

"I'll contact your dad later today," King shouted angrily, as Eileen opened the Jeep's door and got in. Joe shoved her over and took the keys. She had caught his urgency but she barely had time to get her seat belt out before Joe was reversing the Jeep. Gravel stuttered under the tires as they bounded up onto the asphalt of the highway.

"Be careful!" Joe shouted back as the Jeep screamed down Highway 24.

"I'm calling your parents!" King shouted after them, his voice already faint in the distance. Eileen looked in the rear view mirror and saw him standing on the side of the road, looking after them, his hand shading his eyes. Then she saw him shake his head and put his hat back on and he turned away.

"What the hell is going on?"

"The fat man and his friend met Ted at the airport," Joe said. "Ted – well, I'll let him explain later, but he got away and we got away. They followed us but we lost them. Still, they know about your parents' post office box address and I think they'll be coming in after me. As soon as they can figure out where your folks live. Oh, God, Eileen," Joe nearly sobbed. "I put everyone in danger, everyone—"

"Stop it," Eileen said crisply. She removed her SIG-Sauer from her shoulder holster and checked the loads. "Put your seat belt on. King is a jerk, but he isn't a dummy. And these killers aren't dummies, either. They'll want to make it look like an accident, which they can't do with a houseful of people. We'll be fine."

"Right," Joe said, blinking and shifting his shoulders. He rolled his head from left to right on his neck. "I'm about scared to death, Eileen. I couldn't tell Ted and Lucy, because we had Hank in the car."

"Of course," Eileen said. She laid her SIG-Sauer on her lap and placed her hands neatly on top of the warm gun. She stared out the windshield and disconnected from the world. In her head was a jigsaw puzzle, white and clean, with pieces named McBride and Jorie Rothman and Bob, the crystal skull. She boxed them up carefully and set them aside and as she put them away a piece flipped over. The pieces abruptly fell together and just like that, she knew. She closed the box anyway. She swept the table clean with a soft cloth, and set down the new puzzle pieces. Ted Giometti. Rapid City airport. Lucy and Hank and Joe Tanner. Sully the angel and her lance. And the fat man, the murderer, the killer.

"They were in my apartment," she said, her eyes focusing again. "They found out about Ted because Lucy is in the wedding. Something in my apartment."

"Yes, we think so," Joe said. He blew out a big breath and grinned over at her. "Damn, you're good, woman."

"Not good enough to think about warning Ted," Eileen said. "He got a phone call of some kind? Dress color was wrong, or shoes the wrong size?"

"The measurements were lost, they said."

"They're coming after you," Eileen said. "We have to powwow. Cards on the table. We have to get Hank and Ted to safety. My parents and Howie's hunting crew, too."

"Then?"

"Then we set the trap, and when they enter it, we take them," Eileen said. "The turnoff is right up ahead. Don't leave any tire marks on the road that they might be able to see."

"Okay," Joe said. "Okay."

"We'll be fine," Eileen said. She jumped out of the Jeep as Joe came to a stop, her SIG-Sauer in her hand, and she opened the gate. Ted hadn't left tire marks with the Mustang, either, Eileen noticed. She approved. She closed the gate and got back into the car.

"What about your dead guy? McLean, or what was his name?" Joe said.

"Oh, that," Eileen said dismissively. "Dr. McBride. That can wait. I know who killed him."

CHAPTER SIXTEEN

The Reed Ranch

"What's this all about?" Howie asked. "Is this the Agatha Christie scene where you tell us who the murderer is? Shouldn't there be a thundering rainstorm?"

The current inhabitants of the Reed Ranch were sitting in Paul and Tracy's family room, all except Bob the crystal skull. Lucy missed him. The mystery of his origins and the murder of Dr. McBride seemed like a fun little game right now, something delicious and ordinary and safe. Joe had told her that Eileen knew the identity of the murderer. Lucy, under her fear, was intensely annoyed that she still didn't know. She had all the information Eileen had, so why did the murder remain a mystery to her? There was no time to twist her friend's arm, either. No time to think about McBride's murder, at all.

Hank was rolling toy cars up and down the carpet, with Zilla an attentive audience at his side. Ted sat at Lucy's feet, the only spot available in the crowded room. The warmth of his body against her calves and the touch of his hand on her sandaled foot was an entire conversation between them. Lucy knew, if they got out of this alive, that their marriage would be different. Deeper, more complete, with less hidden doorways between them. Provided they made it. She was no longer terrified, but she was still deeply afraid. She'd seen the blinking doll eyes of the fat man. She'd never looked in a killer's eyes before. She'd seen actors portray them on television, and she'd seen pictures of serial killers like Charles Manson and John Wayne Gacy, but she'd never had a living killer look her in the face. Her insides were quivering. She had to get on top of her fear, she kept telling herself. She had to.

"I wish it were, Howie," Eileen said grimly. She stood at the mantle of the fireplace, her khaki shorts wrinkled and the armpits of her shirt soaked with sweat. Underneath her open shirt she wore a tank top that showed an irregular tree shape of sweat between her breasts. Her dark red hair was tangled, and Lucy felt a first flicker of strength and humor when she realized that Eileen looked, despite all this, or perhaps because of it, magnificent.

Paul and Tracy Reed sat on the hearth, Tracy with her hands red and raw looking from a morning in the kitchen. She was rubbing lotion into her hands as Eileen spoke. The sweet smell of the lotion cut through the anxious sweaty air of the room. Paul sat solidly, face impassive, one hand resting lightly on a shotgun. His other arm was around his wife, his hand resting at the curve of her waist. Eileen's parents weren't usually public in their affection. Lucy knew that Paul was very worried.

Howie lounged in the leather armchair. His brother-in-law, Jimmy, sat attentively in the other one. Nolan Simmons, the comedian, and Mark Plutt the software genius sat on the couch. They all looked like bushes. All the hunters and Paul, too, were dressed in camouflage hunting clothes, patterned shirts, pants, hats and boots. Their faces were painted in irregular patches of cream, green, and black. They were planning to call turkey in the early evening, an operation that included masking their scent and sitting, looking as much like shrubbery as possible, calling turkey with a strange device that looked like a metal plate and a sharp stick.

Their ferocious outfits were perhaps why Jorie Rothman stared at them with such loathing. She and Beryl sat on the other couch, both wearing stained clothes but with clean faces and hands. They'd washed up before they came up the hill from the buffalo jump. Jorie's long golden legs slanted from her dirty khaki shorts. One of her hiking boots tapped the floor impatiently. Lucy, who hadn't had time to talk to Ted about Jorie, saw him observing her from the corner of his eye. His initial appreciative gaze was already fading. Jorie was in an even fouler mood than usual. Lucy could hardly believe Jorie had a worse mood than her standard one, but there she was, looking as thunderous as Howie's Agatha Christie storm. Beryl patted her companion's knee occasionally, as though to calm her, her own round face crinkled into a look of deep concern.

Joe Tanner slumped next to Lucy, his head in his hands. He'd removed his bandage and his stitches, clotted with fresh blood, showed at his hairline. He'd broken them open somehow during their chase from Rapid City, and they looked like they hurt.

"Okay, then, I'll try to be as complete as I can, as quickly as possible," Eileen said. "This has nothing to do with Dr. McBride and his murder. My fiancé, Joe Tanner, has a black eye and some stitches. You've all noticed this, I suppose. He was run off the road by a couple of men who then tried to track him down and kill him."

Eileen paused to let this soak in. Hank, unconcerned, wove a bright purple car along an Oriental curlicue of carpet. Coming to the end, he backed the car up with a spluttering motor sound that was clearly audible in the silent room.

"They tracked him here," Howie said. He didn't move but suddenly he was completely aware, completely there, as compact and focused as a big cat. Lucy noticed this with interest. Jimmy, sitting next to him, abruptly straightened.

"Yes, they did. And I'm sorry that you are all involved in this now, but you are. It's a strange turn of events that I was at my parents' house because of Dr. McBride, but there's nothing we can do about that now. These men managed to track Joe down by finding Ted Giometti's airline reservations. So this is what happened today. Lucy and Hank and Joe went to the airport in Rapid City to pick up Ted. When they got there…."

Eileen finished explaining what had happened in a few minutes, her voice crisp and without emotion. When she was done there was a long silence.

"They'll find their way here, you mean," Jorie said.

"Yes, and that means—"

"I'm not leaving," Jorie said hotly. "We have nothing to do with this!"

"I'm not talking about forever, Jorie, just a few days," Eileen said. "If Joe and I run, they may come here anyway and take hostages. Or torture you to find out where we've gone, and then kill you. These men are vicious killers."

"Call the sheriff, he'll protect us," Jorie said. "Just call the police and set up a whatchamacallit, a stake-out. Why do we have to —?"

"These men may have killed upwards of fifteen people," Lucy said.

"So how would you know that?" Jorie said waspishly. "Did you read it somewhere in between changing diapers?"

"I read about them, yes," Lucy said. Ted squeezed her foot and she wiggled her toes silently against his palm.

"So no turkey hunt tonight," Howie said. "Shit fire. I was planning to have my jet pick us up at the Rapid City airport at the end of the week. That's probably not going to work, is it?"

"Gillette is the alternate," Jimmy murmured. "If we can get to Gillette."

"You're just going to clear out?" Jorie asked, eyes wide. "Just run, like that?"

"Jorie," Howie said impatiently. "You really are a silly little bitch."

"We can't sit around and hope they don't find us," Eileen said patiently. "I know you see lots of shoot-outs in the movies, but in real life people can get badly hurt. Killed."

"Could we take Jorie and Beryl on the jet?" Nolan asked. Behind the paint Lucy could see his expression, half-embarrassed and half-defiant. Jorie, whose face was scarlet at Howie's insult, threw Nolan a murderous glance.

"Certainly," Howie said. "The jet seats eight, we can fit Lucy and Ted and throw Hank in, too. He weighs next to nothing."

Hank stopped driving his car and observed Howie closely for a moment. Howie gave him a big wink and a sunny, uncomplicated grin, his teeth bright white in his green-black-cream face. Hank ducked his head back to his toy cars.

"What about Paul and Tracy?" Nolan asked. Behind the paint Lucy was sure he was bright red. Jorie continued to glare at him, her lovely eyebrows drawn tightly together.

"I'll stay," Paul said. "No one is running me off my ranch."

Mark cleared his throat. "I don't mean to one-up Howie, here," he said apologetically. "But I have a Gulfstream Four. It can seat eighteen in a pinch. I'll call up my company and they'll have it waiting for us. It can go nearly supersonic, too. Nobody is going to catch us in the Four."

Howie stared at Mark.

"I suddenly have jet envy," Howie said. "We'll take it."

"But you're going to stay, Eileen?" Beryl asked in her soft, beautiful voice. "What are you going to do? Shouldn't you go back to Colorado Springs where you can get help?"

"We'll do that, once everyone is clear," Eileen lied brightly. Lucy didn't glance at her face so that she wouldn't reflect Eileen's lie. She had no intention of getting on that jet, either. Hank and Ted would go, but she was damn well going to stay. She was going to clear her missile defense file once and for all, if it meant bringing back the fat man's bloody head on a pike.

"Uh, huh," Howie said. He obviously wasn't fooled.

"I have a question," Jimmy said.

"Yes," Eileen said.

"Why do they want to kill Joe Tanner?"

Joe lifted his head from his hands. He looked tired. "I'll answer that," he said. "I'm a computer scientist on a top secret government program. I'm not even supposed to tell people that I'm on a top-secret program. These guys have been killing people like me. I don't know if they're paid to do it or what, but I do know they've killed three friends of mine. And now they want to kill me. And I don't know anything about them."

"Perhaps I can help with that," Ted said.

Everyone turned to look at him. Lucy couldn't see his expression, sitting at her feet with his back to her as he was, but she could see Eileen's sudden stillness.

"What?" Eileen asked.

"Well, in my former life," Ted said, "I was taught defensive driving on a rather intense scale. One of the things we learned how to do was escape a kidnap attempt. And the other little skill we were taught was, well – pick pocketing. If he'd had a gun in his jacket I'd have that too, but all he had was this."

He took something out of his jacket and held it in the air. It was a wallet.

Hulett, Wyoming

"You can't find your wallet anywhere?" Ken whispered to Rene. Rene, sweating and cursing, rose from the back seat of the Chrysler.

"I can't find it, damn it," he whispered back. They were at the lone gas station in Hulett, Wyoming. Rene had all the traveling money in his wallet, a large sheaf of small denomination bills. They never traveled by credit card; it left a trail too easily followed.

"I've got about fifty bucks," Ken said, opening his own wallet. "But that's it."

Rene put his hands on the doorframe of the Chrysler and rested his sweaty forehead on his hands. The July day was baking hot, cloudless and dusty. Wyoming was as empty as Rene remembered, an enormous bowl of prairie and sky. He hated everything about Wyoming, he hated the people and the tiny dusty towns and the way people looked at him, marking him and remembering him.

He thought back. He'd had the wallet in the airplane because he'd purchased a drink from the surly stewardess. There was no first class on the tiny puddle jumper of a plane. Right, then, he'd had his wallet at that point. Did he lose it when they shoved the elderly couple into the back of the Oldsmobile? Was it there when Ted Giometti had—?"

"He took it," Rene said, straightening abruptly. "He took my wallet when he elbowed me in the chest. When he escaped us at the airport."

"Giometti did?" Ken asked. "You sure?"

"Of course I'm goddamn sure," Rene snarled. "He's been trained by somebody, we should have thought that Eileen Reed's little bridesmaid was more than she seemed. They might be FBI or other cops for all we know. Giometti took my wallet. He took my *wallet*." Rene clenched his hands into fist, feeling new sweat pop out on his brow, hating the feeling of sweat running down his back.

"I'll pay for the gas, boss," Ken said. "Then we'll get out

of here and decide what to do."

"I know what to do," Rene said viciously. "We're going to kill them *all*, Ken. And I'm going to kill that bastard's wife and child in front of him before I kill him."

"Okay," Ken said. "That's cool with me. I'll pay for the gas, okay?"

"Yes, yes, okay," Rene said. He got back into the car and cycled up the engine after Ken disengaged the pump. Ken headed into the pathetically small gas station. The air conditioning started blasting cold air at Rene and he let the full force of the air blow across his sweaty face.

"Calm, keep it calm," he reminded himself. "They have nothing. Nothing at all."

Reed Ranch, Devils Tower, Wyoming

"This is everything," Joe said. "This is everything."

"Rene Dubois," Howie read from over Eileen's shoulder. "So we know his name. How do we find out everything about him from a passport and a driver's license and a pile of cash?"

"We can find out about him," Eileen said. "Lots about him."

"That's ridiculous," Jorie snapped. "Don't you have to have a warrant, or something, to collect information like that?"

"He's a dual citizen of France and the U.S.A., looks like," Howie said, reading the passport. "You'd need someone who has all sorts of clearances to access Interpol. FBI, maybe."

"Or a CIA agent," Jorie snorted.

Lucy flushed bright red as Ted, Eileen and Joe turned to look at her. She was changing Hank's diaper. He'd grown tired of driving toy cars around the carpet and was close to his afternoon naptime. Howie blinked as he followed Joe and Eileen's gaze and his jaw dropped comically. After a moment he started laughing.

"This has been the most *interesting* trip," he said.

"What's the deal?" Jorie asked, annoyed. Beryl was looking at Lucy with an expression that Lucy couldn't decipher; was it disgust? Fear? The CIA had a sinister reputation from its very inception, and hadn't much improved its public persona over the years. Lucy knew the work she did was desperately needed. Still, Beryl's expression was hard to take. She finished taping Hank's diaper and slipped his shorts back over his bottom. They were blue, patterned with tiny cartoon airplanes.

"Time to get into the phone booth, Lucy," Eileen said. "Take the Clark Kent glasses off."

"Okay," Lucy said, and sighed. She kissed Hank on his smooth cheek and he nestled into her arms. He was sleepy. She stood and held Hank and looked around the room. Howie was openly grinning, his eyes blazing with delight. Jimmy looked at her with interest. His overwhelming purpose was to get his brother-in-law to safety, Lucy was sure. He sat like a bodyguard with his shoulder behind Howie's back, his eyes constantly searching. Lucy was sure Jimmy didn't care if she sprouted horns and a tail as long as she helped get Howie Magnus to safety.

Nolan and Mark were staring at her with uncomplicated grins, like brothers whose sister had pulled a particularly good practical joke.

"Whoa, *Lucy*," Nolan said.

Jorie looked puzzled and angry, instead of just angry.

"Having a blonde moment, Jorie?" Howie asked sarcastically. Jorie jumped and glared so fiercely at Howie he should have burst into flame. He sat, undisturbed, grinning a particularly toothy and insulting grin.

"No, she's just so used to treating Lucy like she's stupid because she has a child that she can't get her mind around who Lucy really is," Tracy said. Lucy looked in astonishment at Tracy and saw Eileen's mother with her fists clenched and her jaw raised. "If she doesn't get it, I don't care. Lucy, what do you need from us?"

"Paul's study, Eileen and Joe," Lucy said.

"I'll take Hank," Ted said, and reached for Hank. He took the sleepy boy tenderly from Lucy and folded him into his arms. Lucy's throat closed up as she met his eyes.

With my life, his face said.

With mine, she said back without speaking a word.

"Good, you have the study. Paul, you and the hunters get

ready to leave," Tracy said.

"I'll post a watch on the top of the hill," Paul said. "Jimmy, how about you first? We'll get your stuff ready for you. Mark has to call for his jet."

"What happens if I see someone?" asked Jimmy.

"You let us know with your walkie-talkie," Paul said, pointing to Jimmy's small hunter's communicator. Like everything else, it was camouflaged. Lucy hadn't even noticed it until Paul pointed at it. She saw the hunters all had them on their belts. "Then you lie down with your face in the turf. Don't get up. Don't come down here. No matter what. If we lose, you stay alive."

"I don't like the sound of that," Jimmy said without expression.

"Be lookout, Jimmy," Howie said. "We need you up there. I need you up there."

"I'll be lookout," Jimmy said immediately. Lucy didn't know if Paul realized that Jimmy hadn't promised he wouldn't come back down the hill.

"We'll stay in gear," Paul ordered. "Don't clean up the camo. If we get face paint on the seats of Mark's jet, we'll just have to clean it off later."

"We should be ready to clear out at dusk," Tracy said. "I'll pack food and supplies. Jorie, Beryl, you need to secure your site. You'll be back in, say, three days. Bring enough clothing and toiletries."

"We aren't—" Jorie began, but Beryl interrupted her.

"We are. I don't like it, either, but we have to," she said. "We have to get the site tarped and staked; we can't lose a single grain of evidence. Oh my God, what about the skull?"

"We'll bring Bob with us," Joe said with the first smile Lucy had seen from him since early in the morning. "Right?"

"Right," Mark said, already on the phone. "Thirteen adults, one child. Gillette, Wyoming, and I want skid marks on the tarmac, Joyce. I don't care if the pilots are in their pajamas; I want them here by dark. If we're not there, they wait."

"Thirteen?" Eileen said.

"He counted Bob," Joe replied. "My kind of guy."

"We'll be back in an hour," Beryl said, on her feet and

urging Jorie to do the same. Jorie was looking at Lucy with dawning comprehension, and for the first time her habitual scowl was missing.

"You're a CIA agent?" she said. Lucy shrugged and nodded. Jorie's guards were down, her anger gone, and for the first time Lucy saw a real person behind the perfect face and figure. Jorie looked like a girl she could like, open and interested and bright.

"I'm not supposed to tell," she said. "I didn't mean to try and fool you."

"You fooled me," Jorie said, and smiled for the first time since Lucy had met her. "I guess they teach you about that, huh? In spy school?"

Lucy caught a glimpse of Nolan Simmons's face and felt a deep and sincere pity for the poor man. He was looking at Jorie the way Beryl had looked at the crystal skull, as though she were the most precious treasure he was lucky enough to put eyes on. Jorie with her scowls and petulance was attractive, but wearing a simple and uncomplicated smile she was unutterably beautiful.

"Come on, Jorie, we have to go," Beryl said, frowning and tugging at Jorie's arm.

"Let's go, Lucy, we don't know how much time we have," Joe said.

"Tell me about it, later?" Jorie said, letting herself be pulled by the arm towards the door. She passed Nolan without glancing at him, which Lucy thought a kindness. Nolan was not running a line of spittle down his chin, the way Ted said he had when they met, but he was close.

"You bet," Lucy said, and turned away to find Paul's study. Behind her, she could hear Paul talking to Howie and Nolan.

"Lucy works her magic again," Eileen said as the three of them crowded into Paul's study. "That's the first time I've seen Jorie smile."

"I bet she was raised on James Bond movies," Lucy said with a sigh. "She'll be so disappointed to hear that I work in a basement reading reports."

"Make up stuff, like how you saved the world from a terrorist nuclear attack," Joe said, deadpan.

"Or how you discovered the plans for world domination by a failed politician," Eileen suggested.

"Very funny," Lucy said. "Let's just concentrate on Rene Dubois, shall we?"

"Is Mark off the phone?" Joe called. "We're ready to go online here."

"He's off," Nolan shouted back. "Go gettum, cowboys."

CHAPTER SEVENTEEN

Hulett, Wyoming

The post office sat in the broiling sun and Rene sat, broiling with frustration, across the street. Ken had his headphones on and was listening to his music. He listened absolutely quietly, without moving his lips or his body. He was the perfect companion for a killer because he was never annoying. Ken sat motionless, patient as the dead, waiting for Rene to decide what to do.

That was the trouble. Rene had no idea what to do. There was no way for them to get the Reed's location from the post office. There were too many people coming in and out. Since Joe and his friends had gotten back to the ranch, Rene was fairly sure they'd already warned the postmaster. The police, too, although Rene could see no sign of a sheriff. The local bar was crowded with early evening diners. Rene's tentative plan was to go into the one diner after it closed tonight, a clean looking place called the Tower Pub and Grill, and take the owners hostage. Once they'd given Rene the information he needed, he'd kill them, as messily as possible, as one more victim of a fictitious serial killer.

The problem was the sheriff, of course, and time. Who knew what the police detective was cooking up, her and her mysteriously competent friends? Every minute of delay was a minute that help could be on the way, or their prey on the run. Rene had no illusions about the young lioness Eileen Reed. She'd killed a man face to face, a child serial killer who'd been in the midst of a new kidnapping when she happened upon him. She knew how to kill, this detective.

"Hot out there," Ken said mildly.

Rene sat up in his seat. Hot, and cloudless, like each day before. There was a wisp of a thought crossing his mind, a potential plan. Perhaps they could—

"Hey, boss, look at that!" Ken said. Across from them a large, pale yellow truck had pulled up into the post office parking lot. Instantly a small crowd gathered around the truck. The truck was decorated with a drawing of a swan and had many small latched doors along the side.

"Ice cream man?" Rene said, annoyed. The thought that was forming in his head was elusive and now he'd lost it.

"No, a Schwan's delivery guy," Ken said. The small crowd of mostly children was mobbing a man in a uniform shirt who'd gotten out of the tall cab and was opening one of the doors in the side of the truck. He hauled out a box and handed some sort of ice cream treats out to the eager children. "That looks good," Ken said in simple greediness. The Schwan's man smiled and handed the last of the treats to a few adults, locals by the look of them. One of them clapped the Schwan's man on the shoulder and they exchanged a few words.

"Why are you pointing this out to me?" Rene said. "Your reason?"

"Well, it's just that Schwan's delivers food, boss," Ken said. He was chewing on the side of his mouth. "Back where I'm from they deliver in the towns, but if he's out here that must mean—"

Rene held up his hand and leaned forward like he was taking a bead on a rifle. Which, in a sense, he was. The Schwan's man was powerfully built, probably from hauling boxes in and out of his truck, but he didn't have a soldier look to him. He looked like a kindly, capable young man who liked to give out a box of treats to kids. His hair and eyes were brown and with a hat on Rene thought Ken could probably pass for him for a few minutes, at a distance.

A few minutes were all they were going to need. Rene became aware that he was licking his lips, and stopped.

The Reed Ranch, Wyoming

Lucy, lost in the web of the Internet, heard nothing. Joe Tanner, who was watching Lucy's traversal of sites forbidden to him, listened with half attention to the sounds outside the study door. There were thumps of hurrying feet and the constant banging to and fro of the front door.

Eileen chewed her lip while she watched. Lucy, once she was on the Internet, moved to a site that required her name, a badge number, a password and an identification number that she read from a tiny card she carried in her fanny pack. Joe, curious, asked to look at it after she was done with it. Lucy refused, but held it up so he could look at it. The card was a simple liquid crystal display that held a twenty-digit number. As Joe watched, the number changed. Lucy put the card back in her little pack, where there was a small collection of gadgets along with Hank's emergency diapers and a package of baby wipes. Joe suppressed a longing to rummage through Lucy's pack.

"The card's number changes every minute," Lucy said, waiting for her information to be received. "And it's synched with the Central Intelligence Database. You can't touch it because it has a fingerprint reader on the bottom side. If anyone but me puts a finger on the underside, the card goes dead. Permanently. Just another way to try and keep secure. This is my second card. Hank got hold of the first one and I had to fill out about a million forms. Here we go."

The screen flashed and Lucy leaned forward, typing rapidly. Within a few minutes she was entering all the information from Rene Dubois' passport and driver's license. In addition, she had Joe read her the serial numbers off four random bills from Rene's wad of money. While the search engine was looking for information Lucy fired off a rapid e-mail to her boss. She described the attempt on Joe's life, the attempt on Ted and herself, and their current situation in such rapid, clear, crisp prose that Joe was amazed.

"I wish I could come up with reports like that," Eileen murmured, watching Lucy.

"Me too," Joe said.

"Practice," Lucy said, and sent the e-mail. "Best to get this off in case we don't get out of here. One would hope the CIA would follow up and avenge us, but…" she shrugged. "Who knows?" Obviously Hank and Ted were far from her thoughts right now. She was in full analyst mode, thinking not of personal blood and death but of the analysis of her long-dormant missile defense case.

"I'd say we can spend no more than twenty minutes on-line," Eileen said.

"Why's that?" Joe asked.

"Sheriff King might be calling my mommy and daddy," Eileen said sarcastically, then grimaced. "Or he might call to warn us about seeing Dubois and his buddy. Any indication in his wallet who his buddy is?"

"No," Joe said, searching through the empty wallet. "Hey, what's this?"

Lucy leaned back and Eileen pressed in closely on his side. He felt a thin, almost weightless slip of paper in an inner pocket, one of the tiny slits in a man's wallet that can hide any number of important papers. It took him a moment or two to figure out where the opening to the hidden pocket was. When he discovered it, he withdrew a black and white photograph.

"That's an old photo," Eileen said. "Look at the hair styles."

Joe looked at the picture of the happy father and his laughing child. The father wore a very dated turtleneck and jacket. He had a big gold cross around his neck. Despite the garish outfit he was handsome, with tousled dark hair and dark eyes that were full of laughter. He held a toddler in his arms, a boy who could be no more than four. The boy was wearing a polyester shirt with a zipper up the front and bell-bottomed trousers in a horrible paisley print. He was as cute as a button. The boy and his father were gazing at each other, looking very happy and very much alike. The boy's face was recognizable, though years of fat and killing had turned his lovely little features into a grotesque parody. The boy was Rene Dubois.

"Damn, nothing but an old picture of his dad," Lucy said, turning away. "I'm getting some information, let's see what they've got in Interpol for us."

Joe continued to look at the picture as though hypnotized. What had turned that cute little kid into a killer? How could that laughing little face have turned into a man who'd taken Sully's beautiful head in his hands and turned it, snapping her spine as though he were killing an insect?

"What kind of killer carries around a picture of his *dad*?" Eileen asked. She was still at his shoulder, staring down at the photograph. Joe felt a sudden wave of fear so complete and deep that it was almost like a cramp. He had to clench his teeth together to avoid crying out. He had put all these people in danger. He should never have come.

"They might have gotten us both, if you'd stayed," Eileen said, as though he'd spoken to her. "Put it out of your mind. We have work to do."

"Yes, ma'am," Joe said, feeling the fear recede like a cramp coming unknotted. It would come back, though, he thought grimly. It would come back.

"Here's our fat ugly slug," Lucy said. "Rene Dubois. Hasn't been in official trouble with the law since he was eighteen and killed a robber at the wine shop where he worked."

"That sounds like a good guy to me," Eileen said doubt-fully.

"That's just the beginning. The robbers were part of some chintzy low-grade Russian Mafia gang and they took him into their organization. Looks like he branched out on his own a few years after that. The French police keep tabs on him but they've never been able to pin anything on him. He does insurance investigation contract work, all above board. Underneath it looks like he was contract muscle."

"What does that mean?" Joe asked.

"He beat people up for money," Lucy said shortly. "Maybe killed them. This means we have to find out who's paying him. He's a nobody, he's just muscle. Somebody behind him has brains, they're the ones who are paying him and they're the ones I want."

"Time, Lucy," Eileen said.

"I'm disconnecting," Lucy said. She shut down Paul's computer and massaged her fingers, staring at the dark screen as though it were still on.

"I think he's got lots of brains," Joe said firmly. Lucy turned to him and her cool analyst face was gone. She was Lucy Giometti again; Hank's mother and Ted's wife, and she looked scared to death.

"I do too," she whispered. "Let's get the hell out of here."

"You said it," Eileen said. "I bet I can pack my bags quicker than either of you two prima donnas."

"Ha!" Joe laughed. "I have one bag with 'Berto's clothes. I'm already packed."

"Darn," Eileen said. "You'll have to help Lucy pack all her frocks and pearls."

"Ho, ho," Lucy said, her look lightening. "If you think I'm going to let Joe Tanner look at my dainty under things you've got—"

"Let's go, kids," Tracy said, opening the door to the study. She was dressed in hiking boots, tough twill khakis and a lavender tank top. A lavender headband held back her flyaway hair and a pair of sunglasses sat askew atop the headband.

"I'm packed, Mrs. Reed, can I help with anything else?" Joe asked.

"You can help with the horses," Tracy said. "Thank goodness. We're going to let them loose in the backcountry. We'll have to catch them again when we get back, but at least these men won't be able to harm them."

"What about Brumby?" Eileen asked, stopping abruptly. Lucy, who'd gone first, paused in the hallway to listen. Joe could see Eileen's face and she looked stricken.

"He'll be fine, Eileen," Tracy said, but her face looked worried. "He's your father's pride and joy, I know, but he'll be just fine. He'll probably decide he's a stallion again and try to gather up a herd. Now go, we've got less than an hour before we're supposed to leave."

"Mrs. Reed, I just wanted to say—" Joe began, as Eileen followed Lucy up the front stairs. Tracy waved a hand in the air, stopping him.

"I don't want to hear it, Joe. They're bad men and I don't want you trying to take responsibility for what they're doing. Enough. Go help Paul with the horses, and don't watch him release Brumby. He doesn't admit how much he loves that bad-tempered lug."

"Yes, ma'am," Joe said numbly. He went out the front door and tried to hurry down to the barn, but his feet felt like blocks of lead. The day was even hotter than before, a dry shimmering heat that took his breath away and made him break into a sweat almost instantly. He could smell crushed grass and oats and horses.

In the short time he and Lucy and Eileen had been in the study, Howie and his crew had packed their things. They sat by the barn door, waiting to be loaded into the truck. Howie's battered guitar case sat on top.

As Joe entered the barn he saw Paul checking the hooves of an enormous brown horse, his face carefully blank. The brown horse reached around and tried to take a nip out of Paul's backside. Paul elbowed the horse in the jaw without looking around, and the horse shook his head up and down, teeth bared, as though laughing.

The barn was cooler than the yard, and dark. Howie and his hunters still looked like shrubs. They were already in the barn checking the hooves of the other horses. Joe stumbled over a pile of long objects stacked upright by the door. He realized they were compound bows and stepped backward carefully. Each one of the capped quivers, he knew, bristled with razor edged arrows. Best not to fall into that.

"What did you find out?" Howie asked. He was working on a spotted mare, cleaning out the inside of her hoof with a rounded metal scraper. She stood calmly, her head in a bucket of oats, happily munching at the unexpected treat. Paul had evidently gotten all the horses some oats as extra food before they were released.

"Not too much," Joe said. "He's a contract killer, but we don't know who hired him. His name is Rene Dubois."

"Best take him alive, then," Howie said. He dropped one hoof and started on the other one.

"Joe, we've got the horses," Paul said, elbowing aside another vicious bite from Brumby. "Can you fill the automatic feeders in the chicken coop? Make sure the water line is clear. If there's any chickens out, get them back into the coop. They'll be fine for up to a week, if the feeders are full."

"Okay," Joe said. He turned to the barn entrance and stopped. He couldn't believe what he was seeing. He felt as though all the life was draining out of him and soaking into the baking hot ground at his feet. He made a hoarse gargling sound in his throat.

Instantly, Paul was at his side. He held his shotgun in his arm. Howie, Nolan and Mark snatched up their bows.

"What is it?" Howie hissed.

Joe pointed, his throat still unwilling to work.

"Look at Zilla," Paul whispered.

In the space where the road swept from the ridge and into the ranch, Zilla stood. Her tail was wagging uncertainly. Her ears were up, her head high. She was looking up the track that led to the highway.

A voice spoke from the hunter's belts, with no crackle or beep. It was Jimmy, as clear and quiet as though he stood in the shadows of the barn. "Howie, this is Jimmy. We have a truck coming in from the highway. He's moving slowly, but he's coming your way."

Paul lifted his walkie-talkie to his mouth. "What kind of truck?" he asked. His face was ghost pale. His hand trembled slightly.

"Yellow, big, has a name on the side. Wait a second, I'll tell you. Says Schwan's."

Paul's shoulders slumped in relief. "That's Doug," he said. "The Schwan's delivery man. Don't worry, Jimmy, stay there. Did anyone follow him in?"

"No," Jimmy said. "He's alone."

"Why isn't Zilla jumping around like she usually does?" Nolan asked suddenly. Howie and Mark, who'd been at the point of putting down their bows, paused and looked back. Zilla stood at the entrance to the road, her tail wagging. They stood in a bunch, frozen, watching Zilla's tail like a pendulum slowing down. Her tail wagged slower, slower, and then stopped.

"Holy Jesus, it's them," Howie said. Paul snatched another walkie-talkie from his pocket. It was bright yellow instead of being camouflaged and was obviously tuned to another channel.

"Tracy, code red, Tracy, get them to cover," he snapped. "Do you read?"

"I read you," Tracy said clearly. Paul dropped the yellow walkie-talkie into his pocket and took the shotgun into both hands.

"Let's get to the house," he said calmly. "Bows in carrying formation. Let's go."

"So what's this, part of the Underground Railroad?" Ted asked Tracy.

"It was the old pantry, before we remodeled the kitchen and Paul built me the big pantry," Tracy said. She stood with her back to Lucy, a hunting rifle in her hands, looking out the kitchen windows. Tracy had moved a pretty knickknack cabinet to one side. The cabinet was wheeled, and Lucy understood why when she saw what was behind the cabinet. Set into the wall was a narrow door, and behind the door was a small room that held two cots and blankets and a battery-powered lantern. There was a tiny portable privy and even a tiny bookshelf. "I'll explain, sometime, why we hid it."

Ted carried Hank, who was deeply asleep. He laid his son gently on one of the cots and turned around. "Come on, Lucy. I'll guard outside the door."

"You won't," Tracy said firmly. "Both of you, get in there with your boy."

"You're not coming in?" Lucy asked Tracy.

"I'm a fine shot with a rifle," Tracy said. "Ted, Lucy, *my* child is out there. Think of Hank. You have to protect *him*. Both of you, get in."

"Yes, ma'am," Lucy whispered, feeling like a coward. Ted stepped through the door and closed it behind them. He fumbled past Lucy and then there was a dim light. He'd turned on a small battery-powered lantern. They looked at each other as they heard Tracy moving the knickknack cabinet back over the door. The kitchen door slammed shut, faintly, and then they were alone.

"Oh, Ted," Lucy said miserably, and he folded her in his arms. The shotgun got tangled between them as he kissed her. The kiss deepened, became something much more than comfort.

Suddenly she felt completely, electrically alive. Every inch of her skin tingled with her heartbeat.

"I love you, Lucy," Ted whispered to her.

"I love you too," she whispered.

He set the shotgun against the wall and took her back in his arms and kissed her. Lucy pressed herself against him, running her hands up the back of his shirt and over his bare skin. He was hot already, his skin sheened with a light sweat that made her fingers slip deliciously over him. He broke away from her lips and kissed her on the neck, his hands already plundering her breasts.

They'd been apart too long, Lucy thought distantly. She wanted so much to forget everything but Ted, to take him to the ground and make love to him. But there was no time, no time to do anything but kiss. There was desperation in the way he kissed her, the way his hands came close to hurting her as he pressed her body against his. Lucy lost all thought of killers or sleeping toddlers or crystal skulls as she clung to her husband, feeling his heart pound against her own, shoving the world away with all her might.

Joe, unarmed and without camouflage clothing, felt naked as he ran with the other men towards the big ranch house. They reached the deep porch without incident. Zilla stood at the road, head high and her tail, unwagging, held straight out behind her. They were all breathing hard. Mark's eyes showed white in his painted face. His teeth showed white, too; he was grinning and didn't realize he was grinning.

"Here comes the truck," Paul said tensely. "Zilla! To me, girl. Joe, get into the house. Don't present a target. Howie, Nolan, Mark, spread out along the porch."

Joe stepped through the screen door without another word, and then stopped. He had to see. He had to.

"What's going on?" someone shouted, just as Joe's ears caught the faint rumble of engine noise. He looked in the direction of the shout and saw Jorie standing at the far edge of the ranch yard. She had a baseball cap on and was carrying a knapsack. Joe saw Howie make a futile grab at the back of Nolan's shirt.

Nolan leaped the porch railing and ran across the exposed

ground of the ranch yard, his bow held upright in his hand. He'd taken the quiver cap from his arrows and they glinted like diamonds in the sun.

"Nolan, no!" Howie cried, and started off the porch after him. Paul reached out an arm and pulled Howie back as though he were no larger than a child.

"Hold, man, hold!" Paul ordered.

Nolan reached a stunned Jorie just as the engine noise crested the hill. He whipped an arrow out of his quiver and pulled his bow into full, steady position just as he stopped in front of her. He stepped backward into her body, his shoulders and arms covering her frame, aiming at the truck that was about to appear over the hill.

"Nolan!" Howie cried out in a choked voice.

"Good for you, Nolan," Eileen said from Joe's elbow. He gulped in relief as she pressed a gun into his free hand. It was her spare, her small LadySmith, and even though it was swallowed in his man's hand he felt suddenly a part of the battle again, no longer a bystander. She held her SIG-Sauer ready in her hand, standing sideways with only her head showing in the doorway. He copied her and that was all he had time to do before the Schwan's truck came over the hill.

CHAPTER EIGHTEEN

The Reed Ranch, Wyoming

The Schwan's truck lumbered down the hill and it seemed to take forever. Eileen couldn't see through the windshield. She wondered why Nolan didn't pull Jorie to safety, since the truck was taking so long. Then she realized her sense of time had slowed down. She could see Nolan's chest rising and falling slowly; he was still breathing hard. The truck ground to an unsteady halt and the door opened. Zilla barked sharply, started forward, and then backed up on her three feet.

Doug, the Schwan's man, came around the door. He was spattered with blood from his scalp down his face and across the chest of his cheerful Schwan's shirt. He put a hand on the hood of his truck and blinked as though he couldn't see very well.

"Hey," he said in a faint voice. "Help? Somebody? Paul?" He leaned against the truck and looked around, finally seeing Nolan and his bow held at the ready. "Hello?"

"Is there anyone in the truck, Doug?" Paul shouted. Then he moved with lightning speed down the porch, coming to rest less than three feet from Eileen and Joe. His back was to the massive pillar of the front porch, his shotgun held across his chest, his mouth a lipless line of strain.

"No, it's not my blood. That's what I've got to tell you, these guys tried to, they tried to – then Sheriff King came up behind us and – oh, God, they shot him. They shot Rick." Doug scrubbed a hand across his face and looked at the blood on it, his face dazed and horror stricken. "Paul? Help me, Paul."

Paul nodded at Eileen. She burst through the door as he ran across to help Doug, who was leaning against the hood of his Schwan's truck as though he weren't sure he could stand on his feet. She scuttled at shoulder level up to the passenger side of the truck, then popped up and took an instant sweep of the interior, gun at the ready. No one there. She ripped the door open and Joe stepped from behind her and aimed his gun at the interior, exactly as a partner should. She felt grateful for his help and fiercely annoyed that he hadn't remained inside the house, all at the same time.

"Back door," she panted.

He nodded silently and followed her. The back of the Schwan's truck was smooth, without a door. The sides of the truck were lined with small doors, each one for different kinds of frozen foods, evidently. They were all locked. Joe followed her to the other side of the truck as she checked underneath the wheels and undercarriage.

"No one there, unless they're locked in the freezers," she said.

Paul was helping Doug to the porch. Tracy appeared with a glass of cold water and a warm washcloth.

"Tell us what happened, Doug," Paul said. "Mark, Nolan, Jorie, get up here. Tracy, get Lucy and Ted and the baby. Howie, keep an eye on the road. Jimmy still up there?"

"Jimmy?" Howie said into his walkie-talkie.

"Here."

"Stand by," Howie said. When Nolan and Jorie came up to the porch Howie put an arm around Nolan and shook him. "I'd like to kill you, boy," he said fiercely. "Like I'm going to explain to your father, losing a fine son like you." He embraced him roughly and thumped him on the back.

"You're not going to lose me," Nolan said as though mildly astonished.

"You didn't need to do that, Nolan," Jorie muttered. She looked pale and disconcerted. "What's with this guy – is that *blood*?"

"Where's Beryl?"

"Coming up soon, she had to pack away some of her soil samples," Jorie said.

"The sheriff?" Eileen asked hoarsely. "What happened, Doug?"

Doug took a deep sip of water and then took the washcloth Tracy had left. He scrubbed at his face. Eileen could smell the blood on him, the fresh biting scent that made all of them stamp and twitch like horses.

"I was on Highway 24 and I noticed this car following me. They passed me and then a few minutes later they flagged me down. I stopped, because they had their hood up and I thought they might need some help—"

"They did," Joe said bitterly.

"So then they pulled these wicked looking guns and said I was going to help them find the Reed Ranch, did I know where it was? I tried to play dumb and one of them, he took his gun and slapped me across the side of the head with it." Doug winced and touched near his right ear. Eileen could see a blood-clotted gash above Doug's puffed and reddened ear. "So I said yes, I could find it but I couldn't tell them how to get there, you had to know all the twists and forks in the road."

"Good man," Paul said huskily, gripping Doug's shoulder. The path from the highway was a straight track from the road to the ranch, without a single fork.

"I figured I might be able to warn you, at least," Doug said. "Or try and run the truck off the road at the last minute. I wasn't sure what I was going to do."

Doug wiped at his neck with the bloody washcloth, the kind and capable deliveryman who was prepared to give his life to keep a pair of murderers away from his customers. As though there wasn't anything else he could do.

"What happened next?" Tracy asked unsteadily. Eileen glanced at her and saw her mother's expression. She understood, too, what Doug had been trying to do.

"Then they got in the truck with me and the tall fat one held a gun on me. The other one, he started digging in my portable cooler. Said he wanted some of those ice cream bars. Suddenly the sheriff—" Doug cleared his throat. "Sheriff King was in the rear view mirror, lights flashing. He saw the whole thing, I guess. Anyway I pulled over like they said to. He came up to the truck with his gun out and they waited, calm as could be, as though they didn't even care. The thinner one kept digging in my cooler, looking for ice cream bars. He said he wanted the number 5's I was handing out earlier in Hulett. The sheriff came up and did something they didn't expect, though – he opened my door and yanked me out, quick as a snake. I hadn't put my seatbelt back on because I was thinking I might make a run for it. I fell down and he dragged me behind the truck. They had to get out, see, both of them, because they couldn't shoot through the truck."

"He didn't have any backup," Eileen said through tightly clenched teeth. She tried not to see the image in her brain, but she couldn't help it. Richard King, without a soul to help him, taking on two contract assassins.

"No, I guess he didn't," Doug said. He scrubbed at his face again, even though it was clean. "So the sheriff went around one side and shot at one. Then the other popped around the other side and they – he shot him." Doug put his face in the washcloth.

"How did you get away?" Paul asked. Doug lifted his head and spoke, looking at no one.

"The sheriff pushed me away and tackled the fat one, who'd shot him. The sheriff grabbed him and told me to run, and I did. I jumped back in the truck and it was still running so I took off. When I looked back I could see they were still struggling. The thin one was sitting on the road. He had his head in his hands but he didn't seem like he was that hurt. I didn't see any blood coming from him."

"If he's unhurt, they could be here anytime," Lucy said coolly. She was in the doorway with a sleeping Hank in her arms. The old pantry must have been dreadfully hot; both she and Ted had flushed faces. "If he's hurt, or dead, Rene might withdraw and set up another time."

"I think they're coming in," Eileen said. "Or they're going to wait out at the highway and pick us off as we come out. We can't drive out of here."

There was a grim silence as the words sunk in. Nolan

shifted and Mark drew a deep breath. Howie looked unhappy and fingered his walkie-talkie.

"Eileen, what did we learn about Rene today?" Lucy said suddenly.

"That he's a contract assassin?" Eileen said. "You have an idea?"

"He's a Parisian," Lucy said. "He's not an American. He's fat, he's old, he's used to city life. He's probably never been five feet from a paved road in his life. We don't take the road out of here." Lucy pointed at the woods to the south, deep and green in the baking heat. "We go into the forest. He *can't* follow us in there. He won't know how."

Highway 24, South of Hulett, Wyoming

"You're sure you're all right?" Rene asked Ken.

"I'm fine," Ken said shortly. "A hell of a bruise, that's all."

They stood by the sheriff's car, down a no-name track that hid the patrol car and their stolen Chrysler. They were less than a mile from the spot where the sheriff had pulled them over. The sheriff was back at the spot by the highway, face down in the weeds that lined the ditch. Rene hadn't waited to see if he were dying or already dead, he'd simply shoved him into the ditch and pulled Ken, dazed and bruised, into the patrol car. He wanted badly to finish the sheriff off, watch him while he died, but there was no time. After a few moments he'd found the switches and turned off the flashers of the patrol car. Then, calmly and patiently, Rene had driven them back to where they'd hidden the Chrysler.

Ken's injury seemed to be affecting him, however much he protested that he was fine. His lightning reflexes had thrown him back, twisting in mid-air, to avoid the sheriff's gun. The sheriff had made a clean miss but Ken, in his backwards lunge, had slammed his head into the side of the Schwan's truck. His eyes seemed unable to fully focus and he was pale and sweaty.

Rene opened the door to the Chrysler. "Get in," he said shortly to Ken. The day was blazing hot and cloudless. The very air seemed to burn in his nostrils. He held himself under tight control. Now was not the time for a mistake. If, indeed, they hadn't already made one, by killing a county sheriff so blatantly. The Schwan's man had seen both their faces. The only way things could be worse was if Ken had been hurt and the sheriff, not the deliveryman, had gotten away.

Ken, though, *did* seem to be hurt. He got in and let his head rest against the back of the seat as Rene started the car and turned the air conditioning to full blast. Rene took a wet wipe from a box and slowly, methodically, began to remove the stink of sweat from his face and hands. He was bloody, too, from grappling with the dying sheriff, and he regarded his shirtfront with distaste. He would change that, too, but not until they decided what they were going to do.

"The ranch has to be close, boss," Ken said huskily. "You know that's where that delivery man went, to warn them."

"I know, Ken," Rene said quietly. He continued to rub the wet tissue across his face and neck, gazing through the windshield at the blazing hot day. There had to be a way to turn this all around. There *had* to be a way.

The Reed Ranch, Wyoming

"Let's get the horses saddled up," Paul said. Joe nodded, intensely glad that Paul had decided to act on Lucy's idea. He didn't want to drive up that road. Not that he minded seeing Rene again; he had an idea that if he saw Rene first he might just be able to take the fat killer down. But if he didn't, and Rene was quicker, everyone here was going to die.

"But where can we go?" Jorie said. She was ashen-faced at last, her eyes on the bloody washcloth Doug had set by his side on the porch steps.

"I know," Eileen said. "I was planning to take Joe there tomorrow. There's a Native American ceremony at the Devils Tower. They're protesting the rock climbing of the Tower, since they say it's a sacred site. So there's a delegation of rock climbers who are going to be ascending the Tower, and then rappelling down. They're protesting the protest. It should be an interesting event."

"Why —"

"What do you have with protesters, Jorie?" Eileen said with a strained grin. "You have *cops*. Park rangers, anyway, and they carry side arms. If we can get to the Devils Tower, we'll be able to tell them what's going on and they can radio the State Patrol."

"Can't we call the State Patrol right now?" Jorie asked in bewilderment.

"I think we should," Eileen said. "And after you're clear from danger and in the woods I'm going to call in on the phone and then come after you. We have to move. Where's Beryl?"

"I'm here," Beryl Penrose said, walking out of the trees. She carried a knapsack, bulging heavily. Tools of various sorts were strapped across the back. A water bottle rode her hip and she wore a cloth folded over her dark hair. Her face was strained and white. "I've been here since you helped Doug to the porch. I'm glad you're okay, Jorie."

"I'm fine," Jorie said. She didn't look fine; she looked pale and upset. "We're going into the woods, Beryl."

"I don't think so," Beryl said quietly. Her words caused a widening arc of stillness in the small crowd at the front porch. Joe blinked at her, astonished, because Beryl was holding a very large and serviceable revolver. She held it very steady. She was aiming it at them.

CHAPTER NINETEEN

The Reed Ranch, Wyoming

"Beryl," Jorie squeaked. "What – what are you doing?"

"Just trying to get a head start," Beryl said grimly. "Right, Eileen?"

Joe realized Eileen was no longer at his side, and hadn't been since Beryl had come across the yard. Beryl frowned and looked nervously from left to right.

"Please don't do this, Beryl," Eileen said, appearing from behind a pillar halfway down the porch. Her gun was held, level and very steady, aimed at Beryl. Beryl stepped backwards and moved her gun so that it was aimed at Eileen. Joe's heart nearly stopped in his chest. Eileen had drawn Beryl's line of fire from the porch to herself. There was no one behind her, so Beryl's gun would hurt no one but Eileen.

"So how did you figure it out?" Beryl said conversationally.

"We don't have time for this," Eileen said with equal calm. "You're not really a killer, Beryl. You know that. If you keep us here much longer, we're all going to die. You don't want that, do you?"

"I didn't want Jon to die," Beryl said fiercely, blinking rapidly. The gun barrel shook in her hands. "And I want to know how you figured it out."

"I was stirring around the puzzle pieces," Eileen said. "And your piece flipped over. We all knew Jorie was a lesbian. She told Nolan. What I never thought was that you might be one, too. That you were lovers."

Joe's mouth dropped open. Jorie stood, mouth quivering, a foot from him. Her lovely blue eyes filled with tears. "Beryl," she whispered.

"Well you've got one lesbian right," Beryl grinned as though it hurt her. "Me. Jorie's no lesbian. She's a hurt little girl, that's all, visiting the island to soothe her wounds. She won't be the first, won't be the last. It's not her fault that she was the best thing that ever happened to me."

"Island?" Mark Plutt mouthed, his painted face looking comically confused.

"The island of Lesbos," Lucy said quietly. "Thought by the Greeks to be where lesbians originated. The island of women only, peaceful and serene."

"What are you talking about?" Jorie said huskily.

"Oh, Jorie," Beryl said, her gun still aimed at Eileen. Eileen stood with her gun aimed at Beryl, as steady as stone. Her lovely face was calm and unruffled. Joe felt sweat spring out over every inch of his skin, stinking fear sweat. Why did this have to happen now?

"I am too—" Jorie began, but her face was confused.

"Jorie, you had a crush on Jon McBride that you didn't even realize you had," Beryl said in exasperation. "And what a man to leave the island for! I knew you'd leave me, someday." Here Beryl's voice thickened with unshed tears. She cleared her throat. "That's all right with me. Just to love you for a little while, that was enough for me. But I knew what McBride would do to you. He's waded through so many young women. He'd have broken your heart, my little Marjorie. I couldn't—"

"He taunted you, that day," Eileen said. "He taunted you with what he was going to do to your lover. And you knew he was going to do it, too."

"We argued," Beryl said dully. "I didn't know what he'd stolen, but when I came back early from the funding meeting I found him working on the skeleton. It was plainly obvious that something was missing. I could see the gaping hole in the midsection of the skeleton. I didn't know it was the crystal skull. I didn't know what it was, but I knew he'd taken something. He wouldn't tell me where it was, or what he'd taken. He wanted it for himself, he said. Can you imagine, an archaeologist of his stature robbing a site like that?

"He climbed out of the site and I followed him. We were standing by the tables, and we were arguing. We started throwing everything in, tossing insults back and forth, insults about every-thing. His lack of publishing in the field. My department's lack of funding last year. My eyebrow earring and his awful ponytail and then we fought over Jorie."

"Oh, no," Jorie whispered.

"And there was the stone knife, sitting on the table. He'd taken that from the site, too. I picked it up and we were shouting at each other, I was shaking the knife in his face, telling him his career was finished, he'd have to figure out some other career that would supply him with young female students for him to seduce. And he said – he said something so awful about you, Jorie, so horrid, about what he was going to do to you, with his – with his – and I slashed at him, I slashed at him, I was out of my head with thinking how you were going to be so hurt, Jorie. I swear I didn't mean to kill him. But the knife, it was so sharp. It cut into him like he was made of butter. It stuck in him. He staggered backwards and put both hands on it and pulled it out of his chest. I turned and ran. I thought he was running after me. He had the knife. I thought he was going to kill me. When I finally got my breath back and my courage and I went back to the site, he was gone."

The light was changing. The long evening hours were drawing in. Beryl held them trapped against the porch, her face pale as paper, her hands shaking on the gun. Eileen seemed uncon-cerned with Rene and the other killer. She was relaxed and fo-cused, intent upon Beryl.

"Listen, Beryl," she said. "Let's talk about manslaughter."

"I don't want to go to jail," Beryl said.

"Well, I think we're going to talk about jail time," Eileen said reasonably. "But not life. Not life in prison, not a death sentence. Jail, a place where you can write a book about your Aztec warrior and his journey. A *women's* penitentiary, Beryl. Women guards. You can survive that."

"I can't," Beryl whispered.

"I'm not going to let you commit suicide with me as the suicide weapon, Beryl," Eileen said. She raised her gun sideways in the air, very carefully, and then put it inside her shirt. She put both hands out, palm up. "If you really want to be a murderer, go ahead. Start with me."

"I'm not going to kill you," Beryl burst out, her face crumpling into tears. "I'm not going to kill anybody."

"I don't think you meant to kill Jon McBride," Eileen said. "And a jury will see that too. Don't run. Stay."

Beryl stood, gun still trained on Eileen, her face wavering like water, tears running down her face. Then her chin firmed up.

"Joe, give me your car keys," she said. Eileen's shoulders slumped, but she didn't reach for her gun. Joe looked at Eileen and she nodded. He drew out 'Berto's keys and said a brief, silent prayer. Not for Beryl, because he knew she was being incredibly stupid. Rene and his friend had seen the Mustang. Beryl was driving to her death, if she drove out of the ranch in the Mustang. He said a prayer for 'Berto's car, that she wouldn't drive it off the road or bang it up. Or get it riddled with bullet holes and soaked with blood. 'Berto had trusted him with his car and it had saved his life twice, already. He would hate to see it damaged.

"Here," he said, stepping forward carefully. He leaned forward and dropped the keys into Beryl's outstretched hand, not attempting anything stupid like tackling her. Eileen's nod had told him that much. Don't risk it, her eyes had said. "Check the oil when you fill up," he said. "You need to make sure to do that."

"Let her go," Eileen said, fixing Howie with a stern glance. Beryl hurried to the Mustang without another word. She threw her rucksack into the backseat and turned to Jorie. Jorie looked at her, her expression shocked and hurt. Beryl nodded, as though she and Jorie had discussed something and come to a conclusion. She turned away and got into the car and a minute later the Mustang had roared up the track and was gone.

"They'll kill her and be down here in fifteen minutes," Howie said.

"Then we've got to be in the woods in ten," Paul said.

"Let's go, people! Nolan, Mark, take the group over the southern ridge. Howie, call Jimmy down here. We'll get the horses and meet you over the ridge. Eileen, make your phone call to the State troopers. I'll leave Fireball tied to the post for you."

"Let's go, Jorie," Tracy said. Jorie stood stock still, staring where the Mustang had left a rooster trail of dust. Her face was deathly pale. She let Tracy take her arm as though she were sleep-walking. "Ted, Lucy, Hank, come with us. Joe too. Doug, help Paul with the horses."

"Yes, ma'am," Doug said, getting to his feet. The water and the rest had obviously restored him, but he looked stunned. Joe was sure they all looked stunned.

"Why didn't you shoot her when you had the chance?" Howie asked Eileen, as she passed them on the way into the house.

"Because I'm not a murderer," Eileen said shortly, pausing. "Could you see her revolver?"

"Yes," Howie said doubtfully.

"It wasn't loaded."

"Then why did you let her go?" Jorie burst out. "Why didn't you stop her?"

"Because she has to choose her own path," Eileen said. "She's no danger to anyone, Jorie. She'll realize the best option for her. And right now our lives are in danger. We've got to get moving. We can't drag a handcuffed woman with us. We can't wait. Besides, attacking a police officer is a felony. I wanted to avoid that, for her sake."

"But they'll kill her!" Jorie cried. She froze, and looked around at the grim faces that surrounded her. Joe felt that belly cramp of fear again. Jorie believed, finally. And her pretty face was suddenly shocked and fearful.

"It's a damn fast car," Joe said. "If she can drive fast, they won't catch her."

Tracy pulled gently on Jorie's arm. "Let's go, people."

Jorie and Tracy followed Paul and the hunters, all of them hurrying. Joe turned to Eileen and she looked back into his face unflinchingly. He saw the truth of what she'd done in her face, and she didn't look away.

"You let her go, as a *decoy*," he said.

"If she's killed, I'm going to have to live with that," Eileen said, her mouth a thin and unhappy line. "I didn't know what else to do, other than shoot her, to save our lives. Can you live with that?"

Joe took her roughly into his arms, not caring if anyone was looking. He kissed her, hard, and let her go. "See you over the ridge."

"Ten minutes," Eileen's voice came out the darkness of the front hallway as she disappeared into the depths of the house. Joe suppressed the overwhelming desire to go after her, to stand with her and protect her, and headed for the horses.

Black Hills National Forest, Northeast Wyoming

"Okay, here's Eileen," Paul said, his voice rough with relief. Lucy watched in uncomplicated pleasure as Eileen galloped over the ridge on a brown and white horse that Lucy had heard Paul call Fireball. Fireball had white patches around her eyes and splashes of white along her sides that made her look like the victim of a paintball attack. Lucy admired the sight. If Eileen Reed had been wearing a cowboy hat and chaps she would have looked just like a Hollywood cowgirl, so smoothly did she ride the galloping horse. Fireball came to a neat, bunched stop and Eileen swung out of the saddle and bounced to the ground.

There were four other horses, saddled but carrying packs instead of riders. Brumby, the tallest horse, had hooves that looked as big as dinner plates to Lucy. Paul held the reins of Brumby and fended off an occasional attack from the enormous horse's snapping teeth. Zilla sat patiently at Lucy's side. Hank sat quietly on her hip, still silent, his weight a warm bundle. She knew Hank had picked up on the sickening tension that had swirled like a flood. She hoped that the blood on Doug's face and shirt hadn't frightened him too much, but she had no time to engage in toddler talk with him. He would have to wait, and with what must have been the instinctive understanding of a human child in danger, he seemed to know this, and was silent.

Doug had borrowed a shirt from Howie. Horses didn't like the scent of blood, and Tracy had whispered to Lucy that bears did.

Setting out with a bloody shirt into the National Forest was a good way to get unwanted attention from four-footed predators. Doug strained the limits of Howie's faded Bud Lite T-shirt, a tight fit that Lucy appreciated even as frightened as she was. She wished she could nudge Eileen and point out Doug's biceps to her; Eileen was the kind of girlfriend who knew how a woman could be head-over-heels in love with her husband but still admire, um, art.

Eileen, however, was reporting her findings to Paul, her face focused and intent. Behind her the top part of the green, leafy ridge seemed to break away and slide down the slope. Then Lucy saw the piece of ridge was Jimmy Arnold, who had finally left his post and joined the group. He moved to speak to Howie in the near-whisper that seemed to be his natural way of speaking. Lucy couldn't see his expression through the paint but she saw him put a hand on Howie's shoulder. The gesture conveyed a depth of affection that Lucy realized must exist between the brothers-by-marriage. She was fiercely glad, suddenly, that Howie and his friends were innocent of Dr. McBride's murder.

"Okay, folks, we have five horses and thirteen people," Paul announced. "We'll lead the horses and anyone who gets tired can ride. Ted, I want you to ride with Hank."

"I can walk," Ted said. He was standing next to Lucy, his hand on her waist. A sense of the safe, sure strength that was Ted seemed to flow into her like an electric current. They all stood in the hollow of a ridge, a grassy meadow surrounded by pine and oak trees. Lucy realized suddenly that this meadow was where she and Eileen had stood and looked into Hank's diaper, to see an ancient stone knife covered in dried blood. They were out of sight of the ranch buildings but they were very close.

"Hank can't ride," Paul said. "And Lucy has been here at five thousand feet of altitude for longer than you have. We're in a survival situation, folks. We all do whatever keeps us alive."

"All right," Ted said immediately. "I'd love to ride."

"Good man," Paul said, smiling briefly. "Now we need to head southwest, towards—"

"Wait," Jorie said. She was standing with Tracy, her face still pale and upset. "What about the State Police? What did they say?"

"They're sending up the police officer from Sundance," Eileen said. She rubbed her hands across her eyes and through her tangled hair. Her face was powdered with dust and her hands left streaks behind. For a moment she looked utterly weary and frustrated. "I explained that we thought that Sheriff King was dead, that these men were coming after us, but of course they have to have a police officer on the spot. They didn't say they thought I was crazy, no, but they insist that they have to have a report from the sheriff. Who is dead, I reminded them. God help him if the officer from Sundance runs into Rene and his buddy. Anyway, I told them where the sheriff had been shot. We're hours away from any kind of help. No helicopter with a SWAT team, sorry."

"We didn't expect it," Tracy said. "That's why we're going to the Devils Tower."

"Right," Paul said. "I'd like to put at least a mile between us and the ranch in the next hour or so. Anyone at the ranch could probably hear our voices right now if they listened, and I don't like that. I'll lead with Brumby. Howie, you and Jimmy follow and lead Pirate. Nolan, Mark, you're next with Sunny. I'd like Eileen to lead Starlight, she's the gentlest, with Hank and Ted on board. Eileen, explain about bear and lion as we go, please."

Lucy felt Ted's hand tighten on her waist, but he didn't say anything.

"Joe, Lucy, walk with Eileen. Tracy, Jorie, lead Fireball. Doug, I'll have you bring up the rear. Keep an eye out for anything dropped, or snagged or torn. We don't want to leave a trail that's too obvious."

"What about the horses?" Lucy said as Eileen handed Fireball over to her mother and took the reins of a mild looking gray horse. The horse, saddled, carried only small saddlebags. The other horses were weighted down with pack rolls that covered their backs and hindquarters and hung down their sides. All the horses seemed resigned to this, except Brumby. When Paul didn't mount him but took his reins instead, Brumby gave a few vicious kicks and then tried to bite Paul on the shoulder. Paul knocked the horse's head out of the way and then patted Brumby on the nose. Brumby shoved his head against Paul's shoulder, nearly knocking him over, and then followed as meekly as Starlight.

"Dad'll take us up and over the brush on the next ridge," Eileen explained, holding a foot and helping an eager looking Ted onto Starlight. "There are soft pine needles and some hard stone outcroppings along the top. By the time we get off that ridge and down into the next valley, our tracks will be gone."

Lucy looked up at Ted and he was grinning at her, his curly black hair tousled across his forehead, eyes sparkling. He took hold of the saddle horn with a white knuckled grip but he didn't lose the boyish grin.

"Hank, you're going to sit on Daddy's lap," Lucy said.

"Up you go, Hankster," Eileen said, raising the little boy until he was sitting on the saddle in front of his father. Hank, who'd been on a token horseback ride already, was clearly delighted. "Take hold of the saddle around Hank, Ted. Don't hold onto Hank, hold the saddle. Let me get the stirrups for you." With quick, practiced movements Eileen lengthened the stirrups so that Ted's feet, shod in black loafers, fit into the stirrups. "Okay. Let's go."

Lucy looked around and saw that Paul and Brumby had already disappeared up the slope of the ridge and the hunters were close behind. The hunters disappeared so completely into the surrounding terrain that the horses looked as though they were walking alone. Eileen held Starlight's reins and looked up at Ted.

"Okay?" she asked.

"Okay," he said. "Let's go."

Eileen started walking and Lucy nearly went headlong into the sun-heated pine needles as she tried to walk and look at Ted and Hank at the same time. She grabbed Eileen's arm to keep from falling and then paid attention to her footing as the slope quickly became steep.

"Quick lesson about lion and bear," Eileen said, as they entered the blessed cool shadow of the trees. They angled up the slope of the hill, following the hindquarters of the horse ahead of them. Paul was picking a slantwise course up the hill, probably to keep from leaving gouges in the soft pine needles of the forest and marking their trail.

"I'm listening," Ted said.

"Me, too," said Joe, who was walking on the other side of Starlight.

"Horses hate bear and lion. If they smell them, they're going to try to bolt. So if Starlight starts to drop out from under you, that's what you're feeling. She's trying to dislodge you so she can run. If that happens, get your feet out of the stirrups. Hand Hank down to me and then jump off. I'll hold her until you're both free."

"That's the instructions? You jump *off*?" Lucy asked.

"Brumby won't run," Eileen said, "but it's a rare horse who won't go berserk at the smell of a bear or a mountain lion. It's best just to let them go, strange as that sounds. Don't worry, we probably won't run into any predators. They'll smell us a long way off and they'll go the other way. You need to know, just in case."

"All right," Ted said, drawling the words. Lucy looked up at him suspiciously. He was looking up the trail, through the trees, his arms around Hank, swaying back and forth on the saddle as Starlight walked uphill. He was still smiling.

"Ted's going native, Lucy," Joe said solemnly. "It happens. Nothing can be done. Prepare to move to Wyoming and be married to a cowboy."

"Shut up, Joe," Lucy laughed. She was increasingly out of breath as the horses and people climbed to the top of the ridge. The footing was treacherous, covered with pine needles and small rocks that wanted to turn underfoot. The smell of pine was everywhere in the unmoving air, pine and horses and sweaty people. Lucy wondered if Rene could track them by their smell alone. Then she remembered what she'd read about Rene and felt better. Rene probably didn't know how to walk on ground that wasn't paved over.

She glanced behind her, to see Tracy and Jorie walking with Fireball. Zilla's shaggy head poked out of a wide-mouthed carrier on Fireball's side. Tracy reached up to pet the dog and Zilla panted happily. Lucy had wondered how the little three-legged dog was going to keep up, and she smiled to herself. Tracy thought of everything.

"Water?" Eileen asked. Lucy turned to see Eileen offering a bottle. She took the bottle and drank gratefully, noticing with interest that it seemed to have some sort of structure inside it. "Keep it. See, it's got a snap for your belt. It's a water purifier bottle," Eileen explained, taking another bottle out of Starlight's saddlebag. "I fill it anywhere, and the filter takes out germs and microorganisms. We all have them, and Dad has a collapsible tank for tonight. That way we don't have to carry water. Don't forget to fill it when we cross streams."

"A water tank for tonight?" Ted asked. "How far away is Devils Tower?"

"Six miles, give or take," Eileen said. "We'll see it when we camp tonight."

"We can't walk six miles in an afternoon?" Ted asked, puzzled. "Why not?"

"Because we're going six miles as the crow flies," Eileen explained. "But we're not crows, and we're not flying. We're going to walk more like twenty miles by the time we're there. Up and down, around cliffs and ravines and brush that we can't force our way through. Tonight, we'll rest. Tomorrow, by the time we get there, the Park Rangers will be monitoring the demonstration and hopefully the State Patrol will be looking for all of us."

"Tomorrow, we'll be safe," Lucy murmured.

"Then *we* get to be the hunters," Joe said with a wolfish look. Lucy shot him a glance that said without words: *Damn right.*

CHAPTER TWENTY

Outside Hulett, Wyoming

Rene, sitting in his stolen Chrysler with the air conditioning still going full blast, saw that the gas gauge was starting to dip below the full mark. He felt a burst of fresh rage for the thief who'd stolen his wallet. The money was an inconvenience, but the man had taken the picture of his father. Rene had more, but he was fond of that print. It was his good luck and Ted Giometti had stolen it.

Ken, in the other seat, had fallen asleep. His head lolled against the back of the seat and his breathing was harsh and bubbly. Rene wanted to let him rest as long as possible, but he was getting impatient. He had sketched out the outline of a plan, but he needed to discuss the matter with Ken. Ken, despite his sidekick amiability, had great instincts and was always willing to discuss them.

"All right, Ken," Rene said finally, unwilling to let Ken's irritating snores go on. "Let's talk about the plan." Rene reached out and shook Ken's shoulder.

Ken's head lolled over. His eyes, half-open, were blind. One of his pupils was enormous, filling his eye. The other was pinpoint, showing a vast blue iris. A line of saliva spilled from his half-open mouth and ran down his chin.

Rene was suddenly out of the car, in the blazing sunlight,

coughing helplessly. He stumbled to the back of the Chrysler and leaned against the trunk. He wiped a shaking hand over his forehead. The cooler, purchased in a Rapid City supermarket, was in the trunk. Rene and Ken had filled it with water and soda and snacks from the supermarket. He reached back into the car, keeping his eyes fixed so that he couldn't see Ken, and popped the trunk. In a few moments he sighed as cold water splashed over his face and into his mouth. He rinsed, and spat, and rinsed again. Finally he started to feel better, and rummaged in the cooler for some food.

The chilled slices of beef, the soft smoked Brie on crackers, started to bring him around at last. So, he'd worked with Ken for six years now. Only in America, and only a few times a year. Ken was a tool, nothing more, and when a tool broke it was replaced. Ken's head injury had obviously been more serious than it looked. Rene knew what Ken's extra-large pupil meant. The pupil was blown because Ken had hit his head hard enough to start a small bleed in his brain. Blood destroyed brain tissue. If Ken had been in a hospital for the past few hours a CAT scan would have showed the injury and the bleeding, and he would have had brain surgery to correct it. A hospital with a CAT scan was hours away, undoubtedly in Rapid City, and Ken was dead now, anyway. Rene knew Ken was still breathing, but he was dead just the same.

Rene wiped his mouth with a napkin and then folded the napkin and used the clean side to wipe his forehead. It was incredibly hot, hot and dry.

He stopped, looking at the wet surface of the napkin. The elusive idea suddenly fell on him like a rock bouncing off his skull.

Black Hills National Forest, Northeast Wyoming

"Camp here, folks," Paul announced.

"Alleluia," Joe gasped. He meant it, too. They had walked, nothing more, but all the walking was straight up and straight down. Joe wasn't sure if going uphill or going downhill was worse. Downhill gave him a chance to catch his breath, but his toes jammed into the front of his sneakers until they hurt. His shins, holding him upright against the steep slopes, felt like splintered sticks. His calves, on the way up the hills, screamed with pain. His lungs burned, his shoulders hurt, he was, in a word, finished.

Paul had picked a small clearing as their campsite. A rocky outcropping jutted into the center of the small area. Massive pine trees sheltered it all around. There was a pretty, grassy meadow just to the south. Eileen handed Starlight's reins to Joe and helped Lucy and Hank from the horse. Lucy had done quite well, for a girl with sea-level lungs, but she'd grown increasingly tired as the day drew down to evening dark. Ted was obviously exhausted. He'd walked more than he should have for his first day at high altitude. Joe glanced at his watch. The time was nine p.m. and the sky was still light, but the sun was down and the dark would be coming soon.

"We're getting close?" Lucy asked hopefully, as she set Hank down on the soft pine needles. Hank crowed with delight and immediately began taking handfuls of pine needles and throwing them into the air.

"Look," Eileen said, pointing to the south. Joe turned with Lucy and stood, transfixed, as he saw an enormous stone Tower through the trees. He hadn't looked at the sky until Eileen pointed. He'd been too busy looking for their path. The Tower seemed as though it must be just over the next hill, it was so close. It was brightly lit by the setting sun. The lines that marked the sides of the Tower were drawn as sharply as knife scores – or tooth marks. It looked as though it was just through the trees. Then he realized the black specks circling the stone top were actually enormous birds, hawks or eagles of some sort, and the immensity of the Tower struck home. It was miles away from them.

"Yeek," Lucy said in a gulping little voice.

"We're a good two hours away," Paul said. He handed Brumby's reins to Eileen and walked off. Eileen glared ferociously at Brumby and jerked his reins.

"Don't give me any problems, you brute," she said. "I need to stake out the horses in the meadow, Joe. Can you help?"

"Of course," Joe said. "What do we need to do?"

"Strip them of their packs and saddles here. We'll stake them by their halters and strip their bridles from them after we've staked them out. Nolan, Jimmy, Doug, you know the drill?"

"We know," Jimmy said. He already had Pirate stripped of her saddlebags and was working on the saddle. Pirate was a red horse – a roan, Joe guessed they were called – with a black mane and tail. Joe helped Eileen by stripping Starlight as she took on Brumby and they walked them to the edge of the meadow. The horses eagerly stretched their necks to the thick grass. They were munching, green foam around the bridles, before Eileen had tied two ropes from their halters to some widely spaced trees. She stripped Brumby's bridle, glaring at the horse and swearing she'd murder him if he bit her, Paul's affection or no. Brumby looked as though he might just go ahead and take a chunk from her, but then shook his massive head and let her strip the bridle. He then ignored her totally, even as she swept his coat with a currycomb.

"Here, let me do Starlight," Joe said. Eileen gave him the currycomb with a grateful nod and he went to work on the sweaty hide of the horse. The horses must be as tired as they were, Joe thought, particularly Starlight who had carried Ted and Hank. She stood quietly, ears flicking, as he brushed dirt and hair from her smooth sides. The smell of her, warm and horsy and sweet, was as soothing as the touch of a hand. She brought her soft nose back to him as he finished. She nickered softly. Her mouth was foamy green with the grass but he patted her anyway, feeling an absurd rush of affection for her.

Beyond her, Joe saw Jimmy rubbing down Pirate and Doug looking after Fireball. Doug looked worried. Joe knew that Doug was more concerned about his wife missing him than the idea of Rene following them in the woods. Doug's wife was certainly worried by now, but there was nothing any of them could do. There was no cell phone coverage and they'd decided to keep the walkie-talkies off, in case Rene had one himself.

On the other side of the meadow Nolan was patting Sunny, a pale blond horse with long legs and knobby knees. Nolan looked fit and rested, as though he'd spent the day lounging in an armchair rather than walking up and down perpendicular slopes.

"They've been scouting for a week," Eileen reminded Joe, taking the currycomb from his hand. "They've been doing this every day."

"That's why the leftover desserts are missing in the morning," Joe said. "I'm so hungry right now I could eat Fireball."

"No need, that's why Doug was cleaning her up instead of Mom. Mom's fixing dinner. Come on." Eileen pulled at his hand and grinned at him and he took the opportunity to kiss her, tired as he was. Suddenly all things seemed to be possible. The whole long evening was empty of threat and menace, out here in the depth of the woods. For the first time, he realized, he wasn't afraid about Rene and his friend. He kissed her harder. She kissed him back as fiercely as he kissed her.

"I love you," she said breathlessly, as he broke the kiss.

"I love you too, and I want to—" he started, but suddenly there was a small smattering of whistles and clapping. They turned to see Nolan, Jimmy and Doug standing and applauding.

"It's a ten from the American judge, and a, oh, no, it's a four from the Russian judge!" Nolan called. "Too bad!"

"Get a room," Doug growled, shaking his currycomb at them.

"You better finish up quick, or we'll eat all the food," Joe teased, then turned and hurried with Eileen back towards camp. He was barely ten steps into the trees when he began to smell something delicious. As they entered the clearing he saw that Paul had brushed away pine needles and revealed a round circle of stones under the large outcropping of rock. The underside of that part of the rock was burned black. A cheerful yellow and orange flame danced in the pit, with Paul tending it. Paul had cleared the ground around the fire to bare dirt, and the fire was half the size of the rock ring. Joe recognized this bit of dry-weather savvy and was glad, though he expected no less from an outdoorsman like Paul. Sparks from a campfire could be disastrous after weeks without rain. Paul was making sure there would be no sparks.

"This is one of our hunting camps," Paul said. "The flame is under the rock and can't be seen from more than a few yards away, but we still get to yarn around a fire."

"Very nice," Howie said lazily. He was lounging in a canvas chair, watching Paul tend the flame. Ted sat in another chair, Hank in his lap. Hank was chewing messily on a cracker. Ted looked hollow with hunger. He looked the way Joe felt. Zilla sat at Ted's feet, as close as she could to Hank. Beyond the fire Joe could see

Tracy working at a square table that had been erected on spindly legs. Another camp stove sat on the ground, two pots busily boiling something that smelled heavenly. Jorie, beyond them, was pulling canvas chairs out of a horse's pack with a tired, mulish look.

"Let me help," Eileen said. "We're back." She went over to the cook stove and was immediately directed to a saddlebag. Joe went over to Jorie and hoisted some of the canvas chair frames onto his shoulder. They seemed impossibly light and small, but one of them obviously held Howie's weight comfortably. When he figured out how to put together the first one the rest went together quickly.

"We don't have enough chairs," Paul said, scowling. "This is our hunting party set and we never have more than eight in a party."

"Are you kidding?" Joe asked, setting up another chair. "This is like being on an African safari, or something. I'm used to crouching by the fire and eating beans from the can."

"We're a bit better than that," Paul said, his face relaxing. "I guess we can put some sleeping bag pads on the ground for the others."

"Steaks are ready, Paul," Tracy called. Paul dropped a grate – obviously stashed in the clearing and dug up from the needles – onto the rock ring. The grate settled, perfectly flat, on stones that had been placed within the ring, and Joe again had to shake his head in admiration. The smell of pinewood, drifting in the air, was replaced by the heavenly scent of sizzling beef.

"I could eat that raw," Nolan said, entering the campfire ring and staring at the line of steaks Paul was setting on the grill.

"No need," Paul said. "These will be done soon. Let's get washed up, and by the time you fill your plates with corn and barbequed beans, we'll be ready."

Joe thought he'd never eaten a finer supper. The dark came upon them rapidly, cutting off the sight of the Tower that seemed to leer at them over the trees. The stars scattered across the sky as they ate around the fire. Jorie refused the food and ate a crumbly-looking nutrition bar that looked awful. Hank only managed a few small bites of steak but ate ravenously of the beans and the corn. When he was done he gave a tired little sigh and was asleep instantly, his head lolling on Lucy's shoulder. She disappeared into the darkness to change his diaper and put him in the sleeping bag Tracy had arranged for him. There were no tents; they would sleep in the clearing tonight, with the stars overhead their roof.

Eileen helped her mother clean away the few supper dishes. Joe clambered to his feet, managing not to howl with pain at his stiffening muscles, and collected plates. Eileen, scrubbing the plates in a small pan of warm water, refused to look at him as he came up to her.

"What's up?" he asked softly.

"Thinking about Richard King," she said shortly, her face turned to the soapy water. "What a damned fool he was. If he weren't dead, I'd probably kill him right now. You never take a risk like that."

"Not where you come from," Tracy said, squatting beside Eileen and taking the washed plates from her daughter. She nodded at an empty packsack and Joe took the hint. As she dried, he stacked the plastic dishes away. "Sheriff King is – was more than you saw, Eileen. He was a good sheriff and a good man, and he died trying to protect us." Tracy's voice thickened and Joe saw with distressed surprise that she was weeping.

"I'm sorry, Mom," Eileen said. "I didn't mean it that—"

"You never saw him as anything but what he was in high school. But he was more than that. Do you remember the Martinez family?"

"Sure, they worked for you when you started the business."

"They weren't really named Martinez. They were packed in a station wagon that broke down on I-24. They were illegals from Guatemala, Eileen, and Sheriff King brought them to us. They'd broken down in a snowstorm after spending all their money to buy a horrid ancient car and if they'd been returned to Guatemala they'd have surely been killed. Rick brought them to us because they were hungry, and cold, and the littlest one was sick."

"I remember her," Eileen whispered. "Elena. Like my name in Spanish."

"So by the time we got everything straightened out we were part of what is pretty much an underground railroad," Tracy said. "And Sheriff King was a part of it. We found the church that had sheltered them in Texas and now we help people who can't become citizens the normal way. He did it – Rick King."

"You never told me," Eileen said, her face stunned, her hands rewashing the same plate over and over again.

"Hiding illegal immigrants is illegal. I don't want to go to jail," Tracy said. "I certainly don't want you to go to jail. But you have to know now, Eileen, because of Rick King. We'll get a new family, get them fake green cards and start over, but I don't know how we're going to do it without Rick. He was a man in every sense of the word. He just didn't show it on the outside."

"I'm sorry," Eileen said in a low, miserable voice. "I don't know what else to say. I wish I could say it to him."

"Maybe you will," Joe said. Both women looked at him in surprise. "He seemed like a darned hard guy to kill, to me. Just because Doug got blood on his shirt doesn't mean King didn't get away."

"That's a good thought," Eileen said with a smile that meant she thought it wasn't a particularly bright one.

"On that note, let's go sit by the fire, kitchen workers," Tracy said with a sigh. She wiped at her face with her hands. "We're done here."

They walked together to the fire and Joe took Eileen's hand as they walked. She let him hold her hand but she was obviously buried in thoughts, and they weren't good ones.

"This is perfect," Ted said to them as they joined the group by the fire. Ted was leaning back and looking at the sky. Joe saw Jorie's expression as he and Eileen sat down and, for the first time, felt sorry for her. She'd finished her crumbly energy bar and was sitting cross-legged, her hands in her lap, staring into the fire, her face lost and bewildered and tired. Tracy, who took her seat next to Jorie, patted the girl's knee gently. Joe saw Howie looking at Jorie and wondered what he was going to say.

"I've never been the prey, before," Howie commented, rummaging in his carry pack. He pulled a substantial bottle of Scotch from the pack and carefully carved away the lead seal with his pocketknife. "Adds a bit of spice, doesn't it?"

"We were tracked by that grizzly in Alaska, once," Jimmy said. He accepted the bottle from Howie, who'd taken a swallow, and took a mouthful. He passed it to Paul, who took a drink and passed it to Tracy.

"Yeah, we hunted that bear until we realized he was hunting us," Howie said. "That was tense. This is – more interesting. I'm damn sorry about the sheriff."

Jorie, who had been handed the bottle, looked at it without expression. Joe understood how Jorie could be in such shock over Beryl Penrose. Beryl was the last person he'd expected to be Jon McBride's murderer. He had, in fact, thought that Jorie was most probably the killer.

"No meat in that bottle," Howie said in a surprisingly gentle tone. "Just grain."

Jorie put her chin in the air and took an enormous mouthful of Scotch. She choked and wheezed, then said hoarsely: "I've never had Scotch before. Sorry."

"You didn't spit it out," Howie said. The firelight lit his grinning face like a carved pumpkin and he stretched his legs to the fire. "Our guide in Alaska, his name was Dave, and Dave told us all about grizzlies and black bears. With black bears, you wear bells on your clothing and you carry pepper spray to discourage them if they get too close to you. You try to avoid grizzlies altogether, and the best way is to recognize their droppings."

"A bear must leave a big pile," Joe said.

"They do, and Dave taught us how to recognize the scat from grizzly and from black bear. Black bear scat is always full of berries, because that's what they like to eat most. And grizzly bear scat, well," Howie paused and looked around the campfire.

"Well?" Doug demanded.

"Grizzly bear scat is full of little bells and it smells real strongly of pepper spray." Howie concluded his joke to general laughter and grinned. "So, speaking of bears, who's going to tell us the real story of the Mateo Tepee?"

"The what?" Ted said, taking the bottle from Jorie. He'd vacated a canvas chair for a sleeping pad, set lengthwise. Lucy slipped back into the firelight and settled on the pad with Ted. Lucy fitted her shoulder against his chest and sighed deeply. She, too, took a healthy swig of Howie's Scotch after Ted had taken a drink.

"Mateo Tepee," Eileen said. "Bad House, or Black Place, if you will. Named the Devils Tower by Colonel Richard Dodge. He was the commander of the military escort for the U.S. Geological expedition in charge of mapping the Black Hills in 1875. I think Mom should tell the story. She's the best."

The bottle came to Joe. It was the MacAllan Scotch, he saw, a fine brand. Joe was a beer drinker by nature, and that not often. But the Scotch tasted absolutely perfect after the seared beef and the hot sweet corn. He gave the bottle to Eileen, who took a small mouthful. She was sitting next to him on one of the sleeping pads, cross-legged. The diamond he'd given her glittered fabulously in the firelight, like a star set on her hand instead of the sky. She swallowed and handed the bottle to Nolan.

"Tracy?" Paul asked. Joe understood that Howie's set-up had been both kind and generous. A retelling of an ancient legend was much better than talking about Beryl Penrose and whether or not she, a murderer, was already a victim of the other killers who walked the Wyoming night. Or Richard King, the sheriff who hadn't listened to them and who was now dead forever. Stories were better right now. Stories, like sleep and food, were a way to deal with what had gone so terribly wrong.

"All right," Tracy said. "Doug, when you're done with that you can pass the bottle right back down the line." Doug, who was at the end of the semicircle of people around the fire, nodded and raised the Scotch, the level of which was dropping rapidly in the bottle. The bulk of the rock outcropping jutted over the fire, protecting it but also preventing Doug from passing the bottle back to Howie. Doug returned the bottle to Nolan and Mark, both of whom floated like disembodied faces in the dark. They'd cleaned their faces and hands for supper but the rest of their bodies were still camouflaged.

"Here's my story of Mateo Tepee, or Bad Place. I can tell this true story because my grandmother was a native. She was Lakota Sioux and Kiowa and she told it to me."

"Really?" Joe whispered into Eileen's hair.

"Really," Eileen whispered back. She was not Tracy's blood daughter but she looked every inch her mother's child, cross-legged and slender and strong as a strung bow. She reached out and put her hand on his calf. Her hand was warm and gentle, and he felt like pulling her into the darkness and making love to her immediately. He put his hand over hers, instead, and listened to Tracy's story.

"Many thousands of years ago a group of seven maidens were gathering summer berries here. You may have heard that they were attacked by a bear, but no, this is not so. This place has been a bad place since the earth was born. Some places are like this, always dark and evil. Some places are strong and good. This place, even before the Tepee appeared, was bad."

Tracy looked around the fire. She was cross-legged like her daughter, and the light smoothed the planes and lines of her face and made her look ageless. Her dark eyes sparkled but her mouth was straight and firm. Joe's elbow was nudged and he accepted the bottle from Nolan. A second mouthful of Scotch would be enough, he decided. He passed the bottle to Eileen, who passed it without drinking again.

"The story that Richard Dodge heard was a legend of seven maidens and an enormous bear. He understood and repeated only part of the story. The seven maidens were not alone, you see. Their brother, who was gathering berries with them, fell down and began to growl and foam and grow long hair."

"A werewolf?" Mark asked.

"Le Loup Garou?" Tracy asked. "The French called the werewolf Le Loup Garou. But the Europeans only knew a tiny fraction of what we call the manitou."

"Manitou," Howie said dreamily, stretched out in his armchair. "What's a manitou?"

"Some say it is a shape-changer," Tracy said. "A manitou can take a shape; a bear, a wolf, a mountain lion. The wind. The rocks. Or a man. Some manitou are always evil, always searching, always killing."

"Their brother was a manitou?" Jorie asked. Her eyes had lost their dulled, shocked look. Tracy's story had captured her, too.

"Perhaps," Tracy said with a raised eyebrow. "Perhaps not. Perhaps the manitou had been captured, bound to the rocks or the trees, and the brother was somehow – open. A portal that the manitou could use. So the boy became more than a bear."

"A were bear," Ted said. Joe saw that Ted's arm was around Lucy. Beyond them he could see the tiny lump that was Hank, asleep in a camping bag. Two glowing green eyes by Hank's sleeping bag was Zilla, alert and on guard, sitting by Hank's side. Zilla's eyes blinked at Joe; she knew he was looking at her.

"A manitou," Tracy said. "More terrible than we can imagine. The seven maidens ran through the bushes, the thorns catching at their clothes and tearing their skin, and the manitou came after them. They knew they wouldn't escape and they refused to scatter. Some might survive if they separated, but certainly the manitou would get one or more. The sisters wouldn't leave each other. So they scrambled to the top of an enormous tree stump, the remnant of a forest giant that had fallen at last to the ground. There they stopped, exhausted, bleeding, with no more running left in them. They prayed for a quick death, these girls. They didn't pray for help, because that is not our way. They prayed that they would all be taken, and that it would be over soon. And behind them, crashing through the brush, came the manitou, the gigantic thing that used to be their brother but was now much more than a bear."

"Oh, no," Lucy whispered.

"And then the Great Spirit touched the trunk of this giant tree. My grandmother said that the tree was good, as good things can grow in bad places. That the only goodness in the entire forest was the remnant of this gigantic oak, a place where the manitou could not reach with his blank face and hungry claws. And the tree trunk began to grow, and turned into stone, and continued to grow until it was a great monolith in the sky."

"Devils Tower," Mark said.

"Mateo Tepee," Tracy corrected. "The American scout, Richard Dodge, got it all wrong. The evil isn't the Tower; the evil is what surrounds the Tower. If they'd understood the legend they would have called it God's Tower, not the Devils Tower. But they understood what they felt when they were here, when they saw the Tower in the sky."

"They felt uneasy," Lucy said. "Very strange."

"Yes," Tracy said with a sly smile. "But do you feel strange looking at the Tower, or do you feel strange because of *where you are standing?*"

There was a long silence, broken only by the crackling of the fire.

"Oh, that's terrific!" Howie laughed. He held the bottle again, diminished to an inch at the bottom. He upended the bottle and finished it off, then carefully replaced the cork seal and put the bottle back in his pack. "Now we know the real story, don't we? So were the maidens saved?"

"The story you'll hear says that the maidens were taken into the sky, to become the Pleiades constellation," Tracy said. "A group of seven stars. That, too, is not the real truth as we know it to be. Their tribes people rescued the maidens when the manitou had gone back into the earth again. Or how else would their story be known? The truth is, after the girls were back with their tribe they saw the stars appear above the Tower, and realized the Great Spirit had set them there to remind them of His greatness and His mercy."

"The Great Spirit sounds a lot like God to me," Lucy said.

"To me, too," Tracy replied. "And considering where we are, I think a prayer to our God sounds just right." She smiled at Lucy and held her hands out. Paul took her hand immediately. Jorie took a moment to figure out what Tracy wanted, but then she took Tracy's hand. They joined hands, not a circle but a semi-circle, and Tracy bowed her head. Joe bowed his head, his left hand holding Lucy Giometti's hand and his right holding Eileen's.

"Great Spirit," Tracy said, "God the father, as you are to every people on earth, protect us from the evil that walks the earth this night. Help us to safety. Take our brother, Richard King, into your heavenly embrace. Help our friend and sister, Beryl, see a way back to your light and salvation. Amen."

"Amen," Joe said, and heard the whisper from all sides. Tracy's switch from Lakota wise woman to Christian was so abrupt his head spun. There was something in her words that reminded him of Sully in the clouds, Sully with her laser-spear and her laugh. His vision, or dream, of Sully seemed to fit into Tracy's world more than the one he thought he lived in. A God who would make an enormous stone Tower to save a group of frightened girls seemed more like the God that Sully fought for than the vague, white-haired old guy image that he'd imagined in Sunday school.

"So what happened to the brother, Bre'r Were-bear?" Howie asked, after they'd dropped hands. Jorie's head was still bowed. She was obviously struggling with tears.

"That's the unhappy part of the story," Tracy said. "A manitou never leaves a victim alive. The manitou had to go back to earth because it destroys its victim unless it feeds. That's the legend. That's the way we look at the Mateo Tepee."

"What a story," Lucy said.

"Yeah, but the three-quarters of me that's Minnesota Swede says, well, I'm not *sure* about that, dontcha know," Tracy said, adopting a perfect singsong Minnesota accent. "But we Swedes don't have great ghost stories, so I have to use my Lakota grandmother when we're telling stories around the fire."

"A ghost Lutefisk?" Nolan suggested. "An evil Swedish meatball?"

"Off to bed, everyone," Paul said. "I'm going to put out the fire after everyone brushes his teeth and washes up. Sleep in your clothes, I'm afraid. We'll get fresh things tomorrow after this is trip is over."

"I'm being sent to bed," grumped Howie, as relaxed as a cat in his canvas chair. "I want to stay up and listen to ghost stories."

"We need to be well-rested and ready tomorrow," Paul said. His face was quietly stern as he looked around the campfire. "We don't know what we'll be called upon to do."

Joe felt a shiver at the words. Would Rene go home, now that he'd been thwarted not once or twice, but three times? Joe had escaped from Rene's killing jar in the ditches outside Schriever Air Force Base. He'd taken Ted Giometti from under Rene's nose, and Ted had taken Rene's wallet with him. Finally, Sheriff Richard King had disrupted Rene's plans to use Doug, the Schwan's deliveryman, and given his own life in Doug's escape. Somehow Joe didn't think Rene was going to give up. He didn't think so at all.

"We'll take the three o'clock watch, is that okay?" Eileen murmured to him.

"Of course," Joe said. "I was hoping Paul would set watches."

"Then we'll sit up together," Eileen said. "Thanks for taking the worst watch with me."

"For better or worse," Joe said, and he meant the words to be light and teasing and they were not. There was a meaning in there that he hadn't intended, something far too complex for a camp full of people brushing by them on their way to settle down for sleep. Eileen nodded, understanding what Joe was not trying to say.

"For better or worse," she whispered so quietly only he could hear.

CHAPTER TWENTY-ONE

First Watch, Devils Tower, Wyoming

"This is absolutely crazy, you know," Jimmy said quietly to Howie. Howie had propped his bow next to the rocky outcropping. He'd removed the top from his quiver and the razor-edged arrows glimmered in the firelight. He was checking the arrows one by one, examining the feather fletching that made the arrow fly straight and true. The tips, equipped with four angled razor blades, were sharp enough to cut paper. Howie could put an arrow through a whitetail deer at thirty yards. He was better with arrows than firearms, though he'd accepted Paul's .45 revolver.

"Worse than that uprising in Zimbabwe?" Howie said idly, turning the arrow in his hands. He kept an eye on Zilla, who'd been led to his side by Paul. Now Zilla sat quietly at his feet, eyes closed, nose twitching occasionally. Howie had great respect for Zilla's ability after seeing her detect the blood splashed on Doug's uniform shirt. She'd smelled the blood at a distance, and with the bloody shirt inside of Doug's Schwan's truck, no less.

"They weren't after us in Zimbabwe," Jimmy noted. "They were happy to see us get the hell out. We were just sportsmen in the middle of an uprising. They didn't care about us. These two guys are wiping out everyone in their path. They mean business."

"They do," Howie said. "Killing a sheriff isn't regarded too highly in Wyoming, I hear."

"I just mean—"

"I know what you mean," Howie said gently. He replaced the arrow and picked up the next one. He'd never shot a man with an arrow. He didn't want to. But if Joe's serial killers appeared out of the darkness he'd have one shot, maybe, to save their lives. He was better with arrows than he was with bullets. He'd have to shoot perfectly, and at once, or they would all die. Arrows were what Howie knew, so arrows it would be. "We'll be fine, Jimmy, you know that. Stop worrying, brother."

"Not possible," Jimmy said. "But I'll stop telling you how worried I am."

Second Watch, Devils Tower, Wyoming

"I knew she'd packed Pop-Tarts," Mark said happily. "See? A little smashed but they're okay."

"Excellent," Nolan said. "Hand one over."

They sat in the chairs vacated by Howie and Jimmy and munched on strawberry Pop-Tarts. Zilla slept at Nolan's feet now, her nose on her one front paw. Nolan caressed her head absently, his other hand full of crumbly pastry. They talked softly so their voices would be hidden in the crackle of the fire and the sighing of the night wind through the pine trees. Nolan hadn't slept well before his watch. Now he felt totally awake, totally alive, every inch of him aware of every windblown star and shift of pine tree. He thought he could even hear the slow steady sound of the horses, shifting and creaking the leather bands that held them within the dark meadow.

"I have to tell you, man," Mark said eventually, after wolfing down his pastry and taking a deep drink of water. "I've never had a better time in my life. I know that's kind of sick, what with the archaeologist guy and the sheriff and all, but —"

"I know what you mean," Nolan said. He peered into the darkness and counted the sleeping humps in the bags. Everyone was there, and every bag was still. Above them the stars packed the sky, so thickly he could see the frosty glitter of the Milky Way. The night was growing colder as the thin air gave up the heat of the day.

The fire felt good on Nolan's face. "It's like we were dropped into the middle of somebody else's adventure."

"Just as long as we're not the guys in the red shirts," Mark said.

"What's that?" Nolan asked.

"Red shirts. You know, Star Trek. The new crewmember in the red shirt was always the one sent behind the rock to investigate the strange sound. Then gachh – no more crewmember."

"Oh, yeah," Nolan said. "You're a software geek; you're required to be a Trekkie, right? They plant some sort of electrodes in your brain during one of those classes down in the dungeons?"

"That's a closely guarded secret," Mark said. He crumpled the Pop-Tart wrapper and threw it into the fire. It unfolded into flame, blossoming for a few seconds and then abruptly collapsed into ashes. "So are we red shirts, or not? And what's with you and that girl, anyway?"

"Nothing, yet," Nolan said gloomily, poking at the fire with a stick. "She won't talk to me. She's pretty upset right now."

"But we know one thing," Mark said with a grin that was simultaneously shy and wicked.

"I know what Beryl said," Nolan nodded. "My dad's a movie producer. That's why I know Howie. I've known him since I was a kid. There are lots of every type in Hollywood. I thought I had a chance with her the moment I met her. But now, well...."

"Well what?" Mark said. He took a drink from his water bottle and raised his eyebrows at Nolan.

"I think I might be in love with her," Nolan said miserably. "I've never felt like this before."

There was a long silence, broken only by the crackling of the fire and the soft sound of the wind in the trees.

"Sorry, man," Mark said eventually, in what sounded like real sympathy. "I don't think she likes you much. I don't think she likes anybody very much, really."

"Maybe I can change that," Nolan said. "I'm still starving. Is there anything else in there?"

Third Watch, Devils Tower, Wyoming

"Coffee, love," Eileen said, handing Joe a cup. She'd fumbled with the Coleman stove but she didn't have to dig through the saddlebags to find coffee. Tracy had set up the coffee pot before she'd gone to bed. The smell of the coffee, hot and fresh, was enough to wake her up. It was the grave of the morning, three o'clock.

"Thanks," Joe said, taking the cup from her hands. Zilla was with Joe now. He was petting her and rubbing her ears. Nolan and Mark had stumbled off to bed, red-eyed and grateful their watch was over. The firewood was getting a bit low, but it would last until dawn. When Paul and Tracy took the watch from Joe and Eileen they would have a two-hour nap while her parents set up breakfast. Even if there were serial killers after them, Paul and Tracy would have an enormous pancake and sausage breakfast for everyone, with lots of hot coffee to revive them.

There was a late moon in the sky, dim and thin, that silvered the tops of the pines. A thin milky haze covered the stars. Eileen sat in the canvas chair next to Joe and sipped her cup, feeling a glorious rush of hot caffeine through her. The hardest part about a three o'clock watch was getting out of the warm depths of her sleeping bag. That was always the worst. Now that she was up, she felt like tackling the world.

"Nolan said their watch was fine. He said Howie reported no problems either," Joe said.

"I wouldn't expect Rene to come into these woods. He's a city type," Eileen said confidently. "I don't know what he'll try, but being Daniel Boone isn't one of them."

"I think so, too," Joe said. "I'm trying to figure out if I'm feeling uneasy because I'm worried about Rene or if I'm still spooked by your mom's story about Devils Tower."

"She's good, isn't she?" Eileen grinned, curling up in her chair. "She tells stories in such a quiet, reasonable way that you don't realize until much later that she's got you spooked to death."

"That's the real legend?"

"That's the legend," Eileen said. "I've never been on top of the Tower. I heard that it's beautiful up there, that you can see for hundreds of miles. But I've never been into climbing and rappelling, so unless they bolt a ladder on the damn thing, I'll never go."

"I don't know how you could climb it. It wouldn't feel right," Joe said.

Eileen thought of the immensity of the structure, how it looked as though it had just been unzipped from the earth and resented it.

"It looks as though it might just shrug you off while you're halfway up," Joe added.

"Exactly!" Eileen said. "I know Lucy feels that way. It's strange. I've been to the Tower a lot, and every time I'm there I hear tourists talking about how disappointed they are. They're always saying something like 'I really wanted to see this, but now that I'm here I'm kind of disappointed.' Or they say 'I don't like it, somehow. It just isn't what I expected.' Eventually I realized that these people were all saying the same thing: 'I'm nervous. I'm afraid.'"

"They feel it, even if they don't know what they're feeling."

"Right. That's why I was going to take you to the Native American ceremony tomorrow. The natives want us to leave the Tower alone not because they want to keep it for themselves, but because they want to keep the manitou away. That's why you'll see prayer bundles along the paths. They're for protection."

"You just sent a shiver up my spine," Joe said. "And the climbers just want to climb it, right? Because it's a big damn rock, and it's there?"

"Well, if what the Lakota say is true, and the only good and true place in this area is the top of the Tower, what do you think it feels like to climb up and out of evil and into pure goodness?" Eileen asked.

"Oh," Joe said.

"Exactly."

There was silence between them as Joe got up to put more wood on the campfire and Eileen refilled their coffee cups. When they were seated again Eileen held her hand out and Joe took it. They sat together, not talking, as the flames consumed the new wood and the night grew colder around them. The dawn was rushing over the earth, the daylight that would launch them into a new day. She didn't know what would happen, but she knew she was ready to face it.

"I love you," Joe said in a low voice, not looking at her.

"I love you," Eileen said. "Remember when I told you I loved you, in the hospital where my dad was in the operating room and we didn't know if he would live or die?"

"I remember."

"Before then, I ran away from you to try and solve my problem. Now, we stand together. Nobody runs."

"Nobody runs," Joe said, and twined his fingers through hers. "For better or worse."

Morning, Devils Tower, Wyoming

"Mama," someone said, patting her cheeks. Lucy struggled awake and opened her eyes to see Hank, barely an inch away, holding her face in his little hands.

"Hi, Hank," she said groggily.

"Mama awake," he said happily, and jumped on top of her.

"Hank," Eileen said, laughing. "Let go of your mom. She needs to go potty, I imagine. Jumping on her like that isn't going to help."

"No, it doesn't," Lucy said. "Is it morning?"

"It's morning. Dawn is about a half hour away, so you can go pee in the dark if you're quick about it."

Lucy sat up quickly and then groaned. Her bottom and legs felt as though she'd run a marathon. "I'm so stiff!"

"Horseback riding," Eileen said with a shrug. "Best if you get up and hobble around. You'll warm up."

Lucy pulled on her dirty jeans from yesterday, trying not to grimace, and quickly slipped on her socks and shoes. Luckily she'd brought sturdy walking shoes and they were holding up well.

"I'll hang on to Hank. Coffee when you get back," Eileen's voice floated after her. Then she heard Eileen speaking quietly to Jorie. Eileen was getting all the women up first, so they could comb their hair and pee in the woods in peace, before the men got up. Damn men, Lucy thought crossly, crouching in the bushes and trying not to splatter her shoes. There was something wrong with a world where men could pee standing up, writing their names and everything, and women had to squat like setter dogs.

She felt much more cheerful with a steaming hot cup of coffee in her, a comb run through her curly hair and with a warm washcloth to clean her face and hands. By this time Eileen was waking up the men. Jorie was neat and clean. She was wearing fresh clothes. She had her pack with her and hadn't left it behind. She'd carried it all day yesterday too, without complaint. She sat quietly next to Lucy and drank a cup of coffee. Paul and Tracy were busy with sausage and eggs and pancakes.

"Can you eat pancakes?" Lucy asked curiously. She was sitting on a sleeping pad struggling with a diaper, Hank, and his clothes. He was at the age when diapering was a major wrestling match, but he was so intrigued with a pine cone he'd found that his struggles were half-hearted.

"I'm a vegan," Jorie said with some of her old waspish bite. "I won't eat eggs or milk."

"No milk?" Lucy asked, smiling as Hank's face popped out of his shirt. He grinned at her.

"I think milking cows is cruel," Jorie said loftily. She sipped her coffee.

"As a former milk producing mammal," Lucy said, tickling Hank's toes, "I have to tell you I loved making milk and giving milk. It feels *wonderful*. Don't you think cows feel that way, too?"

Jorie looked at her blankly and Lucy grinned up at her. "I just can't imagine going through life without chocolate chip cookies and a big glass of milk."

"Cookie?" Hank said.

"Breakfast, no cookie," Lucy said. "Pancakes, too, Hank! Now hold still while I put your sock on."

Ted kissed her behind the ear, a very prickly one. She turned and kissed his lips, which weren't prickly at all.

"Hi, love. Hi, Hank," Ted said.

"Daddy!" Hank squealed.

"Breakfast," Paul said.

They ate around the campfire, now a few ash-covered coals, and the food was hot and very good. Ted, his black beard and wildly curly hair making him look more like a mountain man than ever, ate ravenously. They all did, even Hank. Jorie, who subsisted once again on an energy bar, used her finger to poke all the crumbs from the wrapper and then unselfconsciously turned the wrapper inside out and licked it clean.

"All right, everyone, clean up and pack up. We need volunteers to get the horses, and then we'll be on our way," Paul said. "First, I want —"

His voice broke off and Lucy, who'd been trying to get Hank to eat the last bite of his sausage link, turned to look at him. Silence fell over the camp. Zilla was standing stiffly, eyes to the north, tail quivering. Lucy had seen Zilla do that once before, when she'd pointed to the crystal skull that Jon McBride had hidden before he died.

Howie reached behind him and in one seamless movement had an arrow to a fearsome compound bow. Paul put his hand on his revolver strapped to his hip, and as Lucy blinked she saw Eileen's black gun appear in her fist. No one else had time to do more than draw a breath.

A bush full of berries crackled and was pushed aside by something huge, a dark shape that wasn't a man; it was bigger than any man could ever be. Lucy thought with a falling sensation of the manitou, the enormous bear that wasn't a bear. She swept Hank up into her arms and stood, trembling head to foot, as the bushes parted.

An elk bounded into the clearing. The elk had an enormous set of antlers. They were thick and furry looking, and Lucy remembered reading how elk and deer grew their antlers all summer, shrouded in thick velvet, and had to rub the velvet from their antlers in the fall. This elk was in velvet, then. It stood like a forest king, head up, large carved nostrils wet and black as it snuffed and snorted. The chest of the elk was a dark brown and the enormous hindquarters were a soft and lovely beige. The delicate looking legs were dark brown too, thin and beautiful like a showgirl's legs. The elk put its nose in the air and the enormous rack of antlers dropped to the elk's back. It leaped across the clearing in one gigantic bound and then it was gone, crashing into the underbrush. Lucy could smell the elk as it passed her, a musky wild odor that filled her nose and made her feel as if she couldn't breathe.

The clearing was totally silent. Howie let his bow down and the creaking of the bow's wheels was clearly audible. He put his arrow back in his quiver with mildly shaking hands.

"That was a seven point bull," he said conversationally. "I've never seen a bigger bull in my life. And he wasn't even out of velvet yet."

"Wasn't he beautiful?" Lucy asked. She realized her voice was trembling. "Wasn't he beautiful?"

"If that's what this forest holds, Paul, then I'm—" Howie started, when Paul held up his hand. His entire body was concentrated to the north, where the elk had come from.

"What is it?" Tracy asked, as everyone fell silent once again.

Paul dropped his hand and turned around. His face was pinched and white and, for the first time since Lucy had met him, he looked deathly afraid.

"*Fire*," he said.

CHAPTER TWENTY-TWO

Devils Tower Junction, Wyoming

Rene watched with satisfaction as the first State Patrol car screamed by, siren blaring. He was parked just north of Devils Tower Junction, a ridiculously small town that existed solely to sell T-shirts and souvenirs to Tower visitors. He'd studied his Wyoming map until he figured out where to set the fire and where to park and wait for his prey to run out of the woods. He had never taken an interest in hunting but he'd gone on a couple of pheasant hunts in France once. The beaters interested him, the way that the men and boys walked the woods and made noise until the frantic animals leaped from their hiding places and ran into the guns of the hunters. He'd used the concept several times since then, but never in an actual wilderness.

And this was a wilderness, he realized. The cooler in the trunk was almost empty and the gas was starting to dip below the halfway mark. He had to have the air-conditioning or he'd go absolutely insane. There were mosquitoes outside, and biting flies. He'd gotten bitten several times while he was setting up Ken's body and starting the fire. The thief who'd stolen his wallet had stolen all his money. He had to have it back or he'd be forced to actually knock off a store or gas station, something he'd never lowered himself to do. He was a contract man, not a common robber, and he had respect for businessmen.

His setup was good. He'd wait while the fire swept down from the north and as the tourists and the Park Rangers ran, he'd wait. Then when his fire flushed Joe Tanner and his friends out of their ranch, Rene would be ready. Though he would regret shooting the detective first, he knew she would have to be the first to go. She would be armed, and capable, and thus too dangerous to keep alive. Once she was taken out the rest would be like panicked animals.

Joe Tanner would be last, Rene promised himself. Tanner was the cause of all of this. Rene was sweaty and dirty. He'd been in the same clothes for two days, and he hadn't had a decent meal. His wallet was gone with his father's picture inside. Ken was gone, too. Everything had been stripped from Rene. He felt odd, disconnected, as though he were in some sort of new dimension that wasn't exactly the earth he'd always known.

A fire engine with "Sundance" printed along the side roared north, men hanging from the sides and back in hastily donned fire uniforms. They looked pale and wide-eyed, even at a distance. Rene checked his map and nodded in satisfaction. The Hulett fire department, if they had one, had discovered that the fire was too large to contain and had called for help. They'd find the fire impossible to stop.

The sheriff's car had been full of gas and Rene had siphoned and then splashed it along a quarter mile of woods before he'd set the vehicle on fire. He'd put the hose he'd used to siphon the gas in Ken's hand. The fire investigation would reveal Ken's body and the arson equipment in Ken's hand, if the fire didn't turn the whole scene into ashes. Rene had set a warehouse on fire once. He knew the drill with gasoline and making sure there was a clear exit before lighting the match.

The fiercely burning sheriff's car had made a curious popping noise as Rene had driven away, after making sure the fire would spread. Rene didn't know anything about setting fires in the forest, really, but how different could a forest fire be?

Now the second Park Ranger truck roared up the road, this time turning into the Devils Tower highway. It thundered past Rene's hiding place, a small turnout that held a parking spot behind part of the crumbling bluffs that dotted the landscape. Rene supposed it was a camping spot for people who didn't want to pay the fee to enter the national monument. If a Ranger checked it while evacuating the tourists, another cop would die. Rene didn't care. He had enough ammunition in his bag to take care of a dozen cops and Joe Tanner's friends, too.

Rene checked his Glock. It was a nice weapon, small and deadly, and he itched to make use of it. He settled back into his seat and let the cold air from the vents blow across his face. It wouldn't be long now.

Devils Tower, Wyoming

"Dad," Eileen said. She stepped close to him. She took his hands in hers and looked into his eyes. "You know what to do. It's hard, but it's okay. We don't have time for anything else."

Paul looked at her and squeezed her hands. For a moment they were alone, the two of them, father and daughter. He was so capable, so intelligent, and he was frantically looking for a solution that would save them all. Eileen knew instantly that this was impossible. There were thirteen people and only five horses.

"They can bring back help?" he whispered.

"They can make a Park Ranger stay, with a truck," Eileen said. Paul's eyes instantly relaxed and his shoulders dropped.

"Of course," he said. He turned away from her. The remains of breakfast lay scattered on the pine needles, where all of them had dropped their plates and forks. Eileen could see her mother eyeing the mess with a distracted air. Tracy never littered. Howie stood, relaxed and alert, while Jimmy worked his hands into fists again and again. Eileen wondered if Jorie realized that Nolan was standing next to her. Her face was shocked, but she seemed calm and her color was good. Mark Plutt and Doug, the Schwan's man, stood next to Nolan, their faces mirrors of dismay.

"Rene set the fire," Joe said flatly. "He figured he couldn't find us, so he'll just smoke us out."

"We'll worry about that later," Paul said. "I'm going to send Howie, Jimmy, Mark and Nolan out on the horses. Doug, I'm going to send you ahead on Brumby."

"Doug?" Eileen asked. "On Brumby?"

"Hush, Eileen," Paul snapped. "Doug's the best rider in the county. He can ride Brumby ahead to the Ranger Station. Have them keep a truck behind for us, when they evacuate. The rest of us will hurry as fast as we can to the Tower, then down to Devils Junction and the highway."

"You're asking us to abandon you?" Howie said incredulously.

"I'm asking you to go for help," Paul said patiently. "We won't get there in time to tell the Rangers that there are people who need help. You can. Don't argue or we'll all die."

Eileen could smell smoke in the air, though the sky remained blue and blameless. The elk hadn't been the only visitor, either. As Paul spoke, a brace of rabbits ran through the clearing, ears erect and bottoms thumping up and down. The forest was alive with tiny, unseen movement. The animals were clearing out.

"I'm not going. Send Jorie out," Nolan said calmly.

"I can't ride a horse," Jorie snapped. "I don't know how."

"Then I'll stay," he said implacably. Jorie stared at him, hands curling into fists, then abruptly turned away and picked up her pack.

"Eileen," Paul started, and Eileen held up her hand.

"No, Dad," she said. "I have to stay with Joe. I'm the only one trained to take on Rene."

"I'll go," Tracy said. She stepped towards Lucy and held out her hand. "I'm the only one besides Eileen who can ride with a child. Will you let me take him?"

Lucy stood, Hank on her hip, staring at Tracy. Her face filled slowly with horrified dismay. Eileen knew what Lucy finally understood. The ones left behind might not make it out. Tracy was giving Lucy a chance to save her son.

"Of course," Lucy said, obviously forcing her face and voice to smoothness. "Hank, you get to take another horsy ride."

"Saddle up," Paul said, and there was a scramble for the horses. Within minutes the five horses were saddled. Doug saddled Brumby himself and vaulted to the back of the huge brown horse with an athletic grace that made Eileen blink in astonishment. Brumby tried to bite Doug in the leg and Doug kneed the horse in the head and yanked hard on the bit. Brumby reared once and then settled down, ears twitching.

Paul stood at Brumby's head, holding the bridle. He was erect as a soldier, his face turned up to the younger man. Doug looked down at him, his face set, his mouth a thin, determined line.

"Run Brumby, Doug. Run him all the way out, if you have to." Paul dropped the reins and gave Brumby a heavy blow to the hindquarters. Brumby launched like an arrow towards the trees. Doug crouched over his back, urging him forward, and they disappeared into the trees. For a moment there was the thudding of hooves and then there was silence.

Paul turned to Tracy and took her in his arms. Eileen looked away as Paul kissed Tracy with the passion he never showed in public, cupping her face in his hands with the care of a man holding a priceless treasure. When she looked back, Tracy was already wrapping a blanket across her chest, tying it in the back in an ungainly, sturdy knot. Lucy kissed Hank tenderly and handed him to Ted, who kissed him on the forehead and handed him up to Tracy, who'd mounted Starlight. Tracy, her face white and set, took the little boy and snuggled him into the blanket. He began to wail as he realized he wasn't going to sit on the saddle, but Tracy's odd sling kept him pressed against the length of her chest.

"We'll get help," she said, and kicked Starlight into motion. Howie and Jimmy followed, then Mark. They disappeared into the trees towards Devils Tower.

Eileen suddenly realized what her father had said to Doug. Doug was going to run Brumby to death to save them. She saw Ted and Lucy standing together, holding hands, looking shocked and lost. Lucy was struggling with tears, lips trembling.

"Let's go, already," Jorie snapped. She had her pack on. "The fire won't even get here for hours yet, I'll bet. Let's go!"

Eileen picked up her own pack and felt the bundle within it. For a moment she considered abandoning her pack and then she decided against it. Jorie was right; they had hours before the fire got there. Probably. Maybe.

"In twos, everyone," Paul said. "Don't stray. Make sure you have a water bottle and don't carry a pack. Eileen. Lose the pack."

"I have to keep it, Dad," she said.

"Drop it if you start falling behind. Let's get moving. Zilla, let's go."

Already the sky was turning white, though Eileen knew the sky would be white miles from the fire. Joe was at her side as she left the clearing. The area was littered with plates and flatware and the saddle packs that had held all the gourmet food and equipment for last night's supper and this morning's breakfast. Earlier, Paul had buried and drowned the fire and neatly set the grill within the rock ring, which struck Eileen as almost funny. She spotted the coffee pot, an enameled metal pot that had seen her through her own childhood, and felt something she refused to name. She tightened her pack and followed Lucy and Ted through the trees.

When they scrambled up the last ridge and saw the well-worn path in front of them, Howie whooped breathlessly. Pirate, nearly done in, shook his mane and managed a trot as they followed the trail towards the Visitors Center. Devils Tower, so close they were literally within its shadow, was wreathed in smoke.

Howie had been to the Visitors Center with Paul just two days ago. It seemed like another life. Two days ago the road and the parking lots were jammed with people and vehicles. Now the parking lot was eerily silent, empty except for a single ancient Subaru that squatted like an abandoned dog at the end of the lot.

"Doug. Brumby," Tracy gasped. Hank had finally fallen silent in the wrapped blanket around her chest. He had wailed and screamed, calling for his parents, then fell quiet. Tracy, fighting a toddler and guiding the horses along the trail, was exhausted. Her hair was sweat-soaked and clung to her forehead and neck. Her eyes were dark holes in her face and her mouth was open in a gasping sob.

Howie looked to where she was pointing and whooped again. Brumby, lathered from withers to rump in white foam, but alive, was tied up at the Visitors Center, and there was a truck there. A big one, some kind of utility truck with a crew cab. It was painted the horrible pale green of the Forest Service, and it was the most beautiful thing Howie had ever seen.

Doug came out of the Visitors Center with a Park Ranger

at his side. The Ranger was old, slender as a cane, with a head of white hair and an enormous mustache that made him look like Mark Twain. The ranger looked at them and waved as they trotted up.

"Paul Reed? Still back in the woods, Tracy?"

"Yes, Don," Tracy wheezed. "Help. Truck."

"Got all that," Don the Park Ranger said with a tense smile. "Afraid I have another worry on my mind right now."

"What's that?" Howie asked sharply.

"Look for yourself," Don said, and waved his hand at the Tower. Howie turned to look and saw nothing.

"Oh, no," Mark said. "On the Tower, Howie. Not in front of it. On the Tower."

There were four climbers on the Tower, bright specks of red, yellow, green and purple, like crayons spilled from a box. They were working their way down, rappelling down the enormous stone columns, but they were still a third of the way from the bottom.

"Oh, shit," Howie said tiredly.

"That's not all," Doug said. "The Lakota here have refused to go, too."

"Four Native Americans, one for each of the climbers. Some ceremony of theirs. They won't leave until the climbers leave. So that's eight people, plus me, plus your seven. Too many for my truck."

"Then we'll ride the horses to the Junction and have them send another truck," Tracy said.

"You'll have to ride to the Junction, anyway," Don said. "I'm the only one left and I need to make sure we get these people out."

"They can fit in your truck," Doug said, mounting Brumby with quick, economical grace. Brumby looked as wicked as ever, despite the sweat and foam that drenched his sides. "They can squash into the back and in the cab. Just wait for them, please, Don."

"I won't leave Paul Reed," Don said to Tracy. "I'll wait until there's no hope, Miz Reed. And if I know Paul, he'll bring them out. And I do."

"You'll probably pass us on the road," Doug said cheerfully.

"Come on, you guys, the Junction is only a few miles away and it's all downhill. They've got helicopters coming in, and Hot Shot firefighters from Montana. They'll have this fire licked by night-fall."

Howie looked back at the Tower as they walked the tired horses down the road. Tracy insisted they walk, giving the horses a chance to regain their wind. The stone column was layered in smoke, more of it now. The top of the Tower was in the clear sky and Howie remembered Tracy's story. There was something else, too, that the sight of the Tower was telling him. Something that resonated with their own situation, about being hunted....

They were nearly a quarter of the way down the long, curving road when he remembered, suddenly, what was nudging at the back of his mind. He kicked Pirate into a gallop and shouted at Doug, who was leading the way on Brumby.

"Yeah?" Doug said, pulling up Brumby. "We can't stop, Mr. Magnus, we have to go."

"The guy," Howie said, hating how out-of-breath he sounded. Well, he wouldn't see eighteen again. "The guy who tried to kill you. Why did he set the fire?"

By this time the rest of the group had closed in, stopping their horses and listening. Starlight, Tracy's horse, had enough energy to prance nervously. Horses hated fire and Starlight didn't want to stop. Fair enough; Howie didn't want to stop either.

"To kill us," Mark said.

"*To drive us out of the woods*," Howie said. "So he can kill us."

"Oh, shit," Doug said, at the same time as Jimmy.

"Get us off this road, Tracy," Jimmy said. "Can you get us to the Junction off road?"

"I can," Doug said. He looked furious. "I can't believe I didn't think of that. I can't believe—"

"No time," Tracy said. "Doug, lead us. Howie, can you fire an arrow from horseback?"

"Yes," Howie said. He'd kept his bow and quiver and they hung, ready for use, at his side.

"Mark?"

"I don't think so," Mark said. "I'm not—"

"Then take this," Tracy said, producing Paul's .45 from her

saddlebag. "I can't hang onto Hank and a gun, too."

Mark took the gun and put it awkwardly into his belt. Howie wondered if he'd have the courage to use it, if the time came. Doug urged a reluctant Brumby off the road and into the thick underbrush. Howie kicked Pirate in the ribs and they, too, left the comfortable road. A branch lashed across Howie's face and he felt a sudden, unexpected rage for that man, Rene, and his pal. There would be dead and dying deer, elk and turkey in this forest before the end of the day. People, too, perhaps. All this just to find and kill a single man, to fulfill a contract that probably paid less than what Howie's stocks provided him each quarter. Howie reached back and fingered his bow. If the time came, he wouldn't hesitate, he promised himself. He'd feel worse about stepping on a cockroach than putting an arrow through that worthless creature's chest. In fact, he'd positively enjoy it.

CHAPTER TWENTY-THREE

Devils Tower, Wyoming

"The trail," Paul said. "We're nearly there."

Lucy gasped in relief. A trail! The glimpse of the paved path almost brought tears to her eyes. She blinked them back harshly. There was no time for tears, not yet. She hadn't cried when she gave her son to Tracy and she wasn't going to cry until she had Hank back in her arms, and they were safe. Then she'd weep like a girl in a three-hanky movie. She'd use a *box* of tissues. Then she was going to get stinking drunk and start another baby with Ted. And go visit Mount Rushmore, because they'd missed it yesterday. And then —

"Stop for a minute," Eileen said to her, and Lucy stumbled to a stop on a smooth, paved trail. They were there. Beside her, Ted breathed harshly, hands on his knees and his head down. He was suffering cruelly from altitude sickness but he hadn't stopped, hadn't sat on the ground and refused to move, the way Lucy was afraid he might, or she might. They were at the very base of the Tower, and Lucy could see south as the ground dropped away. She saw a long and lovely vista of woods and grassy meadows. There was a glint of water too. The Belle Fourche River ran through the valley like a slim silvery ribbon, silvery because the sky was gray with smoke.

"How close is the fire?" Nolan asked hoarsely. The smoke

was thick around them but not anywhere near choking. There was no sign of fire either, no crackling sounds or visible flame. Lucy didn't know how forest fires worked, but she suspected that when things got bad they would get very bad very quickly. She'd seen pictures on television of enormous flaming pine trees and exploding ridges of fire. Somewhere behind them, there was flame like that.

"Don't know," Paul said. He didn't seem tired or out-of-breath. Lucy suspected that if she collapsed Paul would simply pick her up and carry her. There was a certain comfort in that. Jorie still carried her pack, mostly empty now. She'd dumped all her clothes and most of her other supplies a while back, leaving them in a neat little pile by a large, crooked tree. She tied a bright orange scarf to a branch of the tree, to mark her cache. Her confidence that she'd have a pile of clothes to return to helped Lucy's attitude, at least for a while.

"The Visitors Center is half a mile from here," Paul said. He was still looking around intently, head up and forward. Zilla, who'd been sitting on Paul's back in a backpack modified for her, raised her head and put her nose in the air.

"Let's go, then," Nolan said, "We should —"

"Wait," Eileen said. She, too, was looking in all directions. Lucy realized what they were doing in a sudden, heart stopping breath. They were looking for Rene, who might have killed the first group and who might now be waiting to ambush her. The image of Hank, her baby, screaming in agony as he died, was suddenly imprinted with ghastly clarity in her mind. She could see every detail, the blood and the bullets and her tiny innocent boy, bewildered and screaming as Rene, laughing, raised his pistol and —

She made a hiccupping sound and put her hands to her mouth.

"We would have heard gunfire," Joe said quickly. Joe, who'd taken turns carrying Zilla and whose face was as pale and wretched as Ted's, patted Lucy on the arm. His damaged eye socket was a yellowish green, in the most garish stage of healing, and the fading bruise reached halfway down his face. The crusted stitches at his forehead had bled again today and were beaded with fresh blood.

He looked like a comic book villain, half handsome Joe Tanner and half sideshow creature. His eyes remained all Joe. "It's okay, Lucy."

"Let's move around the Tower," Paul said. "Quick as you can, now. Be careful."

They moved in twos after Paul. Eileen and Joe followed Paul, Eileen with her hand hovering near her midsection where her gun was holstered and obviously ready for Rene, no matter what Joe said. Lucy saw Jorie and Nolan fall in behind her and Ted, neither of them speaking. Nolan, a far different young man than the pudgy boy Lucy had met just a few days ago, took a drink of water and shifted his bow on his shoulder. He had it bad for Jorie, that was obvious, but Lucy was beginning to think he had something more than a crush. Lucy wondered briefly if Jorie knew what she had in this young man, or if she cared.

Then they made the turn around the Tower and Lucy saw a dusty green truck at the end of a parking lot. An old blue car sat next to it. There was nothing else in the parking lot except for the ranger himself, a thin elderly man with a head full of white hair. He stood waving at them. He had an enormous moustache that sat atop a grin.

"Haaaalllo," he shouted. "Here, Paul!"

Paul waved and took a quick look back at Zilla, who was unconcerned. She was, in fact, staring at the Tower. Lucy followed her gaze and gasped as she saw four brightly clad people moving quickly on ropes down the side of the stone. Rappelling, that's what it was called.

"Look," she said.

"I hope we all fit in the truck," Joe said. "How far are they from the bottom?"

"Minutes," Jorie said. "I've climbed before. They're almost down. They must be setting up their last rappel. I've heard it takes three rappels to get down the Tower. It's over a thousand feet tall."

When Paul stopped next to the park ranger Lucy wanted to let her legs collapse under her. She stood, quivering, feeling that if she fell down she'd never be able to get back on her feet again. The park ranger was standing next to a Forest Service sign that held a map and information about Devils Tower. Beyond him Lucy could see a water fountain and a log building that probably contained a Visitors Center and a set of bathrooms. There was a large, almost empty parking lot, and beyond that a curving road that must lead to the highway, and safety. The ancient blue car was a Subaru. It was crammed full of tents and bags and clothing. The car must belong to the climbers, who were carefully setting up for their last rappel, a few hundred feet above. Lucy wondered what they felt, knowing that a forest fire was raging from the north towards them. They must want to hurry, yet know that hurrying could kill them far more quickly than the fire could.

"Your family is safe, they're down at the Devils Tower Junction," the ranger said, and Lucy gave a lurch to the side as her legs tried to fold under her. "The rangers called from the Junction and said they arrived just a few minutes ago. They said they went cross-country, that's why it took them so long."

"Howie," Eileen said immediately, and with satisfaction. "He knew."

"I bet it was Doug," Joe said.

"They're safe," Paul said. He took a handkerchief out of his pocket and wiped his forehead with trembling fingers. "Thank God. Now, how about us?"

"We're just about ready to go," the ranger said confidently. "As soon as the climbers are down."

"What's that sound?" Lucy said.

There was instant silence and in the silence there was, indeed, a sound. For a moment it was like a great crowd of people talking excitedly. Lucy was reminded of the audience in a theater right before the lights go dim. Then the chattering crowd sound dissolved into a louder tone, something that sounded more like an airplane engine spinning up to takeoff, or a railroad engine charging at a hill.

Paul spun around to the way they'd come, and he did an interesting thing. He cupped both hands over his ears, as though he were trying to make his hands into ears as big as Zilla's. Zilla, on his shoulder, had her ears up and aimed along their back trail.

"It's coming from the northwest," he said. "Everyone, up to the rock fall. Run!"

Lucy, who thought she had no more strength in her, found she had plenty left, after all. She ran, shoulders jostling with Ted, following Nolan and Jorie as they raced to the very bottom of the Tower, along the trail. They broke out of the trees and into an enormous tumble of boulders. The boulders must have fallen from the sides of the Tower itself. They were the size of automobiles and buses and houses. The trail ran through the boulder field. Lucy skidded to one knee and got up running, ignoring the wet stinging from her leg. Her breath sobbed in her throat and she could think of nothing but fleeing from the gigantic sound that was getting louder and louder as they ran.

The roaring thing burst from the northwest and it was the fire. Lucy stopped to look, unable to help herself. A plume of dark gray smoke streamed from two or three miles behind the Tower and then in the valley to the northwest two trees exploded into flame as if they'd been wired with explosives. The plume of dark smoke flickered as though it were alive with tiny yellow eyes. The yellow eyes were burning branches and pinecones and they flew into the air over the peaceful valley. As they settled, the forest bloomed with flame, the dry forest that hadn't seen rain for the whole month of July.

Lucy was transfixed. The sight was the most awful she'd ever seen, and the most awesome. The dark wind brought the flame, invisible until it touched the trees. The trees waved wildly as they gave up their lives, as though screaming silently. Some of the falling sparks, Lucy realized sickly, were birds. Hawks plummeted into the trees, wings on fire. Small birds fell like pebbles and fire burst up from where their burning bodies landed. Within seconds the whole lower half of the valley was on fire.

"The wind's from the east," Paul said from behind her. Lucy turned to see him standing at her shoulder. They were all stopped. She saw that they were standing in a clearing in the boulder field. She blinked, wondering if she was hallucinating. There were four Lakota with them, three men and one woman. They wore feathers in their shiny dark hair and the woman wore a pale dress of deer hide, decorated with beads. The men wore no shirts but had breastplates of some sort of narrow bones stitched together, embroidered with beads and stones, and pants of soft pale hide. One of the men was so old his hair was white, and it hung in two snow-white braids down his wrinkled chest. He was holding a small staff that had bones and feathers hanging from one end.

"The fire cut off the road," the ranger said. "We don't dare risk trying to take the truck because the wind might shift." He took out a small walkie-talkie and clicked it on.

"Larry, this is Don," he said. "We've got a problem, here."

"No shit!" the walkie-talkie burst. "We can see it from here. Are you cut off?"

"We're cut off," Don said. "You have a helicopter coming in?"

"Got one with water on board," Larry said. "Is the eastern part of the Tower still clear?"

"We'll meet the chopper there. Tell him to hurry, Larry."

"Ten-four," Larry said. "God bless."

"Oh, God, look," Joe moaned. Lucy followed his hand and saw a burning deer racing across an open meadow down by the Belle Fourche River. His back and sides were on fire but he still ran, head up, as though he could escape. Lucy could see his velvet antlers, crowned by a wreath of unholy fire, and she turned her eyes away.

"I'll wait for the climbers," Don said calmly. "You folks need to head on over there. Sir," he added, bowing to the Lakota, "I need you to go with Paul Reed, here. Please."

"We will," the younger man said. There was something about him that reminded Lucy of Dave Rosen, Eileen's partner. He had waist length braids and feathers in his hair and a breastplate of bone over his muscled chest, but there was something of Rosen's straight, short-haired, button-down look to his face. The older man said something and moved his staff, which made a rattling, almost musical tone.

"What did he say?" Paul asked.

"He said, we did our best," the young man said.

Devils Tower Junction, Wyoming

The crowd at the Junction shop burst into a long, sustained ahh sound, for all like it was the Fourth of July and the fire at the

Tower was a light show. Howie put his arm around Tracy, who was holding a teary Hank, and he felt her frail shoulders trembling.

"Look at that!" a woman said, her video camera in front of her face. "It looks like a hundred feet of fire up there."

"That's a crown fire," someone else said thoughtfully. "I'm beginning to get seriously concerned here. How did it become a crown fire so quickly?"

"What's a crown fire?" Howie asked the man.

"When the fire gets up off the ground and into the trees," the man said. "That doesn't happen often. Firefighters say when a fire jumps to the crown of the trees you clear the hell out. Which is what I'm going to do." He turned away from Howie and hurried into the crowd, jostling people out of his way.

"People, I need your attention." The booming voice came from the back of the park ranger truck that blocked the road up to the Tower. Unbelievably, the rangers had been busy turning back tourists.

When Doug and Tracy had led the others to the back of the tourist shop Howie had been astonished at the size of the crowd. There must have been thirty cars stopped on the road, and the shop was doing a booming business in soft drinks and ice cream. Tracy, who knew the shop owners, had entered the business through the back entrance. Howie helped Doug scan the crowd while Tracy bought soda pop. She also bought a carton of milk and a package of cookies for Hank. He'd refused them, his face stricken and tearful.

Doug, who was the only one who'd seen the killers, pronounced the crowd free of Rene and his friend. Despite this, Tracy and Howie had been the only ones to leave the back of the shop and approach the park rangers. Larry, the park ranger who was now standing in the back of his pale green truck, was the one who'd radioed Don up at the Tower and told their families that they were safe.

"People, it's time to evacuate this area," Larry shouted. "You need to evacuate south, towards Sundance. I'd appreciate it if you would drive slowly, and pull over if you encounter fire trucks or any sort of rescue or police vehicles. Let's be smart, people. This fire could reach here in twenty minutes, and I want you all gone. Let's go."

"They'll be all right," Howie said, but his heart told him that the people they'd left behind wouldn't be all right. The fire was enormous, stretching across the northern part of the valley. The smoke was already thickening, turning the sun into a pale burnished coin. The smoke did more than Larry to convince the tourists that it was time to get out of the area.

"Miz Reed, we have a fire service helicopter on the way in," Larry said to them, holding the megaphone away from this mouth. "We'll pick up your family and take them to Sundance. You need to be on your way, now."

"What about the horses?" Tracy asked numbly. Howie could see she was nearly at the end of her ability to cope. She couldn't seem to tear away her eyes from the flames at the north end of the valley, flames that were steadily burning their way towards her husband and her daughter.

"I've got that taken care of," Doug said, appearing at their side. He'd had to push his way through the crowd, now moving rapidly in the other direction, away from the fire. "Come on."

Howie walked with Tracy to the back of the tourist shop. There was a huge trailer backing up along the side of the shop. An enormous red truck was attached to the trailer and as it stopped Doug ran around the front of the truck and snatched open the door. A girl with a long and lovely fall of brown hair catapulted out of the truck and into his arms. Howie caught a glimpse of a pretty face swollen and red-eyed with weeping, now full of relief and joy.

"His wife," Howie guessed.

"They live in Sundance. He called her as soon as we got here," Jimmy said. "And she brought a horse trailer. Let's get the hell out of here."

They were at the very end of the line of evacuated vehicles. They fell into line behind an enormous recreational vehicle with Virginia license plates. Doug drove the truck and his wife sat close to him, still wiping away happy tears. Howie thought of his own wife with a sudden, unexpected longing. He wanted nothing more than to be with her, in bed, naked and in the dark, to make love to her and then talk. He'd talk for hours, he thought, until his voice was hoarse and he'd talked all the poison out of him, all the fright and anger. They'd talk until dawn, then sleep until the kids came in and bounced them out of bed. He looked over at Tracy, sitting pale and silent with Hank in her lap, and he looked away. He knew a good marriage when he saw it. He hoped Paul and Tracy Reed's marriage was not at an end.

As they drove down the highway he searched the sky for the helicopter. From horizon to horizon he looked, but all he could see was smoke and the tiny, indifferent coin of the sun.

Devils Tower, Wyoming

"Sorry, man," the first of the climbers said. "We got down as quick as we could." Joe saw that he was a stocky young man, a boy really, with a sun burnt, dirty face. His teeth were very white and his eyes were a startlingly light gray.

"We're in a bit of fix, here," Don said. He was scanning the sky with binoculars, a red smoke flare held ready in his hands. The smoke was thick enough now to be a problem. The wind, which had brought the fire like a roaring jet down on them, had now given them a reprieve. The fire was being swept down the Belle Fourche River valley instead of burning around the Tower, where they all huddled. But it would get to them eventually, yes it would.

"They've got a helicopter coming in," Joe said to the young man. He watched as the other climbers walked down, ropes hung over their shoulders. The Lakota stood impassively, looking into the distance.

"We can't drive out?" the second climber asked. He was short and had a high, girlish voice. All the climbers wore helmets and windbreakers. They were all filthy with dirt and sweat and wore expressions of fading happiness, as though the fire hadn't quite made an impression yet. They were all barely out of their teens.

"Doesn't look like it," Don said shortly. "And I don't think our chances are good if we make a break for it. The best way to survive if we're trapped here is in the boulder field. There's nothing to burn in the boulder field, so the fire should burn right past us."

"That might work," the third climber said in a worried voice. He wore tiny sunglasses and now took them off and polished them with a distracted air. "But if the fire burns too slowly it'll take all the oxygen and we'll suffocate. Better than being burned, I guess, but still —"

"We might not have a choice," Paul said. "If the helicopter doesn't get here soon—"

"I see it," Don said. He struck the flare against the rock and for a moment Joe thought he'd struck it too hard, and broken the tip. Then the flare sputtered into life and Don ran out into the open, grassy meadow to the east of the boulder field. He set the flare on a circular patch of dirt that he and Joe and Nolan had cleared just minutes ago, then moved back.

Joe searched the sky and saw a tiny speck that rapidly grew to an X, then a staggered cross, then the unmistakable shape of an old Huey helicopter. It carried an empty water bladder underneath it from a long line and it was going so fast the bladder, designed to scoop up water from a lake and hold it, was stretched out and fluttering behind the copter.

"Hey, baby, it's good to see you," Joe said under his breath, then coughed shallowly. The smoke was growing worse, turning the day into a hazy, gray dusk. Worse, Joe thought it was getting warmer. A lot warmer. The fire was working its way over to their side of the Tower.

"Paul," Don said.

"Don," Paul Reed said. They looked at each other, faces grim, as the helicopter grew closer.

"What is it?" Nolan asked.

"Not enough room for us all," Don said. "That's a Huey. It can carry five passengers at this altitude. Lifeboat rules. Women first. Men, we'll wait until the helicopter returns and if it can't come in, we'll ride it out in the boulder field. I was hoping for a larger helicopter," he added gravely. "I'm sorry."

There was a moment of silence, as heavy as a funeral service.

"The pilot won't have time for another run," Eileen said in a high, thin voice. "You can't survive without oxygen in the boulder field. There's got to be another—"

"Eileen," Joe said, and when she turned to him her eyes were desperate, panicked, nearly mad with fear.

"No!" she said furiously.

"Yes," he said.

"No," she whispered.

"Yes," he said, and held her.

It wasn't long enough, nearly long enough, he thought, as her body pressed against his. There was so much he hadn't done. This was the time in his life for a wife, for a home that was more than a bed and bathroom and an office filled with computers. He wanted so much. Marriage, seeing Eileen pregnant, looking at an ultrasound, getting yelled at while she labored, cutting the umbilical cord of his child. All the moments that could be his life rushed past him. A life that he wouldn't have, now.

"It was supposed to be me," she said against his chest. She looked up and her cheeks were flooded with rare tears. "I'm the cop, I'm supposed to die first, I always thought it would be—"

"Hush," he said, and touched her face. "I love you. Be strong."

The wind battered them as the helicopter landed in the field. Joe kissed her, hard, trying to make time stop for just one second more, trying to hold on. Paul pulled at Eileen's arm and he let go. He unwound Eileen's arms and gave Eileen a push. She turned and ran to the helicopter without a backward glance, taking Lucy's hand and pulling her along. Lucy, whose face was chalk white, kept looking backward. She looked as though she, not Ted, were going to die. The Lakota girl stumbled to the helicopter, weeping, and Joe turned to see who was left. Jorie, her nearly empty pack on her shoulders, started towards the helicopter. Then she turned back to Nolan and grabbed his ears in her hands. She pulled his face down to hers and gave him a kiss, something that started, obviously, as an impulse and ended with Jorie sagging against him, arms around him, her eyes closed. Joe had to smile as Jorie turned and lurched towards the helicopter, as though she didn't know exactly how to place her feet. Nolan looked dazed and completely, utterly happy. Pretty good for a first kiss, Joe thought. Pretty good last kiss, too.

He should be more afraid, more frightened. He wasn't. He knew, absolutely knew, that more than inky blackness and nothingness awaiting him. There would be clouds and light and beauty. Perhaps even a laser spear of his own, and dragons to kill. Death was the hard part, he thought, his eyes stinging with the thickening smoke. Death was the portal.

He was jostled, suddenly, as the climbers pushed their way past him. For a moment he thought they were all trying to climb onto the helicopter and felt sick. Then he realized three of them were carrying the other one, the one with the high boyish voice. A helmet rolled off and Joe saw a bright blonde braid fall down the back of the struggling climber. Her companions threw her bodily onto the helicopter and slid the door closed. They ran back away from the rotating blades as the helicopter struggled into the air.

Joe, standing with his hand to his brow, saw a face between the pilots. It was Eileen, and he saw her gesturing frantically and pointing, trying to communicate something to the pilots.

"What's she doing?" Paul asked.

Joe looked where Eileen was pointing. She was pointing *up*. Joe suddenly felt cold and hot all over in a prickling flood.

"Oh my God," Ted said, following the direction of Joe's gaze.

"Don," Paul said. "Will the fire reach up to the *top* of the Tower?"

CHAPTER TWENTY-FOUR

Top of Devils Tower, Wyoming

"I never did like that kind of Titanic lifeboat crap," Eileen said, laughing.

Lucy sat down, feeling at any moment as though she were going to roll off the sloping edge of the Tower and fall, screaming endlessly, over a thousand feet straight down. She'd never been good with heights. The top of the Tower wasn't a smooth, flat surface. It sloped, about as big as a baseball diamond, from north to south. In every direction the earth fell away in a crumbly mix of rocks and soil that ended abruptly and met the sky. Jorie sat down next to her.

"Can you feel it?" she whispered. Lucy saw her face and Jorie looked transported, almost exalted. "Can you feel it?"

The funny thing was, Lucy *could* feel it. There was a part of her that felt euphoric, as though everything was possible. Eileen grinned down at them, feet planted firmly apart, hair blowing backwards in the breeze, her gaze as fierce and joyful as a hawk's.

"Mateo Tepee," the Lakota girl said, her tears gone, her eyes round with amazement. "I'm here. I can't believe it. Can I sit down with you? I have to be careful of my dress, it's my grandmother's dress."

"We better move off this area," Eileen said. "The helicopter is going to land right back here. So let's move a little to the north."

"Oh, great," Lucy said. She could see great clouds of billowing smoke rising into the air from the north and west sides of the Tower, rising into the air and streaming down towards the northeast part of the valley. Looking into the distance made her feel nauseated.

"Here," Eileen said, striding towards where the sky met the edge of the rock. "Is that right?" She addressed her question to the climber, who was holding her long blonde braid in her fists and looking stormy.

"Right, that's the start of the north slope," she said. "You shouldn't go more than fifty feet, it starts to get steep and crumbly."

"Come over here, then," Eileen said, gesturing. "We've got to let the helicopter have some room."

Lucy got up carefully and walked towards Eileen, keeping her eyes on her feet and not on the curious and sickening illusion that she was going to fall off the edge at any second. In spite of her fear of heights she was feeling wave after wave of giddy happiness. Ted, her heart sang, Ted, bring me Ted, the next helicopter load had better have my man on board. Oh, please....

She sat next to Eileen and Jorie sat down next to her. The Lakota girl joined them, carefully sitting down in her grandmother's pretty doeskin dress. The climber came over as well. She had a square face and a stocky body. She was still clutching her lovely blonde braid. It was wheat-colored and thick and fell below her waist.

"They shouldn't have made me get on," she said in a low voice.

Lucy exchanged a glance with Eileen. She reached out and they clasped hands. She felt her eyes fill up with tears and she whispered, "Ted."

"They'll come," Eileen said confidently.

There was a rising, chattering roar, and the helicopter burst up over the cliff edge. It labored higher, clawing for more altitude, then moved over and set a skid delicately on the top of the cliff. Lucy could see the skid mark from their landing, and marveled that the pilot had fit his skid directly into his previous mark. He was damned good.

Then all thought fled her as Ted scrambled from the helicopter. He was followed by Joe, Nolan, and the three Lakota men. The reason for the helicopter's laboring was thus revealed; they'd crammed six men onto a helicopter that should only carry five. The eldest Lakota, old and frail as he was, must have weighed so little that they'd put him on board.

The helicopter, without delay, picked itself up and plummeted off the cliff and out of sight. Lucy stayed seated, waiting for Ted to come to her. She didn't think she could stand, so dizzy was she with the relief of seeing him. He came to her and took her hands, and everything that had gone on in the past twenty minutes was gone as though they'd been nothing but a nightmare. Ted, die? Of course not. How ridiculous.

"They're picking up your dad and Zilla, and the ranger, and the other climbers right now," Nolan was saying to Eileen.

He was standing next to Jorie but she hadn't taken his hand or leapt to her feet. Her expression was confused and mistrustful, and Lucy squeezed Ted's hand and stifled a smile. She'd seen Jorie kiss Nolan, too. Kissing a man like that meant something, meant a *lot*, and perhaps Jorie had done it because she figured Nolan was going to die, and why not? Now Nolan was here, all six feet of him, sweaty and hairy and full of life and air and promise. He was a man, real as could be, and Lucy wished Jorie would stop fighting the river and let the current take her. Let love take her, and a man take her, and marriage, and life. Jorie didn't understand, yet, that *every* woman struggled against the current at some point.

She saw that Joe was holding Eileen and laughing into her upturned face.

"Can't get rid of me *that* easily," he was saying, with his goofy, happy Joe grin. "Your mom was right about this place, wasn't she? I feel incredible!"

The oldest Lakota said something. Lucy looked up and saw his face. He looked stonily into the distance as he spoke. He didn't look happy at all.

"She was right about this place, Eileen Reed," the button-down Lakota translated. "Your mother who is my great-grandmother's descendant. But I am afraid."

He stopped and looked at his elder, who had fallen silent. "Afraid of what?" Eileen asked.

There was no answer, and no time for an answer. Joe could hear the laboring chatter of the helicopter and he felt like whooping as he realized that meant that Paul and Ranger Don and the other mountain climbers were in the helicopter, and safe. There was a sudden, choking gust of smoke in his face as the wind started to shift.

"The wind is shifting," the woman climber said. As quickly as that, smoke started to circle, then blow to the west. Joe could hear the helicopter and then he couldn't and he stood, frozen with horror, waiting for the crash and the explosion.

There wasn't one. Joe started to see spots in front of his eyes and he remembered to breathe again. The helicopter sound surfaced again from the murky smoke and Joe realized that it was further away.

"Look!" Eileen pointed, and Joe saw the cross that was the rescue helicopter, swimming away in the drowning smoke. The pilot had abandoned the attempt to take his last load to the top of the Tower and was now fleeing south, towards Sundance.

"They're safe," Lucy said. "Thank God. Thank God."

"But are we?" the climber asked. She was looking north and as Joe followed her gaze he saw something that looked like an opening directly into hell. Burning trees and undergrowth were being lifted into the air, literally pulled from the earth by the tremendous updraft. Enormous tree trunks were exploding, burning with flames that leaped a hundred feet. In some places the fire didn't start until it was fifty feet from the ground, where it could find oxygen to consume. Joe saw a tiny spout appear on the top of a ridge of fire, a tornado that lifted burning sparks into a merry, whirling dance. The sparks, burning pinecones and bark and branches, spun and fell and were lifted again. Still, the very top of the fire spout was a hundred feet below the Tower's edge. They had a chance.

"We have a chance," he said, trying to take his eyes from the fire. He couldn't. They were all standing, unable to look away, watching the fire as it raged through the valley. Beyond the smoke and the flames Joe could see a long line of cars fleeing south, their headlights on in the artificial gloom. They looked like tiny ants. He wondered if Tracy and Hank and Howie were in that line of cars. He hoped they were. He hoped they were safe.

The elderly Lakota said something again, something in a resigned voice. Joe turned, with Eileen and Lucy and Ted, to the younger man. The young man looked at them with a suddenly ashen face, his mouth slack with consternation and fear.

"It comes," he translated. "He said – it's coming."

Sundance, Wyoming

"Okay, I'm hooked in," Paul said into the helmet. The pilots had wearied of trying to listen to his shouting and had handed back a helmet with a microphone cord attached. Paul had spent precious seconds figuring out how to hook the cord into the helicopter's communication system. The pilots were fighting vicious cross currents as they struggled south towards Sundance, currents caused by the rising winds from the fire. Local weather conditions were affected by a hot fire, as this one was, and the hot, dry July days made for a deadly condition known as dry lightning. The hot air struck cooler air aloft and caused clouds to form. The clouds weren't heavy enough to give needed rain but they spawned fierce winds and vicious lightning strikes. The Huey, overloaded, labored in the increasing gusts of wind.

"Right, then, what's up?" one of the pilots said, blessedly clear, in Paul's ear.

"I think they're going to get fire across the top of the Tower," Paul said. "I've heard that it's happened before. The updraft brings burning material aloft until it hits oxygenated air. You need to drop water on my people or they're going to die."

There was silence from the padded helmet that covered his ears. Paul waited, then realized they'd cut him out of the communications loop. Instead of a hum he heard nothing but silence. He waited patiently, his hands smoothing Zilla's head. She was on his lap, shivering uncontrollably. Something had happened to her as they loaded on the helicopter. She'd pricked up her ears and looked back towards the fire and barked sharply. She was in her carry pack on Paul's back so he didn't have time to see what she was looking at. He didn't have time to think about it because he wanted to get to the top of the Tower and let the pilots take the women with them, into the clear. Even then he knew that the top of the Tower might not be high enough.

When the helicopter was struggling up the side of the Tower Paul became aware that something was wrong with his little dog. Zilla was trembling from nose to tail. He took her from the pack and set her on his lap, where she tried to bury her nose between his arm and his side. She used to do that as a puppy when something scared her, before she grew to adulthood.

He had no time to think of it now, though he patted and smoothed her fur with gentle fingers. His daughter was trapped on the Tower and there was no worse death than fire. None. Even the rock fall at the base of the Tower was a better death than a burning one. There, at least, the death by suffocation was a fairly painless one. If only the fire wouldn't burn any higher. Paul knew that he was hoping against his judgment, and that was against his nature. He knew better, but he didn't want to think about that.

Someone pulled lightly at his shirt. It was the sunglasses climber, who'd introduced himself as they waited for the helicopter. Dennis Patterson he was, and he was a volunteer firefighter. Dennis was pointing to the north and Paul could hardly steel himself to look. Dennis' expression was bleak.

The north end of the valley was a wall of flame. Worse, flaming debris had been thrown aloft with the wind shift and there was another fire line starting at the southwest end of the valley. If the two fire lines converged there could be a fire spout hundreds of feet high, just like two converging thunderstorms can cause tornados.

It looked to Paul as though the fires would converge roughly at Devils Tower.

"Come on, guys, what are you going to do?" he shouted into the smooth silence of the microphone. "Turn on my mike, damn it," he said, tapping his helmet and tapping the shoulder of the copilot. The copilot didn't turn around but the microphone did come alive with static.

"Okay, Mr. Reed," the pilot said. "We decided to give it a

try. We're going to drop you all off at Keyhole Reservoir and fill up the dump bag in the reservoir."

"We're only going to get one shot at this," the copilot warned. "If we miss, that's all the time we'll have. And we're going to have to time it just as the fire sweeps by the Tower."

"It'll be like spitting in the eye of the devil," the pilot said cheerfully. "I don't think this has ever been done before."

"My prayers are with you," Paul said. He rubbed at his smoke-reddened eyes and drew a deep breath. "And may God be with you, too."

"Oh, *that* guy. He's always tagging along," the copilot said, his voice sounding as crazily upbeat as the pilot's. "He just loves the way we fly."

"Get ready to bail right out when we land," the pilot said. "Don't wait around."

"I'll tell the others," Paul said. The microphone went dead as he pulled the cord from the console in the helicopter. The wind still buffeted them but the skies were clearing as the helicopter raced towards the reservoir. Paul gestured the others to lean close. He explained what they were going to do, his voice cracking with the effort to be heard over the chop of the helicopter blades and the full-throated roar of the engine.

Top of Devils Tower, Wyoming

"What does he mean?" Eileen said. She had her hand on her gun, at the back of her waist. If the Lakota became crazed and tried to throw them off the top of the Tower, she was prepared to stop them. That was the only explanation she could think of for the inexplicable behavior of the old chief. He had to be a chief, and one of the Lakota who had never turned to drink. His face was lined with great age but showed no broken red lines across the nose and cheeks. His eyes were strong and his back was proudly erect.

The Lakota who translated for him, as well, was straight and strong and unbroken. He was looking directly at her and his gaze was faintly disapproving, as though he knew what she was thinking.

"He said the evil spirit comes," he repeated, and broke into a few sentences of his native tongue.

"The manitou," Joe said.

"Where?" Lucy whispered.

"I know where," Joe said. "Look."

Everyone turned to look and Eileen turned last. She made a visual sweep of every person in their group before she turned to where Joe was pointing. There was Jorie and Nolan, Ted and Lucy, Joe and Eileen. There was the climber girl, and then the four Lakota; a young girl, an old man, and two very tough looking young men. Eleven people, and not one of them was changing, growing, sprouting hair and fangs and the mask of a manitou. Eileen didn't consider, at that moment, how completely she believed in her mother's ancient story. She was going to keep them all alive, and if it meant shooting a were-whatever, she was prepared.

Joe was pointing towards the Visitors Center. From this height it looked like a tiny matchbox, a miniature building. The climber's Subaru and the ranger's truck were ants in the handkerchief-sized parking lot. The fire had almost reached the Visitors Center and as a tree exploded into flame at the road that lead to Devils Tower Junction, a car shot out of the trees and into the parking lot.

"Oh Jesus," the climber girl moaned. "Someone's trapped."

Eileen felt Joe take her hand. She couldn't feel her feet; she couldn't feel her body. She was pure spirit, floating without emotion and without pain in the smoke and the hazy light, watching the tiny vehicle over a thousand feet below her. She was going to watch someone die, and there wasn't a thing that she could do about it. It was too horrible to think about. She was a cop and she thought sometimes that cops were born, not made. Her duty was to protect, to serve the community, and even if she hunted down evildoers after their deed was done, she still had that most protective part of her at her core. And there was nothing she could do. Her training and her gun couldn't help her now.

The car roared to the very end of the parking lot, where the trail began that led to the rock fall and the Tower, and stopped next to the other two vehicles. The door opened. A man got out, an enormous man. He started running for the path that led to the rock fall. He might, indeed, make it to the rock fall, where he would die as the fire sucked the oxygen from the air or flame swept over him. There was a chance that the fire would burn so quickly that if he found a cool pocket of air among the rocks, he might survive. It was a slim chance, but better than the alternative.

"Rene Dubois," Joe said, in the tones of judge handing down a sentence. His hand was ice cold in Eileen's. "He waited too long."

"It's Dubois," Lucy said in a high, furious voice. She sounded like the eagles that had circled the Tower that morning, voicing their unearthly cries. "He's trapped."

"That's the man who set the fire," Ted said in explanation to the Lakota and the climber. "I hope he lives. I want to kill him myself."

"Can we drop a rope to him, and pull him up?" Joe said suddenly. Eileen looked over at the climber. She spread her arms wide. She had no rope; she'd left it below, to lighten the load.

"No emergency rope up here? No stash of extras, food and water and rope?" Joe asked. "Nothing?"

"We leave it as we found it," the climber said with a sideways glance at the Lakota. She shook her braid over her shoulder and shrugged. "We don't even pick the flowers. Besides, it's an hour and a half down the side of the Tower, with the best of climbers. You need to fix and rappel three different times. There's not a rope in the world that could go over a thousand feet and not break."

"Okay," Joe said. His shoulders slumped.

"He's almost at the rock fall," Eileen said. "The fire is burning the Visitors Center. It won't be long now."

The old chief said something else in his native language. Eileen turned away from the struggling fat man who was racing the fire to the rock fall. The old chief was pointing, and he wasn't pointing over the edge at Rene Dubois.

"Behold the spirit," the younger Lakota translated. "It comes."

Eileen looked, and her breath stopped. The fire burning from the northeast, the one that was whipping the Visitors Center into ashes, had met the other fire burning from the southwest. Something about the air currents, Eileen thought numbly. Something about the air currents was causing this.

An enormous tornado of fire was building in front of them. It was growing from the two fires and it was higher than the Tower.

"A fire whirl," the climber said, and Eileen could see in her face the same dumb wonder and fear that must be in her own. "A fire whirl."

CHAPTER TWENTY-FIVE

Keyhole Reservoir, Pine Haven, Wyoming

"**H**oly smoke, look at that," Dennis Patterson said. He held his hands to his face like a little boy who was watching a scary movie. He looked through his split fingers.

"Please," Paul said, looking at the tornado of fire that they could see clearly from twenty miles away. His face was still wet from the water falling from the belly of the helicopter's water bladder. The pilots had taken the Huey directly overhead as they flew off towards the Tower. They'd gotten lost in the smoke and the haze almost immediately. Now there was only time to hope and pray.

Don, the park ranger, had contacted his ranger partner Larry. Larry, in turn, had gotten hold of Doug at his home in Sundance. Doug was on his way to pick them up, and within an hour or so Paul would see his wife. He didn't know if he could look her in the eye, ever again. He would give his life before he'd let their daughter be hurt, and now he was safe and sound and she was in the gravest danger. He didn't know how he was going to find a way to live with himself, if those young people died and he lived. He didn't know if he wanted to live anymore, if Eileen died.

"Can you see the helicopter?" Dennis said.

"I can't," Paul said.

"I should have been up there," Don the Park Ranger said,

in a self-loathing way that Paul understood all too well.

"There's nothing you could do—" Paul started, and Don cut him off.

"I have *flares*," he snapped. "If the smoke is too bad up there, how are the pilots going to know where to put the water? If they don't have any flares, how are the pilots going to see them?"

There was a silence that seemed long, but really wasn't. It was only seconds now until the tornado of fire swept over the very peak of the Tower.

"Eileen," Paul said in a voice that sounded like a fading radio station, lost in a roar of static. He sank to his knees, hearing the static grow louder and louder in his ears, and fainted for the first and last time in his life.

Top of Devils Tower, Wyoming

"We need a fire shelter," the girl climber said hurriedly. "Quick, everybody to the center. It's going to come right over us."

"We don't have anything like that," Eileen said. "No one even has coats."

"You have us," Joe said.

The tornado was growing with a sound that was unspeakably terrible. It sounded like a thousand people talking and chewing busily on sticks and bones at the same time. Happy, insane people or demons. Or maybe one demon. Eileen tried to clear her head but she couldn't seem to think.

"Last time counts for all," Nolan said to Jorie. They were huddling closer now at the very center of the Tower, and the men were pushing the women to the center as though they'd been rehearsing this idea for weeks.

"No," Eileen said.

"Yes," Joe said to her, and his eyes were kind, and implacable. "Huddle down, close to the ground. We'll cover you with our bodies. If the fire reaches us, it'll get to us and not to you. Best shot we have."

"I—" Eileen said. She thought of making love to Joe in the Mustang, how sweet and perfect that moment was, and that it was their last. She remembered her mother's sad and grim look, when her mother told Lucy and Eileen and Jorie that they didn't know what men were for. She understood with a completeness that felt like drowning that her mother was right. She'd never known before now.

Joe was going to die for her, to give her a chance to stay alive. And she had to let him do it. She had time for one kiss, quick and imperfect, and then she turned and knelt and put her face in the dirt.

"I love you," Ted said to Lucy, and the worst part of it was that all barriers were down now. There were so many things they could talk about, so many things to catch up on, and there would be no time. Lucy took his face in her hands and she burst into tears as she felt his bristly beard. His hair was uncombed and his eyes were red and ringed with tiredness and smoke, but his smile was as sweet and tender as the day they married.

"I love you, too," she said, but no sound came out.

"Tell Hank I love him," Ted said. "Now kneel down, Lucy. Live."

"Maybe we could have made it, you and I," Nolan said to Jorie.

"I won't let you do this," Jorie said. Her face was dirty and her eyes were red and swollen. She was more beautiful than cool water.

"I can't live for you, now," Nolan said with his best wry grin. "But I can die for you."

Jorie put her hands over his. He kissed her and she met her mouth with his, as though it was the first time she'd kissed anyone, ever.

"Kneel, Jorie," Nolan whispered. "Turn around and kneel. We don't have any more time."

She put her hands to her face and she turned away from him and she knelt. The Lakota girl huddled close to her side and Lucy was curled up to her left. Nolan opened his shirt, losing all the buttons in the process, but he didn't give much of a damn, at this point. If he was burned and he could still walk, he promised himself he'd take the thousand foot drop. Better that than three or four days in a hospital, stinking and drowning in his own cast off fluids, his flesh hanging off in flaps. Better to go on his own terms.

The chewing and snapping sound was approaching at a run, at a hungry sprint, as though it sensed the fresh unburnt meat.

"Helicopter," Eileen said to the dirt in front of her lips. "Helicopter. Water bag. I hear the helicopter."

She could hear it through the Tower itself, oddly enough, as though the vibrations in the air were being transmitted to the stone. She realized what the pilots were attempting to do. She realized, as Don had done only seconds before, that there was only one chance for the helicopter to save them, and the water bag wasn't big enough to cover the whole top of the Tower.

They needed a flare, and they didn't have one. Eileen turned off everything outside of her. The clean room where she worked on her murder puzzles was empty, but there was something there, wasn't there? Something she was missing.

She had it! Eileen pushed Lucy roughly aside as she struggled out of her backpack strap. The men were closing in on them, shirts held wide, sheltering them with their bodies, and Eileen had no time to explain. She unsnapped the straps and reached into her backpack.

The sound of the helicopter thudded into her ears and the sound of the demon tornado roared as though it knew what she was going to do.

She pulled the crystal skull from her pack and she rose to her knees. She held it into the air with both hands, held it above the heads and arms of the sheltering men, held it like an Aztec priestess before a sacrifice.

The skull caught the fire and prismed into a thousand gorgeous colors, as radiant and scintillating as a diamond, as bright as a torch. Eileen realized she was screaming. Joe was trying to push her down, and then the helicopter came out of the smoke like a hawk stooping to the kill.

Joe, struggling to push Eileen's head and shoulders back down to the ground, never saw the helicopter and the hero pilots who saved them. He saw the skull itself, sparkling and glowing with unearthly light, and beyond that the fire tornado spewing a gout of flame across the Tower like a tongue meant to eat them all. The water, released from the helicopter's water bag, landed three feet in front of them. Joe saw icy blue and sparkling clear crystal grow magically from nowhere, a wall in front of them. There was no time to blink, or draw a breath. Joe saw the flame draw back to the demon's mouth as though it had been burned by cold, not heat. The tornado flew apart in an instant and Joe saw the tornado's face, a snarling were-flame, as it collapsed and went back into the evil earth.

Then time began again. The Huey went over them so closely Joe felt the air from the blades thudding against his skin. Eileen's arm wobbled and he reached forward and steadied the skull in her hands. She fell backwards into him and he fell down, breaking the circle that wasn't needed any more.

The helicopter circled once and Joe looked up. He saw the grinning faces of the pilots. The copilot was waving and giving them the thumbs-up. Then he tapped his watch and made a circle with his finger and thumb.

"They need to refuel," Eileen said from his lap, looking up. "They'll be back to pick us up after they refuel."

"Look at the fire," Lucy said wonderingly. They were still huddled as closely as frightened puppies, but everyone was looking around now.

Joe saw that the two onrushing walls of flame had burned into each other. As the two walls had met they'd created the fire tornado, but the fire quickly burned all the fuel. Without anything more to burn – and cheated out of burning them, Joe thought – the fire was collapsing into smoke and embers. The danger was over.

"Did you see it?" the Lakota girl said. She looked around at all of them, and Joe thought they all looked the same. Perhaps they would always look the same, forever, as though what they'd just been through had burned an invisible mark into them.

"I don't know what you're talking about," the climber girl said, but she looked away nervously.

They'd all looked at the fire tornado, Joe realized. It was in none of their natures to look away from death. They'd all seen – something.

The helicopter thudded away and the fire burned down, and the silence was as loud as a song sung by a choir of a hundred throats, a thrumming of life and joy that Joe could hardly bear. He tightened his arms around Eileen and kissed the top of her head.

The elderly chief looked at Joe, his gaze clear and birdlike. He looked at Eileen, and then at the skull in her lap.

"Tell him," Eileen said solemnly, "that this is a crystal skull, brought from the Aztecs to your people, for safekeeping. It was lost, and has been found."

The young Lakota repeated her words in their soft language, and the old chief widened his eyes and put his hands to his chest. He bowed his head and when he lifted him there were tears in his eyes.

"Here," Eileen said, and handed the skull to him. He took it carefully, holding the skull so the face looked directly into his own. He spoke, and the younger Lakota translated for him.

"We have legends, some of which you may have heard. The white buffalo. The big wave. We also have a legend of a skull, a magic skull, a skull sent to us, to be guarded and kept until the proper day. Is there anyone among us, now, who will deny we walk the right path?"

"What's the right path?" Lucy asked the young man. She was sitting in front of her husband, who had his arms around her.

"My grandfather and my brothers and sister, here, are part of a movement to restore the tribal nations," the man said crisply, his voice flawless and educated. "We drink no alcohol, we take no drugs, and we accept no government checks. We believe they're tainted like the Cavalry once tainted blankets with smallpox. Our movement is small, but we have the right path."

"The path back," Eileen said.

"We don't wish to go back to the past, but we do wish to free ourselves from a path that was forced upon us. This gift you bring us, at last, may help us show our people the right path." The young Lakota grinned at them and shrugged his shoulders. "Whatever works, right?"

"Please," Jorie said. "I don't want to interfere. But the skull is part of an archaeological dig, and I was hoping—"

She looked around, and Joe waited for the haughty, poisonous Jorie to reassert itself, now that they were safe. He waited for her to tell the Lakota that the crystal skull which had quite obviously been on its way to them was actually property of the United States government, where it would sit in a cardboard box and be studied by graduate students. He thought that Bob, if he had a brain, would much rather sit around a campfire and be sung to than stashed in a box on a shelf and forgotten.

"Well," Jorie said, looking down at her hands. "I was hoping you would let me come and photograph him, and study him. Wherever you decide to keep him."

Lucy, who was sitting by Jorie, threw her arms wide. She moved out of Ted's embrace and wrapped the other girl in an enormous hug. She hugged her so hard that the two women fell over, Lucy laughing and kissing Jorie on the cheek with enormous smacks.

"Hooray for Jorie!" she said, and kissed her again. Jorie looked like she was going to burst into tears, but she broke into a watery smile instead.

"Oh stop it, already," she said irritably, but she was still smiling.

"What a day," Joe said, as Lucy let Jorie go and allowed Ted to put his arms around her and hug her tight.

The old chief said something to the younger man, and the pretty Lakota girl produced a patterned shawl from her carry sack. The elder took the skull from Eileen and wrapped it carefully, speaking to the younger Lakota as he did so.

"We shouldn't let the skull be unwrapped until we're well away from here," the young man translated for them. He glanced over the Tower where the tornado of fire had built and stood, and Joe saw everyone nodding their heads.

"Good idea," Nolan said. "Really good idea."

"We'd be honored to let you study our skull," the young man said to Jorie. "We'd also be honored if you would speak of where you found it, and how you knew to bring it to us."

"We didn't—" Jorie started, but Eileen broke in smoothly.

"We'd be happy to show you everything, once Jorie has the site safe for visitors," she said. Then she bit her lip and looked north, where the smoke from embers still rose into the air. "If there's anything left, that is."

"We'll know soon enough," Joe said. "Best of all, everyone else is safe. It looks like the fire has burned itself out."

"Hank," Lucy said. "I hope he's not too scared."

"He's fine, I'm sure," Joe said. "And now that we're – hey, wait."

"Rene Dubois," Eileen said, as though she'd forgotten, Well, they all had. There had been more important things on their minds than the fate of one nasty serial killer.

"Better not get close to the edge," the climber warned. "He went into the rock fall, and you can't see it from here."

"They're sure going to need a new Visitors Center," Nolan observed, looking at the ash pit, still smoking, that had been a building.

"And a new car," the climber sighed, looking at the burnt hulk that had been their Subaru. "At least we're still alive."

"At least?" Lucy said, and then saw the girl's smile.

"So where's our ride?" Ted asked. "I'm starving. Is anybody else starving?"

"Food," Nolan said hungrily. Joe put his hand to his belly, which hadn't even seen a whole breakfast, and suddenly he was ravenous with hunger.

"Oh, my God," Eileen said. "Don't talk about food!"

"Taxi!" Nolan said, and whistled like a New Yorker hailing a cab. "Taxi!"

This should have been a mild joke, but it struck Joe as the funniest thing he'd ever heard. He started laughing so hard he fell backward, holding his stomach, and Eileen fell next to him on the ground, laughing so hard tears were coming from her eyes and streaking her dirty, beautiful face.

That's the way the helicopter finally found them, eleven people lying on the ground and laughing deliciously, even the oldest one who chuckled and chuckled, holding a wrapped bundle in his lap.

CHAPTER TWENTY-SIX

Visitors Center, Devils Tower, Wyoming

"The gasoline from these three cars must have been the cause of that tremendous fire spout we saw," the park ranger, Don, said. He stood next to a burned out car, the one that Rene Dubois had left in the parking lot. The other two twisted wrecks were once a blue Subaru and a green truck. The air was choking with ash and smoke and Eileen could feel the baking hot asphalt through the soles of her thick hiking boots.

"Yes, surely," Eileen said, trying to sound like she thought so, too.

Larry, the other park ranger, had driven them to the Visitors Center in his enormous Ford truck. Only twice had fallen trees blocked the road, and both of those were taken care of quickly with Larry's chainsaw. An occasional log sent bursts of sparks and sullen smoke into the air, but the fire wasn't going to flare up again.

"You saw him run up the trail into the rock fall?" Don asked Joe. Joe nodded. Eileen fingered her gun, which was drawn and cocked and locked. She didn't want Joe to come. She wanted him to stay behind, where he was safe. Joe won that argument by refusing to argue.

"Ma'am, you're making me nervous," Larry said.

"I'm a very good shot," Eileen said with a cold look at

Larry. "This man killed Sheriff King yesterday, sir. He set this fire."

"I know that," Larry said. "I know your folks and I know about you. If you're that worried about this guy, then I'm worried too. That's why you're making me nervous."

"Oh," Eileen said. "Sorry."

"I've got a shotgun," Larry said. "How about I take that, too?"

"Good idea," Joe said. Eileen looked at him and flicked her eyes to his pocket. Joe blinked at her and dipped his chin in a tiny nod. He still had the gun she'd given him, then.

They'd gobbled nutrition bars as Larry drove them carefully up the trail from Devils Tower Junction, even as Lucy and Ted were reuniting joyfully with their little boy. Time for celebration later, time for food and drink and love. Right now they had to go back into the belly of the beast and see if it had killed their killer. It felt like going back into hell, to Eileen. The miasma that surrounded the Tower was even worse in the smoke and ash. The burnt smell that settled into her nose made her feel like she was going to go absolutely mad.

"Sorry about your truck, Don," Larry said, with a nod to the burned out shell of the park ranger's truck.

"Damn shame," Don said with a shrug. "But now I get a new Visitors Center, don't I?"

"Brand new, I betcha," Eileen said. "Let's walk carefully, folks. If he's alive, and it looks like he needs help, let's just hold back until we're sure he doesn't have a surprise for us, all right?"

"All right," the three men said, and fell in behind her without comment.

They found him in the rock fall, the smartest place to go. The flames shouldn't have reached this far, but the fire wasn't an ordinary one, was it? He lay half under a tumble of enormous boulders, his face buried in the cracks between the rocks. The smell announced him, a smell that made Eileen wish for the cleanliness of the burnt wood. He smelled almost sweet, that was the worst. Sweet, like roast pork.

"I think he's alive," Don said from the trail, in a choking voice. Larry held his shotgun trained on the man curled like a fried snail in between the rocks, a revolted expression on his face. Joe turned and leaned off the trail and vomited the trail bar he'd eaten just a few minutes before. Eileen noticed with distant amusement that it didn't look any different coming up than it had going down. Her own stomach was okay. Not happy, but okay. She'd seen burn victims before, working car crashes on the highway. Rene was by far the worst she'd ever seen. His clothes hung in patches and his skin, underneath, was purple and hairless. Where the skin had cracked it was a deep, roasted pink.

"Don, can you get the stretcher out of Larry's truck?" Eileen said. "Joe, is this Rene?"

"I can't tell," Joe said, his face turned away. "He's tall and fat like Rene, but I don't know."

"We'll see in a bit," Larry said, his shotgun held ready, his face distressed and white. "I don't think he's going to survive, ma'am."

"I don't think so either," Eileen said. She patted Joe on the shoulder. "Hang on, everybody. We've got to get him to the hospital. Think about what he is, later. Right now he's a man who needs our help."

When they rolled him over, grimacing helplessly and trying not to touch his wounded and raw flesh, they saw that his face was almost unmarked. He'd buried his face deeply enough into the rocks that the blowtorch of flame had crisped everything but the skin of his face. It wouldn't be enough, Eileen thought, to save him. She helped strap him in and took a Glock semiautomatic pistol from his belt as they settled the blanket around him. She searched as carefully as possible and discovered he only had the one. Perhaps there were more weapons in the car in the parking lot. That was for later. For right now, there was only wrapping this horribly burned fat man into the stretcher and making sure that there was no weapon that he could bring out, like the last scene in a cheap horror movie, and kill them after all.

He didn't come around until they had him in the back of the truck and Larry was driving as quickly as he could back towards Sundance and the hospital there. He'd be flown to Rapid City, of course, to the intensive care unit there, if they thought they could save him. More likely he'd be stuffed full of painkillers until he died, which seemed inevitable.

Rene's eyes opened. They were black and expressionless pools, the doll's eyes that Lucy had described. Joe, who was steadying him on the other side of the stretcher, bent over him and touched his forehead, which was unburned.

"Hang on, fella," he said gently, and Eileen felt something fierce and warm in her chest, something that was pride and love and astonishment, all at the same time. What a man this was, this Joe Tanner.

"Joe Tanner," Rene whispered in a cracked and thready voice. He smiled. "Been looking for you, *mon ami*." His arm twitched as though he was trying to reach the gun that Eileen had removed.

"So I've heard," Joe said. "We're getting you to a hospital right away, so hang on."

"Water?" Rene whispered. "So thirsty."

Joe held the bottle for him and he drank thirstily until the bottle was gone. Then he threw up with a grunt, ejecting a gush of water out and down the blanket that covered his chest.

"Hang on," Joe repeated helplessly.

"I didn't know the fire would jump the road," Rene said. His voice, though faint, sounded cheerful, as though the pain of his burnt body didn't bother him a bit. Eileen had read somewhere that burn victims were euphoric, the ones that were going to die. The body knew it was over and dumped all sorts of happy juice into the human system. Or something like that. She could hardly stand the smell coming off this man, the smell of cooked flesh and coming death.

"I'm sorry," Joe said. "We would have saved you if we could."

"Up there," Rene said. "I saw you up there in the light. On top of – You took my wallet. My dad."

Eileen, who'd taken charge of Rene's wallet, dug it out of her backpack as Joe helped Rene drink again from his water bottle. This time the water stayed down. Rene closed his eyes as Eileen found the picture of the little boy and his dad. Her throat closed tighter as she looked at the happy little boy.

Rene opened his eyes. She held the picture in front of him.

He smiled gently, and happily, and his inhuman eyes looked odd set in his human face.

"Who paid you, Rene?" Eileen whispered. "We – I, really want to know."

"Just me," Rene said, not moving his gaze from the picture of his father. "Just me. My dad, he was a cinematographer. He was blacklisted, do you know that word?"

"Yes," Eileen said.

"So he got sent back to France, destroyed him. Destroyed – me. Reagan, he – he blessed the movement, made it legitimate to hurt my father."

"President Reagan?" Joe asked, eyebrows raised. Then his face cleared. He understood. Eileen, too, realized what Rene was trying to say. "You wanted to kill the missile defense program. Because it was Reagan's concept, that's why."

"Almost did it," Rene mumbled. "It was my hobby, really. Just for fun."

Eileen saw Joe's hands clench into fists and he shut his eyes as though he couldn't look at the burned, talking thing on the stretcher for one more second.

"So these jobs were on the side?" she asked calmly, to allow Joe to get hold of himself.

"Just on the side," Rene said, closing his eyes. "Just me, just to destroy something of America that I hated. Right?"

"Right," Eileen agreed, but now her own hands were balled into fists. She looked outside the truck as Rene babbled on, describing horrors that she couldn't force herself to listen to or comprehend. But the small digital recorder she had clipped onto her shirt was listening, the recorder that Lucy had pressed upon her as they'd left, an interesting CIA toy that Lucy kept with her in her fanny pack.

She met Joe's eyes across the stretcher and they looked at each other as though they were leaning over an open sewer, a bubbling evil thing. And even though Rene was evil he was also terribly sad. He was dying; a boy who'd loved his father and never found his way in the world, a boy who'd lost his way in a terrible wilderness. In a sense, Eileen thought, the manitou had taken him instead of them, a burnt offering to the evil that brooded in this place. She tried to think of something else, anything else, and found herself looking at Joe, Joe who was even now helping Rene take another drink of water.

"We'll be there soon," she mouthed at him when he looked at her, and he nodded.

Chapter Twenty-Seven

Rapid City Regional Hospital

Eileen walked down the hallway corridor, seeing the little figure slumped on the bench that served as a waiting area here. She felt tired still, even after a few hours sleep and a hurried breakfast.

She'd slept on the ride back from Sundance, slept against the window of Doug's truck with Joe's exhausted, sleeping weight against her shoulder. Lucy and Ted, with Hank between them, were fast asleep right next to them. Hank never stirred, but even in sleep he didn't let go of his mother's hand.

She'd woken in Hulett, after dark, to discover her parents weeping and hugging and laughing as they learned that the Reed Ranch hadn't been touched. Rene's fire, hot and explosive though it had been, had followed a valley three miles to the west of the ranch. The volunteer fire department in Hulett hadn't been able to stop the course of the fire as it raced towards Devils Tower, but they'd contained the fire within the ridgeline where Rene had burned Sheriff King's patrol car and the stolen Chrysler. The fire had missed another ranch on the way, a cattle ranch owned by the Schwartz family. The entire family worked through the day to create a fire line, down to the five-year-old grandson of old Charlie Schwartz. The Schwartz family and the people of Hulett were crying and hugging, too; they thought the Reeds and their clients had perished in the fire since they hadn't been found at their ranch.

She didn't remember the journey to the ranch. One moment she was watching her parents' joy through the dirty windows of Doug's horse truck, struggling to comprehend the excitement, and the next she was jolted awake in pitch darkness.

"Everyone in," Paul said. "Right to bed, and we'll go to Rapid City in the morning." They were at the Reed Ranch, and it was exactly the way they'd left it. Eileen stared through the window at her parents' home, trying to understand that everything was still there, unburnt, untouched. Doug's Schwan's truck sat parked in the yard, just as he'd left it.

"I have to go to Rapid City—" Eileen started to say, then caught sight of her father's face. She stopped instantly and nodded. When Paul wore a look like that there was no arguing. She stumbled into the house and fell across her bed, fully dressed, and remembered no more.

Now the day was bright and she was still tired, but she was showered and dressed and had brushed her teeth before the long ride to Rapid City. The figure on the hospital bench straightened as she approached.

"Hello," Beryl Penrose said.

"Hello, Beryl," Eileen said. She sat down next to Beryl and took her hand. "Thank you."

Beryl looked exhausted. She also looked serene, as though all decisions had been made. She was wearing the same clothes she'd worn when she'd taken Joe's Mustang, and they were spotted with blood.

"He'd crawled back to the highway from the ditch," Beryl said, allowing Eileen to hold her hand. Her voice was rough and unsteady. "He was kneeling, like he couldn't go any further, and I knew who he was, of course. Sheriff King. So I could run, or I could try to save him."

"And you saved him."

"I don't think so," Beryl said, and touched her forehead with trembling fingers. "I don't like the way the nurses look. Are you going to see him?"

"I would like to see him," Eileen said. She found that she was gripping Beryl's hand far too hard. "I'm sorry," she said, letting go.

"It's all right," Beryl said. "I didn't save him to try and get leniency, you know. I just—"

"You couldn't let him die. I know. I'm so sorry this happened, Beryl."

"Me, too," Beryl said. "Are you going to arrest me now? I think – I think I'm ready."

"Not now," Eileen said. "Let's wait a while."

A nurse came out of the room and nodded at Eileen. She was dressed in bright purple scrubs. Her scrub jacket was patterned with purple and brown teddy bears. Her face, above the cheerful garb, looked fixed and sad.

"He can see you now," she said. "You have five minutes, no more."

"Thank you," Eileen said, rising to her feet. "How is he?"

"Are you a relative?" the nurse asked crisply.

"A good friend," Eileen said. "But I'm a fellow cop. Could you tell me?" The nurse shrugged, nodded. They walked a few steps down the hall, away from Beryl.

"He was shot in the stomach," the nurse said. "Perforated his intestines and he lost part of his liver. The surgeons fixed the injury, but he'd eaten a full meal before he was shot."

"A full meal," Eileen said in a voice that didn't sound like her own. She knew what meal it was, too. The meal she'd served him in the Tower Pub and Grill, meat loaf and gravy with French fries.

"So the infection is in his bloodstream now, and that's called sepsis. His liver is damaged and having a difficult time dealing with the infection. We've got every big gun antibiotic we have, but he's not responding as well as he should. Be positive, be cheerful. He needs good thoughts right now. He might turn around, still. I've seen some that do."

"Okay," Eileen said, and found to her surprise that she was speaking in a whisper. The nurse gestured her inside the I.C.U. and she walked in feeling as though she were going before a judge who would find her guilty, guilty.

But it was only Richard King after all, a very pale Richard King who was swathed in bandages from his chest down, with horrid looking drains and tubes seemingly everywhere. King turned to look at her, his head moving slowly on the fresh white pillow.

The whites of his eyes were yellow, bright chrome yellow. Eileen tried not to gasp. She'd never seen someone's eyes look like that. Liver damage, the nurse had said. Other than the yellow eyes, he didn't look so bad. The yellow eyes fixed on her and his lips drew back from his teeth. It might have been a smile, or a snarl.

Eileen dropped into the seat by his bed and took his hand in hers. She bent her head over his hand and tears burst out of her eyes and flooded down her face.

"I'm sorry," she whispered, choking. "I'm so sorry, Rick."

"Tears," he whispered. She looked up and he was looking with amazement at his hand, which was wet. He looked at her face with great effort and she looked back, unflinching, though she desperately wanted to hide her face.

"I should have made you come with us—" she started, and he moved his head back and forth on the pillow, one tiny inch one way and one tiny inch the other way. She stopped.

"Never saw you cry before," he said, his whisper even fainter. "Ever."

"Just learning how," Eileen said, and wiped her chin. More tears followed, making her feel sticky and hot and horrible. "Can't seem to stop, now."

"Loved you," he said, though there was no sound.

"I should have kissed you," Eileen said, and she meant it with all her heart. "I was so young, and I was still hurt over Owen even though I knew he wasn't for me. I hit you. I should have kissed you," she finished miserably. His hand moved under hers and she gripped it, and the tears dripped from her chin and wet their hands.

"Loved me?" he mouthed, his strange yellow eyes slipping closed.

"Yes, I could have loved you, Richard, I could have," Eileen said, and she was lying but she felt as though her heart were breaking. "Don't go, please. Don't go from us. You're everything you didn't know you were, Richard King. You *are* the king."

"Time to go, Miss Reed," the nurse said at her elbow, and Eileen started. She let go of Richard's hand and wiped hastily at her face. "He needs to rest, now."

"Hang on, Rick," Eileen said as she got to her feet. She patted his hand gently and let the nurse lead her from the room. She looked back and saw his sleeping face, smoothed free of anxiety and pain. She might have imagined the slight smile.

When the doctor came into the first floor waiting area three hours later Eileen was calm. She'd washed her face with icy cold water, twice, scrubbing at her face as though the sticky tears would never come off. Joe sat by her side. Everyone was there. Doug and his pretty wife, Howie and the hunters, Lucy and Hank and Ted, Beryl and Jorie sitting side-by-side as though nothing had changed from a week ago. Tracy and Paul Reed sat with the mayor of Hulett and with the Olsens, who had shut down their Tower Pub and Grill and driven to Rapid City. The waiting area was overflowing with Schwartz's and Hammond's and the families that Sheriff Richard King had served. Among them was Owen Sutter, her boyfriend from high school, who'd hugged Eileen and looked, as she felt, bewildered with loss. His wife, Molly, was with him, and three tall boys who looked exactly like Owen.

On the third floor were Richard's parents and sisters, in the family waiting room. They'd already gotten the news that this doctor was going to tell them, and Eileen felt her heart sink as she saw his set, grim face.

"We lost him twenty minutes ago," the doctor announced. "I'm very sorry."

There was silence. Eileen swallowed hard and bowed her head. She couldn't bear it if she started crying again.

"Sir," Paul Reed said. "Doctor? If he'd gotten to the hospital sooner? If we'd found him earlier?"

"I doubt it," the doctor said. He was tall and imposing, an older man who looked as though he was used to telling people bad news. "The injury was extreme. We did everything we could. Thank you folks, for being here for him. He knew you were here, and I think that was a comfort to him. Thank you."

"Thank you, doctor," Paul said. Tracy turned to him and they held each other. The doctor turned and left the room and quietly shut the door behind him.

Rapid City Regional Hospital

"He's going," the nurse said to them. "You want to visit him? He hasn't had any family in."

"He doesn't have any family," Lucy said. They stood like a panel of judges behind the intensive care unit glass: Lucy, Joe, and Eileen. Lucy wondered if Joe or Eileen had thought about what Rene Dubois meant to them. His hobby of killing missile defense scientists had brought the three of them together. Lucy was investigating the murders when she came across Eileen and Joe.

Lucy couldn't help but feel a surge of excitement when she realized she could close an open file that had existed for decades, close it with damning evidence from the killer's own mouth. She'd already made two copies of her digital tape, even though it made her sick and faint to listen. She couldn't imagine what it must have been like to listen to Rene tell of his killings while leaning over his roasted body.

He looked peaceful through the glass. They'd given him enough painkillers to float him away as his burned body shut down. The intensive care unit nurses had wrapped his crisped flesh in special bandages that would help him if he was going to live, and that should at least deaden some of the pain. Lucy thought of the couple he'd talked about drowning in fresh cement and felt her stomach do a slow, unpleasant flip. She didn't want to deny Rene pain medication, though he hadn't bothered with his own victims. Even Sully, Joe's girlfriend, had her neck broken and then was left to die, alone and paralyzed, on a dark country road. Sully died without anyone to care for her, to comfort her as her body shut down and she died.

Lucy realized her nose was pressed against the glass and the nurse was giving her a strange look. She stopped and looked at Eileen guiltily. Eileen looked through the glass silently, her profile proud and disdainful. Joe looked miserable, his body drooping with weariness.

"What a waste," he said. "What a waste."

"Excuse me," the nurse said abruptly. She left them and there was a brief consultation behind the glass. Lucy watched as the bulk in the bed twitched, and the monitors started beeping and hooting. Someone touched her hand and she realized it was Joe. She held his hand, hard, knowing Eileen was holding his other hand and feeling a circle closed and complete and strong.

"He's going," Joe whispered, as the nurses calmly disconnected the monitors and pressed buttons to stop the beeping. A doctor came in leisurely and pressed a stethoscope to the bandages that covered the man on the bed. He spoke briefly to the nurse and they made notes on a clipboard. This all took place behind the glass like a play performed for them, a death play without words.

"He's gone," Lucy breathed.

They watched as the nurses pulled the sheet up to cover Rene's face. Joe squeezed Lucy's hand and let it go. She looked up at him.

"Enough of death," Joe said, with a ghost of his old smile on his face. "Beryl saved the Mustang. Let's get the hell out of here."

"You got it," Eileen said.

"First one to the car gets to drive it," Lucy said, and as they headed for the elevator she wiped unexpected tears from her eyes. Tears, she supposed, for the little boy who loved his father. Tears for everyone that he'd ever hurt. And happy tears, too, because what she felt deepest in her heart was relief. He was dead, the wicked monster was dead, and would hurt people no more.

EPILOGUE

The Reed Ranch, Wyoming

They sat on the porch, feet up on the railing, two pitchers of Margaritas on the table. The empty first pitcher had attracted several bees, which were now flying erratic patterns around the columns of the porch. Eileen snorted, watching them. She would loop around just like the bees if she stood up, which she had no intention of doing. Joe sat with her, his leg draped so that it touched hers. He was sipping his Margarita with his eyes half-closed in pleasure. He was very drunk.

"Good thing Tracy promised to put Hank down for his nap," Lucy said slowly. She pronounced each word very carefully, as though by speaking precisely she could deny that she was absolutely plowed. "I don't think I could walk very well right now." She smiled at Ted, who still hadn't shaved. He was sitting with his feet propped on the railing and a full glass in his hand. He wasn't wearing cowboy boots, but Eileen could see them in his future. She might even get him a pair for Christmas.

The memorial service for Rick King, the county's fallen hero, had gone on well after midnight the night before. Everyone for a hundred miles had shown up, it seemed, all of them bearing food and drink. Rick's parents and sister, having driven in from Gillette, accepted the Reed's offer and had used the ranch for the service. Eileen bore the wake as her own private penance for Rick.

She carried endless cups of coffee and bottles of beer. She served casserole and cake and cleaned up hundreds of paper plates and plastic forks.

She spoke to Rick's parents, feeling their bewildered pain like fishhooks in her skin. She was carefully honest with them, explaining that the men who'd murdered their son were experienced killers. The Rapid City Journal had already drawn the connection between the terrorized elderly couple and the motel guest whose car had been stolen and the killings at Devils Tower. The last picture they'd printed was a shot of Rene's burned body wrapped like a mummy in the intensive care unit at the hospital. Rick's parents at least had the small satisfaction of knowing that their son's killer was caught, punished, and dead.

At midnight Joe had found Eileen in the kitchen, scrubbing glasses with a dazed, abstracted urgency, her face wet with tears. Joe took her by the hand and led her to bed, tucked her in like a child and kissed her cheek. He sat in the rocker until she let go and fell asleep. She slept like a stone for over twelve hours. When she awoke the rocker was empty but a blanket lay crumpled on the floor. They'd broken her parents' rule about sleeping in the same room, but Eileen didn't think her mom and dad would mind, this time.

Now, with a quarter of a pitcher of Margaritas in her, she felt better. She figured she'd pay with a crushing hangover tomorrow, but that was acceptable. She was glad Lucy felt the same way she did, that a good soaking in tequila would go a long way towards helping them all cope. There was certainly enough beer and liquor consumed at the wake last night to float at least a small rowboat. Now the King family and the other mourners were long gone, Howie and the other hunters were napping and a peaceful, sleepy silence hung over the ranch. Even the horses were dozing, heads drooping and tails swishing lazily.

In the shady front yard Hank and Zilla were playing a complicated game of chase, using a blue rubber ball and a couple of reluctant butterflies. Every once in a while Hank would dash up to the porch and jump into Lucy or Ted's lap, looking as though he had every intention of staying there all day. Then a few minutes later, reassured, he would be gone again, and he would chase Zilla and her blue rubber ball around the yard.

"So we all have headaches tomorrow," Joe said, and gestured with the glass. "So what? Now that I'm drinking heavily, I can think of good things. We're alive. And I get to return 'Berto's Mustang to him, unharmed."

"Thank goodness for that," Eileen said. She realized her glass was once again empty. "You think he'd lend it to us for the honeymoon?"

"He'd better," Joe said. "I attract people who want to kill me, it seems. We need a fast car to survive our honeymoon."

"And lots of guns," Lucy said.

"You know, I should just quit my damn job."

"You must be drunk," Eileen said archly. She knew Joe loved his work.

"I mention one thing," Ted said in a professorial tone. He wagged his finger at Joe. He looked almost, but not quite, sober. "You saved the *entire* Chicago Bulls professional basketball team."

"As well as Chicago," Lucy laughed. "And I helped."

"Oh, Joe," Eileen said. "You can't quit your job. America is like a damn cheerleader at Serial Killer High School. Every crazy, person or country, is after us. You'll just have to put up with it."

"And Eileen will save us all, like she always does," Lucy said, with a very exaggerated wink at Eileen.

"With your help, of course," Eileen said, and raised her glass in a toast to Lucy. Mysteriously, it was full again. "Did you like my anan – analogy? Serial Killer High? Huh?"

"Absolutely brilliant," Ted said. "I give it an A. As for—"

"Hush!" Lucy cried. "Listen."

There were voices coming around the corner of the house, voices raised in argument. Eileen listened as the others fell silent. The people around the corner of the house must have stopped, because their voices were clear and loud.

"Why not? I love you," Nolan said cheerfully.

"I don't know that I love you," Jorie said.

"Your kiss told me that you do. Look, it takes people a lifetime to get to that kind of understanding that we came to on that Tower. We can skip all the bullshit and get right to the happy ending."

"What happy ending? Marriage?"

"Yeah, I'm an old fashioned guy. I want to marry you, Marjorie Rothman. I love you. Did I tell you, I love you?"

"You told me," Jorie said in a low voice.

Eileen glanced at Joe and saw his delighted expression. Lucy and Ted, too, were sitting alertly, heads cocked to the side and eyebrows raised, smiling identical smiles.

"So I'll take you to Egypt on our honeymoon. Didn't you say you wanted to go to Egypt?"

"Egypt?" Jorie said, and her voice sounded a bit breathless. "How can we – I mean, I've always wanted —"

"We'll reserve Egypt for the honeymoon. How about Paris for our engagement? Have you ever been to Paris? I'll buy you a diamond in Paris and ask you to marry me at the Eiffel Tower."

Eileen leaned towards Lucy as Lucy tapped on her arm.

"Girls like Jorie *always* get the romance," Lucy grumbled in a loud whisper. "Did Joe ever offer to take you to Paris and propose at the Eiffel Tower?"

"Shhh, don't make me start laughing," Eileen whispered back. "Listen!"

"I'll think about it," Jorie said, but she sounded out of breath and dizzy.

"Think about this," Nolan said, and there was silence.

Joe put his arm around Eileen. "I'm inspired," he whispered. He turned her chin and kissed her, his mouth cold and salty from the Margarita, and she drowned in sensation.

"I think they're kissing," Ted announced loudly, eyes sparkling.

"I think they are too," Lucy chimed in. "Stop it, you two! Get a room!"

A moment later Nolan and Jorie stepped around the corner of the house. Jorie looked flushed and mortified and Nolan looked flushed and happy.

"We've got a pitcher of Margaritas here that we are too drunk to drink," Joe said, waving his hand at the table. "This is our own personal wake and celebration and I think you two doves should get over here."

"No meat in these Margaritas," Eileen added, taking a sip

of hers.

"Well, at least you're not going to turn me away from vegetarianism," Jorie said, as Nolan brought two chairs around and picked up fresh glasses from the table. Then she stopped still, face reddening, as she realized what she'd said.

Lucy burst into giggles and so did Eileen, and then they were all laughing together.

Out in the grass before them Hank and Zilla danced happily, chasing a blue rubber ball. There would be much to do tomorrow, Eileen thought, watching the little boy and the dog. There was her wedding to plan, and a marriage to start. Joe's leg shifted against hers and she took his hand without looking. Jorie would be talking to the Lakota tribes about their crystal skull and Nolan would be romancing Jorie. Lucy would be covering herself with glory at the Central Intelligence Agency, closing her unsolved murder file. Howie and his friends would be leaving tomorrow. They'd be back in the fall; Howie assured Tracy and Paul, if only to see what interesting adventures the Reed Ranch could come up with next.

Jorie and Nolan sat down and Eileen grinned at the other girl. Jorie had changed. She was still beautiful, still annoying, but there was simplicity to her face, a relaxed line to her shoulders, that spoke of bridges crossed and decisions made. After Nolan got through romancing her, Eileen thought she might end up liking the other woman. Maybe.

"I propose a toast," Joe said, "now that Jorie and Nolan have joined us."

"Okay," Eileen said doubtfully. But Joe's toast was not, as she feared, to Sheriff King.

"Here's to our deliverymen. Here's to Doug, who warned us, and here's to our Aztec warrior, who finally got his package delivered. I hope he's up there with Sully, and I hope they're watching us right now and they're laughing with us."

"Here's to both of them," Eileen said.

They all raised glasses, and clinked them, and the sun seemed to darken as they drank. Eileen looked around, puzzled, as the day around them turned from bright to dim.

"What's going on?" Lucy asked. "Hank, come here,

honey."

"I know," Ted said, with a big smile. "You guys have been here in Wyoming too long. It's just a rain cloud."

"A *rain* cloud?" Eileen gasped. She stood unsteadily, then gathered herself and walked out into the yard. Joe followed, looking skyward. Lucy and Hank followed, along with Jorie and Nolan. They looked to the west, where the sun was starting its long afternoon descent, and there was a bank of heavy dark clouds.

"*Rain*," Joe said.

"I can smell it," Eileen said reverently. There was a tang in the air already, a scent that made her want to run and jump in the air like Hank, like the butterflies. "I can smell the rain coming."

Lightning flashed from the clouds and a few seconds later they heard the first rumble of the approaching thunderstorm.

"We better get back on the porch," Jorie said. "We're going to get soaked if we don't."

None of them moved. They stood and watched the clouds build and the heavy sheets of rain come sweeping down over the ridges and valleys to the north, where Rene's fire still smoldered and smoked. They watched as the curtain of rain and clouds moved closer, as the temperature dropped and the wind started to gust. Eileen let the first drops lash her skin. She tilted her face back and let the rain fall on her.

"Come on," Joe said finally, tugging on her arm. She ran with him and joined the others on the porch and they watched the rain pound the thirsty earth. Streams of water ran from the gutters and fell in sheets to the ground, washing the whole world clean.

The End

An Excerpt From

THE QUEEN OF THE NIGHT

By
Bonnie Ramthun

Here's my journal to keep with all the other journals in this cursed Queen of the Night box. Cursed in the classic sense, cursed in the sense of destruction and death. I opened the box, that's what I keep telling myself. I opened the box, just like the other four. They opened the box and they're all dead. I'm not going to end up like them. I'll be really, really pissed off if I do.

My journal is on disk, though I'll print it out as soon as I'm finished. The first journal is handwritten in the beautiful, elegant style of two centuries ago, the ink so faded the words look like spider legs. The second journal was also written by hand, and the third on what looks like a typewriter. A typewriter, if you can imagine that. The last journal is on a reel to reel tape, a medium so arcane I had a hell of a time getting the information translated into script. Note to future cursed investigators: Print out your goddamn journal. You don't know how long it will be before someone tries to avenge your bloody and horrible murder, and if you leave your journal on an archaic recording medium it might be lost forever.

From my quick scan of the contents, the other victims of the Queen of the Night were willing investigators. Not me. I was roped into this assignment by some of the very same people who gutted me, in a professional sense, and left me staked out on a hot rock to die.

Interestingly enough my career took off after I was rail-roaded out of my former life. I ended up in commercial heaven, Louisville, Colorado, a small town north of Denver in a place

I

known as the golden Triangle of the West. Silicon Valley in California is more expensive, more fossilized, and more flabby than the muscular computer companies inhabiting the space between Boulder and Longmont, Colorado. IBM has been here for years. Storagetek, Sun Microsystems, Oracle and Level 3 Communications came in and built enormous campuses that fuel each other and the local economy and draw even more computer companies into the area.

I'm a clownfish in the world of these huge sharks. I pick rotting meat from their teeth, rotting meat being the employees that rob and cheat their employers. This keeps companies healthy and solvent and sends bad employees to jail or at least to the next big shark down the road. I'm a private investigator but I bill myself as a computer security firm, since telling people you're a private detective makes them laugh. Private dicks have been so overused by cinema and television they are their own cliché. Plus, I'm not a cop and I've never been one. The heavy lifting, arresting and so forth, I let the real cops do.

What I am is a programmer. Down all the way deep to my computer geek bones, I'm a programmer. Hacking is a brutal word, like something you do to meat. I'm a surgeon in code. I don't hack, I dissect. I discovered this ability of mine in college and I was so good I was never caught. Until much later, that is, and that was a set-up. Earlier, though, I was unstoppable. I became a peeper rather than a thief or a vandal. I never wrote viruses that destroyed hard drives, or stole credit card numbers from banks. I never hacked the IRS website although I visit it often to see what wildly inventive pornography appears on it next. There was a series of months where every anal sex act was perpetrated on that site, one after another, in vivid filmed pornography with the heads of the porn stars replaced with various administration officials including the President of the United States. I found it hilarious, but I didn't do it. I swear.

I just snoop. I can get into any site, without visible trace, and no one ever discovers me or kicks me out of their systems.

My company is called Sorcha Security Systems. I'm Sorcha. I wasn't born with a great name like Sorcha Stone, of course. My mother, bless her, wanted a perfect and beautiful little girl and so she named me April Dawn Stone. April Dawn is a fine enough name for a laundry additive and I suppose I did well enough with it through childhood and high school. But after my run-in with the big law, the FBI, I went through the courts and changed my name. As April Stone I was just an ordinary girl computer programmer, having fun and writing code and making lots of money. As Sorcha Stone, scorched and reborn, I'm capable of just about anything.

Except maybe this case. Damn it. But my options are few and unpalatable. The suspended charges could be resurrected and I could find myself in a federal penitentiary for longer than I probably have on this earth. I like women fine enough, but not enough to spend a lifetime with them. I don't tilt that way.

I was beautiful once, a standard issue pretty high school girl, popular and bubble-headed and I'm sure I was the subject of many high school crushes from the computer geeks I didn't even see from my high school Olympus. I'm medium height, built the way a girl should be built, with creamy blonde hair and blue eyes and the kind of even, agreeable features that come together in just the right way. This was before Deborah Miller and her Camero, before my freshman year of college and the celebration of Frontier Days, when Deborah killed herself and LeeAnn Parker and almost killed me when she ran off Pershing Avenue in Cheyenne, Wyoming, at a rate of speed exceeding eighty-eight miles an hour. Alas, we didn't go back to the future, we didn't get shot forward or backward in time, we simply corkscrewed through the air and came down with many ugly crunches and splashes of blood.

They shoved me into the flight for life helicopter as an afterthought, shoved me to the side and worked desperately on the thing that had been Deborah which still had a heartbeat of sorts. They didn't bother with LeeAnn. Pieces of her littered the graveyard where we landed, a piece of symbolism that I can still do without. I found out much, much later that her pretty brunette head was impaled on a fence post and hung there just like the pig's head in *Lord of the Flies*.

Me, I'd been wearing my seatbelt. Good upbringing, that's me, drunk beyond belief as we all were but I still fumbled that seat belt on. Thank god Deborah only killed LeeAnn and herself and no innocent bystanders, though I wanted to die, too, when I saw what happened to my face and my left leg.

The scars, once red and swollen, are thin white lines now. My cheekbone on my right side is slightly different than the left, and the long gash that runs from my temple to my ear only shows up when I'm furiously angry. I can't wear shorts though, or those pretty knee-skimming dresses that look so lovely on the girls who float down the Pearl Street Mall in Boulder. And I limp a bit. Not bad, but in our beauty pageant world that's plenty.

Once I healed up I went back to school and found my way into computers. It was the perfect place for me, a girl who'd once been beautiful and now only wanted to hide. Computers became something wonderful for me, and that reaffirms my faith in the Big Guy up there. Whenever things get really dark there comes something amazing, something grand, that takes all the darkness and turns it into light.

The second time I was down and out, jobless and reviled and recently free from jail, I became fascinated with my mother's bread making. She's a great cook, my mom, and I love her dearly though she never really forgave me for wrecking my face and ruining her dreams of a perfect Barbie wedding. I was determined to develop cooking skills, since I thought I might end up in some prison kitchen somewhere. Or at the very least I thought my future in computer programming was over, and a life behind a grill at some diner might be my only career option.

Bread making is a task that begs for metaphors. You knead and knead the dough, mixing in flour until the dough is firm and rubbery and perfect. The dough is placed in a pan and covered with a wet cloth and left to rise on its own. Then when the dough finishes rising, it is punched back down. My mom had to show me how to do this just right. Pressing the dough doesn't work, you have to hit it hard and fast. If the dough were a nose, it would spurt blood.

"You have to really punch it down," my mom told me. "Or the bread fills up with air holes and it's useless."

That was me, I realized, punching down the dough. Maybe this is everyone. We're punched down, pummeled flat, and left to rise again. What rises from the dough is fine and tasty and just right for a toaster and some peanut butter.

IV

After my first punching experience, red-scarred and limping, I rose with computer programming. I love computers. Love them. Before my accident I was floating through life, not loving anything or anyone other than the shallow momentary pleasures of partying, making out with guys, pretty clothes. When I discovered computer programming it was like a muscle I never knew I had started working. Or a third eye opened in my brain and suddenly I could see an entirely different world, more colors than I knew existed, more shapes, more everything. With every physical therapy session I worked to make my leg stronger, but that was only to make me walk the way I used to walk before. With every session on a computer, I walked paths I'd never walked before. I thought I was a pretty air-headed girl, and I found out I was a brilliant scientist. I found out I could fly.

So couldn't God have done that without wrecking my face? Ah, well, that's not my question to ask. He helps me to rise, if I can find the way, and that's what's important.

I was happy after college graduation, happy and beginning to feel less like a freak. The scars were fading and the limp was slight and I still had my blue eyes and blonde hair, after all. I was presentable. There was obviously something else I was supposed to do, though. Some shakeup was supposed to happen. It did. It did with a vengeance, and his name is Dexter McCrea.

Dexter McCrea said he was from the effa bee eye, the lovely organization that gave us Ruby Ridge, Waco, and the career agent and killer spy Robert Hanssen, among other fiascos. McCrea came to our organization when I was working on a team that was developing vision systems for a spy satellite system so incredibly good it could read the fine print off a newspaper crumpled in the gutter.

I don't quite know how I ended up working for the Department of Defense. They paid a lot and three of my friends from the University were recruited, so I submitted my resume and because the work was in Denver, Colorado, close to my parents in Fort Collins, I chose it over my other offers. Plus, lets face it, spy stuff is glamorous. I didn't know what I was going to be working on at the time, but I knew it was secret and hush-hush and all of that. It sounded pretty cool, and spies don't show their faces.

I sat around for three months in an anonymous office

building while my clearance work went through, sat around playing War Craft and networked Doom with my teammates. Finally we got our clearances and we weren't set to dissecting aliens or even checking out their spaceship, as some of us suspected and some of us hoped. We weren't given missile defense systems and told to blow up international terrorists. We were given something even more interesting.

Satellites could take millions of pictures, but ordinary people had to shuffle through all those pictures and make decisions about them. Our job was to develop computer programs that would pick out interesting objects from satellite photos – a terrorist's face, for example, or a tank's gun turret sticking out of sand, or bulky items moved from a Los Angeles port into a Chinese tanker – and bring those pictures to the attention of the flesh-and-blood analysts who might be able to make a coherent pattern out of them. This sounds easy, but it's incredibly difficult. Teaching a program to "see" things is the hardest task a computer can do. The best of them can't do much better than your average cockroach. Ah, computers, I love them.

I was three years into my job and having an absolute blast when McCrea showed up and punched my dough flat. McCrea is tall and dark haired, with a round face pitted with old acne scars. He has kindly brown mongrel eyes and a sweet crooked smile. I liked him immediately. He asked if any of us would like to volunteer for a new assignment, an assignment that involved attempting to hack into the nation's most secure computer systems.

"I need the best computer programmers I can find," he said. "We've got to know where our weaknesses are and I think this is the best way to do it. We're choosing a few volunteers from our best defense programming pools. We're going to put together a new task force on computer crimes. We'd like to give you all a test."

"What kind of test?" I asked.

"Give me all the information you can find out about me. You know my name. You have until tomorrow noon. Anyone who's got a sheet with information on it will be considered for this Task Force. Let me know."

I worked all night. I had no desire to sleep. This was more

fun than anything I'd ever done. I never thought to ask certain crucial questions. I was naïve, bursting with enthusiasm.

I was a chump.

ABOUT THE AUTHOR
BONNIE RAMTHUN

When Bonnie Ramthun was nine years old, she realized that someone actually wrote the stories she loved to read. When she discovered that her favorite author had died and there would be no more Tarzan stories, she immediately started penning her own Tarzan tales in the wild jungles of Africa. She still has those stories.

"They're awful," she says, with a laugh. "Truly awful. Don't ask to look at them."

The desire to write burned stronger as she grew up. Bonnie decided that since her favorite authors were people who led interesting lives, she'd have to live one, too.

A computer science degree led her into military helicopter crash investigations. She then worked in a Detroit factory that used robots to build trucks.

"Occasionally one of the robots would fling a huge, razor sharp piece of metal across the factory floor," she says. "There were other problems, but for some reason the guys in the factory wanted me to fix that one first."

When Bonnie heard about missile defense war gaming, she had moved on from robots and was working on a design feature for the space station.

"War gaming?" Bonnie says. "Shooting down nuclear missiles like a space cowboy, saving the world from destruction? I threw my pencil in the air and said: 'I have got to get myself in there!'"

As a war gamer, Bonnie found her talents stretched to their limits. She spent less time writing and more time working. Then Bill Ramthun came into her life and, quite simply, stole her heart.

Bonnie realized that her life was at a crossroads. She could continue as a computer scientist or she could choose marriage and a family, and try to make her dream of becoming an author come true.

The pencil went into the air. And came down onto the page. Bonnie left for a new life.

Bonnie's first novel *Ground Zero* was a Colorado best seller. *Earthquake Games*, her second novel, was a finalist for Colorado Book of the Year 2001. *The Thirteenth Skull* is her third novel.

"I'm the mother of four children, and I'm married to Bill Ramthun, and I write novels. That is what I am and what I love, more than anything in the world," Bonnie says. "I just love a happy ending."

Title List

Fiction

NEW FOR SPRING 2004! *Hen House* by Sharon Sala
(ISBN 0-9662696-8-3, ˜ 273 pages, 6x9, paper, $14.95)

NEW FOR 2004! *Queen of the Night* by Bonnie Ramthun
(ISBN - TBD, ˜ 363 pages, 6x9, paper, $14.95)

The Thirteenth Skull by Bonnie Ramthun
(ISBN 0-9662696-7-5, ˜ 312 pages, 6x9, paper, $14.95)

Whippoorwill by Sharon Sala
(ISBN 0-9662696-6-7, 264 pages, 6x9, paper, $14.95)

The Spanish Peaks by Jon Chandler
(National Winner - Best First Novel of 1999!)
(ISBN 0-9662696-0-8, 208 pages, 6x9, paper, $15.95)

The Salzdorf Wellspring by Wade Stevenson
(ISBN 0-9662696-3-2, 228 pages, 6x9, paper, $12.95)

Wire-Wrapping

Moods in Wire: 2nd Edition by Ellsworth "Ed" Sinclair
(ISBN 0-9640483-3-7, 144 pages, 8 ½ x 11, Wire-O, $29.95)

Holiday Moods in Wire by Ellsworth "Ed" Sinclair
(ISBN 0-9640483-2-9, 160 pages, 8 ½ x 11, Wire-O, $29.95)

21 Ga., Square Brass Practice Wire, 120 yard coil - $30.00

4 Piece Pliers Set. Box jointed with double leaf springs and cushion grip handles, 1 ea. chain, flat, round and sidecutter in a case.

"How-to" Journaling, Writing and Getting Your Writing Published

The Journal Wheel and Guide Book by Deborah Bouziden
(ISBN 0-9662696-4-0, Wheel, Quick Reference Bookmark and 56 page booklet, $14.95)

The Successful Writer's Guide to Publishing Magazine Articles by Eva Shaw, Ph.D.
(ISBN 0-9662696-1-6, 184 pages, 6x9, paper, $15.95)

Writing the Nonfiction Book by Eva Shaw, Ph.D.
(ISBN 0-9662696-2-4, 286 pages, 6x9, paper, $18.95)

Bronze Sculpture

Patinas for Silicon Bronze by Patrick V. Kipper
(ISBN 0-9647269-0-4, 226 pages, 8 ½ x 11, Hardbound, $69.95)

The Care of Bronze Sculpture by Patrick V. Kipper
(ISBN 0-9647269-1-2, 88 pages, 6x9, paper, $14.95)

Loveland Press Order Form

FICTION

- ❑ **The Thirteenth Skull** by Bonnie Ramthun...............................$14.95 _____
- ❑ **Across the Brazos** by Ermal W. Williamson................................$14.95 _____
- ❑ **Whippoorwill** by Sharon Sala...$14.95 _____
- ❑ **The Spanish Peaks** by Jon Chandler.....................................$15.95 _____
- ❑ **The Salzdorf Wellspring** by Wade Stevenson..........................$12.95 _____

NEW FICTION Available in 2004

- ❑ **The Hen House** by Sharon Sala..$14.95 _____
- ❑ **Man From the Brazos** by Ermal W. Williamson..........................$14.95 _____
- ❑ **Queen of the Night** by Bonnie Ramthun.................................$14.95 _____

"HOW-TO" WRITING AND JOURNALING BOOKS

- ❑ **The Successful Writer's Guide to Publishing Magazine Articles** by Eva Shaw, Ph.D. ....$15.95 _____
- ❑ **Writing the Nonfiction Book** by Eva Shaw, Ph.D. ....$18.95 _____
- ❑ **The Journal Wheel and Guide Book** by Deborah Bouziden.......$14.95 _____

WIRE-WRAPPING BOOKS AND SUPPLIES (check our web site for more supplies)

- ❑ **Moods in Wire: 2nd Edition** by Ellsworth "Ed" Sinclair..............$29.95 _____
- ❑ **Holiday Moods in Wire** by Ellsworth "Ed" Sinclair....................$29.95 _____
- ❑ Ed Sinclair Signature Series Wire Wrap Starter Kit......................$79.95 _____

BRONZE SCULPTURE (check our web site for supplies)

- ❑ **The Care of Bronze Sculpture** by Patrick V. Kipper.................$14.95 _____
- ❑ **Patinas for Silicon Bronze** by Patrick V. Kipper......................$69.95 _____

Item Total _____

Shipping and Handling — US rates $4.00 for one book, $1.00 each add'l book _____
(Please call or email for rates outside the continental US)
Colorado Residents add 3% Sales Tax _____

TOTAL AMOUNT DUE _____

Payable by Check, Money Order, Visa or Mastercard. Call 1-800-593-9557 or (970) 593-9557 fax (970) 593-9911, order on-line at www.LovelandPress.com or mail your orders to:

Bill my: ❑ Visa ❑ MasterCard (exp. date) ___ / _____

Card # ___ — ___ — ___ —

Signature _____

Loveland Press
PO Box 7001
Loveland, CO 80537-0001
www.LovelandPress.com

Purchased by:

Name _____

Address _____

_____

City _____

State/ZIP _____

Daytime Phone # _____

E-mail: _____

Ship to (if different):

Name _____

Address _____

_____

City _____

State/ZIP _____

Daytime Phone # _____

E-mail: _____

Please allow 5-7 days for delivery. This offer subject to change without notice.